WILDEST DREAMS

THE FANTASYLAND SERIES
BOOK ONE

KRISTEN ASHLEY

ROCK CHICK
PRESS

A LOVE IS EVERYTHING SAGA BY

KRISTEN

NEW YORK TIMES BESTSELLING AUTHOR

ASHLEY

FANTASYLAND BOOK ONE

WILDEST
DREAMS

Wildest Dreams

This book is a work of fiction. Any reference to historical events, real people, or real places are used fictitiously. Other names, characters, places, and incidents are products of the author's imagination. Any resemblance to actual events, locales, or persons, living or dead, is coincidental.

Cover Image: Pixel Mischief Designs

I

LOVE IS EVERYTHING

"You are sure?" Valentine asked in her soft, throaty, sing-song New Orleans accented voice.

I nodded.

I was sure. Heck yeah, I was sure.

I could *not* wait.

"Finnie," my friend Claudia hissed from my side, and I looked from Valentine to Claudia to see Claudia looked pale and alarmed. "This is crazy," she went on then elaborated. "Crazier than when you bungee jumped. Crazier than when you jumped from a plane. Crazier than when you swam with the sharks. Crazier—"

I cut her off, saying through a smile, "I didn't swim with sharks. They just crashed the party."

Claudia's eyes got squinty. "You know what I mean. And I'll throw in treasure hunting with that guy who thought he was the Indiana Jones of this generation but who was, I will remind you," she leaned in, "*not*. And that time you nearly got stampeded by elephants when you were on safari—"

I looked to Valentine. "That was unfortunate. And it wasn't my fault no matter what anyone says."

Valentine's eyelids lowered a little, like a cat who was coasting to sleep.

Seriously, this bitch was cool.

"Finnie!" Claudia snapped, and I looked back at my friend.

"I get it sweetheart. You think I'm nuts."

"You *are* nuts if you..." she leaned forward again, her eyes darting with more than a little obvious distrust at Valentine before coming back to me, "think you're going to a *parallel universe*."

"I can assure you," Valentine put in smoothly, "she *will*."

I looked at Valentine. Her hair was a dark, shining auburn, real as far as I could tell. Her skin was alabaster. Her body was long and very thin. Her descent, she declared, was pure Creole. In other words, *her* people were there before *our* people were there (her people being the Europeans and when she explained this to us during our first meeting with her a couple of days ago, after, of course, corresponding with her for months to set up this gig, it was *she* who added the emphasis). She had a kickass place in the French Quarter. She had major class from her perfectly coiffed head to her killer Jimmy Choo clad toes. She reeked of money even more than *me*, and I was loaded.

And, incidentally, she was, I'd learned from a variety of reliable sources, an extremely powerful witch.

"Okay," Claudia stated. "Say you do this. Say you send Finnie there—"

"Her name is Seoafin," Valentine cut in haughtily, her green eyes sliding elegantly to me. "That is far more chic then..." her lips turned down and one nostril quivered delicately, "*Finnie.*"

The nostril quiver, I thought, was a good touch.

"Well, *I*, and all her friends who know her and love her and don't want to see her get gouged by someone like *you*, call her *Finnie*," Claudia returned.

Valentine forced her gaze to Claudia (and made it obvious she did so) and she said one word. The ice dripping from it underlining a meaning the word did not exactly have but could not be missed.

"*Indeed.*" Then she looked back at me and her face warmed, *slightly.* "Sjofn is the Goddess of Love. And love," her eyelids suddenly fluttered dreamily. "*Love*," she breathed then she focused on me with a strange intensity that made me—even *me*—squirm a little. "Love is *everything*."

Okay, this bitch had style and class, but she was *whacked.*

"All righty," I whispered.

"Oh my God!" Claudia cried. "This is insane!"

Valentine's eyes sliced to Claudia and her gaze grew sharp. "It is far from insane. Magic is entirely *natural*. It is not *insane*. And I will remind you of what I've told you repeatedly. This is not something I would normally do. It is because I like your friend, I admire her..." her green gaze traveled the length of Claudia seated in her chair, "...outside her choice in acquaintances, that is, and she carries the name of a goddess, and that goddess is the goddess of love, that I'm doing it at all. She should feel honored."

"I do, totally," I assured her, and Valentine smiled benignly at me.

"Yeah, she should feel honored," Claudia cut in sarcastically. "What with *Finnie* giving *you* a million dollars, *she* should feel honored. Right."

Valentine sniffed delicately and condescendingly as any uppity bitch would do when money was brought up.

Claudia was a dog with a bone. "So, say you can actually pull off this nonsense. Where's she going? What's she going to do when she gets there? And are you sure you can bring her back?"

"She is going to Lunwyn, a beautiful, snow-covered country at the very top of the Northlands. She is taking the place of the Sjofn who lives there who, by the way," Valentine looked again at me, "actually spells it properly." She turned again to Claudia. "She will assume the life of the other her. She will be there for the time we agreed. That is one year to this very day, this very hour, this very minute and then, in this very place." She raised a pale, graceful hand and pointed a long, thin, lethally-rounded, blood-red tipped fingernail at the thick rug on the floor. "I will switch them back."

"Right," Claudia whispered, clearly thinking Valentine was a loon.

I grabbed Claudia's hand and pulled it to me.

"Honey, listen to me. Valentine's been in touch with this, uh...other me. She's on board and she wants this as much as me. I've written a twenty-page report on my life and all she needs to know about it to show her the way, *and* she'll have *you*." I squeezed her hand. "She's going to write to me about what I need to know about her life. It's all sorted. It's all good. But if I do this, which I'm going to do, it has to happen very soon. The window is closing."

Claudia stared in my eyes, and I saw fear in hers. "Okay, Finnie, I get this. I get it. I've gotten it for years. I get what you want from this. I get that your dad, your mom—"

My lungs seized and my back went straight before I snapped, "Don't."

She squeezed my hand and kept at me. "I wouldn't but you're giving me no choice. You're giving this woman a million dollars for something..." She shook her head. "For whatever this is, and you have no idea if it's going to work, *where* she'll send you if it does and *what* will happen once you get there."

I grinned and pointed out the obvious, "That's the adventure."

"This is why I like her," Valentine murmured decorously.

Claudia's eyes slid to the side, aiming a vicious *shut up* look at Valentine, but they cleared when they came back to me. "Your mom and dad—"

I tried to pull my hand from hers, snapping again, "Don't."

She held tight, leaned far forward to get in my space and didn't give up. "Your mom and dad, Finnie, they *died* because of this thirst for adventure. A thirst they taught you and a thirst you've never quenched, not once in all your wanderings and shenanigans. And I fear, honey, I fear you never will until you meet their same end."

I yanked my hand free and looked hard at her. "They died happy," I stated.

"Finnie, they died *young*," Claudia said gently.

"And *happy*," I returned.

She closed her eyes tight and then burst out, "*God!*" She opened her eyes and retorted, "You can't know that."

"No, she can't. But I can," Valentine butted in at this point.

Claudia's face got hard, and she and I both looked at her.

Valentine was looking at me.

"They did die happy. You are correct," Valentine declared.

My heart tightened and Claudia muttered, "Freaking great. Now she communes with the dead."

Valentine continued, totally ignoring Claudia. "Though, you must know, happiness is a line, and that line has degrees. There is bliss at one end and there is contentment at the other. They were not blissful, as I would assume you think they were. Being in love, being together and dying doing something they enjoyed, the sheer exultation of thrill and excitement coursing their veins, life as big as life can be rushing through their systems. They *were* happy but this happiness held weight. And that weight was *you*."

I pulled in a soft breath and heard Claudia do the same.

"They were sad to leave you," Valentine said quietly. "Very sad. And you should know with what we do this evening, there is no guarantee. You *do* take risks with this venture. I do not know a great deal about this world. I know it exists. I get communications from it but infrequently. That said, although interesting, *I* have little interest in it. These communications are a nuisance. There is much going on in my world, I cannot find the curiosity to learn about both. I am also not a seer. So I do not know what will befall you there, what you can expect, if you will be safe or in danger. I do know there is another you and she wants to be here for a year. And I would caution you to understand that her motives might not be the same as yours."

4

"This is true, Finnie," Claudia whispered, grabbing my hand again. "Think about that."

"But you can bring me back?" I asked Valentine, and Claudia's hand tightened in mine.

"Yes, Seoafin. I can bring you back," Valentine answered.

"You can definitely bring me back," I stated, and she inclined her head regally. "So what do I care what the other me wants here?" I asked.

"While here, *ma chérie*, she will be you," Valentine replied with a fluid twist of her hand.

"And I will be her when I'm there. Honor system," I returned.

"There are as many ideas of what honor is as there are people, my goddess of love," Valentine warned quietly.

Hmm. That didn't sound good.

"I will, however, provide you with another service," her eyes drifted to Claudia momentarily then back to me, "*free of charge*, because I like you. I will keep an eye on this Sjofn. And if I have concerns, I will get a message to you."

I smiled brightly. "That sounds cool to me."

Valentine's lips tipped up about a half a centimeter at the ends.

"Oh boy," Claudia muttered, but Valentine again ignored her and continued.

"You understand what I *have* explained about this world? That it is parallel to ours. That most of the same people here are there—"

I interrupted her, "Yes, I understand."

And I understood. I *totally* understood. That was why I was forking over a million dollars for this in the first place.

She studied me then she said softly, "And you understand the people there who look like us, sound like us, are not..." her eyes narrowed slightly, "*us*."

I nodded. "I get it."

"Finnie—" Claudia whispered, and I turned to her.

"It's going to be okay, Claudia," I assured my friend.

"Right." Claudia, as usual, sounded far from assured.

"It's going to be," I shook her hand, "*all right*."

Claudia studied me. I let her. Then I smiled, big and bright.

Her gaze moved over my face, her eyes warming as it did so, she shook her head and whispered, "Just for the record, I do. I totally think you're nuts."

"I know," I whispered back, still smiling.

"But I love you, mostly because you *are* nuts," she told me something else I knew, and my smile got bigger.

"This is, *mes petites filles*, touching. However, we had not much time when you arrived and our window of opportunity as to when Sjofn can make this switch is quickly closing," Valentine warned.

"That's another thing I don't get," Claudia muttered.

"Well, you will have to ask her when she's here in five minutes," Valentine returned coldly.

Claudia glared at her. Valentine accepted her glare, completely unperturbed. Then Claudia gave up, looked at me and rolled her eyes.

I smiled at the eye roll, but I wanted to get on with it.

I was ready for my next adventure.

So I looked at Valentine and declared, "Valentine, I'm ready."

She looked at me.

She smiled an actual smile.

Then she whispered, "Lovely. Shall we begin?"

2

WINTER WONDERLAND

I didn't close my eyes. I didn't want to miss a thing.

I kept them open while sitting in Valentine's elegant chair in her elegant living room, and I gave Claudia another reassuring smile, blew her a kiss and turned to Valentine.

She was sitting across from me, eyes closed, face so relaxed she could be asleep, but her lips were tipped up like she found something vaguely amusing. Her hands were lifted, palms up, red-tipped fingertips curled toward the ceiling and her hands started glowing with green—a beautiful, vibrant, emerald green.

It was *awesome*.

Then the entire room took on the shade of her green slowly, and I watched the room start to fade. Mere seconds went by while Valentine's elegant salmon walls with their intricate white cornices and ceilings got greener, greener, then darker green, then all faded to black.

Suddenly ice-blue sparks shot all around me and I was standing in a room looking out a window.

"Oh my God," I breathed as I stared at the wavy, frosted glass of the diamond-paned window. "It worked."

It worked!

I smiled huge.

Then I studied the window, saw the catch, lifted it and threw the two windows outward to open them. A gust of arctic air shot back at me but that wasn't what made me breathless.

"Oh my God," I breathed again as the scene before me assaulted my eyes with astonishing beauty.

Amazing. Unbelievable. Absolutely freaking *cool*.

Whatever building I was in was on a small rise. I was on the second floor and laid out before me was a Winter Wonderland. A town or maybe small city sprawled throughout and nestled in what looked like a valley if the not too far away, not too close shoots of snow-topped mountains that interrupted the twinkling midnight blue of the night sky were anything to go by.

My head moving side to side, I took it all in.

Most of the buildings that I could see close were one story, topped with a marshmallow blanket of pristine white snow; all the many chimneys had smoke drifting straight into the air. Wavy, diamond-paned windows cast a flickering glow of candlelight on the snow-covered ground. There were icicles hanging from the roofs, glinting in the candle and torchlight. The houses were made of something dark, perhaps wood, at the bottom that went up to the lower edge of the windows and then some light-colored material with crisscrosses of dark beams through them. The buildings seemed planted in the snow, there was so much of it—some of it even blown in drifts up the sides.

Taking it in, I saw there was clearly no city planning. The buildings looked built wherever, dotted here and there. There were winding pathways through them, obviously well used if the tramped snow was anything to go by. Some were narrow, some were wider. All were lit at their sides by torches stuck in the ground, their fire caged with iron, the small blaze dancing around the cage. A light snow was falling, and I had no idea how they stayed lit, but they did.

There were also massive barrels scattered here and there, far fewer than the torches, which also held roaring fires. These too lit the space, and around a few, there were people standing, holding their hands out to the flames and chatting.

But there weren't that many people, two around one fire, three around another in the distance.

Suddenly, I saw a horse gallop through, and I couldn't stop myself from letting out a delighted giggle as the rider's cloak streamed behind him, his head topped with a furry hat.

"That is *so cool*," I whispered as he took a turn on a winding path well down the incline of the town or city-like-place and disappeared around a building.

"The switch, it succeeded?" I heard a woman ask.

I jumped in surprise and turned.

Standing beside me I saw a woman with gray hair pulled back behind her head. She was wearing a voluminous wool cloak the color of cranberries and it had a collar made of black fur.

Her eyebrows were up. Her face was lined in a way that made her look interesting and was a testimony to the fact she'd laughed much in her long life. Her somewhat faded blue eyes were alert, and she was examining me.

"It worked," I whispered then jumped again when a loud banging came from across the room.

I turned my body that direction to see it was someone knocking on a door.

"*Sjofn!*" a woman yelled from the other side of the door, sounding desperate. "Open the door! We need to speak with you now! Your mother approaches."

I stared at the door.

My mother approaches.

I couldn't stop my smile.

"Close this after me," the woman in the room with me ordered urgently. I looked to her then her eyes moved the length of me and back before she smiled and whispered, "Enjoy The Drakkar. I think you will and more, I think *he* will enjoy *you*."

I blinked at her.

What?

"*Sjofn!*" Another shout and loud knock. My body jolted again, I looked to the door as the woman behind it shouted, "*Please!*"

I felt a whoosh and turned back to see the woman in the room with me was gone. I glanced around quickly as more knocking came at the door, more pleas, but I was stunned to see I had no company.

Where did she go?

I turned to the window, looked out and down and saw a cranberry cloak streaming around the nearest building. There, I lost sight of it.

Holy moly, the bitch jumped.

I looked down at the two-story fall and heard the begging, "*Seeeeooohaaahfin!*"

"Shit," I whispered.

I grabbed the windows, pulled them to and set the latch. That stopped the arctic gust of air but the cold still came through so I grabbed the heavy curtains on either side and pulled them closed over the window, succeeding in shutting out the draft mainly because the curtains were a thick, voluminous velvet. Nothing was getting through those.

More knocking that was now more like pounding and it didn't stop. So I turned to the room to hurry toward the door but stopped, arrested by what I saw.

Gleaming dark wood everywhere. Dark plank floors covered by thick pile, wool, patterned rugs. An enormous fireplace, the massive mantel carved from cream stone. More deep carvings in the wood cornices. The carving on both mantel and molding were pears, apples and oranges with leaves and vines, and it was so intricate, even at a glance I saw it was sheer perfection. I could even see dimples in the oranges. With that kind of crafts-manship and that amount of it in the big room, it had to take a hundred artisans a hundred years to do it all.

There was a big bed, four-poster, headboard carved with the same motif with an ice-blue coverlet that had a silken sheen. A fluffy, winter-white blanket was folded across the bottom and six fluffy, European square pillows stacked in twos at the head—two dove gray, two winter white, two ice blue. The heavy curtains around the bed also were ice blue.

There was heavily carved dark wood furniture everywhere. Two night-stands. A big dresser. A long, tall wardrobe. A desk and chair. A full-length, freestanding, oval mirror with the pear, apple, orange, leaf and vine theme at the top and drifting down the sides. A small table with a huge, cushy armchair next to it that I desperately wanted to curl into covered by that fluffy blanket on the bed, it looked that comfortable.

There were pearlescent globed lamps lit not with electricity but flames dancing within on either nightstand, on the desk, on the table by the chair and dotting the walls.

The whole room was freaking *amazing*. Way cool. Unbelievably cool. I'd seen a lot in my life, and I had the money to go for the gusto, but I'd never seen anything *this* amazing.

"*Sjofn! Please!*" Another call and more pounding at the door, so I shook myself out of it and saw a folded piece of paper on the bed.

That must be my note.

I stared at it a second thinking there didn't look like there was much to it.

I started toward it as I could swear the pounding on the door became kicking. I looked that way but caught a flash of something in my peripheral vision, my head turned, and I stopped dead.

Then I stood straight.

I turned to look at myself in the mirror.

And I slowly walked to it, the pounding and begging outside the door muted as I stared with deep fascination at what I saw.

When I got to the mirror, I reached out a hand to touch the cold surface just to be certain it was real. When my fingertips brushed the glass, I changed directions and moved my hand so it lay flat to my belly and I felt it.

It was real.

I was real and I looked like *that*.

"Wow," I whispered.

I was wearing ice blue too.

An ice-blue velvet gown that had this kick-freaking-ass sheen at the tip of the pile that looked iridescent white, like the shimmer on top of new snow.

The neckline was square, had thick, braided embroidery around the edge, and it shoved my breasts up so I was giving some serious cleavage.

The sleeves of the dress hugged my body from shoulder to wrist, a sharp point of embroidered-edged material coming down my hand that hooked at the end around my middle finger. The top of the dress, from bosoms to hips, skimmed my body to perfection.

The skirt had a slight flare and when I tested it by kicking out at the back, a slight train too.

The dress had a no waistline, simply flowing elegantly from bodice to hem and there was an intricate silver or—I peered closer—no, *platinum* chain liberally splashed with aquamarines and dusted with diamonds that hung low on my hips. A long single length of it hanging down, winking through the folds of my skirts, weighted at the hem by a large twinkling aquamarine.

I was wearing a choker necklace that matched the belt and earrings of the same dangled from my ears.

Further, my white-blonde hair was a mass of long, thick twists that were pulled off my forehead somehow but hung down my back, chest and shoulders. I had shimmering pink on my cheeks, a gloss of pink on my lips, an iridescent blue on my eyelids, a dark blue rimming my eyes and a sparkle of pearlescent white around my temples, the same powder but applied less opaque dusted my chest.

But the best—the absolute best—was the crown.

Yes, I said...*the crown!*

I was wearing a crown low on my forehead and however it was fashioned it was heavy but comfortable, something soft and maybe furry protecting my skin from the metal.

And it looked like icicles shooting up and slightly out, crusted with glinting diamonds and sprinkled with glimmering aquamarines.

It was freaking *phenomenal.*

I lifted the heavy skirts and saw a pair of winter-white, low-heeled, supple suede boots that kept going to over my knees. Above that, skintight, woven stockings that were also winter white and looked (and felt) like they were made of cashmere. Up I pulled the skirt and I saw winter-white satin tap pants dripping with icicle lace at the bottoms, over this were satin garters holding up the stockings, but I saw the boned point of the bottom of a satin bustier at my navel and I felt more boning that I couldn't see against my skin at my ribs.

Freaking *great* underwear.

"This...is...so...*cool!*" I whispered as I stared at myself in the mirror.

"*Seeoohaahfiiiiiiin!*" I heard the frantic cry.

I started, dropped my skirt and looked to the door.

I then dashed to the bed, snatched up the paper, folded it twice so it was smaller, and shoved it into my cleavage.

I rushed to the door and had my hand on the skeleton key in the lock when I stopped dead.

"Sjofn, open this door this *instant,*" a cold, imperious, *achingly familiar* woman's voice demanded through the door.

I closed my eyes as warmth spread through me.

"Mom," I whispered.

I opened my eyes, smiled huge and turned the lock. Now *I* was frantic to get the door opened. But when I pulled at it, it didn't budge. I stared at it and saw three, thick wooden planks, one on top, one on the bottom, one in the middle, all thrown to in iron latches, bolting the door shut.

How weird.

I shoved them all aside and yanked open the door.

And I froze again, the smile fading from my face as I saw my mother's body jolt. She blinked then she glared at me.

I stared at her.

Oh God. Oh God. Oh God.

There she was.

My mom.

Looking at her I thought, *Absolutely, definitely, one hundred percent worth a million dollars. Absolutely.*

I took her in, all of her, and I felt my stomach get warm.

I got my light-blue eyes from her, and I was looking right into them. Looking into them again for the first time in fifteen years.

I felt my eyes fill with tears. Me! Seoafin Wilde about to cry.

Impossible.

But there it was.

I was a freak of nature. Where I got my unusual hair, I did not know. My mother and father were both dark and Dad had dark-brown eyes. Both of them were tall, lean and straight. I was average height (a little less than that, if I had to admit it, though not short) and curvy.

And now, standing before me in a gown much like mine but a deep red with a glossy, brown fur ruff around her neck, her still-dark hair (there were only intermittent shafts of gorgeous silver) pulled up in twists, curls and braids with tiny gold clips in the shapes of butterflies everywhere. She wore her own crown, gold with diamonds and rubies, as well as a dripping, gold necklace scattered with rubies covering the skin that her scooped neckline exposed and long, gold and ruby earrings hanging from her ears, skimming the fur around her neck.

There she was...my...*freaking*...mom.

"Mom," I whispered, blinking away the tears, and even doing that, I saw her eyes narrow in annoyance over dark, elegant, arched brows that snapped together.

"I'll countenance none of this nonsense, Sjofn," she snapped with cold irritation. "We should have left fifteen minutes ago. The Drakkar awaits, and all know he is impatient and doesn't want to be where he's standing right this very minute in the first place."

She turned, lifted a hand at four young women who were hanging about, all wearing gowns made of soft wool, nowhere near as grand as Mom and mine, and all in dark colors—navy, burgundy, forest green and dark gray (to be precise).

And all were weirdly staring at me intently.

I didn't get a chance to wonder about that because Mom flicked her wrist and started down a wide, wood paneled hall with more carving and intermittent pieces of glossy dark furniture.

She kept talking as she floated down the hall, not looking like she was walking but drifting.

But doing it *quickly*.

I rushed out behind her. The girls rushed behind me.

"It took some doing for your father to talk The Drakkar into this, as you well know. You give him reason, he'll be gone. We can only hope he hasn't already mounted his horse and rode away. *Then* what would we do?"

She turned and disappeared down a flight of steps and I followed.

"I should have known you would try something like this. Your father *did* know. He warned me. If you anger The Drakkar..." she trailed off, her tone dire, making it to the bottom of the stairs that had a banister, the entirety of which was an elaborately carved hunt scene.

I made it to the bottom too, to see Mom turn to me on a whirl of heavy skirts, another woman already with her, throwing over her shoulders a long, lustrous cloak made of dark brown pelts of some fur.

"Well!" she snapped. "If you anger The Drakkar, who knows what will happen to the realm?"

"Uh—" I started.

"I'll have none of it!" she retorted sharply. Having closed a silken frog at her throat, she tore a pair of gloves out of a hovering woman's hand and whirled again, gliding quickly to the door while pulling them on. "To the sleigh!" she ordered.

Sleigh?

I felt something heavy settle on my shoulders and looked down.

The four girls were encasing me in a cloak of dazzling white furry pelts that was so long, the bottom, which was a hem of what looked like tails tipped with dove-gray fur, skimmed the floor.

One girl stood in front of me and shoved the furred, tall collar of the cloak up my neck and it went so high, it covered my earlobes. She deftly and swiftly closed the frogs that went from chin to just below my breasts as two girls at either side of her reached through some slits in the fur and pulled out my hands. They then shoved a pair of elegant, winter-white suede gloves on them, the inside of which was a soft, plush fur that felt like rabbit.

After all this was accomplished in mere seconds, they started pushing me to the door.

"Sjofn," one whispered to me as we went. "If that is you or if it isn't, I must tell you that your trunks have been packed. They've been loaded on your sleigh. We did the best we could." She stopped me for just a moment, looked up at me with what appeared to be sad but searching eyes, then she whispered, "If you are our Sjofn, or not, but mostly if you are ours, please *try*, at least, to be happy. And if you are not, we wish you the best of luck on your adventure."

I blinked at her then opened my mouth to ask a question, but she shoved me out the door into the freezing cold air. I saw a deep red sleigh with a coat of arms painted on the back sides and curlicue trim. It had two black horses at the front. Mom was sitting in the back against a high button-backed seat covered in what looked like black suede and a man in a cloak and furry hat was sitting on an elevated seat some ways in front of her.

Before I knew it, I was rushed down the steps of the building and up the steps of the sleigh. The small door closed behind me, and I hadn't gotten my bearings yet when Mom's hand snaked out and grabbed mine. She yanked me to sitting and threw a heavy fur blanket over our laps.

"Go!" she snapped at the driver and off we went, and we didn't do it slowly.

I turned to her, taking in her beloved profile, gripping her hand in mine and opening my mouth to call to her name when she snatched her hand from mine and turned her head to look to the side.

"Atticus is likely livid," she noted then, "Would that I'd given him a son."

I blinked at the back of her head.

Uh...*ow.*

"Mom," I whispered.

"Quiet, Sjofn, I must prepare in case The Drakkar has stormed out. I must try to plan what I will do to stop your father from throttling you." Her head turned slowly to me, and she pierced me with her ice-blue eyes, which were, even in the torchlight, *icy.* "Or, perhaps, this time I won't bother," she remarked frostily.

Ow again.

"Uh—" I mumbled, and she lifted a gloved hand.

"Quiet!" she ordered and turned her head away. "The one time she can do something to help her father, help her mother, help her *country*, instead, yet again, my Sjofn creates a nightmare."

Oh jeez.

Something was not right.

I really needed to read that note.

We swiftly slid through the town or city-like-place and then came to a bone-jarring stop in front of a big building. I was so wrapped up in what was happening—and the fact that it didn't seem good—I didn't pay much attention, nor did I have the time to pay much attention. Without delay, Mom threw off the blanket, took my hand and dragged me from the sleigh. Then we were out of the cold and in a somewhat warm building lit softly with a huge number of candles everywhere.

I looked around at what appeared to be some kind of vestibule as more women, different ones this time, came hurriedly toward Mom and me.

Mom asked sharply, "The Drakkar?"

"He is still here, your grace," one of the women taking her cloak and gloves mumbled.

Your grace?

Your grace?

Okay, I should have gotten it before, what with the crowns and all, but it appeared my mother might be royalty.

Which would mean I was, too.

Holy moly!

Two women were divesting me of my gloves and cloak as my mother announced, "I will make haste in taking my seat. He will know we've arrived if I do. Prepare her instantly."

With that she was off.

I blinked at her back.

Then I blinked when a bundle of long, delicate twigs was thrust into my arms. I stared down at them. Most of their length was straight with little knots in the wood but the ends were curved and twirly. That was weird but the bark was weirder. They looked like they'd been sprayed by glitter, but on closer inspection, they hadn't.

They glittered naturally.

Whoa. Wow!

The ends of the twigs were bound tight with winter-white and ice-blue ribbons. There was no big bow to finish, the ends were tucked neatly away.

I hadn't yet processed the bundle in my arms or why it was there when I was pushed gently to stand in front of two double doors, and when I was, I looked up and around me.

"Good luck, my Winter Princess," one of the girls whispered, giving my upper arm a reassuring squeeze then she took off.

What? Winter princess?

Oh my God!

I *was* royalty and apparently my mother and father were queen and king.

Holy moly!

I stood there, alone and stunned at this news when it hit me I was alone and maybe had a second to find out what the fuck was going on.

I held the twigs in the crook of one arm like a beauty pageant contestant and dug the paper out of my cleavage with the other hand. Awkwardly but quickly unfolding it with one hand, I opened it and saw with some shock, and not a little alarm, that not much was written on it.

I took the two seconds it took to read it.

Seoafin,

Tonight, you marry The Drakkar. In the ancient tongue, this means The Dragon.

Good luck,

Sjofn.

Oh shit.

I'd been played.

Oh shit! I'd been played!

Before I could freak out or, I didn't know, maybe turn tail and run, the double doors swung wide, and I saw my father was stomping purposefully toward me.

At the same time, an orchestra struck up pounding a dramatic swell of music as beyond my father I saw what looked like the enormous sanctuary of a church filled to bursting with people, all of whom were standing and turning to me.

Nope, it wasn't an *oh shit* moment.

It was an *oh fuck* moment.

Dad made it to me, snatched the paper out of my hand, crinkled it quickly into a ball and tossed it away. He grabbed my hand firmly, tucked it in the crook of his arm at the same time jerking my body close to his side. He tipped his head down to me.

"Pleased you could make it, Sjofn," he growled.

Without delay, he started to march me down the aisle.

3

THE WEDDING

kay, okay, okay, it appeared I was getting married.

Shit.

To a man known as "The Dragon."

Shit!

Try, at least, to be happy, that girl had said to me.

I didn't think that boded well.

Enjoy The Drakkar. I think you will and more, I think he will enjoy you, the lady who could jump from a two-story building had said.

That didn't bode much better. As in, *at all.*

I clutched my father's arm as we walked down an aisle that seemed to be as long as a football field (but wasn't, it was still freaking long).

I wished that I could concentrate on being with my dad for the first time in fifteen years, but I couldn't. There was a sea of people all standing, all smiling at me or watching me with interest in their eyes and happiness on their faces.

I took them in as the music washed over me and my father marched me quickly forward.

Crap, I was getting...freaking...*married.*

Okay, Finnie, I said to myself, sucking in breath. *Take stock.*

Dad was at my side. He was alive, and except for the somewhat strange outfit he was wearing (dark-brown leather shorts, very high, dark-brown leather boots, a thick but gorgeous dark-red turtleneck sweater, a leather band at a slant around his chest crusted with gold inlaid with rubies, a fur cloak attached to the band that hung on a slant on his back and a big, gold crown with rubies and diamonds, much like Mom's, but masculine, on his head) was walking me down an aisle.

I never expected to have that, my dad walking me down the aisle. Not since I was fifteen and their plane went down. If I ever settled on a guy, I knew there would be no Dad walking me down an aisle.

So, okay, this was good. Or, not really, since I had no clue who I was marrying, but I decided to take it as such.

I looked to the front of the church that was coming ever closer and saw no cross or other church-like thing of my world. Instead, six enormous statues that looked carved out of ivory marble were positioned to form a curve at the front.

There were three men statues and three women starting with a man with legs planted, hands on hips. The next was a woman looking down at her belly where both her hands were resting. The next was a man who had one arm straight out, his legs separated, knees slightly bent, his other arm lifted, hand looking at the ready to pull what looked like a sword from his back. The next, another woman, this one had one arm dangling in front of her, her hand loosely opened at her pubis, her other arm lifted and resting on the side of her neck, a weird smile playing at her lips on her slightly downturned face. The next, a man with legs planted, arms crossed. And the last, a woman standing with her hands loosely cupped together, fingertips touching each other, head slightly bowed, lips to her hands.

Weird.

In front of this display stood a man wearing white robes with a long, wide satin band around his neck and dangling down his front. The band bore stripes starting with dark blue then light blue, red, deep violet, gold then bright green.

Okay, interesting. It seemed in this world they had more than one god. It was going to be cool learning more about that.

I sucked in breath to say something to my dad, anything, and to get him to say something in return. It caught in my throat as a man moved to stand in front of and to the side of the man in white robes.

That man looked down the aisle at me.

My step faltered when I took in all that was him and there was a lot to take in.

"Sjofn," Dad growled, his hand over mine in the crook of his arm tensing. He felt my step falter and he thought I was going to bolt. With effort, I pulled my shit together and kept walking.

But I was thinking, *Oh no.*

And that would be a big, oh no, no, no, *no.*

No.

Was that...? Was he...?

Oh shit. He was. He had to be. He was standing at the front of the church.

It was The Dragon.

It was my groom.

And I got his name. I totally got it with the way he was glowering at me like he most assuredly did *not* like me. He also did *not* want to be there. And further, what he did want to be doing was slaughtering entire villages either with weapons or, perhaps, breathing fire at them and setting them alight.

He was massive.

I was five six. He had to be six three or six four.

His hair was very dark, very thick with a bit of wave and it curled around the turtleneck of his sweater that was a dark brown, so dark it was nearly black.

He did not wear weird leather shorts but wool breeches that fit him snug and did not come near to hiding the power of his massive, muscular thighs. The same could be said for his sweater, which did not hide the breadth and brawn of his shoulders.

He had on boots that went to just below his knees and I saw that he didn't bother shining them for his nuptials. They were smudged and even had dirt and mud on them.

There was a leather band slanting across his chest, under his ribs at one side, over his shoulder at the other, but there were no gold, rubies or anything on his.

I saw the fall of a cloak, this one not a lustrous fur pelt like Dad's, but a simple hide.

I could also see the hilt of a sword over his shoulder behind where the band was and knives on either side of a leather belt at his waist.

His features were tan, sharp, strong and prominent. Heavy brow, jutting square jaw, carved cheekbones, full lips with tons of ridges in them. If his look wasn't so dark and *extremely* pissed off, he'd be hot.

He was not.

He was freaking scary. The bulk of him, the intensity of angry energy he exuded, which I could feel pressing against my skin, the murderous look in his eyes.

Scary.

No. *Terrifying* from top to toe.

And this was saying something, coming from me, Seoafin Wilde, a woman who did not get scared easily.

But no matter how frightening he was, I could not tear my gaze from him, so as we cleared the front of the church, I didn't.

And I saw his eyes were a weird shade of light olive green, not green or brown or hazel but light olive green surrounded by a mass of dark curling lashes.

As I got closer and we stopped a few feet from him, I noticed instantly he dwarfed me, not only in height, but in build. He was two of me, at least.

Oh God.

This was not good.

The man in white robes said something I didn't understand, not because I was freaking out, but because it was in a weird language.

The man known as The Dragon tore his furious, brown-green gaze from me and looked at him then he lifted a fist.

My torso swayed back as the massive thing sliced through the air.

Dad clutched me tighter then forced me forward so I was standing beside The Dragon as he pried my fingers from his elbow and lifted my hand, curling my frozen fingers over The Dragon's fist and holding them there.

God, my fingers got nowhere near covering his mighty fist.

The music stopped.

Oh shit.

The man in robes said something and my dad replied with a loud, authoritative, "Yes!"

His fingers squeezed mine then he was gone.

Gone!

Just like that.

Oh shit!

Without any ado, the man in robes tipped his head to the ceiling and started babbling in a foreign language that was nothing like anything I'd ever heard before. And I'd heard a lot of foreign tongues and knew my way around a few of them.

Crap.

This went on for a while as I stood next to my scary giant groom. Then it went on for another while.

And it went on.

All the time it went on, I stood with my hand on The Dragon's fist and, well...that was that.

Strange.

So strange and it went on for so long, I started to relax. Then I tensed when the robed guy turned abruptly and moved to stand in front the statue of the dude with his hands on his hips. The robed guy lifted his arms to the statue and started droning again.

He droned more. Then more. And some more.

About fifteen minutes later, he moved to the statue of the woman with her hands on her belly and started droning again.

Hells bells, if he prayed to all of them for fifteen minutes, we'd be standing there, hands raised, for over an hour.

The packed church was silent behind us, and the robed guy seemed like he was in trance of ecstasy, chatting it up in prayer with the lady statue. So I figured maybe I should take that moment to get to know the scary guy whose hand I was kind of holding and who would be (maybe, if this wedding didn't last a decade) my husband for a year.

Shit.

I peeked at him out of the corner of my eye.

Okay, slightly less scary. He didn't look pissed anymore. His eyes were aimed at the robed guy, and he looked bored out of his skull.

I could dig that. I was getting bored too. Maybe I could work with this.

I pulled my shit together and shuffled my body a little closer to his.

I stopped when his head tipped down, his green-brown eyes captured mine, and they went from bored to mildly annoyed, which was still super-freaking-scary.

I stared up at him.

But what could I do? Really, I had no choice.

I whispered, "Uh...hi."

His dark brows snapped together.

Yep, that was super-freaking-scary too.

Oh hell.

I plowed on, still whispering. "Uh...do we have to stand with our hands like this?"

His expression didn't change, and he made no reply.

"I mean," I went on, tipping my head to robed guy. "He's kinda into what he's doing so I think he wouldn't notice if we took a break."

No answer but his eyes didn't leave mine.

I kept going. "He's so into it, we could probably go sit down or even," I tried to joke and smiled up at him, "go out, get a beer and come back, and he'd still be at it."

His eyes narrowed on my mouth.

Definitely super-freaking-scary.

I stopped smiling and stopped speaking and his eyes snapped back to mine. I wanted to look away, but for some reason, I couldn't. Maybe it was because, really, upon closer inspection, he could be seriously hot if he didn't look like he wanted to break me in two.

Then I *really* wanted to look away when his eyes started roaming. My face, my hair, my crown and finally they drifted down where they took their time examining my ample cleavage.

Ho boy.

In the middle of this, for some reason, his jaw got hard (or, *harder*), his angry scowl returned, his eyes came back to mine for a slash before they turned back to the robed guy.

Well, that didn't work.

The robed guy moved to the next statue and started jabbering at it.

I tried to figure out my next move but there wasn't one. I was apparently a princess at my wedding to a man known as The Dragon. Both my parents didn't seem to like me much. I was standing in front of a huge church with a shitload of people in it. And I was getting married in the longest, most boring ceremony in the history of time.

Not a single bit of that was good, even the princess part.

Okay, that wasn't true. The princess part was good. So were my crown and my kickass clothes, not to mention my boots and underwear.

And I kinda liked the sleigh and wished I'd had a moment to enjoy the ride because I was guessing it would have been fun.

I held on to those thoughts as I kept my hand curled around his fist and the robed guy moved on to the next statue.

Then, ever game (this *was* my adventure and I had to make the most of it as I always did because that was what my parents taught me to do), I pulled in a breath and braved another step closer to my scary groom. I got so close, our arms brushed, and his chin dipped back down so he could scowl at me.

"Hi," I whispered. "Me again. Your future wife?" I made a lame attempt at a joke.

He did not laugh. He did not even smile. He continued to scowl but said no words.

Maybe he didn't have a sense of humor. Maybe he actually had no emotions at all except being bored and pissed.

"Uh..." I persevered. "What are those statues made of? That looks like marble. I've never seen anything like it. It's gorgeous."

His head tipped slightly to the side, but his eyes went alert.

Uh-oh!

Stupid!

Sjofn would totally know what those statues were made of and likely would have seen them countless times before (unless, of course, she wasn't religious).

Shit!

"Uh..." I mumbled quickly. "I mean, I should know, of course. And I've, uh...seen it before, obviously. I mean, seen those statues before just not um..." Shit! "That marble, uh...anywhere else. But I never thought to ask and, um...well, we seem to have time to chat."

He glared at me. Then he shook his head once and looked back at the robed guy.

Okay, that didn't work either.

I sighed and I did this heavily.

A thought occurred to me. I squeezed my fingers on his fist to get his attention and his head turned and dipped to look at me again.

I fought the fear his scary-assed glower sent slithering through my belly, got up on my toes and leaned in slightly, whispering, "Do you speak my language?"

Again with the brows snapping together and narrowing of eyes, so I dropped back down on my feet and leaned away an inch.

His voice came quiet but deep and growling and just as scary as the rest of him, "Have you been at the drink?"

The bad news was, he thought I was tipsy. The good news was, he spoke English.

"No, I...don't think so," I answered, still whispering.

"If you do not know then you have and have had too much," he returned, still growling quiet.

"Well, I don't feel lightheaded or sick and I'm not swaying or singing, which I do a lot when I've imbibed too much so," I tried another smile, "evidence is suggesting I'm not shitfaced."

He aimed his narrow-eyed, knit-browed scowl at my mouth again before it snapped back to my eyes.

Then he growled low, quiet and now ominous, "Shut your mouth..." his neck bent further so his angry face was closer and finished, "future *wife*."

He spit out the last word like it tasted foul then straightened and looked at the robed guy again.

So did I to see he had fortunately moved on to the next statue.

Hmm.

None of that went well. Not any of it. Not even a little bit.

And I was right when I first saw him. He didn't want to be here at all, but I was getting the impression, especially not with me.

I decided to try again maybe at the reception. Maybe after I had some alcohol and maybe after I got some down him. Maybe he'd loosen up then. Maybe, if I got enough down him, he'd pass out so I could avoid the wedding night, uh...*festivities* until I could figure out how to avoid the marital consummation on the whole.

In other words, hijack a sleigh and get the fuck out of Dodge.

I stood silent as the robed guy kept talking to statues and finally moved back to stand in front of us. He said a bunch more stuff, and at long last, he smiled, put a hand on my shoulder and another one he reached high to put on The Dragon's shoulder. He nodded up at The Dragon happily.

He dropped his hands, and I wondered if that was it or if we would exchange rings or vows. I hoped I didn't have anything I was supposed to know to say, but I didn't wonder long.

This was because The Dragon turned his fist. It opened and his long fingers engulfed my hand. I realized his big body was turning to me.

I turned to him, tipped my head back to look up, and then I felt my stomach drop.

He was smiling, even, beautiful white teeth against tan skin. And his eyes were shining with a light that looked a bizarre and terrifying mixture of wolfish, amused, lethal and heated.

He let my hand go, and before I knew what was happening, his long, strong arms were wrapped around me. One tight at my waist lifting my feet clean off the floor, hauling me up his body, the fingers of the other driving into my hair to cup the back of my head.

I let out a surprised cry as my hands automatically went to his shoulders to hold on. I vaguely heard a few excited whoops from the church but

then he was forcing my head down, his was slanting and...oh God...oh *God*!
—he was going to kiss me!

Nope, he wasn't going to. He did.

And no sooner had he crashed my mouth down to his when his mouth opened, his tongue forced my lips open, and he *kissed* me.

Deep, rough, hard, wet and oh so very hungry.

And last, but definitely not least, *skillful*.

I didn't know this guy and he scared the living daylights out of me but that did not take one *iota* away from the fact that the man could freaking *kiss*.

It was the best kiss I'd ever had. By far.

Wow.

His head jerked back, tearing his mouth from mine, and I stared down at him dazed.

I was wrong. He wasn't scary. He was totally freaking *hot*.

I heard but yet didn't hear the calls, shouts, clapping and whoops as the daze of his kiss slid away from me. I saw I had wrapped my arms around his neck, and he was looking up at me, again scary-pissed, but now also guarded-pissed.

What?

Suddenly he dropped me so heavily on my feet, I instantly had to brace so my knees wouldn't buckle. I barely got my legs under control when his hand gripped mine and he was dragging me down the aisle.

Yes, *dragging me*.

Uh-oh.

I had to run to keep up with his long strides as I heard my father shout from behind me, "Drakkar! What are you doing? Where are you going? The celebration!"

The Dragon didn't slow, not even a little bit as my father called and people stopped cheering and clapping and started buzzing with surprise. But I had to keep up with him or he'd be dragging my prone body behind him rather than my sprinting one.

We made it to the vestibule, and he yanked my cloak out of a waiting girl's hands, another one rushed to me, shoving my gloves at me. I took them reflexively and we were out in the cold.

Then I was up, thrown bodily, yes *bodily*, into the back of a sleigh. My cloak was tossed at me, landing against my chest and lap.

I blinked at my new husband in shock, my heart hammering. He gathered a bunch of leather straps, thrust them in my hands and I automatically gripped them. As people poured out of the church, he wasted not a second mounting a glossy, huge steed, twirling it around, then he leaned to the side, slapping the rump of one of the four horses fixed to my sleigh and shouting, "*Yah!*"

All four horses burst forward and the straps in my hands started slipping so I gripped them tight.

And with my new husband at my side, me in a sleigh, we rushed through the snow of the town or city-type place, right the fuck out of it and into a forest.

Oh.

Shit.

4

HOME SWEET HOME

Needless to say, since I'd never driven one, I didn't know how to steer a sleigh.

Also needless to say, my new husband frowned on this.

So after we cleared town on a fast gallop and kept on going like the devil himself was at our heels and my sleigh kinda went awry a couple of times—necessitating my new husband on his mighty beast circling it closely to right its course, after which, each time, he aimed a ferocious scowl at me that made my heart skip and *not* in a good way—I learned quick.

Eventually, we slowed to a fast trot. As I got the hang of things, I had a look around the sleigh.

There were some hooks in the panel in front of me, so I secured the reins to them and quickly donned my cloak and pulled on my gloves mostly because it was bitter cold and I was freezing my ass off. My dress was awesome, and it was velvet, but I'd never experienced a cold that cold. I never thought I'd say it, or even think it, but I needed fur.

I sat down and saw a big fur blanket on the floor of the sleigh in front of me and also a furry, white hat had fallen there. I exchanged the crown for the hat and pulled the blanket on top of me, shoving it under my ass to tuck it secure as high as I could get it around my body. Then I secured the crown as best I could in the open sleigh.

Better.

I grabbed the reins again and took stock.

I had four beautiful dapple-gray horses pulling me. Behind me in the sleigh there was a shiny black piece of fabric with what appeared in the forest-muted moonlight a gold and red crest stitched into it, stretched over a bunch of bulky stuff and held down with gleaming, gold, what looked like silk ropes.

My luggage, apparently.

Okay. Well, there you go.

Off I was on my honeymoon.

Ho boy.

It was at this point when I thought I really, *really* should have listened to Claudia.

We kept riding, and, well, sleighing through the snow, and The Dragon didn't engage me in conversation as we did. I didn't try either. I concentrated on not steering my horses into any trees. Then I concentrated on my cheeks not freezing off.

We trotted ever onward in newlywed silence that was more than a little disconcerting, but I hung with it not sure I wanted the alternative. Early experience indicated my husband wasn't a skilled conversationalist and considering he gave the impression he didn't like me much, I wasn't sure I wanted to hear what he might have to say.

After some time, we cleared the forest and moved into a vast snow-covered plain that was absolutely gorgeous considering the snow sparkled and the entire vista was blanketed by the twinkling moonlit sky that was filled with what seemed like three times as many stars as any night sky I ever beheld. Then, after some more time, we went through a small village that I wished we'd slowed even a little bit as we went through so I could take in more because it seemed mega cool. But we didn't.

Not even a little bit.

The Dragon led us ever onward through more plain then forest then I started to get concerned about the state of my horses, and his, but he drove us on.

And on.

We went through another town, this one larger, but still no slowing.

That was when I realized I was getting hungry and my hands hurt from holding on to the reins. My body was ensconced in fur so I was actually toasty warm. It was just my cheeks that were cold. So cold, they hurt.

I decided it would probably not be smart to share this as my husband wasn't talkative, and he clearly didn't like me, so I figured he wouldn't want to listen to me bitch (even with justification), thus I didn't share. I just tried to ignore it and didn't quite succeed but didn't outright fail either.

He led us through more forest, and we kept right on going. We had long since left the mountain-town or city-type-place behind, and with it my parents, which I did not think was good. Nor did I like it.

I pulled up the courage then pulled in a breath and started to say loudly, "Uh—"

"*Quiet!*" he barked without even looking at me.

Shit.

I was right. Not a big conversationalist.

Okay, I'll deal with the next second. Then the next. And the next. And so on. Focus on the now. On just the now, I told myself.

I focused on the now and in so doing I noticed I was right. A sleigh ride was fun. Maybe not one that lasted hours through a dark, cold night, but I decided not to focus on that and instead focus on the fun part.

And I discovered that commanding the sleigh was even more fun. I tried things out and found that the horses were obviously highly trained. They adjusted to even the most minimal change of their reins and that was super cool.

I did this for a while and then got over it. It was fun but we'd been going for hours and nothing was fun for that long, certainly not driving a sleigh.

We cleared the massive forest and were on another plain, this one by a sparkling river lit with moonlight, which was pretty cool.

We went through another town, which was also cool, but we didn't slow so I didn't see much of it.

This lasted a long, long, *long* time and I was definitely hungry, definitely worried about the state of my horses because they'd been going at a good clip for what was now hours, and I was closing in on pissed when the sun started kissing the sky and we entered another forest.

It wasn't lost on me that the air was even more frigid wherever we were now compared to the arctic clime we left (in other words, it was now *fucking* cold rather than just *freaking* cold and suffice it to say I had thought it was *fucking* cold before, but now I knew the true meaning of that). I lost my pique when I saw the trunks of the trees, all the way up, were dusted with snow, heavier on one side where the wind drifted it up or lifted it to powder the higher bark.

It was fantastically gorgeous.

What was more gorgeous was, when we hit a sleepy, marshmallow-snow-roofed, icicle-dripping, chimney-smoke-drifting village in a some-what cleared area.

That was, trees scattered the level area and the hillside the village deco-rated, but they were not as thick as the forest. There was a wide-ish glis-tening creek running through the village with several streams meeting it crisscrossing the forest floor and running down the hill to join the river (in fact, my horses and sleigh glided over two such streams). And there were two large streams of steaming water that clearly came from hot springs that glided down the hill and poured into the creek. There were even not one, but two wooden waterwheels.

Definitely cool!

I really wanted to take that village in because it was way cooler than all the rest and all the rest were already cool, but we went straight through it. We kept going through the forest for what I estimated was five minutes before The Dragon turned his steed.

I turned my horses with him, and I had to concentrate because this was not a road. We were going through the forest proper, and I had to focus on steering my horses through as well as not getting hit by a big, low hanging branch (of which there were a lot) or whipped by smaller ones (of which there were a lot more).

Finally, I saw it, up on a rise surrounded by trees. A building with some outbuildings. It looked cockeyed because one side was one story, the other side with what looked like a half a story on top.

The Dragon slowed and so did I. I was pretty pleased how I brought the sleigh around to the front executing a tight curve in the small area allowed (truth be told, the horses pretty much knew what they were doing and obviously did all the work, but I thought we all managed it with great aplomb), and we came to a halt.

By the time I did this, The Dragon was already off his horse and opening the front door to the dwelling. What he was not doing was smiling proudly at me and calling, "Well done, my new wife in her gorgeous princess wedding finery!"

Hmm.

It appeared this was either home sweet home or where we were stop-ping for some rest.

And it appeared that The Dragon was no gentleman and was not going to assist his new bride from her awesome sleigh.

And it also appeared that the next few minutes were going to be crucial. I had to be alert, be smart and handle them right. I had no idea what was going on and I had no idea how to handle that frightening man, but somehow, I was going to have to find out the first and do the second.

My body ached, my hands hurt, my cheeks were numb from the cold. I could eat my way through an entire buffet and then I could sleep for a week. But I still got up, found the latch, opened the door to my sleigh, stepped down into the snow and followed my groom into the house.

He was standing in the middle of it, hands on hips, feet planted wide, staring at me looking fierce and impatient like I'd made him wait for an hour while I tried on a variety of shoes to see which matched my outfit rather than made him wait what was likely around two minutes, if that.

I took as much of the dwelling in as I could in a quick, rounded glance. I saw a kitchen at the back, over it I saw I was right. A low-ceiling loft with short railing that you got to using a ladder. The roof was at a slant, opening wide at the front room where there was no loft. A big room at the front. Stone fireplace on either side. Another fireplace I could see in the loft. And a closed door to a space beside the kitchen.

And everything was filthy, absolutely. There was what looked like a hundred years of dust and even cobwebs all over it (not that I could imagine spiders existing in this climate, but clearly they did at some point). There was furniture covered by graying sheets. Windows so covered in grime you could barely see through them. And there were heavy curtains having caught so much dust, it had actually started *dripping*.

Eek!

The Dragon suddenly spoke, and I jumped, my gaze swinging to him.

"The stable is stocked for your horses. The larder for you. Logs, fuel and supplies out back. More logs in the shed. You should be provided for."

At his words, I blinked at him in confusion as he stalked to a counter that jutted out, separating the kitchen-type area from the living room-type area. He dropped a leather pouch on it. It made a loud, thumping jangle., and he turned, walking toward the door while speaking.

"Coin for you to use in Houllebec for necessities."

I blinked again and turned my body to keep facing him as he moved. He stopped at the door and turned to me.

"When I decide it's time, I shall find a woman who looks somewhat like you, if that's possible, and sire a child on her. We will present this child to your father as his heir."

Uh...what?

"What?" I whispered and his hard face got harder at my quiet, one word question.

"I'll not thrust my cock between the legs of a woman who prefers a woman's mouth there, Sjofn."

Uh...*what*?

"What?" I breathed this time, knowing my eyes had grown wide.

He jerked his chin. "You were drunk and may not remember our discussion, but I bloody well do."

Oh God. Oh shit. Oh God.

Now I knew why Sjofn played me.

She was a lesbian and wanted nothing to do with a man who was more man than any man maybe on two worlds!

Oh shit! Oh God! Oh shit!

"Uh—" I started, not having that first clue what to say.

"Maybe," he cut me off, "as further recompense for this ridiculous, bloody, gods-damned farce your father talked me into and, for some gods-damned reason, I agreed to, I'll watch you at play with a woman."

Oh God! Oh Shit! OhGodohshitohGod!

He went on, "The gods know, a trunk of Sjofn ice diamonds and a trunk of gold is *not* worth being saddled with the bloody likes of *you* as wife for a lifetime. I might as well get what I can out of it and watching a woman take you would be..." his eyes swept me before he finished, "*interesting*."

OhshitohGodohshit.

"Uh—" I mumbled.

He cut me off again saying, "I'll be back in a month." I blinked as my body locked in shock at his words and he walked out the door, starting to close it behind him. He stopped and his eyes locked on mine, "Maybe two."

Then he was gone.

I stared at the door unseeing. Then, slowly, I looked around the filthy house, which was only slightly less cold than the outside and nowhere near as grand as the place I'd started this adventure.

It hit me he said he'd be back in a month...or two.

He was leaving me here.

Leaving me here!

I came unstuck with a jolt and ran to the door.

Throwing it open I saw my sleigh, my horses and no Dragon.

I glared into the brightening sky.

Then I shouted at the top of my lungs, "Goddamn it!"

My horses danced slightly in agitation.

I stood in the cold, glaring at the thick but beautifully frosted forest all around thinking I had not handled that situation, or him, very well.

On that thought I stomped back into the house.

~

I WAS COLD, exhausted and hungry, but I was also Seoafin Wilde. I'd been in some serious pickles in my life, and I'd always managed to survive.

It must be said, sharks crashing a sea dive and elephants stampeding were a lot more serious than a dirty house in the middle of a frozen nowhere. And Claudia hadn't even mentioned that time the natives got *seriously* restless.

So I was Seoafin Wilde and *nothing* ever got me down.

The good news was, I was a lesbian and therefore my husband wanted nothing to do with me.

The bad news was, I was a lesbian and my husband thought he could watch me "at play" with a woman.

The other good news was, he was gone, apparently for a while, so I had time to figure out what to do about that.

But the other bad news was, I was in the middle of a frost-filled forest. I was cold, exhausted and hungry and I had four horses as well as myself to take care of.

So, since I really had no choice, I took care of the lot of us.

Prioritizing, I had to get changed. Many people wouldn't think this was priority, but seriously, that dress *rocked,* and it wouldn't do for it to get dusty or torn.

So I went out to the sleigh. I told my horses I'd get them warm and fed as soon as possible. They whinnied like they knew what I was talking about, and I unhooked the silken ropes that held down the also silk tarp and threw it aside.

Eight huge trunks were in the back of the sleigh and four smaller ones.

I started with the smaller ones because I could carry them, lugging them in one by one and opening them. Quick glances told me there was nothing I could use in the present. So out I went to pull off the first trunk, which was so huge and heavy I had to drag it down off the sleigh. It thudded against the snow, and I dragged it into the house.

I opened it.

Sheets and blankets.

Shit.

Back out I went, and I got the second trunk in.

On top of some folded soft, knit woolen gowns, I saw a note. I picked it up and read it.

Princess Sjofn,

We're so sorry. Your mother supervised your packing. We had to pack only your trousseau. We couldn't pack any of your breeches or the shirts and boots you like.

But all of this is lovely, and we hope you enjoy it.

Write to us and tell us how you're getting along.

We will miss you.

Alyssa, Esther, Jocelyn and Bess.

Well, apparently, Sjofn of this world dressed like a boy.

Perhaps not a surprise.

I had to admit, even though I (mostly) avoided dressing like a boy (unless I was caving or the like) I could use some breeches or whatever at the present time. But if a dress was all I had, a dress was what I would use.

I sorted through them, finding the least fine but warmest looking one, as well as a light wool cloak at the bottom of the trunk. I then changed (with some difficulty for it was buttoned down the back) out of my wedding gown.

Seeing my underwear at its fullest, I was right. It was awesome. The bustier was hot as all hell, my breasts nearly spilling out of it. It was so damned sexy, as crazy as such a thought was, I couldn't help but think my stupid new husband who didn't wait around to get an eyeful of *that* was a moron. But I didn't look long because it was fucking cold, and I needed to get dressed.

Thus, I got dressed and I got busy.

I started fires in the two grates in the living room. Luckily, there were dry logs stacked at the sides as well as kindling. They even had matches that were made of very long, slim pieces of wood that I had to drag across the stone of the hearths, but they made starting a fire a snap.

Out to the sleigh I went to drag in all the trunks.

Then back out to stamp through the snow to the biggest outbuilding. Upon entry, I found it was what I thought it was, a six-stall stable, cleaner than the house by far (my husband was clearly not only scary but also a dick; cleaning the stable but keeping the house in such a state). There was a barrel full of fresh water, plenty of oats and hay.

With effort, I threw open the huge sliding door, stamped back through the snow, got in the sleigh and led them inside the stable. I closed the door and went to work.

It took for-freaking-ever to figure out how to unhook the horses and get their apparatus off. But I damn well did it, led them to their stalls and fed and watered them. I hung the apparatus up on hooks outside each stall and I stamped back to the house.

Once inside, I fed the fires more wood and took inventory.

The kitchen was rudimentary: big, old, battered wooden table with two chairs, big used butcher block in the middle, big black iron stove, wooden sink with (thank God) a pump that, upon testing, worked and pumped clear, clean water. Cupboards, as my dickhead husband said, were not bare, but most of the shit at first glance I didn't know what it was.

I decided I'd spend more time on that later.

There were also other supplies stuffed in the plethora of cabinets: dishes, cups, silverware, wooden spoons and a stack of wooden bowls and other accoutrements to use for cooking, cast iron pots and skillets, candle-stick holders and gas lamps with a few lanterns thrown in.

Using the stack of wood in the kitchen, I built another fire in the stove then out the back door I went.

There was an enclosed porch-type area that ran the length of the house, one whole side lined with stacks of logs so high, they went up to my neck. There were a couple of cupboards too, one I opened was filled with tall candles of all widths. Another one was filled with plugged jugs of what a sniff test told me was some kind of fuel. Probably for the lamps.

Okay, good. I had heat and light and, by the looks of it, a lot of it.

I stamped out the back door to the two remaining outbuildings.

One, to my gloom, was an outhouse.

The other, far larger, was a shed that was also filled with split, prepared logs, a shitload of kindling and another cupboard filled with fuel. There was also a hatchet, an axe, several buckets and other bits and bobs.

Back to the house I went. I opened a door off the living room and entered a room that had a table with a ceramic basin on it, a pitcher under it, an oval mirror on the wall over it and a drum like thing in the middle of the space, this one made of some kind of metal. It was oval and I suspected it was a tub. There was also a small fireplace in there.

Well, bath time wasn't going to be relaxing. But at least there was a bath.

Back out to the living room where I wandered the place, noting there were lots of rugs on the floor, not thick, but they covered the wood planks so the cold wouldn't seep up. As I wandered, I carefully pulled off the sheets covering the furniture, bunching them quickly while doing it so I captured as much of the dust as possible.

Now we were talking.

Finally, something decent.

A big fluffy couch and two deep-seated fluffy chairs with ottomans, all turned to the biggest fireplace. A sturdy desk with chair behind it in a corner. Handsome tables here and there as well as some tall candleholders. It was all rustic hunting-cabin chic, but it looked well-made and definitely comfortable...if cleaned.

I then climbed the ladder and, moving around the loft stooped, which was the only way I could for the ceiling was so low, I saw it had three windows. Two either side of the small stone fireplace that had an iron grate at the front to catch sparks and one at the side facing the back. All were grimy and had heavy, short curtains.

The loft also had a fluffy, down mattress on the floor covered with a sheet I yanked off and I saw it also had four fluffy down pillows. Last, it had a heavy curtain that ran on a rail the length of the space in front of a short railing, likely to ward off the chill from the bigger space and keep in the heat from the fire.

Bent double, I stared at the bed. I thought of crawling into it. Then I wondered about the light, how long the days were here and how I would most assuredly *not* want to pass out, sleep the day away and be in this loft in this stinking house in the dark without having at least set up the candles and probably be, by that time, ravenous instead of what I was right then, starving.

Not to mention, I had two open fires burning downstairs.

I sucked in breath and muttered, "I'm *never* telling Claudia *any* of this."

I went to the ladder and down to see if I could unearth any cleaning supplies.

THERE WERE, indeed, cleaning supplies in the back of a cupboard in the kitchen (if one could call them that). But there was soap, what I took as parallel universe dish towels and rags, which weren't much different from each other, but the towels were slightly finer material and definitely cleaner. I also found a broom and mop on the back porch.

Therefore, hours and hours and hours later, the sun had long since set (way early if I estimated it right), and I was done.

The floors were swept (and, proudly, mopped).

The cupboards wiped down.

The rugs and furniture cushions taken outside and beaten with this kind of enormous bent twig fly-swatter thing I found in the shed.

All the dishes, pots and pans were cleaned. The cupboards (and the dead insects hiding there) wiped out and dishes, pots and pans put back.

The cobwebs were swiped down.

The surfaces of the furniture polished.

The windows were washed to a shine so I could actually see out.

The curtains carefully taken down, pulled outside and shaken to within an inch of their lives. The same with the pillows on the bed upstairs.

I put out candleholders and filled them with candles. I filled lamps with fuel and put those out too. I dragged in a bunch of wood and replenished all the stocks and even found this cool pulley thing that helped me load up a stack in the loft (which I did and then I built a fire up there too).

I found a hunk of meat, a loaf of bread and an enormous wedge of cheese. I sliced into all of it, made a huge, honking sandwich and ate it, washing it down with a cup of the fresh, clean, absolutely delicious and very cold water from the pump.

I inventoried the kitchen and found milk in a jug in a cupboard that jutted out of the house (natural fridge) with lots of cheese, meat (some cooked, some raw), some sliceable sausage (that smelled awesome), a slab of bacon, a bowl filled with eggs and a big urn of butter.

In the cupboards there were pots of jam. There was also a jar of ground coffee (hurray!) and what looked like an old-fashioned percolator to make it in. There was loose tea. There was sugar. There was flour. There was a salt pig (filled) and a pepper grinder (also filled). There were jars of spices, which I made stabs at guessing what they were with sniff tests (oregano, basil, bay leaves, thyme, parsley, cayenne, cinnamon, and nutmeg). And there were big sacks of potatoes and onions, smaller ones of oats and rice, and a string of garlic.

I could totally work with this.

I was set.

At least for a while.

I set about perusing my trunks and found clothes, underwear, boots, delicate wool and cashmere stockings, shoes and cloaks all a variety of fabrics and colors. All gorgeous. All obviously expensive and exquisitely made and not meant to be worn in a cabin in the middle of nowhere but... whatever. I also found some seriously sexy nightgowns (again, my new husband was a moron, the nightwear, as well as every single piece of underwear, was freaking *amazing*).

I found sheets (lots of them), quilts, throws and blankets (lots of those too) so I made up the bed. I also found some china and silver, including an elegant, stunning coffee service. These I put in the kitchen. There were further what I guessed were towels and washcloths, which I stacked on some shelves I wiped down in the bathroom-type place.

There was hair stuff, jewelry and makeup, bath soap, scented powders, perfume and lotions. This entire small (ish) trunk I also carted into the bathroom-type place.

There was another trunk filled with leather-bound books, some printed, some blank (journals?), elegant ice-blue writing paper and envelopes, a wax candle and an elaborate, silver seal to use to close the wax on the envelopes (awesome!), a slim, silver quill pen and a couple bottles of ink. I stocked the desk with these.

And there was even a trunk filled with crystal: wineglasses of three shapes (white, red and flat bowled champagne, two of each), stemmed aperitif glasses (also two) and, overkill but definitely awesome, a beautiful crystal vase.

I knew the perfect use for that.

So I went out to the sleigh, fetched my bouquet of twigs from the floor where it had fallen (as well as my forgotten crown, though how I could forget my crown, who knew, but I did). I took them back to the house, shoved the twigs in the vase and put it on the low table in front of the couch.

It looked good there. A touch of glitter, a touch of beauty. Perfect.

The crown I set smack in the middle of the mantel of the biggest fireplace, the one the furniture faced.

It looked good where it was, too. But it would look good anywhere.

All that I couldn't use or needed to be stored, I carefully packed back up and lined the trunks where they would look nice against the walls. Any empty trunks, I carted to the front door so I could drag them to the stables tomorrow.

I had just loaded all the fires with more logs, lit the candles and lamps and found some folded screens on the back porch that were meant to sit in front of the fires to catch sparks. I set them up and I was currently flat out on the couch, exhausted, hungry again and trying to count how many times I boiled water in that big, iron kettle on the stove when I realized there I was.

Alone, in the middle of nowhere and far away from my parents who I had spent a million dollars to see and who, after seeing, didn't like me.

"Fuck," I muttered, staring into the fire.

Well, at least that dickhead didn't defeat me, which, dumping a princess in this hellhole without even seeing to her animals, I knew he meant to do.

My horses were sheltered and fed. The house was cleaned. I was hungry again, but I was not eating, not because I couldn't feed myself, but because I was too freaking exhausted to get up and go to the kitchen. I'd taken stock and I was sitting pretty (*ish*). The house was warm, the fires, lanterns and candles glowed, and the couch was seriously freaking comfy.

I grabbed a soft woolen throw I'd unearthed from one of my trunks and tossed on the couch, and I pulled it over my body. I held my feet out in front of me and used my toes on the heel of my boot, pushing down, down, down until the thing slid off. Ditto the other boot.

I curled up and stared into the fire.

I pulled in a deep breath.

And I grinned.

"Welp," I whispered, "one could say this is an adventure. *Definitely*."

Then I fell into a dead sleep...smiling.

THE TWO DARK figures shifted soundlessly through the snow toward the cabin.

Once there, they stopped at a window and looked inside.

At what he saw, Frey Drakkar did a slow blink and just stopped himself from muttering an expletive.

In eight short hours, the Winter Princess had transformed his cabin. The bloody thing even had a crystal vase filled with her wedding bundle on a table. The fires were burning strong. Every inch looked clean. There was a warm rug tossed over one of the chairs. And—he shifted to another window for a different view, Thaddeus following him—*she* was sleeping peacefully with an appealing grin on her unduly beautiful face, her abundance of white-blonde hair scattered over the arm of the couch, her delectable body covered in another warm throw.

He shifted his gaze from her to the vase on the table and something about that made his neck get tight as it had done several times since her small hand wrapped around his fist in the Dwelling of the Gods.

Princess Sjofn was not known to enjoy pretty things. Princess Sjofn would throw such a bundle out. Definitely her wedding bundle of adela tree twigs, regardless of how precious they were. Princess Sjofn would not stuff them in a sparkling crystal vase and put them on display.

And Princess Sjofn had not once, on the three unpleasant occasions he'd spent time with her, smiled at him. Or joked with him. Or shown her ample and unfortunately spectacular cleavage. He didn't know she had that in her or that she could even wear a dress without looking like her garments were boiled tar poured on her skin.

At the very least not wear them without looking like she was sucking lemons but wear them with grace and float down the aisle toward him with the bearing of her mother—a woman renowned throughout Lunwyn, hell, all of the Northlands, for her refined manner.

He's so into it, we could probably go sit down or even go out, get a beer and come back and he'd still be at it.

He heard her teasing words and saw her smiling face and he suspected the Winter Princess was up to something.

Something was not right.

He just had no idea what. What he did know was that whatever that woman was up to, he had no intention of falling prey to it.

Her father was king, regardless of the fact that his blood didn't merit the throne. And King Atticus had offered an immensely handsome dowry. The pull of both Frey refused for three years.

But King Atticus was anxious for a son so the kingdom would be secure, going to Sjofn's boy rather than King Atticus's brother, Baldur, who ruled Middleland, the country to the south. Baldur was a known tyrant and a twat. Even Atticus detested him, everyone did.

This last, more than the trunks of Sjofn ice diamonds, gold and the land Atticus had settled on him for strapping him with his man-woman daughter was the reason why Frey had finally agreed.

There was nothing Frey would not do for Lunwyn, including marrying a guenipe, even though he was urged strongly not to do so by powers he should likely not ignore.

It was that and the fact that the blood of Drakkar would sit the throne.

His son would be king. And Frey wouldn't have to wage war to dethrone Baldur or Baldur's own woman-man son should one of them succeed Atticus. Not to mention, Frey wouldn't have to settle his own seat on Lunwyn's throne after he defeated Baldur.

That would be a pain in the arse. Absolutely.

Thaddeus whistled his surprise through his teeth at the sights he beheld taking Frey out of his thoughts.

Frey ground his own teeth.

Then he moved away from the cabin, soundless through the wood to where they had left their horses, and Thaddeus followed.

Without a word, they swung into their saddles, but Frey didn't ride. He sat on his mount, Tyr, staring at his cabin, smoke serenely drifting from four chimneys, a golden, cheerful glow shining from the windows, his bloody *wife* asleep and dreaming of gods knew what.

Frey glared at the house feeling something unsettling.

Then he looked at the windows.

They were opened, the curtains not closed to shut out the cold.

His brows drew together.

The woman had it in her to clean and build fires. This was a surprise and an annoying one. But Sjofn, Winter Princess, who had every whim catered to but who clearly demonstrated she had the wherewithal to fend for herself, would therefore definitely draw the curtains to ward off the cold. Even if she had been reclining, defeated, in his filthy hunting cabin, being Lunwynian, she would know to close the curtains to shut out the cold.

Thaddeus spoke, taking Frey from these thoughts.

"I must say, Frey, I wouldn't give a gods' damn that one preferred tart. *That* was my new bride, she'd be tasting my cock either straight through her mouth or because I was thrusting it so deep, she'd savor it in her throat," Thaddeus remarked quietly at his side.

"Mm," Frey murmured.

Frey felt his friend's eyes. "You don't agree?"

"I've no idea where that mouth has been. Or that cunt," Frey replied.

"Must say, speaking true, I wouldn't care about that either," Thaddeus returned.

Frey thought of her hair all over the armrest, her smile, her cleavage.

Then he thought of her fervent return of his kiss after they were wed. A return that made his blood heat and his cock begin to get hard as her tongue played hungrily with his and her arms glided around his neck, holding him tight.

It wasn't a passable kiss. It wasn't even good.

What it was, was the best embrace by far he'd ever shared.

Something else that did not sit right, for that was something else that was *not* Princess Sjofn.

He'd been infuriated at her drunken admission years ago when King Atticus had started his campaign to win Frey Drakkar as his son-in-law. He'd been infuriated because she was, without a doubt, the most beautiful woman he'd ever seen and he wanted her the instant he saw her, even, maybe *especially* because she was wearing breeches.

His new wife had a spectacular arse and even better legs.

Then he found out what she was.

Frey had no issue with guenipes.

But he wanted no wife who did not want him, no matter her beauty.

However, after that kiss, after she'd demonstrated how very well she could pretend, Frey had to admit, Thaddeus's words held merit.

"The ship awaits, Thad," Frey muttered, putting an end to their short conversation.

"Indeed, Frey," Thad muttered back.

They turned their horses, touched heels to flanks, and they were away.

5

WELCOME HOME

*S*ix weeks later...

"Woo hoo!" I cried, feeling the rush of cold air coming in behind me as someone entered the pub.

I ignored it to crow my victory, my arms straight up over my head. I grinned at the men sharing the table with me before I dropped my arms and leaned in, pulling the pile of coin toward me.

"Are you sure I taught you this game two short weeks ago, Princess Finnie?" Laurel grumbled at me from my right, watching his money come toward my big pile.

"Mm-hmm, swear," I nodded, turned my head, lifted my hand to cross my heart and smiled big at him. "Cross my heart and hope to die."

"Right," Ulysses muttered from my left, and I swung my smile at him to see him smiling back showing me he held no ill-will.

Then again, we were playing for what was, essentially, pennies so it wasn't like they owed me the notes on their cottages.

I reached for the rough deck of cards, my fingers deftly organizing them in order to shuffle as I declared, "My deal."

"Make sure she doesn't do it from the bottom, Uly. She may be the mother of our future king, but I don't put anything past her," Frederick, across from me, said to Ulysses even though I knew he was kidding.

He liked me.

In fact, most of the village of Houllebec did. And the only people in the village (that I knew of) who didn't were people I had not met.

My adventure may have not started all that great, but it got a whole lot better.

First, I found a side saddle in the stable (as well as a big washing tub with one of those grinder things to wring out clothes so I could wash my clothes, and I did, using that thing—though, it must be said it wasn't my favorite chore, especially since I had to hang everything all around the house and it took *forever* to dry and messed with the cozy, rustic cabin vibe I had going).

I knew how to ride, just not side saddle. But I loaded the saddle on one of my grays, figured out how to lug my ass up on it, and the very next day after I arrived, I followed our tracks into the village I quickly learned was called Houllebec.

And I'd gone every day since.

The village was *awesome*. It didn't only look cool, it *was* cool.

It had two warm, clean, fun pubs, both that served excellent food, and both had inns because people traveled there to use the hot springs that were hidden all through the hills—this a moneymaker for the townsfolk as the hot springs were well known and the people who sought them brought loads of "coin."

It had a bakery that made magnificent bread, tarts, cakes and even pastries. They had a butcher, a small dressmaker, a market that had staples and not-so-staples including some fresh veg on occasion and even bright-colored delicious candy and sumptuous chocolate they brought in (stocked all the time!) and homemade fudge they made right in the window.

It had a blacksmith, an iron works, a stable, a mill and other such cool-as-shit remote-village-in-a-frozen-parallel-world stuff.

I wandered the town daily and sometimes stayed as late as dinner (which I ate in the pubs) and beyond so I could have a few ales, chat and play cards with new friends.

I was friendly, talkative and anyway, they knew who I was because they heard about me marrying The Drakkar who, I discovered, was actually *named* Drakkar, as in *Frey* Drakkar.

This I learned luckily, if coincidentally, on my fourth (but not last) stop to buy chocolate croissants from the bakery.

They also knew me because my hair was well known and many of them told me they'd know me from miles away with just one glimpse of my Lunwyn-wide, famous, beautiful white-blonde hair (this I thought was sweet).

And they were in fits of ecstasy because their country's only princess was in their midst, she was friendly and chatty, liked their wares and spent her husband's coin freely.

I was in fits of ecstasy because Houllebec was awesome. No matter how many times I went, there were always new things to discover, they were nice and, when I started to hang, I found they were fun to be around.

So I hung around...lots.

Even when I was at home, I was never bored and found ways to entertain myself.

I tried on all my clothes and underwear (all *fabulous*). And I might have had a fantastic bakery a ten-minute horse ride away, but I'd also befriended Cedric and Audrey, the baker and his wife, and they'd told me how to make bread, cakes and tarts in the oven at home.

I bought the stuff from Maria at the market, and I had to admit the first few goes weren't anything to write home about (this included normal cooking). But I got the hang of the fire-burning stove. It was a pain in the ass, but the results were worth it.

Every day prior to going to town, I also got on one of my grays (they were on a rotation so they could all get some exercise) and started slow circles of the land around Drakkar's cabin. I did this just to check things out and I did it steady and smart, noting landmarks so I wouldn't get lost. My circles widened by the day, and at first, I found there wasn't much. But the good news was, it was all pretty.

That was, there wasn't much until I found Drakkar had his own personal hot spring.

Yep, his own personal hot spring!

It was an oasis in the middle of the frigid forest of gray, slick stone that, because of the spring, was warm to the touch, steam rising from the water, which was sublime.

I went there every day too, mostly because this was where I bathed. It was *much* better than starting a fire hours before to heat the bathroom space, then boiling water on the stove and lugging it to the tub and the back and forth with buckets to empty it. Finally, when I could shift it, dragging the whole damn thing to tip it out around the house where the slosh of water wouldn't make my walkways too icy.

Hell, after I did all that, I was sweaty and needed another freaking bath.

The hot springs were *way* better in more ways than one. I freaking *loved* sitting out in the beauty of the frosty forest and luxuriating in the hot, splendiferous water. It was the bomb.

I had also adopted a cat, a huge, fat, ginger named Penelope.

This was from Lindy, the bar wench, whose new husband was allergic, and she couldn't find anywhere for her cat to go. Penelope had been relegated to the stables, something she did not like, until I took her home. My gray didn't like her much on her back, and Penelope was not all fired up about the ride, but we made it to the cabin without (major) incident and Penelope *did* like the cabin. And she especially liked a momma who liked to cuddle and didn't mind getting up every ten minutes to let her out to explore then getting up ten minutes later to call her in because it was fucking cold outside.

She made sleep a dream because she purred me straight to slumberland and her big fat body was warm on my feet.

And lastly, I had five books that were packed for me, and I discovered that Sjofn had not screwed me as badly as I thought she had (though she did still screw me) once I cracked them open.

The first was a history of the Northlands including Lunwyn, where I was princess, my father was king and my mother queen. The Northlands also included Middleland (where I discovered my Uncle Baldur was king, though I found this strange since I didn't have an uncle at home and anyway, I'd never heard of a man with a name like Baldur).

I also learned the House of Drakkar (which I wondered if my husband was a part of) used to rule the land ages ago. Though I couldn't know about my husband's House for the book focused more on recent history rather than past history. He wasn't mentioned and I reckoned Sjofn chose it so I'd know what I was dealing with in the present.

I'd learned from this book that also in the Northlands there was the country of Hawkvale, a small city-state called Bellebryn and another country at the south border called Fleuridia.

This book was written well and was interesting, and I knew Sjofn chose it not only for informational purposes but also because the information was put forward in an entertaining way. Therefore, I was entertained.

The second was the story of the gods and the third was a slim tome about religious practices in Lunwyn, which explained the whole church thing.

The six statues at the church, or Dwelling of the Gods as they called it here, were their six gods: Wohden, god of power (his color was dark blue, and those who prayed to him or made offerings did so to shrines bearing his color or with gifts in his color), Hermia, goddess of motherhood (her color, light blue), Meer, god of war (his color, red), Adele, goddess of passion (her color, deep violet), Keer, god of destiny, (his color, gold) and Alabasta, goddess of wisdom and overseer of the earth (her color, green).

Holy people, known as Vallees, were all men and all ceremonies, including Friday night sermons, were delivered in what was known as the "ancient tongue" or what the Lunwynian people spoke centuries ago.

The reason for this was traditional, and, in my opinion, a little idiotic seeing as only Vallees spoke the ancient tongue. But usually, they didn't actually *know* it. Only a few religious scholars did. They just *recited* it, which meant that dude jabbering on at our wedding had memorized that whole thing which, I had to admit, was kind of remarkable.

Everyone else in Lunwyn only knew a few words of the ancient tongue.

My bundle of twigs was a traditional bundle held by brides. It was gathered from the adela tree. This tree spiritual belief had it that Adele, goddess of passion, caused to glitter through her magic. And, if you steeped its twigs and drank it, it was supposed to be an aphrodisiac, but seemed, upon reading in the book a description of what it could do, more like something to use simply to have one hell of an almighty trip.

The fourth and fifth books I wouldn't understand until I found my *true* note that Sjofn stuffed in one of them.

They were also slim tomes, but they told the tales of the "Raiders," or what others called the "Voyagers." These were men who sailed the many seas of this world, finding treasure (or taking it by looting and pillaging). They seemed somewhat like what the legends told of old Vikings from my world.

I would understand the inclusion of these because Sjofn's note said this:

Seoafin,

I introduce you to your new husband. He is the most noted Raider in all of Lunwyn. Tales of his exploits have spread across the Northlands and beyond. If you read about it in these books, it is likely he has done it. He comes from a long line of Raiders, his ancestors given the name Drakkar, the Dragon, in ancient times because they were as fierce, mighty and clever as the great beasts of old who plundered the land before their power was leashed by Wohden and used to serve our frosted realm. Though his family have long since ceased these activities, your new husband has again ventured forward as his ancestors did.

It is, however, highly unlikely [she was right in her guess] *you'll see this note until after you are bound to him. You must know I apologize for that. I would guess, by this time, you will also know why I was eager to be away* [another good guess] *and understand the timing which I could not avoid for I was never alone prior to my nuptials for father and mother feared I would try to escape. The girls who serve me managed to open a window for me at the time the switch occurred. It was short, and ill-timed for you, but it was unfortunately the best I could do.*

I hope that Alyssa, Jocelyn, Esther or Bess had the time to explain things to you about me before you were away on your sleigh to the Dwelling of the Gods for the marriage ceremony. If they did not, I apologize for that too. But I will tell you now, you can trust all of them as they know who you are and why you are there. They are not only my servants, but also good friends and I would trust them with my life. And they have sworn to me that you can do the same.

To explain, my father's kingdom cannot pass to a woman, and he has no other children but me. Therefore, if I provide no male heir, at his death, Lunwyn will be ruled by his twin brother, Baldur, who is currently king of Middleland, the nation to our south.

Their father, my grandfather, King Halldor ruled both and split it, for although my father came forth first, my grandfather was a kind and fair man and he thought this was just and right.

It was not.

My uncle is not like my father or grandfather, and it is imperative that our beautiful land not pass into his hands, or that of his son. His son, my cousin Broderick, is a lovely man, but he is no king. Either of these rulers would be very bad for my sparkling, frosty Lunwyn.

Before the House of Wilde secured the throne, Lunwyn saw centuries of dark times, decades upon decades of turmoil. Uncle Baldur's or Broderick's reign would be disputed, most likely violently and by many factions, and everything must be done to secure the throne, thus continued peace and prosperity for Lunwyn.

Considering how I am, obviously, I want no husband. But I knew I had to take one for my country in order to provide them with a ruler who could be molded by myself, and a strong father, to be a good king. Unfortunately, no matter how my parents encouraged me then commanded me to do so, I dawdled in this duty.

Therefore, Father stepped in and found The Drakkar, who he admires greatly and who often successfully performs difficult or dangerous tasks others cannot, and he does this for the realm.

If I were to find a man, he would not be a man like The Drakkar, who frightens me as well as the idea of his advances repulsing me.

But I must do this for my country. I just wanted to...wait. To have some time.

To explore and be able to be me, something I could not do at home—for fear of my secret being discovered. And when the witch came with your communication, giving me information of this whole other world I did not know existed, I'm afraid I jumped eagerly at the chance.

I am sure by this time you have come to know what others have said is true (or at least I hope so) about The Drakkar. He is said to be quite virile, very skilled in this area and many women not like me have noted he is extremely pleasing to look upon. In fact, he is much sought after and considered a very fine catch, perhaps —though I pay no attention to these things—the best in the realm.

I do hope with all my heart you feel this way. It may help you as you deal with him to know that he and I do not know each other very well. We have met only three times. We did not converse far beyond the civilities and therefore, although I am certain he knows much of me, as everyone in the realm does, he does not <u>know</u> me. Therefore, although you will not be working with an entirely clean slate, it is clean enough that I hope you can build the relationship you need to build with The Drakkar to make your time with him enjoyable during your adventure. [Well, she was wrong about *that*, maybe she *was* drunk].

I also hope that you have found a witch to assist you with not conceiving his child or can find the courage to discuss this with The Drakkar who can don a sheath to stop this from happening. This is my duty, one I will bear on my return. You will simply need to find a way to stop the conception of a child until I can offer this service to my country.

Or, perhaps, in a year's time, our return to our worlds can be reconsidered. It would truly break my heart to leave my Lunwyn, but if you were to wish to remain with The Drakkar and any offspring you can provide who would serve my ice-bound nation with fairness and decency, and be happy doing so, I would make this sacrifice for the good of my people.

But we will communicate when that time comes.

In the meantime, I wish you great adventures with your adventurer, Seoafin. From the communications you sent me, it seems you will fit The Drakkar well.

I do hope that is true.

Yours,

Sjofn.

Okay, so she didn't want to *totally* play me, but still, she played me. I had been very forthcoming with her about why I wanted the switch so clearly she'd been (kind of) matchmaking at the same time looking out for herself. She had not been as forthcoming with me including news about her upcoming nuptials *and* her mom and dad not being her biggest fans *and* the duty she had to her country.

It would have been nice to have a choice *and* know what I was dealing with *prior* to having to deal with it.

But I had to admit, reading about the Raiders/Voyagers, the thought that that man was one of them was intriguing. I had the sense from the books that their lifestyle was romanticized more than a little bit (again, carefully selected by Sjofn, no doubt in order to call to my own spirit for adventure, something I'd shared with her). But their adventures on the seas, their wide travels, the people they had to meet, the things they saw— well, I *was* me, the adventurer daughter of two adventurers.

I couldn't say Sjofn was wrong about that.

Still, she could have warned me including the fact that she had told him about herself and that he clearly had not reacted well to this news. Unless she had done it while drunk off her ass and didn't remember, which seemed to be the case.

Nevertheless, he was gone. I was here. I was on my adventure, and as I always did, I was sucking all I could get from it.

I had my cozy little rustic-chic cabin. I could bake an amazing pecan pie *with* a fantastic flaky crust *in* an old-fashioned oven (and I bet none of my girlfriends at home could pull off something like that, and Claudia had proved she could cook on anything—campfire, camp stove, underground hot stones, *anything*). I had my own personal hot springs. I had a fat, purry cat to cuddle (that I hoped Valentine could get home with me when I went back). And when I was tired of my own company, I had four horses to choose to ride and a town full of people to chat with.

I was totally set and having a fabulous time.

And I couldn't wait to tell Claudia.

Though I told myself I wouldn't rub her nose in it.

I expertly shuffled the cards, my eyes on them, as I suggested, "How about I teach you boys poker?"

Although I suggested it, I didn't know how I was going to do it considering they didn't have the same face cards. They had diamonds but they had no hearts, clubs or spades. Instead, they had stars, moons and daggers. But the deck started at a dash or "naught" and also had ones, a ghost card and a sorceress card so I figured we could make ones aces and naughts, ghosts and sorceresses could be face cards.

As I was deciding this, I realized none of the boys had said anything, so I looked up.

It was then I belatedly felt the air in the pub, which was wired.

And it was then I belatedly noticed that Ulysses, Frederick and Laurel were all looking in the direction of the door.

And that was when I felt a weird, pulsing and warm, but very scary energy beating at my back.

Shit, Dad had always told me never sit with your back to the door. And there I was, like Wild Bill Hickock before he bought it, sitting with my stupid back to the door.

Slowly, I turned in my chair. Equally slowly, my eyes drifted up the so dark brown it was nearly black clothing, taking in the knife belt (with knives), leather band across the wide chest, slanted cloak made of hides and angled sword at the back of my now heavily bearded husband.

He was scowling at me.

I was fighting for breath.

Shit!

What did I do now?

I instantly realized my mistake of not, perhaps, taking some time away from enjoying my parallel universe adventure and, say, preparing for his return, considering the fact he told me he would be returning. I realized this as my eyes flicked beyond him and I saw about seven men, all smaller than him (not by much) all dressed a lot like him, all sporting thick beards, all having hair (of a variety of colors) that needed a cut, all of them scary and all of their eyes were on me.

This must be some of his Raider brethren.

Ho boy.

I pulled in a deep breath to fill my lungs.

Then I smiled huge and called, "Hi, honey! I see you're home."

There was some movement around me but not much as that weird, pulsing, warm, very scary energy filled the pub until it was suffocating.

Then he growled at me across the expanse, "Wife, arse over here."

Hmm.

Not sure I liked that.

Nope, I was wrong. I *was* sure I didn't like that.

Nevertheless, he was twice the size of me, and he had seven men of much the same size behind him. I had Frederick, Ulysses and Laurel. Sure, Ulysses was the blacksmith and he had forearms the size of anvils (and likely the consistency, though I hadn't checked). But Frederick and Laurel were lightweights compared to the Raider Party.

And I liked them. I knew they liked me. We'd had some good times. But we weren't exactly BFFs (yet), so I wasn't certain they'd wade in for me.

Not with these guys.

It was probably best that I got my arse over there.

I nodded to Drakkar and turned, putting down the cards.

"Thanks guys, see you all later," I muttered, grabbed my little, satin, drawstring bag off the table, decided to let my winnings sit where they were, and with some haste, I stood.

I snatched my cloak off the back of my chair and moved quickly (trying to do it without appearing like I was moving quickly) through the silent pub, taking every step with every eye in the place on me.

I wasn't certain what would happen once I got my arse to him because one could say I didn't know my husband like, at all. But I would never have been prepared for what *did* happen.

The minute I was within reach, he reached.

With a small, surprised cry, I found myself ass in the air, over his shoulder. Then I found myself out of the pub and into the cold night. After that I found my ass on my horse and my arms automatically came up quickly to catch the cloak I had lost and he had caught and was now throwing at me.

Then he growled two words, "Arse. Home."

"But—" I started but didn't finish.

He lifted a large hand and slapped my gray on the rump, barking, "*Yah!*" and my gray took off at a full gallop.

I didn't even have the reins in my hands!

What a fucking *dick*!

I quickly hooked my leg around the saddle and leaned forward. Holding on to the gray around her neck so I wouldn't fall off, I grabbed the reins then sat back, and as best I could with purse and reins, I flung the fur lined cloak around my shoulders.

I rode home and I did this fast.

This was because I was pissed way *the fuck* off and I knew if I didn't go in that direction, I'd go back to the pub and probably do something that would get me murdered by a giant Viking-type, parallel-universe Raider.

So I went home, straight to the stables where I unsaddled and stalled the gray. I stomped to the house, stoked up the banked fires, dropped logs on them, lit candles and lamps, climbed up and built a fire in the loft, and then I went down the ladder and paced.

What I did not do was calm down.

My *husband* and I had to get a few things straight.

First was that he didn't do anything that threatened to break my neck such as set a horse to full gallop when I was not seated properly and didn't have hold of the reins.

Second was that he had to stop throwing me on or in some type of transport when I didn't have anything to shield me from the freezing, arctic, fucking air.

Third was that he was going to hear how I felt about him humiliating me in front of people who were becoming my friends.

I knew there was probably a fourth through about a five hundredth, but I was fucking well going to start with those.

I seethed and ranted in my brain while I paced for a long time. Then I realized I'd been pacing for a long time. I also realized I'd been drinking ale, had a fabulous shepherd's pie at the pub, and I was getting tired. And I realized this was happening because it was way late, and I'd been home for what felt like hours and he wasn't home.

Then I decided...fuck him.

I was going to bed.

So I went to the trunks, grabbed a nightgown, went to the bathroom-type room, changed, came out, flung my clothes on a trunk, blew out the candles and lanterns, threw more logs on the fires and climbed up the ladder where Penelope was already curled and asleep.

I threw more logs on that fire too and slid the curtain shut. I climbed under the sheet, quilt and fluffy wool blanket and was out like a light within minutes.

~

MY EYES DRIFTED open as something light and lovely glided from the back of my knee up the skin of the back of my thigh.

I came to a sleepy, confused, definitely hazy semi-focus in the firelight, my eyes taking in a muscled, so dark brown it was nearly black, wool breeches-covered knee and thigh resting on the bed.

I blinked.

"Waste." I heard a low male rumble and the finger kept going, pushing up my nightgown, drifting over my hip and then down toward my ass. "Waste," it repeated.

The words registered, the touch registered and the direction it was heading registered.

Holy moly!

I shot up to sitting in bed, one hand in the bed, the covers tumbling off me. The finger moved from me, and Penelope scrambled away on a bee-line to the rope of the pulley, deserting me as she used her claws on the rope to crawl down.

Oh shit. My husband was sitting on the bed facing me. I was half lounging on it. As usual, I'd kicked the covers off one leg and was straddling them. The ones that covered my torso were now at a bunch at my waist.

But I didn't notice this. I was staring in his eyes that were staring at me.

His big hand lifted, and I sat stock-still as it moved toward me, cupped my jaw gently, then it slid down to the side of my neck. There, it curled around to the back, his fingers tangled in my hair and kept moving downward.

"Uh—" I started but didn't continue mainly because I was speechless with fear.

"Soft," he muttered, his eyes on my neck, his fingers twisting in my hair. "Softer than I expected. As soft as it is beautiful. A miracle," he kept muttering, his mind somewhere else at the same time it was on me.

My mind was totally on him, and he wasn't completely in my space but he wasn't far enough away that I couldn't smell the whisky.

Shit.

Drunk guys probably didn't care if you were a lesbian.

No, I knew by the look in his heated green-brown eyes they most definitely did not care.

Shit!

"Frey," I whispered and when I did, his gaze snapped instantly to mine.

"Say that again," he ordered.

I didn't say it again. I asked what I thought was a very pertinent question.

"Uh, are you inebriated?"

At my words, his hand twisted and fisted in my hair. It didn't hurt, a slight pull at my scalp, but he was a very big man with his very big fist in my hair, so he had my attention.

"Say that again," he repeated.

"Um...Frey," I whispered.

Suddenly, he used my hair to pull me to him as he leaned close to me and when he had me an inch away, he growled, "*Gods*, that you'd say that, *just like that*, when you were full of me."

At his words, I felt a little tingle in happy place.

Uh, what was *that*?

I put a hand to the massive wall of his (very hard, I noted on encountering it) chest, and put on gentle pressure, starting to suggest, "Maybe we should—"

"Tonight, we pretend," he muttered, cutting me off.

Ho boy!

"I think—"

Before I could finish telling him what I thought, he let me go. Then he twisted, bent his torso and tugged his boots off. Before I knew it, off went his sweater, and I was treated to a view of a highly tanned, supremely muscled, obviously powerful back. I was still blinking as that vision burned into my brain (and I had to admit, it was pleasant) when, still seated in the bed with me, off went his breeches.

Ho *boy*!

Now frantic, though unfortunately belatedly, I started to scoot back, saying, "Um...would you mind if—?" But I again didn't finish.

This was because, without appearing to move, he was reclining in bed, and I was reclining with him. He flicked the covers over us then both his powerful arms locked around me and yanked me to his side.

"Cradle my thigh," he growled.

I blinked at his chest, pushing lightly against it, registering it was as powerfully muscled as his back and so wide it seemed to go on forever.

"Wha-what?"

"As you did the quilt," he stated then got impatient. His hand, starting at my hip, moved swiftly down my thigh, his torso (and me, I might add, since his other arm was still locked around me) lifting in order to reach. His fingers hooked the back of my knee, and he yanked my leg up until I was doing what he asked, half straddling his thigh like I did the covers.

He settled back down in bed and kept firm hold on me.

"Well, uh...okay, uh...do you think—?" I started, but he cut me off again.

"This is not the welcome home I'd like, wife, but it'll do, and you'll sleep here, like this, until the morning. You don't, I'll take the welcome home from you I'd like, and I won't delay. Do you understand me?"

I understood him.

I was totally okay with sleeping like this because I had a feeling I knew what kind of welcome home he'd like.

And incidentally, I was right about drunk guys not minding lesbians.

"Yes," I whispered.

"Now shut your mouth and sleep."

I pressed my lips together in order not to inform him that he hadn't actually let me open my mouth to say much of anything. I didn't think he'd appreciate that reminder at that juncture.

What I did not do was sleep.

He was out in seconds.

I still did not sleep.

Penelope clawed her way back up the rope, curled at my one free foot and purred herself to slumber.

I still did not sleep.

I knew that dawn had to have touched the sky (though I couldn't see it with the curtains closed), and then, only then, did I find sleep.

And unfortunately, when that happened, in sleep, I curled deeper into the big, hard, stranger at my side. My arm snaking around him and holding tight. My thigh curving around his. My knee and calf falling between his legs. My hips cradled by the side of his. My cheek pillowed on his massive, hard chest.

This was something I did normally in my sleep with covers and pillows.

Something I did that night with something a lot warmer, a lot more comfortable and *a lot* more dangerous.

And when I slept curled tight around my dark stranger husband, I slept *deep*.

6

PHEW

I slept in, but Penelope was still with me when I woke.

And Penelope was my only bedmate.

Phew.

I lay in the warm cocoon of covers that was pulled up to my neck and wondered if my dark stranger husband pulled them up after he left me in bed which would be a surprising indication he could be thoughtful.

I figured he did because I likely didn't.

Then I didn't know what to do with that, so I set it aside and listened to the house.

Nothing.

I couldn't even feel his presence.

Phew.

Okay. Good.

Space to get my head straight.

Penelope sensed I was awake and sauntered up the curved line of my body then jumped down to curl in the warm shell of my belly, lap and thighs and there she started purring. I noted the windows were covered by the heavy curtains and the curtain was still drawn at the railing, but sunlight was coming through there (not at the windows, they didn't mess around in Lunwyn with curtains, total blackout situation, nothing got through, they even had draft protectors to set at the base of the doors).

This had to mean it was late morning for Lunwyn's days were very short, by my estimation, starting around nine or ten and ending around two or three. After that it was moonlight all the way.

I tipped my head and saw the fire was blazing, heating the small nest of space.

Definitely my dark stranger husband did *that* for me unless Lunwyn had heretofore unknown fire fairies.

Another surprising act of thoughtfulness.

Hmm.

I pulled just an arm out of the covers to scratch Penelope behind the ears as I considered my dilemma.

First, I was married, and my husband was home.

Second, I was not a lesbian like he thought I was.

Third, my husband was a renowned Raider, known to be virile and "skilled in that area," but also it was clear he *was* very virile unless you were blind, deaf and lost all your senses of perception.

Fourth, I knew there was a strong possibility the rumors of his "skill" were true with the one kiss he'd given me, the light touch he'd woken me with last night and the gentle way he touched my jaw and neck.

Fifth, he liked my hair.

Sixth, he wanted to sleep with me cuddled to his side.

Seventh, he left me covered and cocooned, stoking up the fire to keep me warm.

Hmm.

On the other hand...

First, he'd married me, hauled me across country for hours upon hours through the freezing cold night and left me in a dirty house all by myself for six weeks (well, the house wasn't dirty for six weeks, but he sure as hell left me there alone that long).

Second, when he first saw me again, he bossed me around right in front of everyone without even saying hello. Granted, he was with his buds, and maybe obviously virile, Viking-type Raiders behaved that way in front of their buds, but he could at least have said hello.

Third, for reasons unknown he'd carried me out like a sack of flour, again, right in front of everyone.

Fourth, he'd sent my horse galloping when I was not secure on her back.

Fifth, he barely spoke to me, didn't let me talk when he *was* speaking and most of the stuff he said when he was speaking, I didn't like much.

And last, he was huge, scared me most of the time and, um...he scared me most of the time (that was worth repeating).

I left Penelope to her purring, put my arm back under the covers, rolled to my back to stare at the ceiling and kept thinking.

I was an adventurer, but I wasn't a *sexual* adventurer.

There were two reasons for this.

First, I had a bunch of money. My father inherited a shitload from my grandfather and after the plane he was piloting with Mom in it went down over the Nile, I inherited his shitload of money.

Money made people do stupid stuff and lots of it was not so nice. And having lots of it made you a target for some not-so-nice folks who did stupid stuff mostly to get you to use your money on them or just to get your money. So, I'd learned early, and Dad had taught me to be careful with my heart (and my money). So I was.

I had good friends, but they were few. Trust was difficult when you were loaded like me.

I'd had far fewer lovers.

Second, I was just plain careful with my heart. I'd lost the two people I loved most in my life when I was fifteen. That hurt. Too much. I didn't want that to happen again, and if I was going to risk it, I was damn well going to make certain I took that risk on the right guy.

That guy, so far, had not made an appearance, and so far, no guy even came close.

So, two and two together meant that I didn't go there. This didn't mean I was a virgin. It was just—you share your body, you open a part of yourself and make it vulnerable. So unless I was sure I could cut ties or I had my head on straight (the latter being a rare occasion with me), I didn't take that risk. Vulnerable was not something I liked to be.

But this situation was something else.

This was an adventure with a limited time span.

In ten and a half months, I was going home to my friends, my house, my money and new adventures. I wasn't staying here, no way. They didn't have planes here or cell phones or sushi.

True, it would have been good after what I read in those books, especially about the Raiders, to discover more than Lunwyn. Hawkvale sounded beautiful, Bellebryn gorgeous and Fleuridia was known to have really good food and it must be said, I liked really good food. To explore it all, I could use two years here, maybe three.

But that would mean leaving behind my friends, my house, my money and sushi for two years, maybe three.

I wasn't about to do that.

And I was loaded but I couldn't throw a million dollars at trip after trip. This was a onetime deal.

So here I was, a princess in a frozen world with a very scary yet very hot husband who could really kiss and liked to cuddle.

And I knew I was going home so there was no risk because I knew those ties would be cut.

Then Sjofn would have to deal as she'd left me to do the same.

And Frey Drakkar...

Well, we'd see how I'd handle that.

First, I had to see if he could communicate in the sense that he listened as well as talked and when he talked he didn't only say scary shit or stuff that pissed me off but other...uh, stuff.

Then I would decide.

I rolled out of bed, banked the fire, shoved back the curtain and climbed down. I found fires burning merrily in both fireplaces as well as the kitchen stove (which, seriously, being iron, conducted a lot of heat, the kitchen was always cozy warm) and there was fresh brewed coffee—strong and good.

He could make good coffee and he could build good fires meaning I didn't have to do either. This meant his plus column was growing. So far there were only four things on it but yesterday there were none, so I had hope.

I heated some water, washed a bit at the basin in the bathroom space and pulled on some undergarments. Cashmere stockings attached to garters and a long, dusty pink, soft wool knit dress that clung everywhere, had a scooped neckline, some serious cleavage (by the way, all my dresses had serious cleavage, this was the way they were made, this was what my underwear also made when I strapped it on, and it had to be said, natural cleavage was the way *I* was made) and long flowing sleeves that belled out at the wrists.

I pulled my hair back from my face with a pink satin ribbon, tied the long, matching knit belt so it hung low on my hips, touched some perfume behind my ears and at my wrists and headed to the kitchen to make Penelope a late breakfast and her momma some brunch.

Penelope was on all fours, belly to the floor and had her face in a bowl of leftover chicken I'd warmed by setting it on the stove when the back door opened, Frey Drakkar prowled through and then he stopped dead when he saw me.

I took him in.

A first, no knives or sword. Another first, his hair was partially wet. He'd also shaved.

Someone had visited the hot spring.

Hmm.

It must be said, I kind of liked the beard.

As I took him in, I realized I kept forgetting how big he was.

By then, I was used to that kitchen. It wasn't mammoth but it wasn't small either.

With him in it, it seemed tiny.

His eyes were on me standing at the butcher block whisking pancake batter. I watched them go down the length of me he could see then they went up.

I swallowed.

Then I said, "Hi."

My word activated him. He moved in, swung his arm around that I hadn't noticed was carrying a large stick over his shoulder and he plonked the dead carcass of a small (what looked like a *baby*) deer on the kitchen table.

I blinked.

Then I gagged.

I controlled my urge to hurl, pulled in breath and looked from the dead deer to him.

"Uh...I have a rule. No dead game on the kitchen table."

His green-brown eyes held mine. He didn't speak. He also didn't move.

Okay, ignore big dead animal carcass and move on, Finnie, I told myself.

I searched for a good strategy and hoped I found it.

"I...well, um...I just wanted to say, uh...before I forget, thanks for stoking the fire upstairs and keeping me warm while I slept in," I said, thinking that was nice, noticing and commenting on something *he* did that was nice.

He crossed his arms on his chest and studied me.

All righty then.

"You, um, came home last night after having a few," I noted and got no response. I waited just in case his brain didn't work as fast as mine, still got no response, so I continued. "You look okay. I hope you aren't hungover."

Nothing.

Okay. Right.

"Would you like pancakes? I'm making a late breakfast of pancakes and bacon." More nothing. "Uh...if you want to eat, you'll have to remove the dead animal."

Finally, a semi-response. He picked up the deer, opened the back door and flung it on the back porch where it landed with a sickening thud.

I winced.

Eek!

He closed the door.

"Thanks," I whispered.

He walked toward me. I braced, then he walked by me, grabbed the handle of the kettle and prowled out of the room.

I relaxed.

I set about wiping down the table (doing this mostly with my eyes closed, and still with my eyes closed and finding it with arms in front of me walking like a mummy, I threw the cloth out the back door) after which I put the slices of bacon I'd already cut into the warming skillet.

He came back while I was fiddling with the pancakes in one skillet and moving the bacon around in another one. He stalked right up to me, slammed the kettle down on the stove, grabbed the percolator, poured himself a hot mug o' joe and then stalked to the table where he sat down, one knee bent, one leg sprawled, king of his rustic-chic cabin, eyes on me.

Dear Lord.

In silence and with a one-man audience, I finished the food, served it up, slapped slabs of butter on the warm pancakes and it started melting. I turned toward the table. I put a plate in front of him, one in front of my seat then I went to the cupboards to get honey and silverware. I gave him his, set mine at my place and put the honey on the table. I then moved across the kitchen to warm up my coffee and I sat down, poured honey all over my pancakes, put it on the table and pushed the honey in his direction.

At this point I tucked in.

I saw him reach for the honey. I heard the jug hit the table then I heard him start to eat.

I looked at him and tried again.

"Frey, I think we need to talk."

His brown-green eyes came to me, his eyebrows rose, and he shoved a gigantic bite of pancake in his mouth.

I took the eyebrow raise as a, "Yes, Seoafin? What would you like to discuss?"

"I'm not a lesbian," I blurted for some *completely* unhinged reason and those raised brows shot together in a scary way.

He chewed, swallowed and growled his first word to me of the day. "What?"

"I'm not a lesbian."

Words two and three came in quick succession. "A what?"

Oh. Maybe they didn't have the term lesbian here.

"I...uh..." Damn you, Sjofn! "I don't prefer, um...my own sex."

He froze.

Completely.

His face. His body. His hand with pancake on fork suspended in mid-air. All of him. Frozen. Even the air around him seemed to glitter with frost.

Okay, maybe I should have left that for later, say, after I learned his birth date, favorite color and preferred way to down a deer.

I hurried on. "See, I was, well, I don't remember it actually, and when you told me about it the other...well...after we got married, I was surprised. I mean, I didn't even remember I said that to you. That's kind of, uh...a crazy thing to say and a crazier thing to, um...*share*. I've tried to figure out why on earth I would say something like that, and I think maybe I was drunk and nervous. I mean, uh..." I faltered. Shit. Think Finnie! "You're a big guy and all and I'm...well, I'm not that big, and you kind of, um, flip me out..." His eyes narrowed at a term he clearly didn't understand. "I mean, scare me a bit. Actually, uh...you're doing it, well...right now."

He dropped his fork on his plate, sat back, crossed his arms on his chest and scowled at me in that way it made me think he wanted to break me in two.

I kept blathering. "And...well, *now*. Actually *more* now. The scaring me part. Since I'm, you know, sharing."

He didn't speak.

Shit! I wished he would talk and not when he said stuff that freaked me out or pissed me off, but when I wanted him to.

I kept going. "I thought, with you home and us being, well, you know, wedded in holy matrimony..." I faltered again because his eyes narrowed telling me they didn't have that and he had no clue to what I was referring so I covered, "of the...um, *gods*," Eek! "that maybe we should start to get to know one another and I thought we should start off on the right foot, with everything out in the open. Being honest."

"Being honest," he finally spoke, and he did it on a low rumble.

I nodded. "Yes, being honest."

"So this is you honest, now, and that wasn't you honest, back then?" he asked a good question.

"I can be a little...*crazy* when I have a bit too much to drink."

"Yes, the wench at the inn said you come in often, drink much ale and get quite loud," he remarked, not looking happy about this, but I was sure glad Lindy corroborated my story.

"Uh...yes," I agreed. "That sounds like me." And, actually, that was no lie.

He scowled at me.

I pulled in breath and said quietly, "Frey, this really sucks to admit but just the way you're looking at me now scares me."

"The Winter Princess Sjofn of the House of Wilde does not easily get scared," he replied quietly right back, but his quietly was distrustful, disbelieving and a bit frightening.

I shook my head. "No, I don't. You're right. I can usually handle myself, but I'm alone in a cabin in the woods with no one even close with a really huge man who could break me in two who doesn't seem to like me much. And you have no problem getting physical. It scares the beejeezus out of me, and when it isn't doing that, it ticks me off."

"Ticks you off?"

"Upsets me, makes me angry," I explained.

He went silent again.

"Frey—" I said softly, but he cut me off and scarily changed the subject.

"So if you do not prefer women, you wouldn't mind if I took you to the loft, stripped you naked and did as I pleased with you?"

I felt my face get hot, my breasts swell and my heart start beating faster.

"Actually, I would," I whispered.

He started scowling again. "Right," he whispered back.

He totally didn't believe me.

"But only because...well, I'd like for us to get to know one another better. Spend time together. Then maybe advance to the next level."

His brows snapped together again, and he asked, "The next level?"

"Uh...the part where you strip me naked and do as you please," I whispered. "That's the next level."

He scowled.

I waited.

He scowled more.

I didn't have anything left.

Then he asked in a low, surprised, unhappier than normal unhappy voice, "By the gods, are you asking me to court you?"

That sounded crazy. The very idea of this big scary guy who was a renowned Raider courting me or anyone sounded absolutely nuts.

And that must have been why I burst out laughing.

He did not laugh. In fact, not one thing was funny to him, and he made this obvious.

I struggled to control my mirth, won my fight and suggested, "How about this? We make a deal. You don't order me around, throw me over your shoulder and carry me out of pubs or other locations, toss me into sleighs or on horses, send me careening through the forest on a horse whose reins I don't have in my hands and maybe we share a few meals together. I'll cook. Then we'll see about the next level. Is that a deal?"

"And how many meals would we share, Sjofn?"

Hmm.

He was considering this.

I wasn't sure if that was good or bad.

"Fifteen?" I tried.

"How about two?" he returned.

Two?

Okay, maybe it was bad.

"Twelve," I suggested.

"Two," he fired back.

"Nine?" I kept trying.

"Two," he stated firmly.

Ho boy.

"So, in your two, does this one count as one?" I asked, pointing with my fork at my plate.

"Absolutely," he answered.

Ho boy!

"Do I have to answer now?"

"Yes."

Shit.

I stared at him and tried not to look like I was breathing as hard as I was breathing.

Okay, this was an adventure, *my* adventure. I'd paid for it, and I knew there were risks. There were always risks. And this was a risk I had to take.

And, seriously, there had to be worse risks than sleeping with a hot guy who could kiss really freaking well and whose touch could be both light and gentle.

Right?

I straightened my shoulders and declared, "Okay, two but only if you throw in not cleaning that deer in the house. I don't want to see it or even *hear* it when you clean it, and I certainly don't want to clean up after it."

He scowled at me again before he noted, "You're the finest huntress in the realm, Sjofn, and known for cleaning your own game."

Gross!

Damn. Time again to cover.

"Well, I had an incident that um...troubled me, uh...*mentally* and gave that up. I'm not a vegetarian." This word got me narrowed scary eyes which meant Lunwynians didn't do vegetarian, so I explained, "I eat meat, I just don't want to think of where it comes from. If you agree no carcass cleaning or carcasses on the whole, *ever*, in the house except, of course, what I cook when it's all good and cut up and doesn't resemble an animal anymore." God! How lame could I be? Time to sum up. "We have a deal. If not, we have no deal."

"Deal," he replied immediately, and my heart clenched, my belly dropped and my breasts swelled again.

"One more thing," I said hurriedly when he picked up his fork to start eating.

His head, partially bent over his plate, tipped back to look at me. "You've already tried me, Sjofn," he warned then he shoved the pancake already on his fork in his mouth.

"Okay," I nodded, "I get that, but...I don't want you calling me that."

He did a slow blink. Then he swallowed.

I rushed on. "I...would you...?" I hesitated. "Actually, I'd prefer it if you called me Finnie."

He sat back a few inches, his hand came down to rest on the table, and after he did that, he studied me intensely for a very long time. It took a lot, but I sat there and withstood it.

Finally, he asked softly, "Finnie?"

And shit, *shit* that sounded nice in his deep voice.

"Yeah, Finnie," I replied softly.

He studied me.

Then he said, "Finnie."

Yep. Oh yeah. That sounded nice in his deep voice.

I took that as a yes, so I smiled at him and whispered, "Thanks."

He kept studying me. Eventually he shook his head and forked into his pancakes, cutting off a huge bite and shoving it in his mouth.

Okay, well, that didn't go great, as in, after dinner I was clearly having sex with someone I barely knew. But it didn't go badly either.

Shit.

"You're known for hunting, skinning your own animals and being a very good archer, wife, you are not known for cooking well," he told his plate. I nearly choked on the pancakes I'd just put in my mouth, and I stared at him as his eyes shifted to me. "I'm pleased to learn this about you."

There it was. A sign, a small one, but one like him keeping me warm that said maybe he was a decent guy, and he was going to try.

"I'm glad," I said softly.

He looked back at his plate and shoved more pancakes in his mouth.

Okay.

Maybe that went better than I suspected.

Phew.

7

MR. CONVERSATION

While Frey's attention was on the deer, I grabbed my stuff and nipped to the hot springs for a quick bath.

One could say the hot springs were awesome, but one could *not* say drying off afterward was. However, I'd done it so often, I'd made an art of it, so I was out, dried off and clothed in record time. Then I wrapped my clean, wet hair in the bathing cloth and nipped back quickly, luckily without him seeing me.

Since I had one day of essentially semi-kinda-dating my husband before we got down to the nitty-gritty husband and wife stuff, once I got back, I lotioned, powdered and perfumed as well as put on some light makeup. I mean, I would *never* go on a first date without making an effort. And I had at least a couple of weeks of dates (according to my own personal philosophy of how long before I considered sleeping with someone) to squeeze in one day so I made an effort.

As I did this, I planned the dinner I was going to make that night and therefore drew up a grocery list in my head of what I needed to get from the store. I wanted something special so he would notice I was making an effort (and maybe he would make one too). I also wanted something chewy. He made light work of those pancakes, chewing approximately twice before each enormous swallow, and I was hoping dinner would last a whole lot longer than that.

I was in the kitchen, all done up but hair still wet (though pulled back in the ribbon again) and I was getting the basket I usually took to town with me to carry my purchases back when Frey walked in.

I turned to the door and again, like that morning, when he saw me, he stopped dead.

Weird how he did that.

"Hey," I greeted. "I'm going to town to pick up some stuff for dinner. Do you want anything?"

He stared at me a moment and I was hoping he wasn't back in silence mode when he stated, "I'll take you."

Hells bells. I'd actually wanted some time alone to psych myself up for what was going to happen after dinner.

However, time alone wasn't going to help me know this guy any better, or get used to having him around, so maybe him going was a good thing.

We could chat.

"All righty then," I replied.

His eyes moved to my hair, and he moved toward the living room, muttering, "I'll saddle Tyr. You get a hat. I don't want my new wife catching a chill."

Hmm.

That was thoughtful.

So thoughtful, I smiled as I followed him and called out, "Tyr?"

He turned at the front door, answered, "My mount," then left.

Well, there you go. I already knew something more about him. His horse was called Tyr.

That was a start.

I went to my trunks and pulled out a cloak I liked especially. It was a light silvery-gray wool with fur in a matching color on the high collar. It had matching gloves and hat. The hat was knit wool at the top, furry around the edges and I'd noticed it didn't give me hat head.

I didn't want hat head. Not that day, or maybe *any* day when Frey was around.

I got ready to face the chill, nabbed my basket and walked to the stables.

When I got there, Frey had Tyr in the middle of the space, bridle on, saddle on (with a longer, very dark brown blanket style thing that hung over his rump, probably to help ward off the cold, something the horse hadn't worn on our long ride there). I noticed now that the horse was like everything Frey. That was to say his coat so dark brown it was nearly black.

He was also huge. Further, he was glossy. And he had extremely intelligent eyes.

He was lastly beautiful.

I went to the hooks on the wall to get a bridle for one of the grays and had lifted a hand to nab it when Frey called from behind me. "What are you doing?"

I dropped my hand, turned to him and answered, "Preparing a gray to ride."

"You'll ride with me."

I blinked before I asked, "What?"

He stood by his horse for about half a second then he walked to me, reached low, engulfed my hand in his and led me to his horse. Before I became unstuck, he'd mounted and leaned down to hook me around the waist and pull me up in front of him.

He immediately clicked his teeth and Tyr walked out of the stable. Once clear of the structure, Frey clicked his teeth again and leaned slightly into me, taking me with him, chest to back, at the same time his arm moving me back into him as it tightened around my belly and Tyr took us from walk to a not fast but definitely not slow canter.

Apparently, Frey Drakkar did not stop and smell the roses.

"Um..." I started then pointed out, "You just broke our deal."

"How?" he asked, his voice sounding in my ear.

"You just put me on your horse," I explained as the forest went past us, and I noticed Frey knew a better, what appeared to be more direct route, because he was now taking it.

"Yes, I did," he agreed.

"Part of our deal was, you wouldn't do that."

"No...*Finnie*, part of our deal was I wouldn't *toss* you on a horse. I didn't toss you on a horse. I pulled you onto a horse."

"That's a technicality," I declared.

"A what?" he asked.

I didn't explain, instead I stated, "I think you knew what I meant."

"And I think, when you're making a deal, you may wish to be more clear in your demands and your expectations," he returned.

Well, it could be said he was not wrong.

I made a mental note to do just that.

We rode through the frozen forest, and it didn't take long for me to come to the understanding that I liked this better, riding with Frey. I could pay more attention to the beauty that was around me (even if it was mostly streaming by) and not where I was going. And he was warm and solid behind me and any warmth in Lunwyn, I had learned, should not only be made use of, but treasured. It was a lazy way to go but it was definitely the better way to go.

Hmm.

I decided not to focus on that and instead, learn about my husband.

Therefore, I set about doing that.

"So," I began, "uh...where have you been the last six weeks?"

"At sea," he answered readily.

My brows went up, but I kept my eyes on the vista before me. "That whole time?"

"That whole time," he replied then went on, "or the part of it we weren't in Middleland."

I twisted my neck to look at him and got an eyeful of strong jaw and masculine throat. Attractive strong jaw and appealing masculine throat.

That was when I looked back forward.

"What were you doing in Middleland?"

"One of my men had an errand to run."

Interesting.

"What was the errand?" I asked.

Frey did not answer.

Hmm.

Interesting.

"Was your errand successfully run?" I queried.

"Yes."

Not informative, but at least an answer.

"Um...how many men do you have?"

"Many."

Again not informative, but at least an answer.

"Are we talking 'many' as in 'more than ten' or 'many' as in 'more than five hundred'?" I attempted to clarify.

"Somewhere in between." Frey clearly didn't feel like clarifying.

I was not deterred.

"So, are you often at sea?"

"Yes."

"Are you going back soon?"

I asked this because I wanted to go with him when he went, though I wasn't going to tell him that then. I just wanted to know how much time I had to convince him to take me.

He didn't know this and thus read my question wrong. I knew this not only from his next words but an arm that got very tight at my belly.

"I'm just home, wife, and you wish to be rid of me?"

"That's not what I meant," I kinda semi-wheezed.

He heard it and his arm relaxed.

"If not, then tell me what you meant," he ordered, and I knew I couldn't say I wanted to go with him, not yet.

So I said softly, "I'm just trying to get to know you, Frey. You aren't a font of information, telling me your favorite color and pouring forth your heartfelt desires. I didn't mean anything except to ask about you."

"I don't have a favorite color," he replied. "And my desires, at the moment, though I would not describe them as heartfelt, but felt somewhere else, all revolve around what I shall do when I first bed my new wife. Would you like to talk about that?"

Ho boy.

"Um..." I swallowed, "no."

He shifted then muttered over my head, "I did not think so."

Okay, so, that went well. Kind of. I learned a few things about my husband. Since I did, I decided that I could take a break and stop talking to Frey.

We made it into town, and I refused to think about the fact that the last time I was here I was carted out of a pub by my just-returned-from-sea husband. Instead, I acted business as usual, smiling, waving and calling out greetings to people I knew. Luckily, they did the same (with glances at Frey, of course, who did not call out greetings, wave, and I couldn't see him, but I was pretty certain he did not smile). He stopped us outside the market.

He dismounted then, with hands at my waist, I came down too.

Then he did something sweet, something unexpected, something I didn't think he had in him even after stoking the fire and saying he liked my pancakes.

His big hand enveloped mine and he walked me to the market while holding my hand.

Shit. I liked that. That was nice.

Hmm.

We walked in and I called out to Maria, "Hi, Maria! It's Finnie! I've come to get some groceries!"

She was in the back room and yelled in return, "Greetings, Princess Finnie! I'll be out in two moments. We've had some green beans come in!"

Freaking cool!

Fresh veg, I had also learned in Lunwyn, was to be treasured.

Green beans just got jotted on the menu.

"I want some of those!" I yelled.

"They're yours!" she yelled back.

"This pleases me," Frey muttered, and I stopped wandering through the store shouting and looked up at him.

"What?"

He was looking toward the back room, but at my question his chin dipped down and his active, assessing, and indeed pleased-looking brown-green eyes came to me.

"You have your mother's grace, something I never noticed before. But you do not have her manner. She is refined but cold. You..." he looked to the back room then at me, "are not."

I wasn't certain, but I *thought* that was nice.

"Thanks," I whispered, kinda embarrassed.

He tugged me through the store, continuing to mutter, "You can teach this to our daughters, if we have them."

Oh shit.

Another item for the grocery list: see if they had a condom section (though I held no high hopes for that). And another topic for discussion at dinner: birth control (though I held no high hopes for that either).

Shit.

Frey let my hand go and I started to pile stuff in my basket making a mental note of what we needed to get at the butcher and the baker.

Unfortunately, while I did this, Frey felt talkative and with what he felt like talking about, I decided I preferred him taciturn.

"It is well known your father, not having a son, did all the things with you that he would do with his son. He taught you archery, swordplay, and you went hunting with him from when you were wee. Our daughters will not do these things."

I clenched my teeth after his declaration, not wanting to think of "our daughters" which was something I hoped we didn't create while I was on my adventure.

I grabbed a jug of golden syrup and decided to whisper, "Okay."

"It is also well known that he kept your mother and you close to his side during all his travels and business, by land and by sea. *This*, I will consider doing."

I looked up at him and froze.

I did this because, first, my dad in this world sounded a lot like my dad in my world. He liked me close, and he never went anywhere without Mom and, most of the time, me. I had tutors when I was young and I was only not with them when they died because we'd been around the world and back again so many times, they decided I needed to have some normalcy in my life and make some friends. Thus, they'd enrolled me in boarding school.

Second, I did this because I was super happy he was already considering taking me with him.

"Really?" I whispered and his eyes moved over my face before locking on mine.

"I see this idea pleases you," he noted.

I nodded.

"Good," he muttered, and looked to Maria who had walked into the shop from the back room.

I grinned at the nuts.

Then I looked up at him and asked, "Do you like pecans?"

Frey looked down at me and asked back, "What?"

"Pecans, nuts. I'm really good at pecan pie and I'm going to make one for us tonight. But if you don't—"

He interrupted me. "I like pecans, Finnie."

Boy, I liked it when he called me Finnie.

In fact, I liked that there were things to like about Frey Drakkar and I was noticing there were a number of things to like.

Therefore, I grinned at him, "See, we're getting to know each other already. This is working out great."

He didn't answer verbally. Nope, he didn't.

He did better than that.

His eyes dropped to my mouth, his big hand lifted to cup my jaw and his calloused thumb slid lightly across my curved lower lip.

This felt good. So good, my belly dipped, and my breasts swelled again.

Yes, his touch could be light. Very light. And very sweet.

Ho boy.

I noticed his gaze had lifted to my eyes and then I knew those eyes were hazy from his surprisingly sweet touch when he bent so his face was close to my own.

"I very much like the curve of your mouth, wife," he whispered. The nipples in my swelling breast started tingling and my body swayed slightly closer to him as if he had some invisible pull and it was reeling me in. "I also like to watch it move, to hear it speak words of teasing or jest, or just any words at all."

Oh man, that was sweet too.

He got even closer and kept whispering, "I wonder what else it can do that I will like."

Now that wasn't sweet, that was *hot*.

"Um..." I mumbled for no reason whatsoever and when I did, I watched his eyes go sexy lazy at the same time they smiled.

It was a good look. No, it was *the best* look I'd ever seen. On him or *any* man.

Uh.

Wow.

I was about to do something, I didn't know what, maybe throw myself at him or toss the basket aside and demand he take me home immediately, strip me naked and do as he pleased when his thumb slid back across my lower lip, and he straightened.

"Your pecans, wife, my pie," he murmured.

I blinked then my body jerked, and I pulled myself together.

"Right, pecans, pie, uh...dinner," I muttered and turned to the nuts thinking maybe this adventure was going to be a lot better than I ever imagined.

Maybe even beyond my wildest dreams.

I SPENT the afternoon baking and cooking (and letting Penelope in and out a gazillion times).

Frey spent the afternoon lugging logs in to replenish the supplies by the fires as well as reloading the back porch. After that he set about chopping more.

I was seeing it was good having a husband around because in my six weeks there, I'd already gone through the stash on the back porch and spent an hour of back and forth to the shed restocking it. This meant the supply in the shed was half gone and I'd been getting worried. To keep warm and cook, you went through a hell of a lot of wood. I wasn't looking forward to another hour of back and forth. My favorite chore wasn't lugging wood into the house. And I was pretty pleased I'd done well roughing it but was not hankering to hone my currently nonexistent skill with an axe by chopping down trees.

With Frey there, I didn't have to worry about any of this.

Bonus.

The bigger bonus was, even in the frigid temperatures, evidently chopping wood was hard work because Frey took off his sweater to do it and he did it at a stump that was clearly visible from the kitchen windows.

Watching this, I could see why my husband was seriously buff.

Watching this, I could also get distracted from cooking (and did).

So I stopped watching.

I went all out, using the china, silver and crystal in my trunks for the first time. It looked kinda silly on a farm table, but this was our first dinner as husband and wife, this was our first dinner ever (for me) and this was our pre-consummation dinner so I wanted to make it an occasion. And nothing said occasion like delicate china, heavy silver and elegant crystal, even in a rustic cabin.

So I used it.

I roasted a piece of beef, somehow pulled off potatoes dauphinoise and boiled green beans, which I was serving with fresh bread from the bakery, and after, my homemade pecan pie with cream for dessert. I called out to Frey at his stump (by this time, the sun was long gone so he was chopping in the totally frigid, totally dark evening and doing it by torchlight) twenty minutes before I reckoned it would be done. He quit ten minutes later and came to the table washed.

That was good.

He sat at the table and scooped out food on his plate without really noticing (and definitely not commenting on) the obvious effort I'd made.

That was bad.

When he was about to commence eating, I asked quietly, "Can you open the wine?"

That was when he looked at me. He looked at the table, half of his mouth hitched up for a millisecond before he got up and opened the wine we'd bought in town. He poured it, sat down and commenced eating.

I started eating too and was pretty pleased with the results. The potatoes were burnt a little on the top, but the roast was done to perfection, nice and brown on the outside, nice and pink on the inside.

Frey made light work of it, and even after tasting it, didn't say a word.

This was bad too.

Or, perhaps, chopping wood gave you an appetite.

I decided to think of it that way.

He had refilled his glass of wine (and topped up mine) and was reaching for seconds when I decided conversation was in order.

I also decided what we were talking about.

And I'd spent a great deal of time while baking and cooking deciding *how* I was going to talk about it.

"Uh...Frey?" I called.

He showed me he'd heard and was listening by looking at me.

"Can we talk about something important?" I asked.

He stopped cutting into a slice of meat and gave me his full attention. "And what's important to you, wife?"

"Um..." I started and stopped.

Frey put his silverware on his plate and aimed a minor scowl at me. It wasn't terrifying but it wasn't his best look either.

"I have manhandled you," he made this surprising and maybe a little weird admission then went on to explain why he did it, "but I have never hurt you. This..." he paused, "*hesitancy* in speaking to me has not been earned."

Well, it was interesting he thought that, but...

"And," he continued, "it's beginning to be trying."

"I—" I started, but he kept talking.

"Indeed, what you said this morning, I will agree with for it is visibly obvious. I *am* a big man, and you are *not* a big woman. But I have never given you cause to think I'd do you harm."

That was interesting he thought that too. And not entirely true.

"So," he concluded, "it would please me greatly if you would stop with your 'uhs' and 'ums' and just say what's on your mind."

"Okay," I returned swiftly, mainly because, after having spent hours cooking, making dessert and setting it all out nicely, as well as deliberating on how I was going to say what I needed to say, only for him to hijack the conversation and be a dick about it, I was suddenly *wicked* ticked off. "What *was* on my mind was that I was going to tell you I liked you."

Frey did a slow blink, showing surprise, but I didn't care. That was just how wicked ticked off I was.

"Now," I carried on, "I'm thinking...not so much."

"Finnie—" he started, but this time, *I* cut *him* off.

And I did it by throwing out my hand holding my fork then going right back to cutting my beef (though I did it this time more like hacking) all the while talking.

"You have my leave to call me Sjofn. I'm thinking, now, I prefer *that* from you, a man who tosses me around and leaves me in a filthy house after driving ever onward through the freezing cold countryside." I speared my meat with my fork at the same time I speared him with a look. "*For hours.* Then taking off without even helping me with my *four*," I jabbed my fork with meat in his direction, "*very tired* horses. A man who made it clear he didn't like me much, considering our wedding night I spent *alone*, and he was off *at sea*, missing, I might add, some really freaking fantastic underwear."

He did another slow blink, but I kept right on going.

"So if I'm a little hesitant with that man, I beg your pardon. I'll endeavor not to be so in future."

I chomped down on the meat on my fork, yanked it off and started chewing.

Frey didn't reply and I looked anywhere but him as I continued to saw into my meat, fork into my potatoes with far more vigor than needed and suck down healthy gulps of wine.

The instant I'd cleaned my plate (which was about three minutes later considering I wolfed down the remainder of my food), I jumped up, snatching it as I went while asking, "Are you done? Do you want pie?"

I didn't wait for his answer as I dumped my (probably priceless, or at least, by the looks of it, exorbitantly expensive) china in the wood sink and going back to grab the serving bowls.

"Finnie," he said softly.

I turned my eyes to him and held up the bowl of green beans.

"Would you like to finish these off or do you want to move on to pie?"

"Put down the bowl," he ordered.

I did as he ordered but did it after walking back to the sink. I had cleared the meat and potatoes and was going back for his plate when suddenly two big hands closed around my hips, and I was sitting in his lap.

I put my hands on his chest and tried to push up at the same time crying out, "Hey!" but I got nowhere because his arms had locked around me.

I stopped struggling as it was undignified and my mom taught me no matter what pickle you were in, never lose your dignity.

Instead, I raised my eyes to glare at him and demanded, "Let me up."

"No, my new wife. Take a moment, take a breath, calm yourself and let us go back to what you wished to discuss ten minutes ago."

"I don't want to go back there," I returned.

"Take a moment, take a breath, calm yourself, and maybe you will," he suggested.

I shook my head. "Nope. I know myself pretty well and I'm pretty sure I don't want to go back there."

He grinned. It was a good one. I had rarely seen him do that, in fact, I wasn't certain I had *ever* seen him out and out grin.

It wasn't lost on me that it looked good on him, but I was still too pissed to care before he said, "It would seem, Finnie, you have no problems with 'ums' and 'uhs' when you're vexed."

"Yes, it would seem that way," I agreed then asked, "Do you want pie?"

"Yes, I do, but not now. Now, I want you to calm yourself and then I'd like to listen to what you had to say."

I glared at him a moment before I guessed, "You're not going to let me get up until you hear what I had to say, are you?"

Another grin. It was again good. It was again not lost on me. And I was still too pissed to care.

"No, I'm not," he confirmed my guess was accurate.

"Fine," I snapped.

I shifted my booty to settle in his lap. Crossing my arms on my chest, I looked right into his green-brown eyes and launched in.

"Waking up this morning, I liked you. To be totally honest, I liked you last night, *not* when you were being a *jerk* at the *pub* but when you came *home*, and you were being kinda *sweet*. I liked you more when I woke up and you'd proved you could be thoughtful. And I liked you more throughout the day because, well, you aren't exactly Mr. Conversation, but at least we could have conversations without you freaking me out or pissing me off, which I thought was a plus considering we *are* married and having conversations that freak me out or piss me off for decades upon decades would *not* be a good thing. You also demonstrated you could be sweet again in town and it must be said I'm glad you carried in logs because that isn't what I call fun and it's nice to share the load. With all that and the way you kissed me after we got married, which I liked, a *whole* lot, and the way you were at the market today, I was thinking maybe tonight might be good. And I was thinking that I wanted to talk to you about that and how, maybe, if I kept liking you and maybe started liking you more and if I *really* liked tonight, it might be nice if we had that for a while. Just the two of us. And ask if you'd help me with that."

I gave my hair a short toss and kept right on going.

"But now I've changed my mind. I *don't* like you because you have again

80

been a *jerk*. I'm reneging on the deal and there won't *be* a tonight. You'll get pie. I'll do the dishes, and if you won't let me have the bed then I'll sleep on the couch."

He had no reply, he just stared at me.

Thus, I concluded, "So that's it. That was what I was going to say. I've said it. *Now* will you let me up?"

"No," he replied, and I rolled my eyes to the ceiling and muttered, "Great."

"Finnie," he called.

I rolled my eyes back to him and glared. He pressed his lips together and I'd never seen him do that so I didn't know what that meant but I didn't care about that either.

Then he spoke again.

"You enjoyed my kiss at the Dwelling of the Gods?"

"Uh...*yeah*," I said like I'd say, "uh...*duh*." "Frey, I'd wrapped my arms around you. You're a jerk but you can kiss."

Another lip press and then, "Explain what you mean about me helping you with us having what we have tonight just the two of us for a while. It is my understanding, unless you're unusually broad-minded, what I have planned for tonight is *always* just the two of us."

Yeesh. Men. Their minds, no matter what world they live in, always wandered down the same paths.

"I'm not talking about a threesome, *Frey*. I'm talking about *children*. As in, I don't *know* you, but I was thinking that I was really liking *getting to know you* and that when that extra *component* was *added*, you were giving all the signs I would really like *that too*. So, I thought, if I did really like all of that, I'd like to have all of that with you for a while, just the two of us, before we start thinking of daughters and sons and who's going to teach who swordplay and all that jazz."

I felt the pads of his fingers dig into my hip and noticed his eyes had gone weird, but I didn't pay much attention to that either.

Then he asked, "You wish to delay providing your father with an heir?"

"Not *forever*. Not even for very long. A few months, enough time I could learn about you, you could learn about me, we could learn about...uh...how we are together and maybe I could ride on your ship."

Another slow blink then, "Ride on my ship?"

"Or take a trip on it or whatever you call it. I mean, you know, go voyaging with you. That might not be so much fun pregnant, and if I have a kid, I'd have to stay home while off you go on your adventures and that would suck. I was thinking maybe we can squeeze in an adventure or two and then we can have sons and daughters and provide heirs to the kingdom and all that stuff. It's not like I'll be this age forever and it won't be as much fun when I'm old and decrepit and struggling along with my cane only to slip on a deck one of your men are swabbing and break a hip."

He did yet *another* slow blink.

Then he threw back his head and burst out laughing.

I stared because, first, I didn't know the man *could* laugh. Second, I was staring at his throat which I'd already noted was a nice view. And third, he had a great laugh.

I, however, did not laugh with him. I was still too pissed.

He eventually stopped laughing (though, I will note, he took his sweet time doing it) and returned his attention to me.

And when he did, his eyes roamed my face before he said quietly, "When my wife gets vexed, her cheeks get pink."

I fought the urge to struggle out of his lap *and* the urge to cover my cheeks. Instead, I simply continued to glare.

"I like it," he went on talking quietly.

"Can I get up now?" I asked snappishly.

He didn't answer nor did he let me up. Instead, he remarked, still quietly, "I'm intrigued about these wedding undergarments I missed."

"Sorry, Frey, that was a onetime deal. I was all decked out in my wedding finery, and you took off. You missed that boat, totally."

He grinned again, then whispered, "More fool me."

"Uh...hello?" I called then requested, "Can I get up now?"

One of his big hands drifted up my back and he said softly, "I must tell you, Finnie, I like you here. You fit well in my lap."

Uh-oh.

"Does it matter that I don't like being here?" I asked.

"Indeed it does, wife, let's get you somewhere where you're more comfortable. I'm thinking the loft."

Uh-oh again.

"Frey, I think I told you, the deal is off."

He grinned and shook his head. "You know, my Winter Princess, you never renege on a deal with a Raider."

I blinked.

Oh shit. I'd read that in *both* of those books. You made a deal with a Raider, you went back on it, you regretted it.

Big time.

Shit!

His hand was now wrapped around the back of my neck, and he held me still while he leaned into me.

Once there and he had captured my gaze, he said quietly, "You have ten minutes to prepare yourself and meet me up there. We will see how it goes as to whether we guard against conceiving or, perhaps, forget."

Ho boy. I knew what that meant because I figured that meant the same thing on *both* worlds.

"You haven't had pie," I pointed out in an attempt to stall.

"We'll have it later..." he paused and grinned. "Maybe. We might be too busy, or we might need sustenance to keep going."

Ho boy!

"Frey—" I whispered.

He cut me off. "You now have nine minutes, Finnie."

Shit! Shit! Shit!

"That wasn't a minute," I argued.

He pressed his lips together, but I knew what it meant this time because his eyes were so close, I saw them dancing.

Then he warned softly and effectively with one word, "Finnie."

I stared into his eyes.

I saw there a clear indication that there was no way I could delay.

This was happening and it was my choice whether it happened in the loft or on the farm table. Since that was my only choice, I definitely needed the loft.

So that was why I muttered, "Oh, all right."

That got me another grin. It also loosened his arms. And this meant I scrambled off his lap and hurried out of the room trying not to look like I was hurrying. I hit the trunks, found what I was looking for and went to the bathroom space not bothering with the lock on the door because he could easily break it down if he had a mind to.

Only then did I start hyperventilating.

8

ELVES

I stood in the bathroom space thinking that I really needed fifteen meals.

Maybe twenty-one.

Or, perhaps, ninety.

I was *so* not ready for this.

And I had been in the bathroom *way* longer than nine minutes. I was pretty certain Frey was going to bust down the door any second.

I totally shouldn't have lost it at dinner and thus made Frey skip pie.

I needed pie.

I needed to think!

How to get out of this?

I stared at myself in the mirror.

For reasons unknown to me, probably nervous energy, I had decided to arrange my hair loosely at the top of my head with one of the scads of ice-blue ribbons that had been packed in my beautification trunk.

I didn't know what I was going for, sultry vixen or innocent virgin (probably the latter in hopes that Frey would take it slow and be gentle). And to get this to look even slightly good, it took what had to be nineteen minutes, not nine.

I had also changed into the nightgown I was pretty sure Sjofn was supposed to wear on her wedding night. This was because you didn't sleep in this nightie. This nightie was an occasion nightie. It was meant to be seen and it was way too delicate to sleep in.

It was beautiful, elaborate winter-white lace over ice-blue satin. The thin straps were ice-blue satin too. It had an empire waist and showed serious cleavage and leg. This last was because the skirt only fell low enough to cover my rear...barely. It was mostly simple but that made it elegant, the lace made it extraordinary, and the ice-blue satin made it beautiful (not to mention it felt great against my skin).

But I thought, at that moment, it was too short, too suggestive and way too sexy.

Not that I had to suggest anything, and everything was sexy when you were essentially a sure thing.

But it had been purchased for Frey. And for some crazy, stupid reason (even though he could be a very big *jerk*), when I'd been considering what would happen that night, I decided to wear it. And I did this because I thought even men should have what they looked forward to on their wedding nights. Like women, they only got one and it should be a good one.

So he messed up his first shot. But before my nerves overwhelmed me, I felt some weird drive to give it to him just the same.

And he sure wasn't going to get anything like it when Sjofn came back.

Thus, I'd picked that nightgown.

Shit.

I stared at my reflection, my mind whirling.

I realized I had no choice. I made the deal, I had to do it. I couldn't go running into the night. Frey would find me, and anyway, I'd freeze to death. I had to go to the loft and when I got there, maybe I could talk him into taking it slow, as in, making out tonight for a while, getting the hang of each other and then seeing what tomorrow brings.

I could do that. I could make out with him. I already knew he was a good kisser. That would be nice.

Hell, that would be *great*.

My mind came back to reality with a, *Fat chance of convincing him of that, Finnie.*

I stared at my face in the mirror.

Well, nothing ventured, nothing gained. That was what Dad (and a bunch of other people) always said.

I blew out the candles in the bathroom space and walked out to the living room.

All was dark except the fireplaces that had been fed and were blazing big and bright. The curtains had been pulled by me, way earlier, to shut out the draft after the sun went down. I'd learned that early, as in, after the first night I slept there when I woke up on the couch with a stiff neck.

The curtain at the railing at the loft was mostly closed, light was coming through where it was opened at the end.

By the ladder.

Eek!

I tried to remember if Penelope was in or out when I saw her rise to all fours where she was curled on one of the fluffy throws on an armchair. She stretched her back, sat on her ass and blinked through the firelight at me. Then she looked up at the loft like she knew what was about to happen there. She looked back at me and blinked again. She then jumped off the armchair, landing with a fat kitty thump and waddled into the kitchen.

Well, guess she wasn't going up there with me to assist in talking Frey into a make-out session.

With no choice, I went to the ladder and climbed up.

When I got up, I didn't look. I entered the space bent double (because I had to, though this was not good considering my major cleavage and the fact that it made the nightie ride up my ass) and turned to shut the curtain. I sucked in a deep breath while hiding sucking in a deep breath and let it out while turning back.

I had put three candleholders in each corner to light the space. When I read at night, I moved six of them beside the bed, but I kept them in the corners normally to keep them away from the bedclothes.

All of them were lit, the fire in the grate was blazing, the space seemed warm and cozy, and Frey was wearing nothing but breeches and he was crouched before the fire.

He looked hot. His muscled shoulders looked broad. His defined lats looked powerful. And his eyes were on me. Or, more accurately, they were on my nightie.

Ho boy.

I should have crouched, though that wouldn't have been much better.

"Uh...hi," I whispered.

At the sound of my voice, Frey blinked then he moved. Slowly, his big body shifted, and he crawled on all fours into the bed as I stood still and watched without blinking.

There was something animal about that, the way he moved, the unhurried way he did it, his muscles bunching, the fact that he didn't tear his eyes from my face.

It *was* animal, graceful, predatory...*fascinating*.

My mouth went dry, and I totally forgot about talking him into just making out.

He dropped to a hip and said gently, "Come here, Finnie."

For some reason, without hesitation, I went there. Falling to my knees when my toes hit bedclothes, I moved across the space, stopped two feet away and put my rump to my calves. My body stilled when his hand came up. It went to my hair, and with a gentle tug, the ribbon was gone, and my hair tumbled down.

Well, so much for that effort.

His hand curled warm around my neck.

"I wish to feel it all over me, wife," he whispered.

Hmm.

I liked that.

"Okay," I whispered back.

When I spoke, his eyes did what they did in the market that day. They got lazy and they smiled.

My belly dropped.

Wow.

His hand at my neck curled around to the back and his other hand came to my waist, fingertips only, gliding in, sliding back. I felt his whole hand then, pressing at the small of my back, he pulled me toward him slowly.

I kept my eyes glued to his as my breath started coming faster and my body started trembling—from fear, definitely, anxiety, you bet, and something else, absolutely.

As he pulled me closer, his hand at the small of my back wrapped around my waist, tugging me gently so I fell from my calves to my hip and thigh. Then I was pulled closer...my head tipping back...closer...his head dipping down...closer...my eyes dropped to his mouth right before they drifted closed, and he touched his lips to mine.

That was it. A gentle touch then he used his hands and his torso to push me until my back was to the bed, my head to the pillows. He settled at my side on his forearm, the hand that was at my neck sliding down my shoulder, my arm, in, over the lace and satin at my ribs, down, over my belly, curling at my waist, down, over my hip. All of this slow, all of this taking his time, all of this while his eyes watched.

That felt nice, even relaxing, but I was in no state to relax. The heat in his eyes and the expression on his face were both communicating to me in a way that made my skin heat. And his chest was right there, all of it, there was a lot of it, it was fantastic, and I wanted to touch.

But I was terrified at the same time.

Still, he was touching me so I should get to touch him. And I wanted it, so I lifted my hand and slowly moved it toward his chest as his hand slid back up to my belly. Suddenly my hand was arrested in mid-air because his fingers had curled around my wrist.

My eyes went to his to see his on my hand.

They came to mine as he pulled my hand to the warm, sleek skin of his chest, pressing it flat as he leaned closer to me.

With his face a couple inches from mine, my hand pressed to his skin, he asked softly, "Why do you tremble, wife?"

I licked my lips before I whispered my admission, "I'm nervous, Frey."

His lazy, heated eyes got lazier and more heated as he slid my hand up his chest, over his shoulder and around his neck, gently pulling my torso up with it. He left my hand there and his arm curved around my waist. He dropped down fully to his side in the bed as he turned me into his arms and his mouth came to within a breath of mine.

"I'll be gentle, Finnie," he whispered.

"Promise?" I asked.

His hand slid warm up my spine to tangle in my hair, making me tremble anew, and not with nerves, as it traveled along its path, and he pressed into me.

"I would not hurt you, my winter bride." He slid his nose along mine, and I liked that. It was sweet. It was hot. It felt nice and my body softened under his. "Ever," he growled to finish and that was when he finally kissed me.

There it was. His tongue in my mouth, that skill I remembered, it was all there. But this time he was giving it to me, not using it to take from me. It was slow, it was about discovery, exploration, showing, telling, reward-ing, and I softened more. Pressing closer as his hand moved light over my nightie, warm, not invasive, soothing at the same time heating.

And I was heating, slowly, very slowly. Because that was all he did, building the warmth, stoking the fire. He had time and he was going to take it. So he did.

And I did too. Hesitant, I explored his thick, soft hair and the muscles of his shoulders and back. All the while I explored his mouth, his tongue, tasted his lips, and he explored me.

I liked what I discovered. It was freaking *fantastic*.

Finally, his big hand roved over the cheek of my ass and feeling it, feeling him so hard and warm pressed against me, his mouth so generous, his skin so silky sleek, fire suddenly shot between my legs, my hips pressed into his, and I made a soft noise in his mouth.

Frey broke our kiss, but his lips still touched mine and his fingers cupped my ass. "My wife likes this," he whispered.

"Yes," I whispered back because it was true.

Unhurried, his fingers pulled the material of my nightie up.

I stared in his eyes, my body warm and still, my mind focusing on everything all at once. The feel of him. The smell of him. His lips so close. His eyes so gorgeous. His eyelashes so thick. The room lit with candlelight. My lips feeling bruised. My mouth wanting his back. The brilliant feel of my breasts pressed hard against his chest. The better feel of his hard cock pressed against me. He finally got the material up and slowly, like he had all the time in the world, as I held my breath, his fingers slid back down inside my panties.

Fire seared through me.

Oh my God.

Why was that so, unbelievably, *phenomenal?*

I didn't know. I didn't care.

I just knew I wanted more.

The instant I felt him skin against skin, my eyes drifted closed, another noise escaped my throat, I pressed tight to him, everywhere I could get, and slow was a memory.

His hand clenched my ass, his torso pushed my back to the bed, his mouth slammed down on mine, not slow, not making out, not generous, but hot, wet, hungry and *amazing*.

He shoved a knee between my legs, but he didn't have to. I opened them and bent my knee, pressing the inside of my thigh to the side of his hip as I arched my back to connect with him. Tightened my arms to pull him into me. And I moaned into his mouth.

He kissed me hard and deep then his mouth went from mine, down my cheek to my ear and I pressed into him. My fingernails grazing the skin of his back, I pushed my foot into the bed so I could shove my hips against his.

"You want me," he growled in my ear.

My head turned so I could touch the tip of my tongue to his earlobe, my brain and other parts of me noting I liked the taste of him, and I whispered, "Yes, Frey."

His hand left my ass. Trailing around swiftly, it was suddenly between my legs over my panties, the touch light but definitely there and unbelievably enticing. His head came up, his eyes locking on mine.

"Gods, you want me," he repeated, his voice thick, and I knew he felt the damp evidence that proved this between my legs.

"Yes," I breathed, moving my hips to grind down on his hand, and he instantly cupped my sex and took my mouth in another hard, wet kiss.

I whimpered as he kissed me while his hand slid up, fingers pressing in, God, so freaking awesome. Then up to my belly, I could feel the tip of his middle finger pressing in just above my panties, preparing. He was going to go skin to skin, and I could *not* wait.

I drew in a deep breath of heady anticipation, sucking his tongue deeper in my mouth, and his entire body froze.

His head came up and I blinked as I watched it turn just a little like he was listening.

Then he growled, deep and low and seriously freaking pissed off, "Gods *damn it.*"

I blinked again.

Oh no.

What did I do?

He pulled away.

Oh God!

What did I do?

"Frey?" I called as he maneuvered his big body over mine.

"Stay here," he ordered. "I'll return."

I turned with him as he quickly moved to the overhang of the loft, not the ladder. He wasn't going to waste time. He was going to drop down, which was crazy, but I was stuck back thirty seconds ago.

"But..." I whispered, eyes on him, voice trembling with disappointment, "what did I do?"

His body arrested at my tone and his eyes came to me. They took me in quickly and then he was right there, his hand cupping the back of my head, his face all I could see.

"Nothing, Finnie, everything is fine. Stay up here. Don't leave this space. I'll return as soon as I can. Promise, wife."

I stared into his eyes. He must have seen what he needed to see for he moved to touch his mouth to mine. Then he shifted swiftly and disappeared under the curtain, throwing his big body over the side of the loft.

I heard him land on his feet and I stared at the flickering candlelight on the curtain. Still staring at the curtain, I heard the front door open and close.

What just happened?

Did my husband in an alternate universe who I barely knew just turn me on more than I ever had been *in my life* then take off for what seemed like no reason, throwing himself off the side of a loft?

It hit me that *he* was turned on too. I could see it in his eyes, hell, I could *feel* it pressed against me. He wanted me. Bad.

Then he was gone.

He'd heard something.

Oh God.

He'd heard something.

Did Raiders have enemies?

Oh God!

Of course they did! I read the stories. Maybe they *weren't* romanticized. Maybe the sea was filled with perils. Maybe he'd looted and pillaged and now it was payback time.

And he was out there in nothing but breeches!

I rushed across the bed, threw back the curtain and went feet and ass first out of the loft to the ladder. Foot by foot, hand by hand, I quickly descended the ladder, rushed to the dark kitchen and went directly to the knives. Pulling out the biggest, scariest, sharpest one, I ran to the front door.

I heard his voice, not what he was saying, but he sounded pissed.

Shit!

I couldn't rush outside in a nightie without knowing what I was rushing into *and* what Frey was facing.

Crap.

I went to the window, quickly pushed the heavy curtain aside and looked out.

I froze.

I stared.

I fought against passing out.

Then the teeny, little man with pointy ears and an upturned nose wearing a strange dark-blue hat that looked like a cap with a straight white feather poked in the side, and whose whole body was weirdly glowing ice blue, turned to look at me.

I heard him say to Frey, "Your Ice Bride has seen us, Frey Drakkar."

My eyes shot to Frey standing out in the freezing cold in nothing but breeches but the teeny, little man didn't have to tell Frey that. Frey was staring at me and shaking his head.

He moved to the door.

I jerked from behind the curtains and hyperventilated.

The door opened and I turned to face my husband.

Eyes on me, he said softly, "I asked you to stay in the loft, Finnie."

"There are little fairies outside," I breathed, forcing out the words through quick breaths.

His brows drew together in a way that wasn't scary, but instead, surprised, and he replied, "Those aren't fairies, wife, those are elves."

Elves?

Elves.

Holy moly!

My head slowly turned to the curtained window I could no longer see out of, but my mind conjured the vision of what was essentially our front yard that I'd seen littered with about a dozen, maybe more, teeny men and women glowing ice blue.

Elves!

Oh my God!

How cool! This world had elves!

I looked back at Frey and whispered, "How *cool*!"

He held my eyes and told me his mind was not on elves when he asked quietly, "Can you explain why you hold a knife?"

"You're a Raider," I said without hesitation, wanting to get my explanation over with so we could talk about elves. "You probably have enemies. I thought, with the way you took off, that they'd found you. It was payback time. You were unarmed so I wanted to see if I could help." His face again registered surprise for an instant before it softened, but I didn't really notice mainly because my mind was on the elves outside, so I asked, "Are those really *elves*?"

He moved toward me, and my head tipped back as he did. When he got close, his hand carefully came to mine, took control of the knife then, when he had it, his torso twisted slightly, and he tossed it so it landed with a soft *funf* on the couch.

With free hands, I lifted them and curled my fingers on his shoulders, shaking him a little to get his attention.

When he turned back to me, I leaned close, went up on my toes and whispered excitedly, "Frey! Seriously! Are those really *elves*?"

His hands settled on my hips, and he peered down at my face, one side of his mouth hitching up before he said, "Yes, Finnie. It's been centuries but they have returned."

I instantly pressed in deeper, chest to chest, fingers digging in his shoulders as I felt my eyes go wide, a big smile split my face, and I cried, "How *cool!*"

He grinned then he said, "I must go with them."

I blinked before I asked, "What? Why?"

"They have come to me with a message. It's important. I must go to the adela tree."

Whoa. Wow. Cool again!

I *totally* wanted to see an adela tree. Not to mention, hang with elves.

I pressed closer and asked through my still bright smile, "Can I go?"

He kept grinning into my face but shook his head as his fingers gave me a squeeze, "No, wife."

I felt my mouth turn down and asked, "Why?"

"They have a message for me, not you or us. And it is only me they expect at the adela tree."

"But—"

"Therefore, it will only be me at the adela tree."

Hmm.

Bummer.

As was my way, when adventure was afoot, I didn't give up.

"Can you go out there and maybe...*ask* if it was cool if I came with you? I could stand out of earshot," I offered, and he gave a short chuckle but shook his head.

"It must only be me."

"But you're big and scary and they're teeny and not scary and you can stomp on them with your feet if you had a mind to. Maybe you can just *tell* them I'm coming."

His brows drew slightly together again, and his hands slid from my hips to the small of my back as his head dipped to mine and his voice went low.

"Finnie, it is true. I am their lord, but this is not their only form. They have awesome power and I command them but only because they have returned to the surface. They can retreat and I do not wish them to do so. If they want only me, as their lord, I should hear what they have to say and decide, during ensuing meetings, if I will take my winter bride."

I was staring up with him with what I knew were big eyes when I breathed, "You're their *lord?*"

He studied me then said, "Finnie, you know that. Everyone does. The Frey of the line of Drakkar always commands the elves."

Ho boy. I *didn't* know and Sjofn hadn't seen fit to share *that* tasty morsel in her note.

"They await, wife," he prompted me on a slight squeeze of his arms.

"Right." I nodded. "Of course."

I started to push back and realized my hands on his shoulders and body pressed to his were not encountering cold. He'd been inside for a while, but it wasn't like we had central heating. It was always a wee bit nippy, even with the fires blazing.

And his skin wasn't cold. Not even a little bit.

I dropped my head to stare at his chest, it shot back, and I stared at him.

"Why aren't you cold?" I whispered.

His head tipped slightly to the side for a second before he quickly righted it and replied, "I do not suffer the cold, Finnie. This you also know because everyone knows it. I do not suffer in heat either."

Uh.

Wow!

And.

What?

Unfortunately, I couldn't ask because clearly I was supposed to know. Also unfortunately I had to cover.

"Right," I said quickly. "I forgot."

He examined my face while repeating, "You forgot," in a way that said he didn't believe me and in a way that said he either thought I was slightly unhinged or highly untrustworthy (or both).

"Uh..." I started to cover further, "I'm kinda freaking out about the elves being back after centuries, Frey. It slipped my mind."

He stared at me before he whispered, "Right."

Totally didn't believe me.

So I covered more by smiling at him and I did it big. That worked. His eyes dropped to my mouth, his arms convulsed, and the tension went out of his big frame.

I gave him a light push with my hands and said, "You better go. The cool-as-shit elves are waiting."

That got me another hitch of one side of his mouth before he nodded and let me go.

When he did, I turned and looked around the room, saw his stuff tossed on a trunk and hurried to it.

He followed me and I handed him his sweater. He took it and pulled it on while I blathered.

"When you get back, I want to know everything. This is *so* cool. I *love* this. I can't wait to hear what they have to say."

"Finnie—"

I handed him his socks and cut him off. "No. Don't say you can't tell me. If you hear what they say and you can't tell me, okay. But maybe you can. Don't burst my bubble now. You can burst it later if you have to."

He took his socks but didn't put them on. He just stared at me.

Then he hooked me with an arm around my waist and I was suddenly plastered against his body and his mouth had crushed down on mine. He gave me a short, hot kiss (with tongues) and let me go.

After that he ordered, "Loft, wife. I'll be back soon."

I smiled at him and agreed, "Okay."

I rushed to the ladder and up.

Once in, I stuck my head out and called to my husband as he tugged on his boots, "Have fun with the elves."

His head tipped back, and his eyes caught mine. He shook his head. Then he grinned.

I grinned back and slapped the curtains closed.

I rushed to the bed, sat cross-legged in the middle of it and listened to the door open and close.

I giggled.

Holy freaking *moly*! This world had elves and I was married to their lord, a man who, for some reason (magic?), didn't suffer cold or heat.

How...freaking...*cool*!

This adventure was *totally* worth a million dollars.

Totally.

9

THE MESSAGE

Tyr's hooves pounded through the snow taking Frey Drakkar over the rise behind his hunting cabin and beyond. Through the trees that grew thicker and thicker and into the heart of the forest, the part that was so dense, even Tyr and The Drakkar had to slow to navigate it.

They finally entered an opaque, drifting white mist that only The Drakkar and his steed could penetrate. Any other human attempting it would be cast back.

The elves were present.

Tyr and The Drakkar moved through the thick stand of trees and heavy vapor. They saw the light of the adela tree piercing the mist and shafting around the dark trunks of the forest well before they arrived at the clearing that held the wide, tall, sparkling adela with its many narrow branches rising straight from the stump. Its bark glittering. Its twirly-ended twigs profuse and shooting out to the sides and straight into the air.

The Drakkar pulled back on Tyr's reins at the edge of the fifteen-foot circular clearing surrounding the adela and dismounted. The elves were already there, moving to the adela, touching its bark at the base where the tree rose from the earth, instantly transforming from their diminutive size to human size—stopping at a height not near as tall as The Drakkar, but as tall as his winter bride.

Drakkar approached with Tyr's jaw close to his shoulder and stopped halfway to the glittering, magical tree.

Nillen, Speaker of the Elves, moved instantly to him, stopping two feet away from his lord.

He bowed his head by tucking his chin to the side of the neck before his ice-blue eyes, Drakkar's new bride's same eyes, moved to his lord.

"Thank you for coming, my lord, Frey Drakkar."

"This had better be good, Nillen, I was ten minutes away from consummating my marriage when your elves arrived."

Nillen's lips tipped up at the ends and his eyes sparkled like icicles. "We have bad timing," he murmured.

"Immensely bad," Drakkar agreed on an impatient growl. Nillen's lips tipped up farther, but The Drakkar wasn't in the mood to share his amusement. "Your message?" he prompted.

Nillen held his eyes.

Then he whispered, "You know our message."

This was true. Drakkar knew his message.

They were there to discuss his new bride.

A bride who smiled at him, laughed and joked.

A bride who he woke up to curled tight around his body.

A bride who quailed at the sight of a dead deer on her table when she'd not only brought down numerous in her time on this earth, she'd cleaned them and stripped their hides.

A bride who cooked food like she'd been doing it her entire life, rather than having it served to her already prepared at every meal from the time she stopped suckling her wet nurse's breast.

A bride who said strange words and uttered bizarre terms such as, "freaking out," "ticking me off," "flip me out," "pissing me off" and "all that jazz" as well as "technicality," "beejeezus," "cool-as-shit," "jerk" and "the next level."

A bride who wore dresses and perfume and made up her face doing the former two with natural ease and the latter with obvious practice when everyone in the realm knew she did none of these.

A bride who had an immensely graceful bearing but an unreserved and friendly manner, again, something she'd never had before.

A bride who did not know the difference between elves and fairies nor did she know her husband held elf magic and was immune to heat and cold although this had been known for century upon century as the House of Drakkar birthed Freys into their line.

A bride who returned his kisses with exuberance, melted in his arms and grew immensely heated merely at his hand moving over her rounded arse.

And a bride who moved nearly immediately to assist him in defense when she feared he faced danger then behaved with unbridled delight when speaking of the elves.

A bride who was most definitely *not* the Winter Princess Sjofn of the House of Wilde.

"My bride," Drakkar grunted.

Nillen inclined his head.

"I assume," Nillen started, "considering your reported..." he paused, "*activities* prior to my brothers' and sisters' arrival, she has touched you?"

"She has," Drakkar confirmed.

"May I read?" Nillen asked, and Drakkar tilted his chin up in an affirmative.

Nillen did not come closer but simply lifted his hand, laid it on Drakkar's chest for a mere moment and pulled it slightly away. A vaporous, ice-blue handprint remained on The Drakkar's chest even after the elf's hand had moved away, sparkling, ice-blue sinews stretching between The Drakkar and Nillen's hand as he held it up.

Drakkar saw that Nillen's eyes were closed as he took his reading. Then the connection was broken, the print on his chest fading when Nillen's hand dropped, and his eyes opened.

He smiled.

"She is indeed the Ice Bride," he whispered and the elves in the clearing roused, the air filling with anticipation.

"Explain," Drakkar ordered curtly.

"She is not of this world," Nillen stated.

Tyr shifted his bulk and butted his master's shoulder with his jaw, for his horse had long since communicated this same impression. Indeed, the night of his wedding as she inexpertly (at first) drove her sleigh at his side.

The elves standing in the clearing continued to stir but Drakkar said nothing.

Nillen continued, "The elves have known of the existence of another world, different than ours, in some ways more advanced, in other ways very short-sighted, for many millennia. That world holds very limited magic."

Drakkar remained silent.

Nillen went on to explain.

"Humans have twins that live in each world. In fact, nearly every human has a twin save, fortunately for both worlds, those who carry evil.

Those with extreme malice in their heart, enough to act on that wickedness freely and without scruple, only have one being in one world. There are others who do not have twins but these, too, are not birthed only due to extreme circumstances. Those who do not hold malice or their mothers have not endured extreme circumstances in one of the two worlds have two. Although the twin will look like the other, sound like the other, they are *not* the other but two separate beings."

Nillen paused, Drakkar nodded once, and Nillen kept speaking.

"You have a twin in that world and Sjofn of the House of Wilde has one. And she conspired to switch places with her twin on the night of her wedding to you."

Drakkar's jaw went tight but he said nothing.

Nillen carried on, "The Sjofn of this world wished to escape you. The Seoafin of our parallel world came here for much different reasons."

"And those are?" Drakkar asked.

"Primarily...grief," Nillen answered, and Drakkar blinked as his gut grew tight.

"Grief?"

Nillen nodded.

"Many years ago, she lost her mother and father. They were beloved by her. She has not recovered from this loss, such was the weight it settled on her soul. She became aware of our world and the understanding there were twins to those living in her world." He paused and his eyes stayed unwavering on his lord. "She wished to see her parents again and took a great risk and paid a great treasure in order to do it."

Drakkar felt his gut tighten further as he muttered, "Bloody hell."

Nillen lifted his chin. "I'm afraid that although your Ice Bride was clear about her reasons for voyaging to this world, the Sjofn of this world was not forthright with your new bride. She shared very limited information prior to your bride's travel as well as leaving select information for her to understand after. The switch was accomplished just ten minutes to her being forced into the sleigh that would take her to the Dwelling of the Gods. Amongst other things, she had no idea her parents of this world had grown impatient and even angry with her, and she had no idea that she was facing imminent marriage to you. Indeed, even now, after reading Sjofn of the House of Wilde's communications, she holds incomplete information about you."

Drakkar glared at the elf as he felt his neck muscles contract before he urged in a tight voice, "Go on."

Nillen's head dipped to the side before straightening.

"Your bride is..." another pause, "*unusual* for a female in this world and even one, it is our understanding, in her home world. Although she was faced nearly instantly with these inauspicious circumstances, she has rallied, and while she does wish to spend time with her parents, she has enjoyed her adventure on this world very much so far."

That did not surprise The Drakkar. Not after seeing her greet the townsfolk that very day or walking in on her in the pub last night as she cried out in delight, arms straight in the air, smile beaming from her beautiful face while clearly engaged (successfully) in wagering in a game of chance.

Nillen kept speaking though his voice had grown soft.

"You do remember, my lord, that although we understood your reasons for accepting the king's request, the elves cautioned you strongly against binding yourself to Sjofn of the House of Wilde."

Drakkar kept his gaze aimed at the elf, but he felt his entire frame get tight.

He did remember. The elves went beyond cautioning him. Their concerns at this alliance with Princess Sjofn were communicated in a tone that was nearly desperate. Their warnings were dire that such a union would anger Keer, the God of Destiny, who had foretold that the Lord of the Elves would marry his Ice Bride, a woman who shared, like The Frey of the Drakkar, elf magic, for through her veins coursed traces of elf blood.

A woman that Keer, with aid from *all* the gods, Wohden, Adele, Hermia, Meer *and* Alabasta, had searched for and chosen in order to unite the elf and the dragon to create a child who was a true, rightful heir to the throne of Lunwyn. Something which the gods felt crucial though they had not explained why through prayer, Vallee or the elves.

But, for Drakkar, it was foretold the particular woman destined for him was chosen by the gods as a handsome reward for his endeavors and the weighty responsibility of the commands he held, for she also shared Drakkar's lust for voyaging and his thirst for unending quest.

All of which would be impossible for Finnie to be if the world of the winter bride waiting for him at his cabin held little magic for she, clearly, wouldn't either.

After sifting through this knowledge in his brain, finally, The Drakkar lifted his chin.

Nillen's smile beamed from his face before he announced, "The Great Keer and Destiny have prevailed."

Drakkar blinked and the elves around the clearing twittered.

100

"Explain," he demanded.

"Why, my lord, you've married your rightful Ice Bride."

Drakkar's eyes narrowed. "I thought you said her world holds little magic."

"It does but that doesn't mean it holds *none*. She's of the elves, albeit the elves of *her* world, she's still of the elves, our kind there long since gone to their realm deep within the earth, never to return. Princess Sjofn holds her coloring from traits passed down naturally through her parents. Although latent in each parent, they have come out in her by pure chance. Your Seoafin holds her coloring because she carries the blood of elves."

Drakkar studied Nillen's happy face and noted, "I see this pleases you."

Nillen lifted his chin and replied, "Indeed it does, my lord."

Drakkar thought of Finnie, but he didn't need to do so. He already knew she pleased him, which was why, although he proceeded cautiously with a woman unknown to him, he continued to proceed. Until now, he hadn't known if she was a Sjofn of the House of Wilde bewitched (probably, he had thought, by her mother) to be to his liking, if the gods were at work or if a double had been created for fiendish reasons. What he did know was that he was enjoying testing all these theories, therefore, warily, he proceeded to test them.

Now, he knew he had Sjofn's beauty in his bed but with Finnie's grace, Finnie's humor and Finnie's fire.

Yes, this very much pleased him.

What didn't please him was that, albeit good news, tonight's message wasn't urgent and the elves who approached his cabin had told him it was of grave import.

This news as it stood could wait to be passed on.

At the very least, it could have waited for a bloody half hour.

"I'm uncertain, Nillen," Drakkar drawled, "why I was taken from my bed, and *my wife*, to hear this news. It is good, is it not? And it will not change."

Nillen's smile died, and he shook his head but said, "Yes, my lord, it is good. But I'm afraid, not at present, but in future, it will change."

Drakkar crossed his arms on his chest. "How?"

"Your Ice Bride is not in our world for good, Frey Drakkar. She returns to her world in ten months and two weeks, switching back with Sjofn."

The Drakkar's body again grew tight. So tight, it went statue-still, and it felt like the area around his heart squeezed. Hard.

"She returns?" he said softly, his voice low.

101

"Yes, a deal was struck. They were to remain switched for a year then return to their worlds. Sjofn has warned her of you and explained her reasons for your union. She has also warned her not to get with child as she will see to that duty on her return."

Duty.

The Drakkar did not like Sjofn of the House of Wilde. He liked her less and less the more he knew of her, including her casting his Finnie into a situation that had to terrify her when she only wanted to voyage to an unknown world in order to spend time with her parents.

This in particular was a circumstance he was trying not think of for this type of voyage was gravely hazardous as evidenced by her finding herself in the situation she faced practically upon her arrival.

As a man, he regularly sought such ventures. As a powerful, experienced and skilled man, he bested many perilous situations.

His Finnie was not a powerful, experienced and skilled man.

Bloody hell, his wee wife could have been hurt.

And that didn't bear thinking about. Not then. Nor did his actions after he'd wed her bear thinking about. He'd think about it later.

And, much later than that, he'd discuss her behavior with her *and* the fact she would desist in it immediately.

Drakkar turned his mind from these thoughts and focused on Nillen.

"Then I will not let her return," Drakkar decided, and Nillen shook his head.

"The witch from her world who made the switch is extremely powerful. She holds more magic than most witches on *this* world, witches able to practice openly and share with and instruct each other. True magic is hidden in that world for reasons I do not understand. But *this* witch, your Ice Bride's witch, holds the magic of fifty of *our* most powerful witches. This switch between worlds does not occur very often. It is *extremely* rare and the reason why it is rare is that it takes an inordinate amount of magic to perform it thus any witch attempting it will be depleted of all her power once the switch is made, placing herself, I'm sure you understand, Frey Drakkar, at grave risk. If a witch of that world, or this one for that matter, gathers enough magic to perform the switch, they will be drained, and it would take *decades* for them to regain such power."

Nillen paused as if waiting for The Drakkar to acknowledge he understood, and when he jerked up his chin, Nillen continued.

"The witch who switched your Ice Bride with Sjofn of the House of Wilde will not face this same weakening. She holds enough magic to make the switch and switch them back with only a small dwindling of power and will be at her full strength again in a year's time in order to perform the switch again. You could consult a witch, my lord, but it is unlikely any witch in our world could bind your wife here with enough power to subvert the efforts of your bride's witch to perform the return."

"All right," Drakkar agreed, "I can see this. But no witch, no matter how powerful, has magic enough to rival the elves."

And this was true. A single elf held more magic than the evil she-God Minerva of Hawkvale and the benevolent Lavinia of Lunwyn, witch servant of Alabasta, Goddess of Wisdom and overseer of the earth combined. The magic of all the elves was only rivaled by the gods...and the dragons.

Slowly, Nillen smiled.

Then he whispered, "You wish us to bind your Ice Bride to this world?"

"Immediately," Drakkar replied without hesitation.

Nillen's smile widened.

But it faltered.

"You should know, at this time, your bride does not wish to remain in this world. If we bind her here, she will never go back, and you know a spell cast by elves cannot be withdrawn without sacrifice. She has ties there, acquaintances she cares for deeply, dreams she wishes to fulfill, belongings that matter to her. She may not wish this, to be bound to this world, a world where she has no ties and a world that is *very* different from hers."

"Leave that to me," Drakkar stated.

Nillen studied Frey Drakkar.

Then he cautioned, "This is your Destiny, and you know it is our duty to fulfill your command, but you should also be aware that if you bind your Ice Bride to this world, so she can permanently take her place, you must also relegate Sjofn of the House of Wilde to live her days in the other."

"And I should care about this?" Drakkar asked.

"My lord, it is your due to command us and it is your duty to make such decisions about your Destiny, for it is known by all elves straight from Keer that the destinies of Frey Drakkar, Lord of the Elves and his Ice Bride's intermingle with every citizen of Lunwyn and every elf who resides deep in the earth under our frosted country. That said, these are weighty matters you decide in a heartbeat."

"This nation's only princess fled her country for selfish reasons, thoughtlessly throwing an innocent into an unknown situation and placing her at risk. Already, my bride shines a different light on her people than that of her twin, and from what I've seen, they bask under her glow. I do not make this weighty decision without consideration, Nillen. And you know I never do."

"No," Nillen replied quietly. "I know you never do. I am simply cautioning you that you may wish to delay. Your union with your Ice Bride is new and there may be consequences to your actions."

"Leave those to me too," Drakkar returned.

Nillen studied his lord before he inclined his head and again smiled.

"As you command," he muttered.

Drakkar inclined his head briefly in return and stated, "I expect my command to be executed by the time I join my new bride in our bed."

"Of course," Nillen murmured.

"My thanks," Drakkar murmured back then asked, "Do you have more?"

"No, my lord, Frey Drakkar."

Without hesitation, Drakkar turned to Tyr. "Good. I bid you farewell and safe journey back to your realm."

Nillen lifted his chin at his lord after he mounted his horse. All the elves watched him as he wheeled the steed and set his heels to its flanks, clicking his teeth. The powerful beast shot into the trees and the elves didn't delay in moving to circle the adela.

They immediately cast the spell that bound the Ice Bride to their lord and his world, at the same time consigning Sjofn of the House of Wilde to the other world everlastingly.

Once this was accomplished, they moved to the base of the adela, bent low to touch its bark where the tree rose from the earth and with a flash of ice blue ending in the pop of a white spark, they disappeared to their realm.

FREY DISROBED before he mounted the ladder.

As he pulled the curtain back and spied the loft, he saw the candles still lit but the fire needed to be fed. He also saw his wife asleep, the long, thick mass of waves of white-blonde hair on the pillow, her shoulder, down her back and even in her face.

As she did last night, she straddled the bedclothes, something that stirred the blood in his veins. This likely had a great deal to do with the sight of her exposed, shapely leg. And it likely had even more to do with the sight of the curve of her rounded, generous arse exposed by the short night-dress that had ridden up, revealing a pair of tight, miniscule underwear. Underwear he had felt soaked with her excitement caused merely by the play of his tongue in her sweet mouth and light caresses that rarely even touched skin.

This made him wonder what deeper tongue play and more intimate caresses would bring forth from his Finnie.

But becoming as she was slumbering in his bed and as enticing as the stray of his thoughts, Frey determined that he and his new wife would be having a conversation much sooner than the other he intended to have with her. And this one would be about leaving the candles burning while she was asleep.

He moved with practiced ease through the loft, extinguishing the candles, and then he fed the fire.

After that, he moved to his wife.

He'd detangled the bedclothes from her limbs, settled them over their bodies and himself on his back, at the same time pulling her to his side when her head came up.

She blinked at him sleepily in the firelight.

"Finnie—" he started to order her to go back to sleep, but in a flash, her face brightened, her eyes twinkled with excitement, and she exclaimed, "You're back!"

"This I am," Frey agreed to the obvious.

She shot up to sitting and he barely had time to contract his muscles to brace when she slapped his chest then bent over him. Her hand at his chest, her hair framing her face, her eyes dancing, her cheeks pink with excitement and her voice was breathless with enthusiasm when she demanded, "Tell me everything that happened!"

Frey stared into her animated face as it settled in his gut that this magnificent creature in his bed bravely voyaged from a whole other world for reasons of her own, reasons that weighed in his stomach, but also because their destinies bound them together.

And there she was, after he'd deserted her in his filthy cabin and left her for weeks, angry at her twin for her proclivities and frustrated that he was greatly attracted to her beauty regardless of them, thinking, but not much caring, that she would struggle.

But she did not.

Not his Finnie.

She fed on the challenge, bested it and ended up enjoying herself immensely.

Something about this humbled him as his eyes moved over her face.

"Frey!" she cried, her hand at his chest pressing in to get his attention.

He lifted a hand, pulling back the thick, unbelievably soft curtain of hair and tucking it behind her ear.

When this was accomplished, her body gave a small, surprised jerk, but her lips softened and her eyes warmed in that way he was getting used to and liked very much.

"They needed to explain a situation to me and ask for my command. They did, I commanded and hopefully," he lifted his hand again and tugged at the ends of her hair, "they've executed my command."

"What was the situation?" she asked then didn't wait for an answer before asking, "And what was your command?"

"This I cannot tell you, my new wife, not now," he said softly and watched her face fall.

But, as he was becoming accustomed, she did not give up.

"Why would they need your command?"

"So they would know how to proceed."

"And how do they proceed?"

"With magic."

Her eyes got wide as did her smile.

"No joke?" she whispered, and his body shook slightly with his laughter.

"No joke, Finnie."

Her face grew dreamy, a look nearly as endearing as her delighted surprise as she whispered, "That is *so cool*." She focused on him again and asked eagerly, "Do you get to watch?"

"If I wish."

Her eyes got big again. "Did you watch?"

"No, and I never do."

Her face fell again right before it immediately brightened.

"Did you ask if I could come next time?"

"No, but I don't need to. They are at my command. Sometime in future, when it's appropriate, I will take you to meet the elves."

Her smile got so big, it seemed to light the space as she cried, "Awesome!" Almost immediately, she asked, "Would it be okay if I talk to them?"

"I'm certain they'd enjoy that."

She smiled down at him before whispering, "Thanks, Frey."

"You're welcome, wife."

She kept smiling and he lifted his hand, hooked her behind the neck and brought her closer. As he did so, her smile faltered but her eyelids lowered, her cheeks started to pink for a different reason, and he heard her breath catch with anticipation.

He liked that, all of it, very much. But she mistook his intent.

He brought her close but stopped when her face was an inch away, and he whispered his order in an attempt to soften it, "It is not wise, my wife, to sleep with the candles burning. Do not do this again."

She stared in his eyes, and she whispered back, "I was trying to wait up for you. I was so excited about the...uh, return of the elves I didn't think I'd fall asleep."

"Well you did," he pointed out and she bit her lip. "They're easily relit, Finnie. Extinguish them next time. I like you as you are, that is to say, alive and breathing, not burnt to a cinder."

Her eyes locked with his, hope flared before she hid it, and she whispered breathlessly, "You like me as I am?"

By the gods, he'd been a bastard.

Then again, in his defense, he did not know she was who she was and *all* that she was.

"Yes, Finnie," he replied gently.

She pulled in a breath he felt as her chest contracted against his.

Then she said, "Well, I'm with you. I like myself alive and breathing and not burned to a cinder. So I promise to blow out the candles next time."

He pulled her close enough to touch her mouth to his then loosened his grip to allow her to move back an inch.

Then he muttered, "Good."

He used his hand at her neck and his other arm around her to settle her at his side, cheek to his shoulder and ordered, "Cradle my thigh."

He felt her body still even as her hand drifted to rest on his chest. "What?" she asked.

"I wish to sleep and do it with you curled into me as you did last night. Cradle my thigh."

She hesitated.

Then she whispered, "Sleep?"

Frey felt his mouth twitch as he looked at the firelight flickering on the ceiling. At the same time he gave his bride a squeeze.

She'd enjoyed what they shared earlier, very much, and wished to have his mouth back, his hands, and likely more.

He liked that she wished this, and he would give it to her.

But after he gave her a few more meals in order for her to be comfortable with her new husband.

"Yes, wife, sleep," he gave her another squeeze. "Your husband is weary," he lied for he would be dead before he'd be weary, lying with her next to him not having taken her at least once. "Now, do as you're told and cradle my thigh."

She hesitated again before she lifted her thigh and rested it on his, her weight settling into his side.

However, she did this muttering, "Apparently, Raiders are bossy."

That earned Finnie another squeeze and a, "Bossy?"

"Domineering. Dictatorial. Imperious. Commanding. *Bossy.*" The chuckle that caused was both audible and physical and Frey knew she heard it when she grumbled, "I wasn't being funny."

"No," Frey replied after he contained his mirth. "But you *were* talking, and I told you to sleep."

Her body tightened but it then relaxed with a sigh.

Then she muttered, "Whatever."

"You're still talking, Finnie," he noted.

Her body gave a small jolt, but her mouth didn't make a sound.

Frey grinned at the ceiling again.

And he lay in his bed with his wife, and he did this deciding he would take her home to see her parents very soon.

After sharing a few more meals with her, he'd be certain to see to that.

He knew she slept when her weight settled into him, curling deeper, her arm wrapping around him, holding close for a moment as if tucking him into her body before she relaxed and gave him her weight.

Then, Frey Drakkar fell asleep.

IO

JUMPING FROM FIRST
BASE TO THIRD

T*hree days later...*

I STOOD IN THE KITCHEN, frozen, staring at Penelope sitting on the kitchen floor by the door.

Then she did what she'd done only moments before, opened her mouth and meowed but in my head, I heard, "Let me out."

Clear as day, I heard the words, "Let me out."

But out of my cat's mouth, I heard, "Meow."

In all the time I had her, she didn't make a mew. She just purred.

Now she'd meowed twice and twice I'd heard it like I understood it in my head.

I stayed frozen and staring and she did it again.

"Meee...*ow*," which I heard as scary, freaky, cat-can-talk-to-you, getting *really* impatient, "Let me *out*!"

I dropped the dish cloth and ran straight out the back door Frey had walked out not five minutes ago.

I kept running straight to the hot spring where he'd told me he was going to bathe.

And I kept going as fast as my booted feet would carry me, freaked *way* the hell *out*. The hot spring wasn't far, but it wasn't a two second walk around the side of the house either.

I ran hell bent for leather all the way there.

Frey heard me crashing through the trees toward him. I knew this because he had his sweater off, his breeches on and was pulling *on* his boots, which meant he'd already taken them off.

I ran straight into his arms without slowing and his body rocked back a foot on impact, but his arms locked around me as he asked urgently, "What's given you a fright, Finnie?"

I was sucking in breath, and I pulled back a bit to wheeze, hand pressed into my chest (like that would help) and I forced out, "Penelo-Pen...the cat... my cat..." I pulled in a deep breath and pushed out, "I know...this is going... to sound...nuts...but I think my cat...is *possessed*."

I stared up at him to assess his reaction to this dire news as he gazed down at me, brows knit.

"Possessed?" he asked.

"*Possessed!*" I cried. "By Satan, demons, pure evil, I don't know! She said, 'meow' and in my head I heard, 'let me out' and I know," I shook my head and waved my hand between us, "I know, Frey, that sounds utterly *unhinged*. But I kid you not, that is *exactly* what I heard not once, not twice but," I leaned into him, grabbed both of his biceps and got up on my toes, "*three times*. I've had that cat for nearly a month and not a peep, not the barest *mew* and now *this*! Maybe there's evil in this world..." Oh shit! "I mean, uh...this forest. Maybe people come here to devil worship or hatchet men live out there!" I swung an arm out to the trees then back to slap my hand on his chest. "Or maybe *the ghost* of a murdering hatchet man who killed dozens of villagers before they caught him and strung him up lives out there and he's pissed and he's possessing *my cat*!"

Frey's face got that look I was getting used to. Like a weird sort of understanding (of what I did *not* know and never really did, but at that moment I did *not* care because my fat, ginger cat was possessed by the ghost of a murdering hatchet man) and he said softly, "Finnie, take a breath and calm yourself."

"*I can't calm myself when my ginger cat is possessed by a murderer!*" I shrieked and I swear, I swear *to God*, Frey looked like he was trying really hard not to laugh before he spoke again, and I *knew* he was trying hard to quell his laughter when his voice trembled with it.

"Wife, *as you know*," his face got closer to mine, "women can under-stand cats, deer, rabbits, mice, small birds and other such animals."

I blinked at him as my body locked in shock.

Frey spoke on.

"And men can understand horses, snakes, hawks, falcons, other birds of prey and predatory animals as well as those used in work or war, for instance, wolves and ox."

I blinked again.

"Apparently, considering you'll jump at any indication that Penelope has the merest whim, you didn't move fast enough, and she felt the need to tell you she wished to go outside. Since she actually had to tell you rather than you stuffing her full of chicken and fish before she got the least hungry and gathering her close to nuzzle before she even knew she wished a cuddle and moving to let her out, or in, before she shifted her great bulk fully toward the door, she hasn't had to share her desires. If you were busy or not paying attention, she would do so. I'm sure you've heard the call of a variety of animals."

I kept blinking.

So Frey finished, "Perhaps, out here in the forest where animals do not near the house due to our activity, you've forgotten since you haven't heard it in some time."

"Right," I whispered. "I'd forgotten."

His mouth twitched then he muttered, "That's what I thought."

My gaze on his mouth unfocused as this news hit me.

Holy freaking *moly*! They had *elves* and animals *talked* to you in this world.

That was just...plain...freaking...cool!

"Now are you all right or do you wish for me to find a witch who will scour the forest for traces of ghosts and expunge them?" Frey asked and now he was smiling so I *knew* he thought I was highly comical.

That was when *my* brows knit (though, I kinda wanted to hear about witches who could expunge ghosts).

"I'm glad to see my cat scaring the beejeezus out of me causes you such mirth, husband," I snapped.

His arms gave me a squeeze and his mouth moved to kiss my forehead.

Once he'd done that, his lips still against my skin, he muttered, "You cause me much mirth frequently, wife."

I blinked at his throat as his words caused my heart to flutter.

He let me go and moved away.

Then what he said next caused my belly to drop and my heart to clench.

"Since you're here, disrobe and join me in the spring."

I stared at him as he pulled his boots off, and I tried to get my heart started again, and, I might add, my lungs working because panic had filled me.

The last three days with Frey had been good. So good, I'd added so many things onto my list of why I liked him, I quit bothering to add them.

I just liked him.

First, he laughed at my jokes.

Second, he had a really fantastic laugh.

Third, he smiled or grinned at me, like *loads*. It was like he was a whole different person. He still wasn't exactly Mr. Conversation but in the last three days he'd said not one thing that pissed me off or freaked me out.

Fourth, he was the kind of guy who was busy a lot, had his own things to do and he did them. He was in the stable or shed quite a bit when we weren't in town.

But even so, when he was with you, he was *with you*. You had his attention and his concentration, and you had these in a nice way.

He didn't lie when he said he liked to see my mouth move, he listened to me talk, and although he didn't pour forth bountiful information, he answered questions about the elves, himself, his travels and all sorts of stuff and he was a really interesting guy.

In fact, he was *way* more informative than any of the books Sjofn had left for me, telling me stuff about my mom and dad (of this world) in a way that was nice, like he was sharing memories with me, though he couldn't know they weren't my memories and that he was giving me insight into my parents.

And it was cool to know that, although they seemed off with me, they were well-loved by their people. They were known to be a love match even though their marriage was arranged like Frey and mine. They were both respected not only by their citizens but by rulers of other lands. And Frey held my father in high regard, considering he thought he was intelligent and a fair and just monarch.

Fifth, he wasn't a great kisser, he was a *great kisser*, and I knew this because he kissed me lots, during the day (everything from lip brushes to quick, deep wet ones to mini-make-out-sessions) and we *totally* made out in bed every night. He never let it get hot and heavy (okay, so it got heated and the petting was relatively heavy and *very* nice but not out-of-control). Then he'd stop, hold me, stroke me and chat with me quietly for a while until I was relaxed and drowsy. When he heard that in my voice, he'd order me to cradle his thigh and go to sleep.

In other words, if we were in my world, Frey would totally be in there and I wouldn't make him wait the couple of weeks of dates my personal philosophy dictated happen prior to serious hanky-panky that involved the exchange of bodily fluids.

Then again, when I started seeing a guy I didn't fall asleep in bed with him every night and make him breakfast, lunch and dinner when we weren't in town having dinner at a pub, where Frey had taken me last night so I could have a break from the stove, that was.

I'd figured out on day two what he was doing, and what I'd figured out made me like him even more (and, incidentally, that was when I stopped making my mental list).

And what that was, was that he saw I was nervous that first night, I told him straight out he and his size scared me, and he was being cool about taking some time to let me get to know him and get used to him before we got down to the nitty-gritty of marriage business.

And, by the by, on top of all that, he seemed to like me too. And, since I'd decided I liked him, I *really* liked that.

So now, I had to admit, I was stunned he wanted me to get naked and get in a hot spring with him. That was like jumping from first base to third without even buying a girl dinner.

I mean, I could think he was in there when I was making out with him in our bed by the light of a fire. But out in a frozen forest by a hot spring when I had breakfast dishes to do and I was terrified of him seeing me naked, uh...not so much.

"Um..." I mumbled as he dropped his last sock, straightened and his hands went to the waistband of his breeches.

Eek!

"Finnie," he called gently, and my eyes shot to his. "You sneak to the springs every day after I've returned from my bath in order to take your own. You're already here so we might as well bathe together. Strip and join me."

I blinked.

Then I protested, "But I don't have my soap here. A bath cloth—"

"Use mine." His head jerked to a cake of soap and a large towel sitting on a rock.

I looked to it and looked to him, scrunching my nose. "But your soap smells like boy."

Not that that smelled bad, not at all. It smelled good, especially on him. It was a fresh, clean smell, not much to it except it somehow was entirely masculine, and this was probably because it didn't smell like flowers or fruit like most of my stuff did.

At my words, or perhaps the look on my face, Frey burst out laughing and his hands shot out to me, gripping me at the waist and pulling me to him.

He dipped his still smiling face so it was close to mine.

"Even smelling like a boy, it's impossible for you not to be appealing." I blinked as his words again caused my heart to flutter and he lifted up and kissed my forehead before looking in my eyes. "Now, I'll give you my back and twenty seconds to strip and join me in the springs. Don't delay," he cautioned, letting me go. "I'm starting to count now."

Then he turned his back to me, and his hands went to his breeches.

Shit!

I looked down at the water to see what I always saw, steam coming up where the heat of the spring hit the frigid air. This was good. There was also a constant bubble as the spring renewed the pool, agitating the water. This was good too.

I heard water splash and noticed out of the corner of my eye that Frey was entering the pool.

This was bad.

Well, I was Seoafin Wilde, and this was my adventure so...what the heck?

I quickly untied my belt, yanked off my dress, boots and underwear and dropped them on the rocks by the pool. Pulling my ribbon free from where it held the front of my hair away from my face, I lifted my hands to hold up all my hair as I stepped in and settled myself on a natural seat in the rocks, the water up to my chest. Once there, I started to redo the ribbon holding my hair at the top of my head to hold it clear of the water.

As promised, Frey's back was turned, and he waited until the water settled after I'd moved in to shift around. Then he sat across the misty pool from me, the water, I could see through the steam, coming up to his ribs.

I secured the ribbon in my hair, dropped my hands and tried to let the water relax me.

This didn't work partially because I was naked for the first time with my husband but mostly because he called out, "Come here, wife."

Hells bells. He was *definitely* trying for third, running straight there and forgetting all about first and second.

"Uh..." I hesitated and water splashed. Frey's fingers were suddenly wrapped around my wrist and water was flowing around me as he pulled me to him.

Once he got me close enough, his strong arms curled around my waist, and he pulled me even closer. *Much* closer. So much closer, my calves hit rock and I had no choice but to bend my knees and straddle his lap.

Ho boy.

"Frey," I whispered, my hands going to his chest as his hands moved up my back, pulling me closer, imprisoning my arms between us and I started to deep breathe.

One of his arms locked around the middle of my back, the other hand drifted up my neck, fingers gliding in my hair as he pulled my face closer to his.

"Relax, my wee Finnie," he murmured and, just for your information, he'd started to call me his "wee Finnie" the day after the elves came calling, and that was on my long list of things I liked about Frey too because I thought it was really sweet. "You know I'll be gentle," he finished, speaking as gently as I knew he could be.

"Yes," I whispered as my eyes dropped to his mouth, a mouth that was coming closer.

"And you know you'll like it." He kept murmuring and he wasn't wrong about that either.

So, I breathed, "Yes," right before his mouth touched mine and he kissed me.

Yep, he wasn't wrong. I liked it. Sweet, slow, deep but gentle, his hands moving on me through the water, slick, soothing, light. And the only semi-invasive move was when his thumb trailed up the side of my breast tantalizingly, making me want something not slow, gentle, light or non-invasive, but the *opposite* of all those.

My hands slid up and around his shoulders, the fingers of one hand gliding into his hair, the other arm wrapping tight as I pressed my chest into his and kissed him back.

Yeah, oh yeah. I definitely liked this.

He broke our kiss but didn't take his lips from me. Trailing them down my cheek, they worked my neck and ear, making the skin tingle, making me highly conscious of the power of his body surrounding me, the heat of the water, the slick of our skin, all of it nice. *Way* nice. The best.

Okay, I'd give him third base. Hell, he could slide into home, and I knew I'd love every freaking minute of it.

And that was exactly why I turned my mouth to his ear and whispered, "I like being here with you, Frey."

His arms tightened around me, pressing me deep into his hard body, but his head went back, and his lazy, heated eyes found mine.

"This pleases me, Finnie," he replied quietly, and I smiled at him, dipping my head closer. He slid his nose along mine, something else he did frequently that I put on my why I like him list before I quit making it. Then he again pulled back so I lifted up. One of his hands started roaming my back while the other one slid up my neck to cup my jaw and he went on, "It pleases me, but do you not miss your Winter Palace in Fyngaard?"

No. I did not miss my Winter Palace in Fyngaard. Mostly because I had no idea what my Winter Palace was, or what Fyngaard was for that matter. Though, truth be told, I was intrigued. But nowhere on his earth *or* mine at that moment, would be better than those springs in that frozen forest with Frey.

"I—"

His thumb swept my cheek. "And your parents?"

I stared down at him as my heart jumped.

"I do miss my parents," I whispered the God's honest truth and watched his eyes go soft.

"As you know, the Bitter Gales is in two weeks' time. What you don't know is I have business I must see to after that. Today you spend packing your trunks. I'll load them and tomorrow morning, first thing, we'll be away. You can spend two weeks at the Winter Palace with your parents. We'll attend the Gales and then I'll show you my ship."

My heart jumped again, and it started skipping.

The Winter Palace, the Bitter Gales (whatever that was, but whatever it was sounded cool), my parents *and* his ship.

I'd just hit the mother lode!

Or, more accurately, my husband just offered it to me.

"Really?" I asked.

"Really, my wee Finnie," he whispered, his arm wrapping around me and giving me a squeeze.

Something he said struck me and I felt my excitement start to fade. "You said I could spend two weeks with my parents. Are you going away again before the Gales?"

He stared into my eyes, his soft and warm, and his thumb slid over my bottom lip, "No, wee one. I'll be staying with you at your Palace."

My heart started skipping again and it was definitely not playing it cool, not that a girl, no matter how good she could play it, could *ever* play it cool, naked, straddling a naked man in a hot spring, but still, I couldn't contain my smile.

My husband smiled back and that was so good, I decided that playing it cool was for idiots.

Then it occurred to me that he was probably talking about wherever it was we'd been married, which meant I'd probably get to go back to that awesome room with all the beautiful carving and that armchair I wanted to try out. And if it was a Palace, it *had* to have a library, which meant more books and more learning about this world. Not to mention, a new town (and a definitely bigger one) to explore.

And lastly, seeing my parents again.

And all of this made me melt into my big, handsome, so-not-scary-it-was-not-funny husband and whisper, "Thank you, Frey."

His hand at my jaw slid back and up into my hair and he pulled my mouth down to his for a hard, sweet, deep, but short, kiss.

Only when he let me go did he whisper back, "You're welcome, Finnie."

Oh yeah, it was official. I liked him. A whole lot.

"Now climb off me, wife, soap up and dry off so I can do the same, we can get back and you can pack. The sooner you get done, the sooner we can get to town so you can bid farewell to your friends."

Okay, one could say even though I was relaxed and happy, pressed naked to my naked husband, I wasn't all fired up to "soap up" in front of him.

But the minute I slid off his lap, whispering, "All righty then," his body slid down deeper in the water, and he lounged back against the rocks at the same time lifting the bathing cloth so it covered his face.

He looked like a man relaxing in a hot spring. Or, to be more precise, a really freaking gorgeous guy relaxing in a hot spring.

But what he was, was a kind man giving me privacy to bathe when he knew it would embarrass me to have him watch.

Yeah, oh *heck yeah*. I *really* liked my husband.

I soaped up and told him I was done by pressing the cake to his chest. He took it, his head coming up as he pulled the bathing cloth away. Then he turned his back, and he soaped up while I rushed out of the water, drying off quickly and getting dressed.

I heard the water surge as he got out when I was smoothing my woolen stockings up my thighs. I had my boots on and was turning to him when he tossed the wet towel over his sweater-clad shoulder, and I saw he was fully dressed.

He gave me a sweet smile, hooked me around my neck and pulled me into his side so I slid my arm around his waist and moved with him as I stayed pressed to his long body.

And that was how we walked home through the glittering, frozen forest.

We didn't say anything, we didn't need to, and our silence was content.

But I wasn't content.

No, I was happy in my winter wonderland adventure where you could understand animals and they had elves and hot guys who were awesome and I was on my way back to my Winter Palace, Fyngaard and, best of all, my parents. Then, after that, to his ship and even more adventure.

And my hot guy husband was the one who was giving all that to me.

Oh yeah, in Valentine's line of happiness from bliss to contentment I was not even close to the contentment side of the line.

I was smack in the middle of happy.

II

THE MEASURE OF A MAN

T leaned forward, grinning, and pulled the pile of coin to me. Then I settled myself back in my husband's lap, grabbed my horn of ale and took a big drink.

"I'm certain our Winter Princess deals from the bottom of the deck," Laurel grumbled then his eyes shot around me to Frey who was one-handing the cards, his long fingers expertly sorting them into a pile while his other arm stayed wrapped around me and Laurel clarified hurriedly, "No offense, Drakkar."

"Why would I be offended when it is clear my bride cheats?" Frey noted, and I whipped my head around to glare at him.

We were in town, currently at the pub, having come into town for Frey to send a messenger off to my parents to tell them we would be heading back and would return to Fyngaard in less than three days' time.

He'd also taken me around so I could visit with the people I'd come to know, let them know we were leaving and give them my good-byes.

This kind of sucked because good-byes always kind of sucked. But also, since I liked them, they liked me, they were surprised we were going, disappointed *I* was going and told me they would be glad when we returned, it sucked more because I didn't know if I would.

Then we'd gone to the pub, eaten a dinner of bowls of thick, rich, tasty beef stroganoff that had an abundance of flavorful, succulent mushrooms and was served on a bed of herbed noodles that was not only delicious but also, I was happy I didn't have to slave away at an iron, wood-burning stove in order to put in front of us.

And now we were drinking ale with Laurel, Ulysses, Frederick and two of Frey's huge, well-built men, Thaddeus and Ruben. All of these men had wandered in while Frey and I were enjoying an after-dinner ale and all of whom had been invited to join us at our table.

Thaddeus was younger than Frey, my guess, by at least five years, maybe more (not that I knew how old Frey was, I figured that was something the other Sjofn would know, and I hadn't figured out how to cleverly ascertain this information without out and out asking).

Thaddeus was slightly less tall than Frey and Ruben, and powerfully built, but he didn't have the bulk of either man. He had blond hair, blue eyes and was really cute in a boy-next-door kinda gone wrong sort of way.

Ruben was Frey's age, maybe slightly younger, or perhaps slightly older, I couldn't really tell (Frey's natural air of authority was putting me off, he seemed older but looked younger), and he was a mountain of chocolate muscle with friendly black eyes and an easy grin.

And, to fit us all around the table, considering Frey, Thaddeus and Ruben would have trouble just the three of them fitting their big bulk and long legs around a table, necessitated me sitting in my husband's lap.

Or, at least, this was what Frey told me.

I did not quibble because I didn't mind. I was working on my fourth horn of ale. The beer in that world was strong and flavorful. Frey was right when he said I fit in his lap (I did, *perfectly*), it was comfortable, his body was warm against mine, and I was having the time of my life, playing cards, gabbing and gaming with my friends and my husband's.

Until, of course, right then.

"I do not cheat!" I snapped.

"Wife, you've taken the last three hands, lost one and took the two before," Frey spoke the truth. I'd been having totally awesome luck all night. "I should point out, my wee one, that if you're going to cheat, you shouldn't make it so obvious by winning every hand. People will suspect," he finished helpfully.

"I am *not* cheating," I returned heatedly.

And, really, I wasn't! I didn't even know how.

Frey grinned, obviously not only oblivious to cold and heat, but also oblivious to heat directed at him from *me*.

"She deals from the bottom of the deck, I, too, am certain," Thaddeus put in, his tone teasing, his eyes, I saw when mine shot to him, smiling. "I have not seen it, but I've lost enough coin to her I know it to be true."

"Well, I haven't *dealt* every hand, have I, Thaddeus?" I asked.

"Perhaps she hides cards in her cleavage?" Ruben suggested, brows raised, eyes twinkling.

That did it.

Clearly, I was being ganged up on.

I gave Ruben a squinty look then called loudly, "Lindy!" and craned my neck to find my friend.

"Yes, Princess Finnie," Lindy called back from somewhere behind Frey.

I twisted my torso to him but peered around his frame and shouted at Lindy, "Six horns of beer here, fill them to the rim. I'll be making a point by dumping them over heads once they get here and I want to be certain my point is well made!"

I yelled this across the room and Lindy grinned at me, shook her head and put some horns on the table she was at giving the appearance she thought I was kidding when I was *not*.

"I didn't say you were cheating, your grace," Frederick pointed out, and I turned back around.

"Nor did I," Ulysses stated, smiling at me.

"Okay, well, this is true so you two can drink your horns when they come," I allowed.

"Obliged," Frederick muttered, grinning at Frey.

I felt Frey's lips at my ear where I heard him whisper, "Pour a horn of ale over my head, wee wife, I'll be forced to go back to the springs, and it won't be *me* who'll be soaping it off."

When he was done, I turned my head, caught his eye and asked, "Are you trying to talk me *out* of pouring ale on you, husband?" I leaned in close and shared on a grin, "Because if you are, you're *failing*."

He smiled, it was lazy and heated, and I felt it in a variety of places, all of them good.

I smiled back.

Noting my short-lived pique was *way* over, Frey unwrapped his arm from around me and leaned toward the table to shuffle the cards. I took another sip of ale and caught Thaddeus's eyes on me, or, from what it seemed, me *and* Frey. When he noticed my gaze, I smiled at him even though he looked pensive in his study of us. When he saw my smile, his thoughtful look disappeared, he resumed his usual cheerful one, lifted his chin slightly to me and winked.

I had long since decided that Thaddeus was a good guy. So was Ruben. They were funny and their gentle ribbing was cute, in a brotherly way. I'd never had a brother, so I liked it. In fact, I liked *them*. And I was glad to know them before I got on a ship with them. It would be good to know more than Frey when I started that part of my adventure.

Once he'd dealt the cards, Frey sat back with his new hand. I set my horn on the table and reached out to collect mine.

I twisted my body so Frey nor Ruben, who sat on my other side, could see mine as I turned the cards to face me, fanning them out in one hand and lifting the other to arrange them as I needed. I'd moved two cards before what I had in my hand registered.

I stared at it.

We were playing tuble, and in my hand I had a two of diamonds, a three of stars, a four of moons, a five of daggers, a sorceress card and a ghost card, the highest hand you could be dealt. It was akin to a royal flush and like a royal flush, virtually impossible to be dealt one on the first round of cards.

I looked at my hand then I looked at my husband's profile to see his attention seemed devoted to his own. But I knew he was completely and totally full of it.

I also knew he was one hell of a cheat.

Therefore, I burst out laughing, slapped the cards on the table and fell forward so my forehead was on my cards. I kept laughing so hard my body was shaking with it and I added my fist banging on the table for good measure.

"How much ale has she had?" I heard Thaddeus mutter, and I shot up straight and turned over my hand for all to see, then twisted to my husband.

"You," I poked him in the chest, "are the *cheat!*" I declared, still giggling into Frey's smiling face.

It was then Frey informed me, "You should probably know, my wee Finnie, that Ruben, Thaddeus, Frederick *and* Ulysses have been dealing you excessively good hands on purpose. The only one not essentially *giving* you his coin is Laurel."

My eyes got wide, and I swung around to look at the men at the table.

"No," I whispered.

Thaddeus winked at me again. Ruben grinned slowly. And Frederick and Ulysses were smiling flat out.

"Why didn't anyone tell me?" Laurel asked, pushing slightly back in his chair and looking around at the men, his expression disgruntled at being left out.

"Because you're unskilled at stacking a deck, Laurel." Ulysses pointed out. "The last time you tried, Gerard broke your arm."

"Yes, well, *that* was cheating to win coin *for me*. This is different and our Winter Princess obviously would never notice," Laurel returned.

"She'd notice when you dropped the cards on the floor or pulled them out of your cuff, just like *everyone* notices when you drop the cards on the floor or pull them out of your cuff," Frederick stated then looked at me. "He's very bad at trickery, your grace."

Laurel's torso shot back in clear affront, his mouth opening to deliver his retort, but I got there before him.

"I should hope so and you all should be ashamed," I declared only to see slow blinks and eyebrow raises all around, all filled with mild shock, even Laurel.

I thought this was strange until Frey's mouth came to my ear where he said quietly, "It's the measure of a man, Finnie, how good he cheats. No game is played without trickery. It is the man who can best cheat who wins not only the game but the respect of his opponents. Many complain during the game of being swindled while they themselves are swindling. Others keep aloof and let the cards speak for themselves. And if you're bad enough and get caught, you may catch something else, like a challenger's ire. It's all part of the game." Then he paused a moment before saying, "I'm sure you know that."

My body jolted slightly, and I whispered my lie, "Of course, I was just trying to be funny."

"Of course," Frey mumbled, sounding like he was stifling a chuckle and his mouth went away from my ear.

I took in the table seeing all the men were still looking at me and I shifted my rear in Frey's lap as I hurried to cover what was clearly a gaffe.

"Obviously, you don't know that princesses, being princesses, and thus royal, are taught to be fair and trustworthy in *all* endeavors," I lied through my teeth. "Therefore, I've never been taught to cheat. It would reflect badly on the House of Wilde." I smiled at the group even as I felt and heard Frey lose his fight against his chuckle, something I chose to ignore. "So now you'll need to teach me."

"Excellent," Ruben muttered, grinning at Frey.

"You need look no further than the man at your back, my princess," Thaddeus stated, and my eyes went to him. "Frey has the quickest fingers

I've seen. You married the master card sharp. I've played many a game of tuble or meerkin with Frey and never won a single hand he dealt, nor could I ever make out how he does it. Bottom dealing, false shuffles, stacking—"

Ruben cut him off to say, "How about all of those and add culling, center deal, second dealing and sleight of hand."

"The Drakkar can't do them all," Laurel breathed, his eyes huge. "Not without detection. No one can."

"By the gods, *he* can," Ruben told Laurel, tipping his head to Frey. "Though I've never seen it, I know it to be true."

"If you've never seen it, how do you know it to be true?" Thaddeus asked Ruben.

"Because *I* have never won a hand to him and *I* am a far better cheat than *you*," Ruben returned, bragging shamelessly about cheating.

"Then why did I walk away with the entire contents of your purse two nights ago?" Thaddeus shot back.

"Because when you've had much ale, you never give up. You keep at it no matter how drawn your purse. You won't let a man leave a table until yours is gone or his is gone and I had a wench waiting for me whose company I preferred to yours. It was either risk standing from the table and you pulling your blade, and I didn't feel like drawing your blood or dragging your carcass home and dressing your wound, or let you have my purse so I could get to my warm, soft bed and my warmer, softer wench," Ruben replied.

Oh dear, I wasn't sure, but those seemed like fighting words to me.

Thaddeus's eyes narrowed and his body got visibly tight. "That is simply not bloody true."

Ho boy.

There it was. They were definitely fighting words.

"If it's not, then why did I win *back* my purse and *half of yours* last night?" Ruben returned what I thought was a fair point.

Thaddeus's mouth got tight, and he granted the point but changed the direction of the burgeoning argument. "Even full in my cups, you could never draw my blood."

Ruben sat back, a bright, white smile on his face, he leveled his gaze on his friend and challenged, "Care to consume a bottle of whisky and test that belief?"

"Wench! Whisky!" Thaddeus accepted instantly, shouting yet not taking his eyes from Ruben.

Laurel, Frederick and Ulysses inched their chairs back from the table.

I didn't move a muscle and stared in fascination.

Frey threw his cards face down on the table and muttered, "I think this is my cue to get my bride home."

He stood, lifting me up with him and setting me on my feet. When I was standing, I turned to him and laid my hand lightly on his abs, my neck bent way back to catch his eyes.

At my touch, he bent his neck way down, gave me his gaze, and I whispered, "Shouldn't you do something about that?" I jerked my head at the macho Raider stare down still in process at the table.

Frey answered immediately, "Thad could drink two bottles of whisky while still consuming ale and not be full in his cups. If Ruben waits for Thad to get arsed, it will be a long night. And if Ruben has the patience for Thad to fall full in his cups and Thad's fool enough to challenge, his blade work will indeed be shoddy, and Ruben will have his blood."

My eyes got big, and Frey kept talking.

"Don't worry, wee one. Ruben will be certain to stick him, so he makes his point but doesn't do damage because he knows we set sail in two weeks, and he doesn't want to court a knife fight with *me*. Which is what he'll get if he sticks one of my men badly enough to lay him up prior to a voyage."

I blinked up at him but said no words.

Frey leaned in so his face was close to mine. "This will not happen, Finnie. And it won't happen because that warm, soft wench is *still* in Ruben's bed waiting for him. There is no chance he'll sit here waiting for Thad to get tossed. We won't be halfway home before he'll be at his cottage just down the street, joining his woman."

I knew this was true mainly because of the confident way Frey relayed this information. It was clear he knew his men, he read the situation and there was no cause for alarm.

"All righty then," I whispered, and he grinned.

Then he lifted a hand to the side of my neck and gave me a squeeze before he urged softly, "Bid farewell to your friends and let us get away home."

I nodded, suddenly liking the idea (very much) of "getting away home" with my husband. That meant making out (or better) so I accepted the cloak Frey threw over my shoulders and fastened it at my neck as I moved to Ulysses, Frederick and Laurel to give them all hugs and cheek kisses, thanking them for teaching me tuble and spending time with me.

"Until you return, your grace," Frederick said on a squeeze during our hug.

"It was a pleasure, Winter Princess," Laurel muttered, holding on to my upper arms and smiling at me.

"Honored to do it and will be honored when we do it again, Princess Finnie," Ulysses murmured in my ear while proving his arms were indeed very strong for he squeezed the breath right out of me.

When I pulled away, I smiled into his eyes and wondered if I'd be back this way before I went home. I looked through the three of them and hoped I would. I didn't know them well, just like everyone I'd said farewell to that day in the village. But everything I knew I liked so it would be cool to know more.

Frey came around the table and claimed me. I called good-byes and see-you-laters to Thaddeus and Ruben as I yanked on my gloves. Thaddeus grunted his good-bye, still clearly peeved. Ruben smiled at me and gave a good-bye flick of his hand, still not peeved at all.

I wrapped the fingers of both my hands around Frey's bicep (or kinda did, they didn't get anywhere near going all the way around) and leaned into him as he led us out of the pub and down the snow-covered ground toward where Tyr was waiting.

"So," I started, "do you really know how to bottom deal, stack the deck, false shuffle and all of that?"

"Yes," Frey answered, and my head snapped back to look up at him.

"Really?" I asked.

He looked down at me and grinned. "Yes."

"Will you teach me?"

Without hesitation, he repeated, "Yes."

"Awesome," I breathed, his grin became a smile through which he chuckled. He disengaged my hands from his arm when he moved it to slide around my shoulders and pull me to his body.

I slid both my arms around his middle and walked semi-sideways as I pressed my cheek to his chest.

It had been a good day, a good night, and it had been six good weeks (mostly).

And it kept getting better.

I sighed as Tyr came into view wondering how much better tonight might get (and hoping it got a *whole* lot better). But my step stuttered when I felt Frey's body suddenly get tight at my side.

In a flash, he flung me away from him. I went flying and landed against

Tyr who had shifted quickly to the side in a way that it seemed like he was breaking my fall.

But even as I reeled, I saw it.

I saw.

I *saw.*

Lightning fast, Frey's hand went to his knife on his belt, his knees bent, and his arm swung overhanded, launching the knife down the walk.

And I saw that knife lodge right in a man's throat.

I stared at the man as he fell backward, hands lifting to his neck, blood spurting from the knife and rushing down to stain his sweater. But I sensed more movement, looked back and saw Frey had his other knife out. A man was approaching him, blade drawn. Frey's hand snaked out and wrapped around the man's wrist that was holding the knife. Frey whirled him and yanked him back against his body and, without hesitation, on another hideous gush of blood, Frey sliced open his throat.

Saliva filled my mouth as the air hollowed out of my lungs and I pressed back hard against Tyr.

I heard running footsteps and saw another flying knife as Thad went down to a knee and released one in what appeared to be my direction. My head jerked around to see a man who had been rounding Tyr and nearing me drop to his knees, Thad's knife in the side of his neck.

I whirled immediately the other way as I heard scuffling feet and saw Ruben had hold of yet another man. One arm wrapped around the man's chest, pinning him to Ruben, Ruben holding his own knife close to the man's throat. The man in Ruben's hold was pressing back to get away from the knife and grunting with the effort even as his feet shuffled underneath him. But only his toes were touching the snow because Ruben held him off the ground.

I stood frozen, every inch of me, including my mind and my lungs...but not my heart.

My heart was hammering painfully in my chest.

Tyr was pressing his bulk against my back, which was a good because if he didn't, there was a good chance I would pass out.

"We saw them follow you out of the pub," Thad explained, striding forward casually and bending over to yank the knife out of the not quite dead man lying in the snow not three feet away from me. And when he did, the man's body jerked as he made a horrid gurgling noise and a new flood of blood poured out of the wound.

Another surge of saliva filled my mouth at the sight, but Thad completely ignored him as he straightened and turned to Frey.

"They've had eyes on you and Princess Finnie all night," Ruben put in.

"Felt them, saw them. Not skilled. Unwise, but interesting," Frey muttered distractedly then jerked his chin at Ruben. "Find out what he knows, and I'll want to know everything he says the minute you break him."

Ruben grinned in a very scary way that told an equally frightening tale about the new activities he'd be engaged in that night, activities he appeared to be anticipating with great relish, but Frey was already looking to Thad.

"Go to the constable, explain. Go to the men, I want four at the cabin on patrol outside. All night. Do it now but not in that order. Finnie and I are away home. Tell the men we leave for Fyngaard at dawn. We'll need a guard. And send someone to the king."

Thad nodded, turned and disappeared in the shadows.

Ruben was already yanking the still struggling man away and he too disappeared in the shadows.

I stood still frozen, but my head swiveled woodenly to the side as Frey walked calmly to the dead man to collect his knife, putting his boot to the base of his neck to do so.

He sheathed it after wiping the blood off by stabbing it twice into the snow.

I swallowed back a sudden surge of vomit and my head got light.

Tyr whinnied and suddenly I was caught in Frey's strong arm. He mounted his steed at the same time dragging me with him. I stared blankly ahead of me as Frey touched his heels to Tyr's flanks and we took off at a full gallop.

Frey held me close with his arm around me, his torso pressed into my back so we were both leaning over Tyr as we cleared the town and the darkness of the forest, which was shot by the bright gray of moonlight on snow surrounded us.

My husband just killed two men.

Right in front of me.

And one of his men killed a man.

Right beside me.

And they didn't pause, check for pulses, call police, or anything.

And they were good at killing. Very good. Remarkably skilled. Unbelievably. They wasted no time. They didn't hesitate. They didn't blink. And they didn't even get winded or break a sweat.

They'd done it before. Often.

I started trembling but not with the cold that bit at my cheeks and ears. It was fear. Pure fear the like I'd never felt in my life.

I closed my eyes tight and my trembling tore through me deeper, turning to shakes.

Frey felt it.

"Wee Finnie, it's all right," Frey whispered in my ear. "You're safe, my winter bride."

I opened my eyes for two reasons. One, because I saw the remembered and probably never to be forgotten vision of the man's body jump and his blood flood when Thad unceremoniously yanked his knife out of his neck. And two, because I didn't feel safe.

Not at all.

What I did feel safe was saying that Frey definitely had enemies. Four men had come at him.

Four.

And he'd dispatched them without a thought and left them dead or dying in the snow of a sweet, quiet, winter village that had two awesome waterwheels, and he did this without a second glance.

Oh God.

At a gallop and using Frey's shortcut, we were home in five minutes. Frey took Tyr right to the door, dismounted the minute Tyr came to a stop and hauled me off the horse. He held my hand as he guided me to and through the front door but used my hand to position my back against the wall right at its side.

"Stay here, wee one," he muttered.

I watched blankly as he moved about the room, the bathroom space. He climbed to the loft and down again then moved through the kitchen, out through the back door then back through the kitchen.

He came to me.

I automatically tipped my head back when he got close, and I stood there stupidly as his big hand curled around the side of my neck and his mouth came to my forehead for a light touch.

Then his eyes caught mine.

"I need to stall Tyr and my men will be here soon. I'll need to speak with them when they arrive. Feed the fires, wee one. I'll meet you in our bed."

Before I could open my mouth to make a noise, he was gone.

I stood against the wall staring into the room. After a while, I lifted my hands and saw they were shaking. Even in the weak light of the dying fires I saw them shaking.

Shaking so bad it was out of control.

I closed my eyes tight for a moment before I opened them and wandered to the fire, stoking and feeding it then putting the grate to and turning to the other one. Once finished with the second one, I fed a few logs to the kitchen stove. Then I took off my boots and, still clothed, I climbed to the loft and fed the fire up there too. I lay down on the bed, over the covers, back to the railing, pulled a pillow to my chest and held it tight.

Faster than I would have expected, I heard the front door open and close meaning Frey had come back and my body tensed.

I didn't know what to do, what to think.

This world might have elves, animals that could talk to you and trees that had glitter bark. But it also had men who could take a life without hesitation and without even the barest hint of remorse.

And my husband was one of them.

Thinking of the Frey who had been mine for the last three days, my only thought was, how could that be?

Thinking of the Frey I had first met when I came to this world, I knew the answer.

I felt his presence hit the loft then I felt it hit the bed.

I heard his voice come at me softly, "Finnie, you've not changed."

And that was when I felt his light touch pulling my hair off my shoulder.

So that was when I moved, swiftly rolling away from him and gaining my knees. I shuffled back to the end of the bed, pillow still held tight to my chest.

"I don't...don't..." I shook my head, "I don't think I want you touching me, Frey."

He was on his knees too, but settled back on his heels, and his eyes were on me.

He studied me for a moment before, still speaking softly, he asked, "What's this, wee one?"

I didn't delay in replying. "You killed two men tonight."

He moved as if to come toward me and I shuffled back another foot, my feet clearing the edge of the bed and he stopped so I did too.

"Finnie—"

"You didn't blink," I cut him off. "You didn't...you didn't..." I shook my head and my throat clogged. I swallowed and whispered, "You didn't even *blink*."

"Wife—"

"No," I shook my head again, closed my eyes tight and looked away before opening them and looking back. "No. I...I don't know what you've done to get enemies like that, but I can guess, considering you killed them without hesitation and then rode away while their warm blood still melted the snow. And, I can't say...I can't even think...I don't know...I don't know, but I don't think I want anything to do with a life like that."

"Finnie, come here," he ordered, extending an arm to me.

"No." I shook my head. "No way, Frey. I'm sorry, but no freaking way."

"Finnie, come here," he repeated, and I shook my head. He dropped his hand but held my eyes and said gently, "My winter bride, those weren't my enemies."

"And whose were they?" I fired back. "Thad's?"

"No," he replied carefully. "*Yours.*"

My mouth dropped open and I felt my eyes get wide.

Then I breathed, "What?"

"Come here," he ordered quietly.

I stayed still and unmoving.

"Love, come here."

"They're...they're..." I stared in his face. "They're *mine?*"

Oh God. If that was true, Sjofn *totally* left a lot out of her note.

A *lot*.

"Fin—" he started but that was when I lost it.

And I lost it by throwing down the pillow and shrieking, *"What did I do to make enemies who would come at me with knives?"*

I barely got out the last word when Frey moved. His arm darting out, fingers wrapping around my wrist, he yanked me so I fell forward then he shifted. Whipping an arm around my waist and one down my legs to haul them out in front of me, my bottom swung out. I landed in his lap and his arms were around me before I could even twitch.

I twisted to face him, my head tipping back, and I whispered, "Frey, I—"

"You have been sharing my bed for five nights now, that's what you've been doing, my Winter Princess," Frey finished for me, and I blinked up at him. "And your uncle and, perhaps, spies from dozens of different Houses would know this."

I blinked again and whispered with confusion, "My uncle?"

"As far as he knows, and now I know he is watching, though he nor any of the others have approached the cabin, I would know this, but even if they have, they cannot see through walls. But as far as they know what we've been doing in this bed could conceive a child. And he, nor any of them, wishes us to conceive a child. I was afraid someone would attempt something like this, and if it is as I suspect and it is your uncle who has done this then he has, as usual, made his play and shown his hand without delay."

I stared at Frey.

Then it hit me.

My Uncle Baldur, who stood to inherit Lunwyn upon my father's death, wanted me dead before I could birth a child to succeed the throne.

Oh my God.

"Oh my God," I whispered.

"I see you have some understanding of this," Frey muttered, and I focused on his face to see his eyes alert and *very* focused on mine.

"He's not a good man," I guessed.

"No, Finnie, you speak kind, but you do not speak true. He is instead the *worst* type of man. No honor, filled with greed. He is selfish, grasping, avaricious and underhanded."

Sjofn had written, *My uncle is not like my father or grandfather and it is imperative that our beautiful land not pass into his hands...*

I turned my face away and whispered, "Oh my God."

"Look at me, my wee one," Frey demanded gently, and my eyes returned to his. "Those were assassins. Not good ones. It is my guess your uncle wishes you dead and tonight he declared his intent to see to that. Even if it is not him, obviously, someone else wishes this so."

"Oh God." I was still whispering, and I was again trembling. It was again violently and try as I might (and I was trying), I couldn't seem to stop it.

Frey gathered me closer, and when he'd achieved that, he held on tight.

"Listen to me, Finnie, concentrate on me," he urged, and I nodded, staring in his eyes as he kept holding me tight. "I will not allow you to be harmed. My men won't and your father's men won't." His arms gave me a tight squeeze. "You will *not* be harmed, love. If it is your uncle, I don't know why he announced his intentions in this way for those men were not skilled. But I will find out and we will deal with this, your father and me. In the meantime, you will never be harmed. You will not even be touched. I promise you that." I kept staring at him and said nothing, so he whispered, "Do you believe me?"

"I've never seen a man die, Frey," I whispered back, and he closed his eyes.

He opened them and said softly, "Yes you have, Finnie. Remember when our engagement was announced? An attempt was made on your life then. You dispatched the assassin yourself at the steps of your Winter Palace." His arms gave me a squeeze. "Remember?"

I stared into his green-brown eyes, stunned at this news, news Sjofn should have shared with me. *All* of this news Sjofn should have *totally* fucking *shared* with me *way* the fuck before we even made our deal. But even as this freaked me out, scared me to death and pissed me right the fuck off, I found it in myself to answer quietly, "Oh yeah, right. It was... unpleasant, so I blocked it out."

He nodded before saying, "Because of that, my wee one, I'm sorry you saw that tonight. If it were to happen again, my men and I will do our best to shield you from seeing it so you experience no further..." his eyes held mine before he finished, "unpleasantness."

"That would be good," I replied softly.

His lips tipped up slightly before they moved in to kiss my forehead.

When he moved back, I asked, "Is that how you knew this was going to happen, I mean, if an attempt was made before?"

He shook his head but said, "I do not know how your uncle's mind works and do not wish to know. What I do know is that I would not put anything past him. Though, that said, I will admit to being surprised if he has made this decision or anyone has done, if it is not Baldur. When the last assassin was dispatched, an assassin neither my men nor your father's could successfully trace back to your uncle, or anyone, your uncle declared outrage at this action and we had to pretend we believed his indignation on behalf of his niece. But both your father and I publicly promised retribution should another attempt be made, and we both vowed to ride in war against anyone if their motives were political, should they actually succeed."

I felt my body tense and I breathed, "Succeed?"

His arms gave me a squeeze. "This will not happen, Finnie."

"But, what if it—"

Another squeeze then, "It will not happen, my love."

"I know, but what if—"

His face dipped close to mine and his voice was quiet but low and fierce when he said, "It will not, for you will never be far from my side. It is a measure of a man, my wife, how he cheats in cards. And it is a measure of a man, any man, be he married to a pub wench or a princess, how he cares for his bride. I am a Drakkar. My measure is different than any man's and there are many facets to that, but one of them explains why I turn away without a thought from those whose lifeblood seeps into the snow. Those who moved with intent to harm my bride. And I won't think of them, ever. I will only turn my mind to how I can best care for my bride and that now includes undermining any threat that may loom for you. And I vow to you, my princess, if it means my own life, this will *not* happen."

I stared into his eyes and whispered, "Okay," because really, what else could I do? He sounded pretty freaking serious.

His expression shifted from serious to soft and finally he smiled.

Then he repeated, "Okay."

I sucked in an unsteady breath and said, "Though, um...just to say, if you're going to vow to keep me safe, I'd kinda like you to vow to keep *you* safe too." His soft eyes started to warm, and I rushed on, "You know, because...well, who'll chop the wood and lug it into the house if you're assassinated or something?"

The soft warmth of his eyes took on another smile and he muttered, "My wife does not like carrying wood."

"It isn't my favorite chore," I admitted. "My time is better spent baking pies."

The smile reached his mouth before he murmured, "Then I best stay around to chop wood."

"I'd appreciate that."

He moved his head and brushed his nose against mine.

Staying close, he whispered, "Then I'll vow to keep me safe too..." he paused, "so I can be around to chop wood."

"And lug it in the house," I added.

"And lug it in the house," he agreed.

I stared into his eyes, so beautiful, so close, and felt his arms, so strong, so tight, and his body, so big, so powerful, all of it making me feel so... very...*safe*, and the trembling stopped.

I slid my face to the side and tucked it in his neck as I slid my arms around him and held on tight.

I felt Frey tip his head so his lips where at my ear when he asked, "Are you all right now, my wee Finnie?"

"No, not really, but give me a minute and I'll get there."

He kissed my neck.

That made me feel better.

He held me and I held on until I felt totally better. Or, at least, better enough to change into my nightgown.

Then I whispered, "I'm good now, Frey. I need to go change for bed."

"All right, Finnie," he agreed, his arms loosening. "Hurry."

I pulled away, looked at him, gave him a small smile and leaned in to give him a quick lip touch.

Then I moved away and hurried.

I was back in bed, held tight to my husband's side, cradling his thigh in less than five minutes.

It took me a lot longer to find sleep.

But eventually I did it.

"Frey?" I called.

"I'm here," he whispered, his arm around my back giving me a squeeze. "You're trembling again, wife."

"Bad dream."

He rolled into me, and both his strong arms went around me.

"Hold on," he ordered gently and my arm already around him tightened.

He held me and I tried to find sleep.

I couldn't so I called, "Frey?"

"I'm here."

I hesitated.

Then I said so quietly, I wondered if he heard me, "You were so *good* at it."

He heard me, his arms got tighter, but he said nothing.

"You've had lots of practice, haven't you?" I asked.

"Sleep, wife," he said on a squeeze.

Yep, he had lots of practice killing people.

Ho boy.

"Just tell me one thing," I said softly. "Were they bad guys?"

He didn't say anything for a moment then I heard his head shift on the pillow and with his lips against the top of my hair, he whispered, "Most of them."

Oh God.

"No enemy is all bad, Finnie," he told me gently. "They're just the enemy."

I nodded my head on the pillow for this was undoubtedly true.

Frey kept talking. "But the men tonight were paid to kill a newlywed man and his wife." His arms gave me a squeeze. "I lose no sleep for them, and you shouldn't either."

"But you were awake," I pointed out.

"Yes, I was. Because my wee wife trembles against me in her sleep," he informed me.

God, that was sweet.

"Sorry, Frey," I whispered.

"Do not be sorry, be drowsy," he ordered.

I smiled and pressed closer to my husband.

"Thanks for saving my life," I whispered.

He didn't answer.

He just gave me another tight squeeze.

12

RETURN TO FYNGAARD

We didn't leave at dawn. We left three hours before it. But considering the sun kissed the sky around nine in the morning, this wasn't *that* early. Nevertheless, with a restless night of sleep that included several awakenings, I was exhausted.

Luckily, I had packed the trunks and Frey had loaded the sleigh the day before. However, even if we hadn't done this, it would have been made light work of by the tall, burly men who were to ride with us.

Before leaving, I met them briefly. Thad and Ruben were among them. Then there was Annar, Orion, Stephan (pronounced Steh-fawn), Gunner, Maximilian (but he told me everyone called him Max and invited me to do so too), Lund and Oleg.

Oleg, I learned when Frey pulled me up in front of him on Tyr, was driving my sleigh that had the horses set to and was ready to go by the time I wandered sleepily outside wearing a cloak Frey chose for me (due to its warmness) that was made of white fur pelts dusted with black and gray hairs, gloves and a furry hat that matched the cloak.

By the way, all of my fabulous outerwear was over a gown I chose for the purpose of meeting my parents. A softer than soft winter-white cashmere that had an intricately crocheted, low, square neckline and a matching crocheted belt, so long its ends hung to the hem of my skirt. I'd added a pair of fabulous fur-lined, over-the-knee charcoal gray suede, low-heeled boots and select pieces of very elegant but understated jewelry.

Yes, it was the wee hours of the morning when Frey woke me and told me to get ready. And yes, we were going to be traveling all day, on the back of a horse no less. But also, I would be seeing my parents at the end of our journey. They didn't seem to like Sjofn much and I wanted to make a good impression.

So off we went, the sleigh led by a big, black horse added to my grays (Oleg's mount).

The day before, I had asked, and Frey had agreed to take the ride slower so we could stop in some of the villages on the way because I wanted to have a closer look and so we could have a break (and the horses could too) and something to eat. We were even going to spend the night in one of them so I could be rested and have the time to get presentable to meet my parents.

This plan went out the window with the assassination attempt (understandably) and we were to press on swiftly and get to Fyngaard without delay.

And this we did.

Surprisingly, for the first couple of hours, I turned and curled as best I could into my husband's big, warm body and somehow managed to fall asleep in the cradle of his arm.

Once I woke, Frey ordered a halt and we all stopped to eat sandwiches Ruben's woman made for us filled with cold, lean roast beef that had been stacked on slices of thick, chewy white bread while the beef's juices still flowed, soaking the bread with flavor. It also had a spread of creamy horseradish sauce that was delicious but so thick it made my eyes water. Though none of the men even made a face as they wolfed the sandwiches down.

This was followed with long pulls on wineskins that were filled with smooth whisky that, no matter how smooth, still made my eyes bug out. But Frey gently urged me to drink it to "keep warm inside." So, since he was being gentle and Lord knew I needed to utilize every tactic to keep warm, I sucked back three big sips.

He was right, it worked. After that, I was definitely warm inside.

As we rode (and Oleg sledded with Penelope curled in the fur rug at the floor of the sleigh, oblivious to the ride, the scenery and everything, in kitty cat la-la land of warmth and definitely liking the sleigh better than riding on a horse and I knew this because she...freaking...*told me*), the men did not converse at all.

They were alert and wary, and Thad and Stephan often galloped away from the group, disappearing in front of us, obviously assessing if our path was clear. Lund and Annar often rounded back, clearly assessing if we were being followed. And Orion rarely rode with us, obviously out in the countryside somewhere, assessing if we were safe at our flanks.

But Ruben, Gunner and Max stayed put. Gunner riding steady to Frey and my left, Max riding steady to Oleg's right, Ruben at the front, our constant guard.

As we rode through forest and over plain, Frey spoke to me, mostly telling me what the area we were in was called, the name of the river I'd seen on our way out, what each village was called and adding information such as which gods and/or goddesses they worshiped.

News: some villages chose specific gods or goddesses to revere above the others. Sometimes it was one, but it seemed to be on average three. And their preferences were known easily for they had that god's or goddess's colors displayed in the town, or the town's common places had statues, busts or their faces were carved into buildings (this, Frey pointed out to me, and this, by the way, was cool, and this, I decided, was why there was a lot of green and light blue in Houllebec because clearly they prayed to Hermia and Alabasta).

Although Frey told me this, he didn't explain why. He simply seemed to be talking to me to keep my mind off things.

And he did, including the fact that he was telling me information that it was likely, as princess of this country, I should know.

It didn't occur to me once that this was weird.

Not once.

In fact, that thought didn't enter my mind.

Night fell as it usually did in that world. That was to say in early afternoon, and we were riding through another forest when it did it. I was *way* over the ride by then, and as much as I liked Tyr, I wanted *off* that horse and *in* a place that was warm. So that forest seemed to last forever until suddenly we came out it and the torchlit city of Fyngaard was laid out in the valley in front of us, surrounded by tall mountains, their snowy tops piercing the night sky.

Where I had entered this world.

Where my parents were.

I again noted its beauty, but I instantly grew anxious, and I must have tensed or pulled in a breath for Frey's arm around me grew tight but he said not a word.

To take my mind off the impending meeting, as we rode through Fyngaard, I looked around and saw it appeared most of the city had attended our wedding for the night I entered this world, it was mostly deserted.

But now, there were people out and about. Quite a number of them, walking, riding, standing around the big fire drums, holding their hands to them and chatting.

There were also some sleighs, none as large as mine, one-seaters or two-seaters, some with an area at the back where you could put stuff, some without, some being pulled by two horses, most only one.

All of the people were dressed differently than they were in Houllebec, their clothes more refined. Some of the men and women here had fur trim on their outerwear and there was none in Houllebec. And most of the women in Fyngaard wore elegant fur-trimmed hats and slim leather or suede gloves whereas in the village, the women wore knit caps and mittens.

There were also several long lines of two-story, connected buildings that had shops on the first floor with people in them or outside looking in, perusing the wares. They definitely had more of a selection than our little Houllebec, including yarn shops, a number of dressmakers, milliners, tobacconists, wine and spirits, bookstores, stationery shops and shops that looked like they sold leather and fur.

There were even two shops that we passed whose windows were decorated with what looked like spun, colored glass that was fashioned in all shapes from butterflies to hummingbirds to hawks, horses and wolves and even sleighs and ships. And one of them had a large, elaborate and definitely cool dragon in its window.

It was all so fascinating, my head often turned or my body twisted to keep sight of something we passed and when we passed the glass shops, I decided I was definitely checking *those* out, as soon as I could.

There were a number of restaurants, pubs and even what looked like cafés, some with sturdy, wooden furniture outside surrounded by torches, elegant, but large firepits where warm blazes snapped and big fire drums where people sat drinking coffee or maybe cocoa, some of the men smoking brown-paper-covered, thin cigars.

It was, I noted, definitely a city and what appeared to be a cosmopolitan one at that.

Our entourage, now including all our riders, did not pass through the city unnoticed. In fact, we caused quite a stir. When eyes came to me, men would bow slightly or women would bob in a graceful, short curtsy. But if eyes caught or moved to Frey, men would lift their hand in a fist and touch their chin and women would tuck their chin down and to the side of their neck.

This was strange, but it was cool, and for both reasons, I wished I could ask Frey about it. But, alas, I should already know so I couldn't.

We made it out of the commerce area and were winding our way through what seemed a residential area when our party made a turn around a house, and I saw it.

The Winter Palace.

It had to be for it was huge and it was extraordinarily gorgeous.

It sprawled along the rise at the base of an enormous mountain and the outside carried as much beautifully carved wood as I'd noticed inside. The many, varied-height, narrow-angled gables were all decorated with intricate dark-wood carving mingled with long, glistening icicles. Most of the diamond paned windows glowed with candlelight, at their tops the light glowed through the carved wood adorning them, and the rest of the façade was made of massive wood planks.

And I could see this even in the night for all along the front of the Palace there were big drums with roaring fires probably every six feet, and closer to the building was a row of tall torches only maybe a foot apart and there were a vast number of torches that were affixed on a slant on the Palace itself, all of them bearing cages around the fire and all of them lit.

It was freaking *magnificent*. Every inch of it and there were a lot of inches. The place was huge.

I was frozen in awe, but my awe slid away as I saw on the wide, stone steps that swept down and widened gracefully as they ran from top to bottom there were a bunch of people standing and waiting.

For us.

And the two people at the very top, right in front of the huge, lancet-arched, square-paneled, wooden double doors were my parents.

Eek!

I stared at them and deep breathed wondering why I was so freaked out.

I didn't know why and had no time to figure it out. Oleg drove the sleigh off to a side and the other men fell back. But Frey rode Tyr straight to the foot of the massive flight of steps and stopped. He did not delay in dismounting nor did he delay in reaching up, grasping my waist and pulling me down. Further, he did not delay in engulfing my gloved hand in the hugeness of his and guiding me up the steps.

Nervously, my eyes took in the people standing along the steps, and I noticed there were at least thirty of them, none of them in the fine clothes my parents wore. These included the four girls who had been there that first night, all wearing cloaks of the same colors their dresses had been that night, all of their eyes on me.

Frey stopped us two steps down from my parents and directly in front of them. I tore my eyes from the girls and looked into my parents' blank faces (though, Mom looked kind of peeved for some reason, then again, my mom of this world had so far only looked peeved). But as I took in their expressions, I watched my father lift a fist to his chin and at the same time my mother's chin dipped to the side and into her neck.

Both of these gestures were for Frey.

How weird.

Seriously, I wondered what that meant and had to find some way to find out.

When my father dropped his hand and Mom's chin righted, Frey suddenly bowed at my side. I looked at him to see his bow was not deep, but shallow, just a slight bend of his waist and his head was tipped back, his eyes on my parents. But his hand still in mine squeezed then he gave it a gentle jerk.

Oh shit. I was supposed to curtsy.

Crap.

I dropped into an awkward curtsy, seeing as I was doing it on a step that was deep but not deep enough to execute a curtsy, something I'd never done before in my life. I pulled it off, thankfully, without falling over or something equally embarrassing, and I bowed my head.

"Rise, my daughter and new son," Dad muttered.

Frey straightened and his hand held mine firmly so I could use the strength of his arm to pull myself up.

I tilted my head back to look at my parents while my nerves jangled. But before anyone could say a word, Frey spoke.

"My Ice Bride has been traveling long and she is chilled. We must get her inside."

He didn't wait but led us up another step. I saw both my mother and father jerk in some surprise then, when Frey kept right on going and was about to bowl through them, they turned toward the doors. One of the people standing around rushed to them and pushed both open. Mom and

Dad strode through, Frey and I following close, and some of the people from outside followed us in while others disappeared to places unknown.

The doors barely closed behind us when Frey let my hand go and turned to my dad.

"Atticus, we must talk. Now."

Dad blinked up at him. I turned my head to blink up at him too. His voice sounded firm, fierce, and maybe a little ticked off. I didn't get that. He didn't seem ticked off while we rode.

Dad rallied and replied, "Of course, Drakkar. My study."

Frey turned to my mother and ordered, "The princess does not leave the Palace unless she has my leave."

I blinked again.

Uh...what?

Mom looked up at him and nodded.

Frey wasn't done. "You will attend my conversation with my king."

Mom's eyes flashed to me then to Frey and she nodded again.

Frey turned to the four girls hovering close. "See to your princess."

Then, without looking at me, he stalked away.

I stared at his back, stunned at his tone, behavior and more bossy than his normal bossy commands.

Dad followed Frey.

Mom came straight to me, her fingers curled around my arm tight, and she leaned to my ear to hiss, "*Now* what have you done?"

I didn't get to say a word before she let me go and hurried off in the direction Frey and Dad had disappeared.

What on earth?

Before I could ask, the four girls surrounded me and started herding me toward the carved stairs.

One who was close to my side and had her hand on me, peered at me and whispered, "Sjofn?"

I looked at her, shook off that strange, weirdly troubling scene and whispered back, "No. Finnie."

She blinked then she smiled slightly and pulled me up the steps as she introduced herself, "I'm Alyssa."

The girl walking close at my other side grabbed my hand and squeezed.

"Jocelyn," she whispered.

"Esther," one of the girls at our backs said, and still mounting the stairs, I turned to smile at her.

"Bess," the last one peeped, and I smiled at her too.

"Gods," Jocelyn breathed, giving my hand another squeeze as I turned to face forward because even though they were guiding me, I *was* climbing stairs and I didn't want to fall flat on my face. "We're *so* glad you're back."

We ascended the stairs, and they started leading me swiftly down the hall.

Alyssa got even closer to my other side and whispered, "We've been so worried."

"Yes, we didn't have time to tell you *a thing*," Bess said quietly from behind and another glance back showed she and Esther were right on our heels.

"We're *so* sorry about that," Alyssa stated. "But the switch was supposed to happen ten minutes earlier. I don't know what caused the delay, but whatever it was, we lost our opportunity to warn you what was to come."

Hmm.

Seems it was not so good that Claudia and I prattled on when I should have been transporting. If we hadn't, things might have gone better for me, apparently.

Crap.

We stopped at a door, but just barely before it was opened, we were through it, and I was back in the room where I'd started my adventure. It was again lit, it now had a roaring fire in the grate and it was still freaking gorgeous.

I barely got a chance to take it in and definitely didn't get a chance to open my mouth before my hat and cloak were gone as were my gloves.

And while they did this with practiced ease and uncanny quickness, they kept talking.

"We wanted to send a messenger, but no one knew where you'd gone." This was Esther.

"Everyone was abuzz that The Drakkar rode into the night with you right after the ceremony. They're still talking about it. I mean, obviously, you're beautiful and equally obviously, he's The Drakkar, so they think he couldn't wait to get his hands on you. Especially after your conjugal kiss, which everyone is also still talking about." This was Alyssa and she went on to state, "But your mother was livid. She'd spent months planning the celebration that was to happen after the wedding ceremony. She didn't get over The Drakkar hauling you away for *weeks*."

"She's still not over it," Esther muttered.

"Yes, it was frosty in the Winter Palace, believe me." This was Bess, her eyeballs moved around the group as she finished, "And still is."

As they talked, they led me to the bed and pushed me on it and *in it* and then they climbed in, surrounding me close.

Jocelyn spoke before I could get a word in edgewise.

"Where did he take you anyway?" Jocelyn asked. "Rumor had it he was on his ship the very next night, away on crucial business."

"Oh gods, I hope he didn't take you on one of his ships," Bess muttered.

My wide eyes moved to Bess.

One of them?

They finally paused enough for me to speak. "Uh...he was. Before he left, though, he took me to a hunting cabin, I think."

Jocelyn looked to Alyssa. "His hunting cabin. I told you."

"This I cannot believe," Esther muttered. "His *hunting cabin?*"

"I know!" Bess exclaimed (but her exclamation was subdued, like she didn't want anyone to overhear). "His lodge in Kellshorn is fit for a princess. Balls to that, I've heard it's so grand, it's fit for *a queen*. Even his chalet in Skarnwyld would be better than his hunting cabin!" She looked to Jocelyn and noted, "I've heard it's quite lovely."

"She's just lucky he didn't take her to his fishing cottage in Tylgould. The smell..." Alyssa's cute, pert nose scrunched up.

Jeez, how many houses did Frey own?

"Tylgould is lovely," Esther stated. "My parents took me there as a child. And I hear his cottage is right on the Winter Sea. The properties right on the sea are very old but very quaint and *very* exclusive."

"Yes, but even so...the smell," Alyssa repeated as she shook her head.

"Uh—" I tried to cut in, and all attention came back to me including Jocelyn's hand that curled lightly on my thigh.

"Please tell us he's been kind to you," she whispered.

"Well..." I started but clearly didn't speak quickly enough for Esther spoke.

"Bloody hell, he hasn't."

"Well—" I tried again.

"*I knew it,*" Alyssa hissed and looked at Bess. "If he was away on his ship so quickly that means everyone was wrong. The Drakkar would never leave a woman in his bed who he wanted to be in that bed with, balls to crucial business. We should have *done* something."

"What could we have done? The queen was in a state. And when Queen

Aurora gets in a state..." Bess trailed off, saying it all without saying a thing then finished, "We didn't have *time*."

Alyssa's hand came up and she squeezed my arm so my head turned to her and she said softly, "I'm so sorry, er...other Sjofn."

"Finnie," I urged her to call me on a smile. "Please call me Finnie."

"Finnie," she smiled back.

Okay, well, I was definitely going to like these girls. That I knew right off. But I wished they'd let me talk.

"Finnie," Jocelyn said, and I turned to her. "That's very sweet."

"Oh, we have so much to tell you!" Bess exclaimed in that restrained way again.

"Yes, including the fact that Sjofn's witch has been here *three times*," Esther stated.

I grew tense at this unexpected news and blinked at her, but before I could ask, Alyssa spoke.

"That Agnes, she has something of great import to tell you," Alyssa shared, and I turned my head to stare at her.

Great. Just great. I wondered what that was, but I was thinking maybe I didn't want to know. Who knew what Sjofn was getting up to in my world?

"But she'll only tell you," Bess stated, and my eyes went to her. "Still, it seems rather urgent."

Ho boy.

"Well! Enough of this!" Jocelyn finally announced. "It's clear The Drakkar is in a mood and he and his men have been traveling a long way. We need to prepare Finnie for dinner without delay."

"But—" I started as they scrambled off the bed, tugging me with them.

"Bath first," Alyssa mumbled. "Bess, off you go to see about her trunks. We need to unpack her immediately."

Bess scurried away without a peep.

"The sky-blue satin, I think," Jocelyn mumbled as they led me to the wall, which I saw had a hidden door, the doorknob barely noticeable in the wood.

"Ice blue," Alyssa disagreed. "He called her his Ice Bride."

Esther opened the door in front of us and in we went to another room. This was clearly a bathroom slash dressing room. It had a fabulous light-blue, suede-covered chaise lounge in the corner and a three paneled screen that had a beautifully stitched tapestry depicting a snowy-mountain land-scape with a cloud-free sky.

It also had three dark-wood, carved wardrobes on three different walls, a table with a gorgeous porcelain basin adorned with delicate blue flowers and a matching pitcher on a shelf underneath it.

There was a roaring fire in another beautifully carved, stone mantel fireplace, another heavily carved, full-length oval mirror and a big, oval copper tub in the middle with one side swayed back with a fluffy, ice-blue, cotton-covered pillow tied to holes in the copper where you could lay your head when you lounged back.

I stared with mouth open, rendered speechless by the room rather than the girls' chatter.

Only two syllables described this room: awe...*some*.

"He must be blind or just mad, I cannot understand why he wouldn't see our, er...princess's charms," Jocelyn muttered, and my attention went back to the conversation.

"Well, it's hard to be beautiful in a hunting cabin, no matter how beautiful you actually are," Esther stated in a voice that held an edge of ire. "Especially when you don't have your maidservants to assist you. I cannot *believe* he departed without taking us with her...*wherever* he was going."

"Uh...ladies—" I tried.

"Well, he'll see her *now*. We'll be sure of it, *and* he won't be blind any longer," Alyssa stated firmly. "And it will definitely be the ice blue," she told Jocelyn. "*Not* the sky blue."

"The sky blue is lovely with her eyes, none better," Jocelyn shot back.

"Neither, the winter white with the Valerian embroidery," Esther declared.

All right. I needed to get in there.

"Girls!" I said loudly when both Jocelyn and Alyssa opened their mouths to retort to Esther, and all eyes came to me. "You don't need to make a match," I told them. "Frey likes me just fine."

They stared at me. Jocelyn even blinked.

Then Alyssa breathed, "What?"

"He did take off on his ship, but when he came back, we made a deal, and since then, he's been lovely. We get along great. I like him. He likes me and, um...things are progressing very well," I assured them.

At that, *all* of them blinked, and I braced because they suddenly rushed me as one.

"Oh Finnie," Jocelyn breathed, holding on to my arm hard. "Has he bedded you?"

"By the gods," Alyssa (also) breathed before I could utter a noise. She was holding on to my other arm, her eyes on Jocelyn, "I can't believe this.

This is *wonderful*." Her eager deep-blue eyes came to me. "Is he as skilled as they say?"

"I know he is," Esther, standing close to my front, her hazel eyes dancing. "He took Viola, to his bed. You remember." Her eyes moved from Jocelyn to Alyssa. "That maid, the pretty one who serves the princess's table? She says he kept her there *three days*, three *busy* days, and when he released her, she did *not* wish to go."

Oh my God.

Was I hearing them right?

My heart started banging in my chest as my stomach clenched.

"I *do* know," Jocelyn whispered. "*Everyone* knows. Her stories of his varied and *vigorous* talents kept me warm many a night after I heard them."

Everyone knows?

"Don't forget his stamina," Alyssa added on a wicked grin.

Stamina?

All three giggled.

I tried hard to recover from what felt like a punch in the stomach.

Frey had fucked a maid?

One from *my house*?

For three straight days?

Again, a maid who worked in *my house*?

I mean, what the fuck was that?

"Gods!" Jocelyn cried suddenly, and I jumped. "Water! Oils!" She grinned at me and gave my arm a squeeze. "Even though he," she leaned in, her grin getting wider, "*likes* our princess, tonight, we still get to show him the fullness of her beauty."

"I'll see to the water," Esther stated, peeling off.

"I'll go see where Bess is with the state of the trunks," Jocelyn mumbled, also peeling off.

"I'll press the ice blue," Alyssa muttered, hurrying to one of the wardrobes.

"Lounge and relax, Finnie," Jocelyn called from the door. "We'll take care of you." She smiled big. "It's what we do."

I nodded distractedly to her and then wandered to the lounge, suddenly exhausted and not in a good way.

And this was because, first, Frey had dumped me in a hunting cabin when he had an apparently fabulous lodge and a slightly less fabulous but still lovely chalet where he could have taken me. Not to mention a quaint cottage on the Winter Sea, whatever that was.

Second, I could understand this (slightly) considering he hated Sjofn, but he didn't hate *me*, and he still kept me at his hunting cabin where I cooked for him, kept the place clean, and one day, washed his bloody clothes, another of my *not* very favorite activities.

Third, I had gone out of my way to dress nice for my parents and they hadn't even seen me with my cloak off. I had no time to make a good impression or *any* impression before Frey ordered their attendance (*he* ordered a *king and queen*, and *they* did his bidding—what was *that* all about?) and stalked off with them scurrying to follow.

And now, we were back at my palace, but Frey prowled away with my father *and* mother without a kind touch, word or even look. And my maid-servants were sweet, but they were preparing me to eat dinner with my mother, father and husband at a table that would probably be served by a girl my husband had fucked with varied and vigorous talent, and let us not forget, *stamina* for *three* days.

I felt a headache coming on, not a real one, but a violent one nonetheless. So violent it would keep me in bed for about three weeks.

Maybe four.

Unfortunately, this kind of thing would probably incense my mother, who already clearly did not like me. And my father, who I didn't think liked me a great deal more because he'd barely said a word to me, few of the ones he'd spoken were nice and earlier he had hardly even looked at me.

I dropped to, then curled up on the lounge as these things moved through my brain.

Shit.

I tucked my hands under my cheek on the armrest and watched Alyssa disappear out of the room carrying a flash of extraordinary ice-blue satin, the fullness of it I could not see.

But it was extraordinary ice-blue satin that likely was an extraordinary ice-blue gown that, normally, I would be in fits of excitement to see.

At that moment I absolutely was not.

I closed my eyes, deciding I needed Penelope.

I also needed to find out what the witch named Agnes needed to tell me so pressingly.

And I further needed to figure out why the idea of Frey sleeping with one of my maids hurt so damned much.

Shit.

Then I decided not to think of why Frey's sexual antics hurt, and indeed, not to think about Frey at all.

149

Instead, I decided to think of a nice hot bath, donning a probably extraordinary dress and then putting one foot in front of the other until I could actually get away with faking a headache, which would be around the time I was again alone with my husband. And that headache would be so intense, he'd need to leave me alone in my bed and go the fuck away until I had time to sort my shit out.

13

THE DRAKKAR WILL RISE

"I do not believe this," King Atticus whispered to the night-filled window, and Frey Drakkar turned his eyes from his king's openly ravaged expression to look at his queen.

Queen Aurora had her gaze averted from Drakkar's shrewd eyes, her expression hidden, but what he could see of her face, it was carefully blank.

Neither reaction to their daughter's grave actions was a surprise.

King Atticus didn't often hide his emotions. He did not need to. He was king and those around him catered to his whims.

Queen Aurora was another story.

Atticus turned from the window, his openly wounded gaze finding Drakkar's, and he whispered, "This is...this is...this travel to another world... it is...it's akin to—"

"Treason," Aurora finished for her husband, her voice cold, emotionless and Atticus turned to his wife.

"Aurora, my love—"

She cut him off. "I told you, time and again, Atticus, I *told* you not to raise our girl as," she leaned toward her husband, "*a boy*."

Atticus's jaw got tight. "I did *not* raise her as a boy. She simply enjoys those things. It's her nature. And she enjoys being with her father doing them. But even so, that has nothing to do with it and you know it."

"It doesn't?" Aurora shot back and crossed her arms on her chest, turning fully to face her husband. "You always wanted a son. Always. And not having one, all her life she's been taught as you would have taught a son, a future king. And that is to be headstrong and do whatever she can to get her own way, when, of course, she doesn't naturally *expect* her own way. These, my love, are not traits of a girl. These are most assuredly the traits of a boy."

"Aurora—" Atticus started, color rising in his face as his anger did the same, but Drakkar was done.

"Does your conversation at this point have any meaning?" he asked, and his king and queen turned eyes to him. "Princess Sjofn has done it and in so doing she betrayed her parents, which means she betrayed her king, queen and country, the House of Wilde *and* she betrayed *me*. I'm sure we're all agreed that this action is unforgiveable."

Both king and queen stared at him, and Drakkar was surprised to see the flash of pain in his king's eyes was mirrored, though hidden far more quickly, in his queen's.

They loved their daughter. Although everyone knew this to be true of Atticus, that flash in Aurora's eyes and the fact she had not been able to hide it meant she, too, cared deeply for her girl.

Atticus lifted his chin to Drakkar in assent. Aurora's eyes drifted to the floor, her way to show she, too, agreed.

Drakkar went on, "There is more."

Aurora's gaze moved back to him. Atticus shifted closer to his wife and stood beside her in front of his desk. Once there, he leaned into a hand.

"More?" Atticus prompted.

Drakkar nodded. "I have had a message from the elves."

Both husband's and wife's gazes grew sharper and the tension in the room, already wound tight, stretched taut.

"I assume they are even less happy you've wed a Sjofn from another world," Atticus guessed wrongly, and Drakkar knew his king was concerned about the elves being troubled or, worse, angered by this occurrence. This could mean another century of retreat.

And they most definitely did not want the elves, again, to retreat.

Not now.

Not with a Frey and The Drakkar both embodied in one man and what that occurrence might mean for Lunwyn.

Atticus knew, for Drakkar had used it on numerous occasions to refuse the arranged marriage with Atticus's daughter, that the elves were against the match. And he was not wrong to assume they would be violently opposed to his union to a soul from another world.

"On the contrary," Drakkar stated. "They are well-pleased."

Atticus blinked. Aurora's gaze grew even more intense.

"Well-pleased?" she asked quietly.

"The elves told me the Sjofn upstairs is my true Ice Bride. They were against the match to your daughter, but they are delighted I am bound to her twin. Apparently, Keer's wishes for me have come true through my Finnie. *She* is my destiny."

"By the gods, man, how can that be?" Atticus asked incredulously. "She isn't even of our world."

"She carries the blood of the elves, as do I," Drakkar informed him. "They are the elves of her world, but she inherits her eyes and hair from those of that realm. Because of this, we will mate, create a child, and fulfill Keer's demands that the blood of the elves and the blood of the dragon unite and sit yet again on Lunwyn's throne throughout eternity."

"This is...this is...*shocking*," Atticus breathed.

"This is destiny," Drakkar returned.

"So, clearly, it was destiny for our Sjofn to make her decision and then take her action," Aurora put in smoothly, as she often did in an attempt to soften the circumstances her daughter's actions caused.

Drakkar looked to her.

"She had no idea her leaving would be to the will of the gods," Drakkar retorted. "She had no thought for anyone but herself. She also did not explain to my Finnie why she was leaving or what Finnie would be facing the very moment of her arrival. As I told you, the switch was accomplished right before she left this Palace to ride to the Dwelling of the Gods to be bound to me. Sjofn orchestrated it that way, throwing my Finnie into what I know was a frightening situation for, not knowing who she was, I behaved in ways that terrified her, but Sjofn would take as a matter of course. I know this because Finnie admitted it to me."

Aurora pressed her lips together and Atticus was smart enough not to speak at all.

"The gods' will has been done but it is not Sjofn of the House of Wilde who assisted in seeing destiny fulfilled," Drakkar stated firmly, and Aurora pulled in a delicate breath. Drakkar continued, "And it is partly for that reason that I've commanded the elves to bind my Finnie to this world, which in turn binds your Sjofn to the other. Neither will return to their home world, not again. And this command is everlasting."

Aurora shifted, her arms uncrossing so she could lay her hand palm flat on the desk, a casual stance that many would misread as thus, but Drakkar did not. There was nothing casual about it.

She did it to hold herself up in her sudden grief for her lost daughter.

Atticus did not hide his reaction. He flinched and his face paled.

Drakkar felt for them, but he did not feel much. This was because Sjofn's actions were, indeed, reprehensible as treason always is. This was also because Sjofn was what they created as any child always is. And lastly, this was because he was still enraged at what their daughter had done to Finnie.

"Everlasting?" Atticus whispered.

"The elves explained that to bind Finnie here, Sjofn would need to remain there, never to come back and Finnie never to go home. This is my decision. It is made to fulfill my destiny and that of Lunwyn. It is also made to punish Sjofn for her treachery," Drakkar declared.

"We'll never see her again?" Atticus asked quietly.

"Never again," Drakkar confirmed.

Husband and wife glanced at each other then they looked to The Drakkar. This time, both were smart enough to stay silent on the subject for the decision of a Frey that led to his command of the elves was never questioned.

But Aurora did speak.

"Your Finnie," she said softly. "She pleases you?"

"Indeed," Drakkar again confirmed.

Atticus looked to the ceiling then to The Drakkar before he asked quietly, "What is..." he hesitated, "your Finnie like?"

"Nothing like your daughter," Drakkar replied.

Atticus winced and Aurora pressed her lips together.

Drakkar carried on, "She is soft. She is sweet. She smiles often, talks more and never has anything to say that isn't interesting. She teases and she jokes, and she is good at both. She is an excellent cook and has a strong spirit. People fall easily into her life and like being there. And she enjoys living, immensely, and does not hide it."

"You care for her already," Atticus observed.

"It would be difficult not to. But I wouldn't know for I have not tried," Drakkar replied.

Atticus's lips twitched and his eyes lit but Aurora's expression stayed closed.

"I am The Drakkar and you both know what that means," Drakkar said quietly. "But I cannot command your emotions. However, I urge you to find it in your hearts, even as you grieve the deeds and the loss of your daughter, to open them to Finnie. Sjofn escaped this world for selfish reasons. Finnie sought it for entirely different ones."

"And will you share those?" Aurora asked instantly.

Drakkar answered just as instantly. "Her parents, your twins in her world, died when she was young."

"Gods," Atticus breathed, his torso rocking back and even Aurora's back straightened slightly.

Drakkar nodded. "She grieves them still. She misses them. The elves told me she paid great treasure, and we all know she took grave risks simply in order to see them or..." he paused then stressed, "*you* again."

This moved them both. Drakkar knew it because Aurora turned her face away to hide her expression and Atticus dropped his eyes to look at his boots in an effort to do the same.

Drakkar kept talking.

"She enjoyed her time with me at my hunting cabin and would have been happy to stay there, this I know. But upon offering the opportunity to spend time with you, she was eager to leave a place she liked and a village where she had made friends. Nevertheless, she carries great anxiety about seeing you. I can only assume, not knowing she was who she is, and being impatient with your daughter, you may have acted on this with Finnie in the brief time she was in your company, and this is what causes her unease. But if you cannot find it in your heart to let her in, then I request you at least find it in your heart to show her kindness. She paid dearly and risked much simply to spend time with you. I wish for her to have this and to enjoy it and would look upon it favorably if you do."

Atticus immediately inclined his head. Aurora slowly turned hers to face him again and she regally lifted her chin.

"I will go on to share something else I know to be true. That is, if you do open your hearts to her, she will reward you," Drakkar stated quietly and saw Atticus's jaw clench before he again inclined his head once more. Aurora gave a single nod. Drakkar nodded back and then continued, "There is more you need to know."

Atticus pulled in a breath. Aurora patiently waited.

Drakkar went on, "She does not know I know she is not of this world. And she will not know until I tell her. You will keep this secret and behave as if she is Sjofn of the House of Wilde. However, obviously, you will naturally adapt your behavior to her as she earns your regard."

Drakkar accepted his king and queen's keen gazes as his mind moved to his request, for this was something that had started to concern him.

At first, he did not share his knowledge of her coming from another world with Finnie because he was still adjusting to it himself. Then he found her consistent blunders endearing, her cover ups even more so, and her reactions to things that surprised her deeply amusing. He enjoyed them all...greatly.

Too greatly.

Time had passed, not much, but enough that it had gone beyond when he should have shared he held this knowledge.

Now, it seemed uncomfortably like he was keeping something from her. A secret that was important, so important, keeping it from her was a lie.

However, she'd just the night before witnessed him and Thad taking lives. She had not reacted to that well and took the news of her life being in danger even worse. With the additional anxiety she carried at again spending time with her parents, it was now not the time to discuss the knowledge he held about her.

But he knew he must find the time to do it and the words to explain why he didn't do it earlier.

And he must do it soon.

"I don't understand," Atticus called Drakkar's attention to him. "Why—?"

"An attempt was made on her life, Atticus," Drakkar explained. "She is not, to my knowledge, a princess in her world and from observing her closely, seeing her immensely friendly demeanor with others, this bears true unless royalty is vastly different in her world. She has never had, nor foiled, an assassination attempt on her life. She has not ever seen a life taken, and in one night, she saw three. She reacted to this negatively and this reaction was fierce. She is not your daughter. She does not hunt. She has not been trained in swordplay, knives or archery. From what I understand from her speech, behavior and reactions to things, her world is infinitely different from ours. For instance, animals do not speak to humans."

Both Atticus *and* Aurora's eyes widened in surprise at this unusual news, but Drakkar carried on.

"She is getting used to a great deal. In fact, with the frequency things surprise her, it would seem nearly everything around her is new or unusual.

After she settles and hopefully after we uncover who is behind the plot to take her life, and, it would seem, mine, for the first two assassins targeted me, I will speak to her about what we know of where she comes from, and I will explain to her that she will be staying in this world with us without return."

The king nodded then stated, "It is good you mention the plot, Drakkar, for we need to discuss it. Your..." he again hesitated before again trying out the name, "*Finnie* may be from another world, but in this world, she is my daughter. And her life has been targeted twice."

"Yes," Drakkar agreed unnecessarily and impatiently to a statement he very well knew.

"Obviously, I do not like this no matter who she is. My realm is in the balance," Atticus pointed out.

"And my wife's life, Atticus," Drakkar returned.

Atticus glanced at his queen, but she did not return her husband's look. Aurora's gaze stayed steady on Drakkar.

"True," Atticus agreed after he looked back at Drakkar. "So what have you learned and what has been done?"

Drakkar answered swiftly, "Ruben interrogated the man he captured last night. The man who hired him is Lunwynian." Drakkar watched both king and queen's faces get tight at the news the conspirator was a citizen, not a foreigner, but he kept speaking. "I have sent Quincy and Balthazar to find him. They will make short work of that, as you know. Once found, he will be brought before us."

Atticus nodded and Drakkar continued speaking.

"In the meantime, those of my men who do not have to stay to see to my ships will come to Fyngaard. I assume you increased the guard at the Palace as I asked?"

"Of course," Atticus crossed his arms on his chest and leaned against his desk, "it is doubled."

"Excellent," Drakkar muttered then went on, "My men will stay in Fyngaard to increase the watch on Finnie. She does not leave this Palace, not even to wander the grounds, unless she is in my presence, or she has at least four of your guard and four of my men with her directly as well as scouting for danger that may be around her."

"That seems excessive," Aurora put in, then threw out a graceful hand in a way that was uncannily like Finnie. "This *is* Fyngaard."

"And it was on the steps of this Palace in which we now stand where the assassin was felled by your daughter's dagger, was it not?" Drakkar returned and he saw Aurora's teeth clench.

Atticus butted in, "This is true, Drakkar, but the Fyngaardians are sophisticated and cultured. A doubling of the king's guard and the men of The Drakkar wandering the city will cause unease. They are unused to this. Especially if their Winter Princess wanders her city under heavy guard. Normally, she wanders it freely, and her guard, as it didn't need to be," he stated this unable to hide his pride, "was never heavy."

"They can have the guard, my men and a secure princess or they can have Baldur's rule," Drakkar clipped. "Which do you think they would choose?"

Atticus closed his mouth.

Drakkar continued and when he did, his voice was low.

"I will remind you of what I am sure you will never forget. Finnie is not Sjofn. She has not, from a very young age, participated in the hunt. She has not felled numerous deer and other wild animals. Indeed, the sight of a dead deer made her visibly retch. She does not carry a dagger on her person at all times, and if she did, she would have no idea how to use it. Your daughter proved she could defend her person and her guard understood even before she proved it that, in such an event, she could handle herself." He paused to drive his point home. "My Finnie *cannot*."

"We understand, Drakkar," Atticus replied, his voice low as well, but his was placating.

Drakkar swept his gaze through Aurora before he locked his eyes on his king.

Then he said what he had called them both there to hear, what they both needed to understand and what they both needed to repeat into the right ears until the words swept Lunwyn and, indeed, the entirety of the Northlands.

"Indeed, I believe you do but you must now understand this. I have vowed to my Finnie that nothing will harm her, nothing will even touch her, and that I will keep myself from harm." He bent at the waist taking himself forward two inches toward his king when he finished, "If she comes to any harm, if she is even *touched*, I will command it instantly and the drakkar will rise."

Even Aurora pulled in an audible breath as Atticus's eyes grew wide and his face again paled.

"Drakkar—" Atticus started, his tone now downright soothing, but Drakkar shook his head.

"I will call the dragon, Atticus. I vow to you I will call them all. They will sweep this land at my command, and I'll have your throne. You know I do not wish it, but I will take it and the fire of my dragons will melt every flake of snow and every sheet of ice across this land and with it everything in their path, and they will do this as my vengeance for any harm coming to Finnie. If you do not do all in your power to see that my wife is safe, regardless she is no longer a daughter who has your blood in her veins, which means a child without your blood will eventually sit on your throne, I will call the dragon. I will not delay. I vow this to you."

"You are heard, Drakkar," Atticus whispered.

"Be certain the right people hear it too," Drakkar replied.

Atticus nodded.

Drakkar's eyes moved to Aurora, and she was observing him closely but did so giving nothing away.

But he knew she heard him too. Aurora always heard. Aurora made an art of listening.

He straightened and nodded to his sovereigns by name but not by right then turned to go, muttering, "We are done. I'm away to bathe and then get to my bride."

He'd almost gained the door when Aurora called his name.

He turned and caught her eyes.

"Your..." she too hesitated before she said softly, "*Finnie.* How did her parents die?"

"I do not know," Drakkar replied. "The elves did not tell me."

She nodded and he started to turn again when she again called his name, so he stopped and raised impatient brows to her.

"She came to..." another pause then a very soft, "a whole other world just to..." she pulled in a slight breath, "see them?"

"Indeed," Drakkar answered. "And in doing so, to see you," he reiterated.

Aurora held his gaze before she observed quietly, "She must have loved them very much."

"No," Drakkar stated. "In the last days as I told her of you, any mention, even in passing, of your names, her eyes would light, her cheeks would pink with excitement, her attention, always avid, would grow intense. She did not love her parents very much, my queen. They were her world. And she journeyed from that world to have them back. That is something beyond love, but I don't know what it is. What I do know is that they must have been remarkable to deserve that devotion."

Aurora held his eyes, and as she did, she gave him something she'd never given him nor had he ever seen her give anyone else, even her husband.

She visibly showed vulnerability.

Drakkar watched Queen Aurora pull her lips between her teeth as her eyes got bright with unshed tears. She released her lips and swallowed, blinking and the brightness in her eyes disappeared.

Then she said quietly, "I look forward to knowing your Finnie, Drakkar."

"I can assure you, you do," Drakkar replied quietly as well, dipped his chin to her and to his king then he walked out of the room.

BATHED AND DRESSED FOR DINNER, Frey moved down the hall to the door of the rooms he would be sharing with his wife in order to have a brief moment with Finnie prior to escorting her to dinner.

He was pleasantly contemplating how he would spend that brief moment as he turned the knob and entered their rooms.

He got two steps in, caught sight of his wife, and stopped dead.

Finnie was sitting in an armchair across the great space, her knees tight to her chest, a winter-white blanket tucked around her, and her cat Penelope was curled in a ball in the seat by her hip. Her head was bowed to a book, her white-blonde hair had been curled in a riot of waves and ringlets that fell down her back but was pulled up at the sides in jeweled clips. Her face was made up in a way that managed to succeed in what, until gazing on her, Frey would have thought was the impossible task of enhancing her already significant beauty. And he could see her even more generous than normal display of cleavage coming forth from a gown of shimmering ice blue that was exceedingly becoming to her complexion and coloring.

All of this was to such an extreme, he had to stop dead to give himself a chance to take it in.

Her head came up and her eyes slowly turned to him. When the fullness of their beauty hit him, Frey considered skipping dinner altogether. And as he considered this, he decided that later, much later, they could have something sent up.

This idea fled his mind when she said softly, yet listlessly, "Hey. You're back."

She then returned to her book.

These actions made Frey stay frozen for an altogether different reason as he studied his wife and her demeanor and registered a tone she'd never used and one which by no means suited her.

He closed the door and walked into the room, saying, "Your parents would like us to meet them for a drink prior to us sitting down to dinner."

Her head came up again, and she turned her eyes to him briefly, not indicating even a hint of excitement at this idea, before she looked away, nodded and reached to grab a ribbon to put in her book. She did this, closed it, set it on the table beside the chair and then gently nudged Penelope, who gave a sleepy, disturbed "mew" before jumping to the floor.

Frey had come to a stop in front of her when she tossed the blanket aside and stood, her gaze averted. She attempted to scoot out from in front of him to pass him.

His arm instantly moved to hook her at the waist and pull her in front of him, his other one curving around to hold her there.

Her head tipped back to look at him, and he felt his gut tighten when he saw a blankness that fitted her mother of this world far more than his Finnie.

"Is something amiss, wee one?" he asked, and she shook her head.

"Just tired and hungry," she spoke her lie before again looking away and moving to break from his arms.

They tightened and her gaze went back to him.

"I asked what was amiss, Finnie," he said softly.

"And I told you. I'm tired and hungry," she lied again. "Can we go to dinner?"

"In a minute," Frey stated. She pulled in breath and let it out, holding his gaze, waiting. Then he queried, "What's the matter?"

Her body grew tight in his arms and her brows inched together with irritation.

"Frey, I *told* you. I'm tired and hungry."

"This is not it," he replied.

"Yes it is," she returned.

"You're lying, wife," he stated, and she blinked, and after she blinked her cheeks flushed and her eyes flashed.

"Did you just say I was lying?" she whispered.

"I did because you are," he stated.

Her brows snapped together, and her irritation grew to visible annoyance. "I am not and anyway, if I was, you don't know me enough to know when I am."

"You're hiding something," Frey told her. "And I wish to know what it is."

She pulled against his arms and was nowhere near strong enough to dislodge them but was smart enough to give up before she snapped, "I'm not hiding anything."

"Wife," he gave her a gentle squeeze, "I have seen you tired, hungry, and tired *and* hungry. You do not lose the light in your eyes or the cheerfulness with which you hold your frame even when you are one, the other *or* both. Now, you're hiding something, and I wish to know what it is."

She glared up at him but didn't speak.

Therefore, he guessed, "Are you nervous about dinner with your parents?"

Her glare narrowed and she asked, "Why would I be nervous? They're my parents. We've had thousands of dinners."

This was a lie too, though he let that particular one pass.

"All right, if you're not nervous about your parents, then what are you not sharing with me?"

It was then she stated with not a small amount of ire, "Okay, Frey, actually, I *am* hiding something and it's *my* something to hide and you can be a big, strong guy, but if I have something on my mind I don't wish to share, I don't have to share it. So, suck it up because I'm *not* going to share it. All right?"

"Suck it up?" he asked quietly.

"Man up or..." she shook her head with frustration as she searched for words from both their worlds he would understand, "I don't know. You're just going to have to deal with it."

He dipped his face closer to hers and said carefully, "My wee Finnie, I do not like that you would keep anything from me."

"Tough," she retorted immediately, and his head went back as he again saw the flash in her eyes.

And he suddenly understood what that flash meant.

"Are you angry with me?" Frey asked.

"No," she lied again.

"Gods." He stared in her irate, still beautiful eyes. "You are. You're angry with me."

"I said I'm not, Frey."

"You lie again, Finnie. I see it in your eyes. Your anger is very clear and you're not hiding it. What, by the gods, I would like to know is what I did to deserve it. I've been gone not two hours."

She glared at him and kept her mouth shut.

"Finnie, we'll delay joining your parents until you tell me."

That was when her cheeks flushed, her eyes blazed and her jaw got tight, and before she could rein the words in, she spewed, "That's okay by me. I'll just call my maidservants and order trays to be brought up. Maybe, if you're lucky, *Viola* will bring them."

Bloody hell.

Her bloody maids had been talking.

"Finnie—"

"Let me go, Frey," she demanded, now pushing at his arms with her hands.

"Wife, look at me," he ordered, she did, and she stilled.

Then she suddenly lost control and shouted, "*I said, let me go!*"

At her losing hers, Frey felt his temper snag and therefore growled, "Calm down, wife."

She stopped pushing and glared at him.

"I see, you're done with her," she stated. "Three days, was it? That's a long time. I can see that you would be. Perhaps I should talk to my mother and father, see about letting her go. Would that be good for you?"

Damn it to hell.

Her *bloody* too informative, gods-damned *maids*.

"Finnie—"

"Well?" she cut him off to demand.

It was then he clipped, perhaps not cleverly, "*As you know*, wife, the Winter Palace is *yours*. *You* live in Fyngaard. Your parents reside in their castle in Snowdon and have returned here to prepare for the Gales. The lovely Viola is in *your* employ, and if it is your wish to let her go, then you've every right to do so."

"Then I'll see to that without delay," she returned hotly.

"That is your right," he shot back and continued, most definitely not cleverly, "Though it would be a shame to lose her charm serving your table."

She went completely still in his arms, but the pink fled her cheeks as the pain flashed in her eyes.

Gods damn it to hell.

"You didn't just say that," she whispered.

He tried to gather her closer, but her hands went instantly to his chest to hold herself back.

"Finnie, my love, this discussion is ridiculous. That was years ago. She's a servant. Just a servant. She didn't mean a gods-damned thing. They never do."

This, although she would have no way to know it, for a woman of his world, a princess especially, and Sjofn of the House of Wilde definitely would understand that a man like him would freely dally with a wench like Viola without thought or shame.

But apparently, a woman of Finnie's world did not think the same thing.

And he belatedly understood that it was very clearly the *wrong* thing to say.

He would learn this because her beautiful eyes closed down, shut him out, and she replied quietly, "Then let me educate you, Frey, if it was years ago or yesterday, if it was a servant or a duchess, to your wife, no matter what you think of her or what you think she thinks of you, it means everything. Now, let me *the fuck* go so I can have dinner with my parents."

The ugly word he didn't understand but she emphasized so tersely caused him to loosen his arms and she pulled instantly away. She then didn't delay in moving directly to the door.

She opened it, stood at it, turned back to him and called, "Are you coming?"

She needed him to guide her to the dining room for she had no earthly clue where she was going, and she didn't wish him to know she didn't.

And suddenly, their game annoyed him, but Frey moved across the room to his wife. However, when he got there, he carefully shut the door.

She glared at it then tipped her head back to glare at him.

He lifted a hand to curl around her neck and bent so his face was close to hers.

"We'll finish this discussion after dinner," he said gently.

"No we won't," Finnie retorted immediately, her voice a snap and it whipped across his frayed temper like a lash, causing him to lose hold on it so he squeezed her neck and got closer.

"Yes, wife, we will." His fingers again tensed at her neck, he dipped even closer to her, and his voice was a low rumble when he decreed, "We'll finish a number of things unfinished between us after dinner."

Her eyes widened, her face paled and her lips parted.

She understood him.

He let her neck go, opened the door, took his wife's hand and pulled her into the hall.

Then he dragged her down it, his strides long and angry, and as he did so he thought dinner with her parents was going to be interesting.

And it was going to be long.

Too long.

Therefore, he was going see to it that it ended as soon as possible.

He and his bride had vastly more important things to do.

14

SLEEP WELL, WIFE

"I've a marvelous idea," my dad announced as we stood outside the dining room having just finished a sumptuous five-course dinner that was sitting like a weight in my stomach. "I'll order a sleigh brought round and we'll go to Esmeralda's for a mug of that warm, liquid chocolate my Sjofn loves so dearly."

I thought this was a *great* idea mainly because both my mother and father were acting a lot more patient and even kind to me, if weirdly watchful. Though I put this down to them wondering how things were going with me and Frey.

And they *would* wonder since I didn't speak to him (at all) and barely looked at him all throughout dinner except to glare daggers at him when he specifically asked for Viola to serve him personally.

Yes, oh yes, he did exactly that.

The freaking dickhead *jerk*.

And, by the way, Viola was *very* pretty, and she didn't look a *thing* like me.

Ugh!

I also thought this was a great idea because it would mean delaying being alone with Frey. This was something I did *not* want because I was pretty certain I couldn't strangle him to death, but if I was lucky, I might get in a well-aimed kick that, if I did it as hard as I wanted, might mean the end to everyone's hopes that he'd provide a future king.

I also thought this was a great idea because a mug of warm liquid chocolate sounded pretty good regardless of the dinner sitting like a weight in my stomach (as, everyone knew, chocolate in any form sounded good no matter what) and a place called Esmeralda's sounded worthy of exploration.

I opened my mouth to agree wholeheartedly with this idea, but my freaking dickhead *jerk* of a husband got there before me.

"I'm afraid not, Atticus. Finnie explained she was tired prior to us joining you for dinner. So now I think it's best if my wife and I retire."

I turned stiltedly to him, tipped my head back and glared more daggers at him.

He looked down at me, completely impervious to my mental daggers and crossed his arms on his chest.

"Understandable, Drakkar," Dad mumbled then I felt him coming close to me as he continued to mumble, "It's been a long day for you both."

I wiped my face clean, turned to him and smiled what I hoped was close to genuinely as he leaned in and kissed my cheek distractedly.

But as his lips brushed my skin, I felt their touch like they were lasers. I closed my eyes at the beautiful pain and kept them closed as I memorized it.

He moved away and I opened my eyes to see Mom gazing at me, the skin around her eyes and mouth soft. Her expression, however, was blank, but I could tell she was thinking. About what, I didn't know.

She moved in and I braced because, although she'd been okay during dinner, I didn't know what to expect.

But I would have never expected her to give me a warm, albeit very short hug and say to me during it, "It's so lovely to have you back, my dear."

Then without further ado, as my mind imprinted the feel of her arms around me, they bid Frey a far less familiar but still relatively friendly, yet definitely watchful (see? way weird) goodnight, and they took off.

I watched them go.

Great.

Frey grabbed my hand and started dragging me to the stairs.

Great again!

I let him because I wasn't going to fight him out where servants, such as, say, *Viola* could see. I let him because it was undignified to struggle, and Mom taught me never to lose my dignity and all that jazz. But I *was* a princess in this world so *that* had become a moral imperative as everyone knew all princesses should do their utmost to keep their dignity. And, lastly, I let him because it sucked, but I knew if I fought, I would so totally *lose*.

He dragged me up the stairs and directly to my rooms, in through the door, and he closed it behind us softly. He leaned against it, arms crossed on his chest.

I had walked in several steps and turned to him. Seeing him settle, I crossed *my* arms on *my* chest.

Then I spoke.

"I'm afraid after living the simple life for nearly two months, all that rich food and wine have made me unwell, husband," I informed him, chin up, shoulders straight. "Although it was *served* with great skill." I watched his eyes flare as he caught my meaning, though it would have been hard to miss. "It's not sitting well in my stomach. I'll thank you to leave me to my bed and find your own chambers..." I paused then finished, "*Immediately.*"

A muscle ticked in his jaw scarily before he returned in a quiet, deadly voice, "You're my wife, Finnie. What's yours is mine and that includes your bed."

"All right," I returned instantly. "However, tonight, considering I feel unwell, and this place is gargantuan and *highly* populated, I'm sure for my sake you'll be able to find somewhere else to sleep. Or, perhaps, *not* sleep depending on whose bed you fall in."

That muscle ticked again. It scared the freaking beejeezus out of me mostly because the air in the room was stifling from the heat of Frey's anger. But I ignored it and held his eyes.

This lasted a long time, and I was about to give up and look away when he spoke again in that soft, lethal tone.

"I will take the time to explain a few things to you, wife. And I'll take this time before I peel off that charming dress you're wearing to *finally* discover what you wear under it and after that I'll peel off what you wear under your gowns to *finally* see the entirety of your charms. And after that I may or may not take my time to finally *enjoy* the entirety of those charms."

I felt my chest swell with panic, but I kept my stance, held his gaze and kept my mouth shut.

"I am Frey Drakkar," he announced oddly but his voice held weight. "And you know this, Finnie, *you know*," he stressed, his eyes flashing with anger, his voice rumbling with it, "but I'll explain what that means."

Ho boy.

I had a feeling this was not going to be good.

He kept talking.

"There has not been a Frey of the Drakkar for centuries. In ancient times, every generation birthed a Frey. That was, until one Frey betrayed the elves, betrayed his line and betrayed his country. The elves retreated to their underground realm, not to be seen for centuries. That was, not until my birth to the House of Drakkar and the Vallees declarations that I was, indeed, the first Frey for seven hundred and fifty years."

I had no idea what he was talking about, but I still sucked in a shocked breath because, obviously, that sounded important not to mention interesting.

"But the Vallees did not simply declare me the Frey. They also declared me *The* Drakkar."

I kept his gaze and kept my mouth shut, hoping despite myself he'd go on because I *still* had no idea what he was talking about.

Luckily (or unfortunately, depending on how you looked at it), Frey went on.

"This land and the House of Drakkar have not had A Drakkar for over fifteen hundred years."

Hmm.

That was obviously important and interesting too.

Frey kept speaking.

"And the Frey and The Drakkar have not been embodied in the same man since *before* ancient times. The gods...they learned not to do that. It would make one man too powerful. Even, if that man commanded his power right, more powerful than them."

That was when I sucked in breath and held it.

Oh my God.

I didn't know what that meant, exactly, I just knew it was big.

"As you know, the Frey commands the elves but The Drakkar...it is The Drakkar, my wee wife, who commands the dragons."

I let out my breath, but I couldn't stop my eyes from growing wide.

Dragons?

Frey kept going, "Over fifteen hundred years ago, after the last Drakkar died, the dragons entered their caves high in the mountains where no one can climb. They entered them to slumber and await the next call of their Drakkar. That call has not come for there has been no true Drakkar birthed to the House of my line. Not until me."

Now I was breathing heavily and staring at him because I couldn't pull my eyes away.

"The elves magic is powerful, mighty, more than any witch in any land.

More than the combined powers of the most accomplished witches of all lands. But the dragons...their power is without measure. They are immortal. Their scales cannot be pierced. Their talons are sharper than razors and cannot be broken. Their teeth and horns and the spikes on their tails are tipped with poison they can discharge at their command. Poison so strong, a drop would fell an elephant in seconds. And their tail carries so much strength one swipe and it would cut your Palace in two, leaving splinters in its wake. They are bigger than a house and they fly through the air. And I know, my Finnie, I know you know the tales of the heat of the fire they breathe."

I kept breathing hard. It wasn't fire but it burned my lungs, and I continued staring at him, not moving a muscle.

Even though he said I knew, he explained anyway. "That heat would incinerate a man in less than a second. It melts iron like candle wax. It could remold mountains."

Oh.

My.

God.

"And all of that, my wee wife, *all of it* is at my command."

Oh.

My.

God.

"The Frey who betrayed the elves also betrayed his throne, something else you know. He betrayed his throne and Lunwyn descended into turmoil. Wars were fought. Countless men, women *and* children died. Our beautiful Lunwyn descended into chaos for centuries as the throne passed from House to House until, finally, the House of Wilde secured it two centuries ago. But the rightful seat in that throne all in the land know is a," he leaned slightly forward, "*Drakkar.*"

Okay, one could say this wasn't getting any better.

Frey kept at it.

"And the Drakkar sitting that throne would definitely be The Frey and it would *most* definitely be *The* Drakkar. That means, wife, your father is king, and you are princess at *my* bidding. If I moved on your father's throne, the vast majority of your father's own army would either lay down their swords or carry them to fight for *me.*"

Yep, definitely not getting any better.

He leaned back and continued, "However, I do not wish these obligations. But I am Frey, I am The Drakkar. But even if I was not, I am of the

House of Drakkar, an aristocratic line that goes back farther than any other. But, even if not, nevertheless, we are *aristocrats*. I am not only a nobleman, I am *the* nobleman, Finnie. And in this land or any other, a nobleman does what he wishes *with whom* he wishes, without compunction, without shame and most definitely without *question*."

It was then, *I* leaned back, but I did it in a wrench like he'd struck me.

He saw it, his eyes narrowed, but he didn't relent.

I knew this when he said quietly, "Even if that question came from *his wife*."

I stood stock-still and stared at him.

His voice got quieter when he stated, "But you were not my wife then, Finnie. I barely knew you, but what I knew of you..." He hesitated then said, "We did not get along. This woman is a servant, and I can see you have a manner where you treat people equally, but she is *not* equal. She is a servant. I am an aristocrat. She knows her place and I was born to mine."

I swallowed.

Frey kept talking.

"No nobleman would take any woman against her will. If he does, he is not noble and will be stripped of his banner and the protection of his House. But I did not take her against her will. I enjoyed her and she enjoyed me—"

That was when I lifted my hand and whispered, "Stop talking."

He shook his head and pushed away from the door, saying, "You must understand this, wife."

"I understand." I took a step back as he started advancing. "I totally get it. You can stop talking."

Frey kept advancing while he kept speaking. "There are men who pledge to honor their wives, and they do, because their wives give them reason." I moved backward as he kept coming at me. "It could be you give me that reason and we grow into this type of marriage," he stated, and I kept retreating as he kept moving toward me.

And I did this staring at him in shock, and I had to admit, not a small amount of despair.

Grow into that type of marriage?

"But what I do, Finnie, and who I do it with is none of your concern, be she servant or duchess. I'm explaining this to you patiently so the next time you learn of something like this, you won't show me the same disrespect you did at your table with your parents, speaking not one word to me and withholding your eyes from mine."

The next time?

I hit wall and Frey hit me, his body in my space, his big hands spanning my waist, his head tipped down so his eyes could hold mine prisoner.

"You..." I started, cleared the frog that was all of a sudden in my throat and kept going, "just last night, you told me the measure of a man is how he cares for his bride."

His brows knitted and he agreed, "I did."

"So," I whispered, "what does it say about a man who dumps his bride in a filthy cabin, leaves her there to fend for herself, comes back and shows her gentleness and kindness, which, incidentally, she practically has to beg for, then brings her home to a palace only to make her sit at a table and watch while his ex-lover serves him food? Tell me Frey, what measure is that of a man?"

His fingers tensed into my flesh, and he whispered back, "I thought we'd come to an understanding, you and I, about what was past and what we were moving toward in our future."

"I did too," I replied. "But apparently, I was wrong."

Really wrong.

Heartbreakingly wrong.

His hands slid up to rest under my ribs and they again tensed when he started, "Finnie—"

But I cut him off. "You left Finnie back at your hunting cabin, Frey. I'm Princess Sjofn here to you. But, make no mistake, husband, *you* left her back there. I was willing to bring her with us, but she is now *gone*."

His eyes flashed and his hands slid up to span my ribs as he growled, "Wife."

"Careful of your hands, Frey," I whispered. "A nobleman doesn't take a woman against her will."

That gained me another flash before he stated, "I see, you have a tantrum about me bedding a servant at the same time you threaten to withhold from me. Does that make sense to you?"

"Absolutely," I replied. "Because earlier this evening, you walked in on me, hurt about what I'd learned about you and that you were the kind of man who felt free to humiliate me in my own home. *Then*, not an hour later, you *further* humiliated me at the same time you rubbed my nose in precisely what was injuring me. For five days, you stopped at nothing to convince me you are a kind man, a thoughtful man and a gentle man. But I know I should never forget what my father drilled into my head for years and years. And that is that first impressions never lie, and you may command the power of elves and dragons, but you are none of those kinds of man."

His eyes flashed again, and if I read them right, he seemed even more pissed than before.

In fact, infuriated.

"Tell me you jest," he rumbled and that was when *my* brows knitted.

"Why on earth would I jest about that?"

His fingers dug into my ribs and his face dipped so close he was the only thing I could see.

"Was it *you* I humiliated, Finnie? Am I treated to this behavior from you tonight due to *your* injury?"

I held my breath and stared in his eyes.

Good God.

Did he know I wasn't Sjofn?

He couldn't know. There was no possibility.

Could he?

I held his eyes, and he held mine unblinking, but he looked strangely like he was waiting for me to say something.

When I didn't, suddenly Frey let me go, turned and stalked to the door, saying, "Prior to joining Viola, who I know will gladly give me what I should be getting from my wife, I'll send her up with something for your stomach."

That stomach contracted physically, my back pressing against the wall as if I'd suffered a physical blow.

He opened and stepped out the door but stopped, turned and seared me with one of his ferocious scowls that I'd forgotten could be so terrifying.

"Sleep well, wife," he called.

Then he was gone.

15

WE WOMEN CARRY
MANY BURDENS

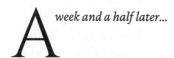 *week and a half later...*

I watched my arrow fly over the huge target and get stuck in the trees beside the Palace.

I bit my lip and slowly turned to my dad to see his gaze was pointed in the direction of where my arrow landed, and his shoulders were slumped.

I'd disappointed him.

Again.

Crap.

"I seem to..." I hesitated when his attention came to me, it did it before he could fully hide the disappointment and my heart wrenched. "Pull up right before I let go." I finished.

Yeah, pull up, and to the side, and one time down so the arrow embedded in the turf five feet in front of the target.

"Indeed, daughter," he muttered, sighed and stated, "Why don't we finish for today?"

He jerked his chin at a boy standing close who came forward hurriedly to take my bow. I pulled the quiver that was strapped across my chest over my head and handed it to him with a smile.

Then I looked at the target that had three of my arrows in it, none of them in any of the lines and another boy was rushing around gathering arrows, but he was rushing around *behind* the target.

I sucked at archery. Totally. Playing it on Wii did *not* set you up for the real thing.

And Sjofn obviously didn't, and my dad was obviously proud of her skill.

"I seem to have lost my touch," I muttered to Dad.

He put a hand to my elbow and started to lead me through the snow to the side door of the Palace.

"Yes, this is what it seems," he muttered back.

"How about we come back out tomorrow?" I asked, forcing brightness in my tone and I watched him turn his head to me.

And that was when I saw what I saw more than once when I was with him—a weird kind of sorrow that hurt to see. I didn't get it, but it was definitely there.

Maybe it was a father's natural reaction as he was coming to terms with his daughter getting married and moving on to another man in her life. But it didn't seem like that. And it got stronger every time we came out and tried this archery business, and we'd been out four days in a row.

I'd been super excited when he'd approached me and asked if I'd like to go out and shoot arrows. First, I wanted to shoot arrows, I'd never done that before except on a video game (which obviously didn't count). Second, I wanted to spend time with my dad and the last week, Dad had seemed hesitant and distant with me, so I jumped at the chance.

Contradictorily, Mom had warmed towards me.

Well, as warm as my mom of this world could be, which wasn't super warm.

My mom was giggly and cuddly, always teasing and tickling and snuggling, both Dad *and* me, and she had given these traits to me.

Queen Aurora was nothing like that.

Still, she no longer seemed infuriated or impatient with me and often sought my company, though we spent our time together while she embroidered, which I found mind-numblingly boring (embroidery, that was).

Mom, however, was *not* boring. Although reserved and not very talkative, she had a skill with drawing people out, and not often, but in moments that surprised you that made it even better, she displayed a very dry wit.

And she had taken me into Fyngaard several times and that was when we had (borderline) fun together. Clearly, she liked shopping. Definitely, I liked it. And one could say the liquid chocolate at Esmeralda's was *brilliant* (it wasn't hot cocoa, like I expected it would be, it was actual *liquid chocolate*—a thick, rich, dark chocolate you could spoon up or dunk in the almond biscuits and glazed, fried, cake-like fingers they served with it, and it was freaking *divine*).

Fyngaard was most assuredly a cosmopolitan city with high fashion, which meant the dressmakers and the ensembles of passersby were out of sight, and then there were the sophisticated cafés and elegant restaurants that served fabulous food.

I loved the city, and I liked my mom. It was weird she was so different and sometimes it freaked me out. But, even so, it was wonderful to spend time with her, hear her voice, sometimes see her small smile or her eyes light and rarely, but they were treasured, feel her touch on my arm or hand.

Dad was easier to like. He was much like my father in ways that made my heart swell and clutch at the same time. He was gregarious and had an open, broad sense of humor. I heard his laughter quite often in the Palace and frequently saw him smiling at people.

Just not with me.

Another boy rushed to open the door for us (I had learned royalty didn't do things like open doors, or, well, pretty much anything but walk to get places, eat food people served and breathe on their own).

Dad replied distractedly as we entered the Palace, "Yes, Sjofn. I'll look forward to that. Tomorrow, same time."

He started to turn down a hall and I called, "Da...I mean, Father."

Shit!

My girls kept telling me I didn't call them Mom and Dad but Father and Mother.

He turned and looked at me, visibly forcing a smile.

My heart clutched again when I saw it.

"I'll find my way again," I promised softly yet fervently. "So much has happened and I just, um...lost my focus. With practice, I'll find it again, even if I have to come out every day. I'll do it, and I promise, I'll find it."

He studied me with something working in his eyes then he walked the two steps back to me, lifted a hand and touched the side of my hair while his gaze never left mine.

Then he said softly back, "Thank you, Sjofn, but maybe now that you're married you have another focus. Perhaps we can spend time finding something new we enjoy sharing together. What do you think of that?"

My heart lightened and I grinned at him before I admitted, "Well, I kind of actually *like* archery." His eyes brightened at this news. I took heart and I went on, "I just for some reason have become not very good at it. I'm totally into keeping it up and getting better again if you're happy to help me."

His eyes stayed bright when he replied quietly, "I'm more than happy to help you, daughter."

My grin became a smile.

Father smiled back and finally it wasn't fake.

"Until tomorrow," he muttered.

"Cool," I muttered back.

His head jerked a little at my word (and I reminded myself that I really had to speak like they did in this world), but he kept looking at me smiling. Then he bent and touched his lips to my cheek, turned and walked away.

I stood in the hallway watching him go and grinning to myself.

Well, that went well. Finally. Thank God.

I turned and started to make my way to my rooms because I knew, soon, the dressmakers would be there to do a fitting for my gown for the Bitter Gales.

I had learned from my girls that the Gales was a big, resplendent ball that was preceded by a huge hunt—this one of two hunts and balls the King and Queen of Lunwyn threw every year. The Bitter Gales was held on the shortest, coldest day of the year, the hunt in the forest around Fyngaard and the ball in the Winter Palace. And the Solar Gales was held on the longest, warmest day of the year thrown at the king and queen's castle, Rimée Keep in a city called Snowdon.

One could say I was looking forward to the Bitter Gales like I would look forward to having bamboo shoots shoved under my nails. That was to stress *attending* it, not dressing for it, since my gown was kickass.

This was because I would be attending with my husband.

In the last week and a half, I had barely seen Frey and I had not spoken to him once, and obviously, he had not spoken to me. I'd seen him three times, all from a distance, all only in passing and only once did his head turn to me. When his eyes caught mine, he gave me a minor chin lift then he looked instantly away.

That hurt. A lot. Too much. More than it should.

But it did.

And the fact he kept away not only from my person, but my bed also hurt.

A lot. Too much.

More than it should.

I now had four girls to guide my way and help me to understand this world better and they took this job seriously, were very informative and what made it fun was that they thoroughly enjoyed learning about my world too.

So, in the last week and a half, I'd learned a lot about Lunwyn, about this world, and mostly about Frey.

The good news was, my girls had asked around and he wasn't sleeping with Viola as he had threatened, or with *any* of my servants (the girls checked, they were, I was learning, thorough).

The bad news was, they had no idea where he was sleeping. But it wasn't at the Palace.

The good(ish) news was, in learning about my husband, I'd learned why my maidservants were so keen for me to hook up with him.

This was because sex was not at all taboo in Lunwyn. Brides were not expected to be virgins and sexual exploration for boys and girls started early, around fourteen or fifteen. In fact, it was encouraged in order to prepare you for a fulfilling sex life during marriage.

"Dalliances" (as my girls called them) amongst unmarried people were frequent, often short-lived and were without any disgrace. "Affairs" or relationships between unmarried people lasted longer and were also frequent.

And, as a matter of course in their culture, with a man like The Drakkar on my hook, with his looks, wealth (and he was wealthy, I'd learned that too), aristocratic line and the sheer power he held, my girls expected me to be all for that. To want it (badly) and work for it—beyond anything.

They were, they made clear, there to help any way they could.

And when it became painfully obvious I wasn't getting it, they did not pry, but they exuberantly went about trying to get me to thaw my chill toward "The Drakkar" (as Frey was known and always referred to) and they did this by sharing a great deal about him.

I had learned he was thirty-six (shocking, he had the manner of a man much older though he didn't look it).

I had learned he commanded a fleet of five ships (five!) and all the men it would take to man those ships plus his own highly trained, personal raiding party of which Thad, Ruben and the other men I had met were members.

I had learned that along with his lodge, his chalet, his hunting cabin, his fishing cottage and his ships, he also owned a chateau in the country of Hawkvale and apartments in a city in Fleuridia.

This made it more of a bummer that we were not talking, and it didn't seem we ever would again because, I had to say, I would have liked to see *all* of these places.

Intriguingly, I learned that, although Frey was a Raider, he was not like the other ones who traveled long distances to pillage foreign, often more primitive lands, lands that did not have the resources to seek retribution against the Raiders or even Lunwyn for their raids.

No, Frey's raids had purpose. They were, as the girls informed me firmly, *just*.

This was because the Frey who had betrayed his throne and cast the country into chaos had also sold or lost Lunwyn's many treasures and sacred relics and those that weren't sold or lost disappeared in a variety of ways in the ensuing centuries of turmoil.

And often, when not sailing on some secret mission for his realm (the girls and everyone knew of these but did not know details, obviously, because they were secret), he was sailing to retrieve Lunwyn's lost riches. These included priceless scepters, chalices, crowns, orbs and objects that held Lunwynian, dragonian or elfin magic.

Frey had been very successful with these endeavors, and on top of the extraordinary things he'd shared about himself, which would clearly demand the respect of all of Lunwyn for obvious reasons, he'd actually *earned* their respect by returning these important national treasures to their homeland after centuries of them being lost.

I had to admit, I respected him for these endeavors too. Not to mention, him going after them and securing them was cool, *way* cool, like out-of-an-action-movie cool.

I had also learned from my girls that the House of Drakkar might be the longest running noble House in Lunwyn and the first known rulers of the land (which, at that time, included Middleland where my Uncle Baldur now ruled), but it was currently the least respected and most definitely the least liked.

This was because, when the Frey that went astray did his dire deeds, the House of Drakkar, like Lunwyn on the whole, descended into chaos. Without A Frey or A Drakkar born to the line, the males of the House stopped their raiding. Unrest and infighting prevailed, and from the stories my girls told me, it was *far* from pretty. Brothers killed brothers. Wives poisoned husbands and (the very next day on one occasion) married her husband's brother, uncle, cousin, who she'd conspired with to take over the House. Sons plotted against fathers. And sisters competed bitterly to make the best match to strengthen the line of Drakkar.

Although the House of Drakkar held vast wealth and property across Lunwyn, they were known to be ruthless in business, and more often than not untrustworthy and autocratic with their servants and those who worked their lands.

They were also known to be superior, condescending and dedicated to the order of things.

That was to say they were nobles and everyone else were little people and everyone knew their place, stayed in their place and served their purpose.

This, clearly, they'd instilled in Frey.

But that was, strangely, all they instilled in Frey. For the first time in over seven hundred years, his birth heralded a true leader in the House of Drakkar, and it was known widely his mother and father were overjoyed. Not to mention filled with conceit that they had created the undisputed head of their House.

But, to my shock, the girls told me that at thirteen, Frey had walked away from all of that. He'd walked away from his family, his home and the House of Drakkar, boarded a ship, talked its captain into employing him and turned his back on that life and his House.

And he never went back. In fact, to this day, he had very little to do with his House except carry their name.

Although he went on to own many properties, amass great wealth (for when sailing, Frey didn't only raid, he also loaded his ships' stores with goods and brought them back to Lunwyn to trade), command his own fleet and the men who sailed it, he had nothing to do with his House. Except the fact that he bore their name, the stamp of aristocracy they drilled into him growing up and the command of elves and dragons he'd somehow inherited through their blood.

This, I had to admit, considering the stories about his family, I respected too.

And, I had to admit as I made my way through my Palace to my rooms, it was becoming clear to me that I might have overreacted a *wee* bit about Frey and his dalliance with Viola.

He couldn't know it (though, I couldn't shake the uncomfortable feeling he did even though this was impossible), it was not *me* he'd humiliated but the other Sjofn. And he'd thought she was a lesbian, or, the girls told me, they were referred to here as guenipes.

And the girls knew all about Sjofn's tendencies, which also, considering the sexual openness, were not frowned upon in either sex, unless of course the guenipe happened to be a princess and needed to bring forth a future king. Therefore, Sjofn had not only hidden her preferences, doing so for her country and her father, the king, she'd never allowed herself to act on them and vowed to her girls that in this world, for country and king, she never would (which was extremely sad).

Because of this (and Frey knowing it), it was doubtful Sjofn would care about Frey getting it on with Viola, if Viola was her servant or not. And it was definite that Sjofn wasn't really allowed to care even if she would because what Frey said held true from my girls. He was a man, he was an aristocrat, and he could do as he wished, when he wished and with whom he wished.

Although dalliances and affairs before marriage were commonplace, after marriage (yep, you guessed it), the wife desisted in these behaviors, but it was not expected for the husband to do the same. It was common-place for husbands to honor their wives and only their wives, most specifi-cally amongst those of the lower classes, but also some aristocrats. But it was not unheard of for a husband to do as he would, and the wife was expected to turn the other cheek.

This did not sit well with me. But I had to remind myself that I was not in my world. I was here. And Frey could have no idea I was from another world, how that world was and how it looked on these things and unfortu-nately was justifiably livid that I had an expectation that any Lunwynian woman, and especially a wife, should most definitely not have.

This sucked.

It also meant, as much as it chafed, I was in the wrong.

I just didn't know what to do about it.

Because, although he was within his rights to do as he wished, espe-cially since we were not married at the time he took Viola to his bed, he *had* asked her to serve the table right in front of me.

There was, of course, the small fact that, back when the deed was done, I had no clue he or his world even existed, and he still had no clue mine did. So he was right in his weird questioning if he had actually injured *me*. He had not. I had just grown into my place in this world, and I forgot that it actually *wasn't* my place.

But still, Frey rubbing my nose in his dalliance and the mean-spirited way he did it, well...*that* was *not* nice.

And *that* was what was holding me back from doing anything at all.

Because that hurt. A lot.

Too much.

I'd ascended the stairs and was moving down the hall toward my rooms thinking that what sucked the most was that I missed him.

A lot.

Too much.

Logically, in the recesses of my head, I recognized this distance was probably good. Although I enjoyed spending time with the Frey I'd come to know and would have definitely enjoyed spending more time with him doing more things with him, specifically some of the things we could have been doing, the smart thing to do was keep a distance.

I'd been getting in too deep.

Illogically and in the forefront of my mind, I wanted what we had back.

And that, too, was a lot.

Too much.

My girls were fun to be with. They laughed often and Sjofn was right. It was very clear they were trustworthy, and they had been immensely helpful. I had a great time with them. I was enjoying spending time with Mother and discovering Fyngaard. I definitely liked learning more about this world because it was all very strange but *very* cool. Being a princess in a Palace, I'd learned, pretty much rocked. And I was making inroads with Father, which pleased me immensely.

But on Valentine's line of happiness, I was no longer anywhere near bliss. I was no longer smack dab in the middle of happiness either.

I was definitely at the lower end, hovering around contentment.

And I was there, I knew, because I didn't have Frey.

I opened my door and stopped before entering when I saw Mother in the armchair across the room, her legs crossed, her long fingernails scratching Penelope's ruff. A Penelope who was lying on my mother's thigh with her eyes closed, purring.

Hmm.

This was unusual. If Queen Aurora wanted to spend time with me, she sent a servant to tell me she wished my attendance.

I wondered why she was there, and I worried the reason was not good.

Her regard came to me, and she greeted, "Hello, my Sjofn."

I took her in. Her face was blank thus gave no clues.

Damn.

From past experience with her, I did not know if this was good or bad. She'd been warmer, but I'd also learned from my girls that Queen Aurora could be moody, her expectations were high, and those expectations were significantly elevated when it came to her daughter. Who knew what I could do to make her minimal warmth disappear and the frost return? It could be anything.

Therefore, I decided to tread cautiously.

I closed the door and moved into the room, replying, "Hello, Mother."

She stopped scratching Penelope and motioned with a graceful sweep of her hand to the bed.

"Sit with me, daughter."

I nodded and went to the bed, sitting on the side. Penelope opened her eyes slowly, took me in then jumped down. She waddled across the floor, hunkered in preparation to shift her massive bulk from floor to bed then she jumped. She waddled to me and settled with her booty to the duvet but paws and chest on my thigh, and I started scratching her ruff.

Penelope knew who her momma was, and I knew this because she purred, "Mrrrr, hullo, Mummy."

"Hullo, baby," I whispered to my cat. She purred louder. I looked to Queen Aurora.

She looked down at Penelope then up at me and her lips tipped up slightly. It wasn't the first time I thought she was a lot like Valentine, except without the edge of creepy and weird.

"The dressmakers have already arrived with your gown, but I've asked them to wait for a few minutes so I could visit with you," Mother announced.

I took in a short preparatory breath and nodded. But I didn't say anything. I wanted to see what she had to say.

She didn't delay, and when she spoke it was soft and almost gentle.

"I needed to discuss with you something that has been troubling me."

I tipped my head to the side to encourage her to go on but spoke no words.

She took this in and continued, "I cannot imagine, Sjofn, that you would think it escapes me or your father that there seems to be..." she hesitated, studying me closely, "*distance* between you and The Drakkar."

Ho boy.

I was afraid it was something like this. And I was afraid something like this was something that would herald the return of the frost.

I bit my lip and nodded my head slightly to agree with her observation without saying anything and thus giving anything away.

She read my agreement and took in a slight delicate breath.

"This troubles me for it seems very..." she hesitated, "*odd*. Especially coming so close on the heels of your return. A return upon which, immediately, The Drakkar demanded your father and my attendance to inform us that he was infinitely disturbed at the attempt on your life, and we were to do everything in our power to keep you safe. Something," she rushed slightly to say, "we would do, obviously, since you are our beloved Sjofn."

I kept my eyes firm on her and didn't speak, mostly because I didn't know what to say nor did I know what to feel at what she'd said about Frey.

I didn't need to say anything. Queen Aurora was not near done.

"This disturbed him, as I am guessing with your detachment from your new husband you may not understand, because in the short time you were with him, he made it very clear that he'd come to care about you."

I felt my heart clench at the same time my breath started escalating.

She kept talking.

"It would seem, the way he spoke of you, he'd come to do this deeply. Perhaps," she paused and continued to study me, "even more deeply than he understands. Definitely," another pause, "more deeply than it would appear *you* understand."

I kept silent and this was mainly because I'd started semi-panting and I was thinking I might be in the early stages of cardiac arrest.

"He called you sweet," she whispered, her eyes intense on my face, which I knew had grown pale at these words. Words I liked. Words that meant the world to me. "He said you had a strong spirit. He said everything you say, he finds interesting. He told us he enjoys your humor and your smiles."

I swallowed, shocked these words could even come out of Frey's mouth, even if he *did* feel that way. I was also stunned and experiencing the weird sensation of being both heartbroken and immensely pleased that he actually did.

As all this hit me, I pressed my lips together as my throat started to clog.

Mother kept going. "And he shared with us that he had vowed to you to keep you safe from harm and while doing this, he told us if anything were to befall you, he would unleash the dragons as vengeance."

I blinked, not in confusion, but in total shock.

Queen Aurora didn't miss it, as I was guessing she didn't miss much, and she nodded.

"Yes, my dear, that is what he said. The Drakkar promised to unleash the dragons, beasts that have not flown across this land for well over a millennium. Beasts that could cause damage and havoc the likes of which cannot be borne. Beasts that are not called upon except to defend our frost-covered land or to utilize their awesome power as service to our people. Your husband made it clear that *we* were to make it clear to anyone who would listen that if anything were to harm you, he would call upon his beasts to wreak vengeance. And this, my daughter, is not an idle threat to make. This, Sjofn, is extraordinary."

Oh my God.

Oh my *God*.

I said nothing and she moved. Uncrossing her legs and shifting to the edge of her seat, she leaned forward, elbows to knees in a casual pose the like I'd never seen her adopt.

And then she kept speaking.

"It is my duty as queen of this land to service my husband who rules it, but also to be a good wife, to stay quiet, listen and *observe*," she said softly. Then even more softly, she got to the meat of the matter by saying, "I know of Viola."

I sucked in an audible breath, and she nodded.

"I know of her, Sjofn, and I saw your face when The Drakkar ordered she attend the table."

I couldn't stop myself from closing my eyes and looking away in an effort to hide what her words were making me feel *and* the intensity of it.

I opened them and looked back at her when I heard her shift. I watched her move to stand in front of me, looking down.

"My dear Sjofn," she whispered. "We women carry many burdens. This is one of them, I'm afraid."

I held my breath as she lifted her hand and tenderly cupped my cheek before she continued.

"I, too, had an arranged marriage and I, too, struggled in the beginning to build my relationship and earn the love of your father. I was enamored with him on sight. He was the most beautiful man I ever beheld, but he was also so full of life, so full of humor, it was immensely appealing."

She unusually shared these juicy morsels, and I felt my eyes sting with tears as she went on.

"But he was king and could do as he would. That said, even though I understood, his dalliances wounded me, and they did so deeply."

She leaned slightly closer and kept whispering.

"And thus, my Winter Princess, I learned to do all I could to make it so he would not need such encounters. I did this instead of making it clear they offended me, something your father disliked." She leaned back and smiled a smile that almost, but not quite, reached her eyes. "However, he did *not* dislike my efforts to make him no longer seek these relations and..." she paused, her hand shifting to my jaw, her thumb then sweeping my cheekbone, her smile finally reaching her eyes, "he *still* doesn't."

I stared up at her silent, but I felt my lips twitch.

Apparently, Father got it regular.

"Do you understand me, my darling girl?" she asked softly.

I nodded. I understood her. Totally.

Her face went soft, and she murmured, "Good."

She dropped her hand and moved to the door while I turned to watch, her sweet, soft touch still tingling on my skin, her smiling eyes burned on my brain.

She stopped at the door and looked at me.

"The dressmakers have left the undergarments they have made for you to wear under your Gales gown in your dressing chamber. You may don them now in preparation for the fitting. I will find one of your maidservants to bring the dressmakers to you so you can be done with this chore and get on with whatever other..." she paused with meaning, "*pressing matters* you intend to see to today."

Not exactly a subtle hint so it wasn't lost on me.

It was time to seek out The Drakkar.

Shit.

She waited and she did this with obvious expectation.

I gave her what she expected.

"Okay, Mother," I whispered.

She lifted her chin majestically and I decided I had to practice that. The way she did it was way cool.

Then she moved gracefully through the door like she floated on air rather than walked on rug-covered wood, and she was gone.

16

SHE MISSED YOU

I stood in my dressing room wearing a pair of skintight, delicate, black silk undies that had an abundance of exquisite lace at the seat of my ass. I also had on a black satin, boned corset that tied up the front with a blood-red ribbon that pushed up my breasts. Under this was a red silk, loose-fitting, camisole-type thing that had a short, dense, lace ruffle around the edge, a black ribbon that drew it tight against my flesh and showed serious cleavage.

I had one foot on the lounge because I was connecting the second of a pair of the silkiest, flimsiest, most *divine* black silk stockings to the back garter that ran from the corset over my booty to the hose.

And I was thinking that the underwear in this world rocked in a big way because not only was all this hot, it was also impossibly comfortable. And those silk stockings, even in a parallel universe nowhere near as advanced as mine, were the most extraordinary pieces of hosiery I'd ever touched.

And I was also thinking that any man, especially one who commanded dragons, would dig this underwear.

In a big freaking way.

Yes, that was exactly what I was thinking, at the same time wondering how in the hell to find that man and then find the words to apologize to him in order to sort our shit out (and I was thinking the underwear might be useful) when the door opened.

"Hey," I started to say, turning my head to who I expected to be one of my girls leading in the two dressmakers.

But instead seeing Frey standing statue-still, hand still on the door handle, eyes aimed at my ass.

I went statue-still too and took him in.

Okay, it was safe to say from the look on his face he *definitely* liked the underwear.

And it was also safe to say from the panic that seized my innards that I was *definitely* not ready for him to see me in it.

This was why I put my foot down, whirled and ran across the room to the screen that had my robe thrown over it.

I got there. I even got my hand on the robe. But the silk was soon gone from my hand because Frey got there with me, and he jerked it right out of my grasp.

Ho boy.

I turned to face him, eyes wide, breaths coming fast like I'd run a two-hundred-yard dash and not across a room, my mind reeling for the right words to say to sort our shit out. But with one look in his eyes, both heated and enraged, not one word came to mind.

"I think," he growled, "don't you, that at the very least I'm entitled to see the woman who is supposed to be my wife without cover."

I stared up at him, close to panting.

Yep, definitely enraged.

That was when I did the smartest thing I could do.

I retreated.

Quickly.

And Frey advanced just as quickly, invading my space with every backward step I made until I slammed against the wall. He pushed right in. Hips to my belly, he pinned me to the wall.

Oh shit.

I had to arch my back to tip my head to look at him, which pressed my belly into his hips.

Shit!

"Frey—" I started, and his name was breathless. But I stopped saying whatever it was that was going to come out of my mouth when I heard gasps from across the room.

And I knew the dressmakers had arrived.

I knew Frey heard them too, but he didn't release my eyes and I couldn't look away as he barked an obviously impatient and equally infuriated, "*Out!*"

My body jerked with the noise.

Oh shit, shit, *shit!*

The door closed.

Shit.

"Frey—"

He cut me off this time by saying, "I've come to inform you..." He paused, his eyes moved to my rising and falling chest then back to my face. "*Wife*," he spat, and my stomach clenched. "That I'm away in an hour. Business. I'll be gone at least a month, likely longer."

That was when my stomach wrenched, searing pain up through my lungs and even in my throat.

And because of this, all I could manage was a whispered, "What?"

"I'm away in an hour," Frey repeated.

He was away in an hour.

In an hour he was away.

Without me.

"But...but the Bitter Gales—" I started.

He interrupted me to bite off, "Is there reason for me to escort you to the Gales?"

"Uh..." Oh shit. Think Finnie! "Yes, you...you're, um...my husband. A husband—"

"I'm not, Sjofn. There are many things I am but one thing I know I am not and that is your husband."

That hurt. God, it hurt so bad, I had to close my eyes and turn my face away from the anger in his.

And it wasn't him saying he wasn't my husband.

It was him calling me Sjofn.

I was not Sjofn. I was Finnie. His wee Finnie. I was not the Sjofn he knew and hated.

I was not.

But I'd asked for that.

Shit. I'd asked for it.

I felt my throat clog as my breaths kept coming fast, my breasts brushing his chest as they came.

Then I felt the tip of his finger glide along the dense ruffle at the edge of my camisole, light against my skin. Gentle, sweet and unbelievably sexy.

I closed my eyes tighter, and my breaths came faster as hope budded at his touch.

His finger went away.

I missed it when it was gone and clenched my eyes tight as the tears rushed up my throat.

"Enjoy your Gales, Sjofn," he said softly but his tone wasn't gentle. It was distant and that hurt too. "I'll see you upon my return."

He started to move away, but I looked at him then, and I knew, hells bells, I knew when I opened my eyes there were tears there.

Tears!

From me!

But they were there, and I didn't have it in me to make them go away.

And this was because I really, *really* did not want *him* to go away.

My chest still moved, rising and falling rapidly as my mind went blank to everything but the thought of him going.

But he not only stopped moving away, he had grown completely still as his eyes stayed riveted to mine and there was no way to stop the one tear that dropped and slid down my cheek. I watched him watch it as it went all the way down, falling from my jaw and landing on my chest.

His gaze came back to mine when I decided what I needed to say.

And when I did, I whispered, "I change my mind, Frey. I really don't like it when you call me Sjofn. Please don't call me that anymore."

I barely got out the last word when he was back in my space. One of his arms sliced around the small of my back, the other hand plunged into my hair, fisting and pulling back as well as tilting my head to the side.

Then his mouth slammed down hard on mine.

Instantly his opened, mine reciprocated, and there it was.

I was back. He was back. And having him, I shot straight up the line of happiness toward bliss.

But this was not a gentle kiss. This was not sweet. This was charged, greedy, and that was coming from the both of us. I took, he took, and the way we took I knew there wasn't ever going to be enough.

My arms had wound around his neck, and I pressed deep into him. When I did, Frey didn't break the connection of our mouths as he leaned deep into me, arching me back as his arm slid over my ass and I knew what he wanted.

I helped by hopping up and circling his hips with my legs. Even before I got them around him, he was turning, walking, still drinking from my mouth as he prowled to my bedroom.

Then I was on my back in the softness of my bed, his heavy weight on me. I arched up, tensing my limbs around him to push deep like I wanted him to absorb me.

It was then he tore his mouth from mine and his blazing eyes locked with my own.

"Do not let your body ask for that which you aren't ready, my wee one," he growled his warning.

And he did it while calling me his wee one.

God, I missed that.

"I know what I want, honey," I whispered, watched his eyes flare then his arms went from around me. I felt his fingers at the sides of my panties and then I heard the material tear.

Yes.

Oh yes. Yes, yes, *yes*.

My hands went to his sweater at the back, clenching in, pulling up as his fingers went to the gusset of my undies, yanking them free.

"Hurry," I whispered.

"Patience," he muttered then he lifted his arms for me.

I pulled his sweater free, baring his fantastic chest. His hand went immediately to his breeches.

"Hurry, baby," I pleaded, pressing into him with my hips and rounding him again to hold him tight in my arms, loving the feel of his sleek, hard-muscled skin against my hands.

"Gods," he muttered, eyes on mine and I knew my gaze was filled with all the hunger I was feeling for him. Then his head dropped, his mouth captured mine and his tongue invaded as his cock thrust inside.

My back arched and my low moan drove down his throat.

Oh yes. Yes. Yes, *yes, yes*!

God, he felt so *fucking* good.

He thrust into me, hard, fast, deep and not close to gentle. I lifted my hips to get him deeper, encourage him to go faster, help him to ride me hard.

I broke my mouth from his as it built, fast. God, so fucking fast. And hot, God, the heat was going to reduce me to ashes. And because of that I couldn't take his tongue anymore.

I shoved my face in his neck, held on and gloried in the fierce jolts his deep thrusts scored into my body as I begged against his neck, "Harder."

I barely got out the word before my head flew back, pushing into the bed, my neck arching, my back arcing, my limbs tightening, and I cried out as it seared through me, burning brilliantly.

"Gods." I heard him grunt as he kept driving into me. "Gods, you're beautiful, my wee Finnie."

I opened my eyes to see his on me, burning me anew. And I held them as he kept driving into me, again and again, until he thrust hard, deep, my body jerked powerfully with it, but he stayed planted and his head went back, the veins in his neck stood out and his groan of release filled the room.

Yes. Oh, *hell* yes.

When he was done, he collapsed on me, and my lungs compressed at his immense weight. But I held it not but a second before he rolled so I was on top, and he was still inside me.

My cheek was to his chest and that was all I could see. But I could feel him inside me, the ache from his thrusts so freaking sweet, one of his hands was in my hair and his other arm was wrapped around me.

And all that was him under me, in me, all around me, I touched the top of the happiness scale and hit bliss.

Then I blinked.

Then I thought, *Okay, shit. Now what did I do?*

Before my mind could sort it out, my mouth decided.

"Um...suffice it to say, I don't want you calling me Sjofn anymore."

His body stilled under mine for a long moment then it started rocking like he was laughing. His fingers fisted gently in my hair and tugged even more gently, but I knew what he wanted. I sucked in breath, and with it, courage, lifted my head to look at him and saw his beautiful eyes warm on me.

Yes.

Oh, hell yes.

"Does this mean my Finnie is back?" he asked quietly.

"Yes," I answered quietly then my mouth kept talking. "And she missed you."

At my words, his eyes closed, and he rolled me, disconnecting us (sadly). He laid me on my back, but his big, warm body stayed pressed close to mine and I watched his eyes open.

God, I'd missed his beautiful brown-green eyes with their dark, thick fringe of lashes. Especially when they were looking at me like they were looking at me then. Not that I'd ever seen that particular look, exactly. It was warmer, sweeter, and definitely better since it said he knew the feel of the most intimate part of me, and obviously, he really freaking liked it.

"Um...just for your information," my mouth, clearly detached from my brain, kept going, "I'm not all that into this Gales business. So, you know, if you feel like company on this gig you've got going, um...I'm available."

Frey grinned.

Then he said, low and rumbly, "Wife, if you think I'm going to further discover your significant charms in my cold cabin on a ship filled with my men, I must inform you that you are very wrong."

I felt my eyes get wide and my heart swell.

"You're not going?" I whispered.

"Gods, no," he answered instantly.

He wasn't going!

And he wasn't going because he wanted to stay with me.

Woo hoo!

I grinned before I admitted, "Uh...that's good since I actually *was* into all this Gales business, mostly because I have a fabulous dress."

That was when Frey's grin became a fantastic smile.

Thinking about what he did on his ships, I tipped my head to the side and asked, "Isn't your business important?"

"It was," he stated. "It isn't anymore." My heart swelled so big, it felt like it was going to burst. His head dipped and his mouth touched mine before he pulled slightly away and muttered, "Ruben can deal with it."

I nodded, agreeing eagerly. "He can. I don't know him very well, but he seems really competent to me." And this, actually, was no lie.

His eyes held mine and I felt his body move the entire bed as it rocked with his laughter before he fell to his back, taking me with him so I was again on top. I lifted my head to look down at him and his hand held back my hair as his other one drifted down my spine.

Then he told me, "I'm afraid, my wee Finnie, your dressmakers are in for a long wait."

Oh yes.

Hell yes.

"Maybe they'll come back tomorrow," I suggested.

His hand drifted over my ass, my eyes instantly glazed over as I felt his touch cause a spasm between my legs and he muttered, "I don't think there's any 'maybe' about that, wee one."

I forced myself to focus on his face to see his focus was entirely on me.

Hmm.

I liked that too. *Seriously.*

His fingers gripped my ass and his voice growled, "Kiss me, wife."

I'd gone dazed again, but that didn't mean I didn't whisper, "Okay," and then, immediately, I did what I was told.

～

I stood between the door and the doorjamb, hiding the room from view but in no way hiding the fact I was wearing nothing but Frey's huge sweater from Alyssa, who was standing out in the hall and looking at me with her eyes dancing.

"Uh..." I mumbled, fighting the heat that was in my cheeks. "Could you do me a favor and bring up some food?"

"Of course, my princess," she said enthusiastically.

"Thanks," I whispered.

She winked, smiled brilliantly and hurried away.

Eek!

I closed the door and turned to the room.

It was hours (and hours) later. Frey was asleep in bed. After I'd carefully left his arms to pull the bell to order some much-needed sustenance, he'd rolled to his side, commandeered a pillow and his arms were wrapped around it. His hair had fallen on his forehead and the covers were down to his waist.

He looked very hot. Hotter than ever. It was a wonder the bed didn't spontaneously combust, he was that hot.

I kept watching him as I walked across the room and only pulled my eyes from all the glory that was my husband when I made it to my armchair. I scooped up Penelope who gave me a, "Mrrrr, Mummy, I was mrrrr sleeping."

"Hush, baby," I muttered.

Penelope hushed but only after I started scratching her ruff.

Cradling her close, I walked to the window and slowly and silently pulled the curtain open. The rush of the cold draft hit my bare legs and crawled upwards, but although I felt it, I didn't really feel it.

I had other things on my mind.

I took in Fyngaard.

Night had fallen. Torches were lit. People were out.

Life was going on in this world as it undoubtedly was in mine.

And I had finally become wife to my other world husband. There was no mistaking it now. I had five orgasms as proof (the first, two more with Frey inside me, one from his fingers (fabulous) and one from his mouth (so freaking good, I thought it might be supernatural and this was possibly not be wrong, considering his command of elves and dragons)).

And now that he was asleep, the lamps shining a glow on the room, the huge fire roaring in the grate banishing the cold but not quite holding back the chill, it came to me that I was screwed. And not just in one way, in *all* ways.

In our love fest, birth control had not only not been mentioned, I didn't even think about it.

And that was not smart.

In fact, I was wondering if *any* of this was smart.

It could not be denied it was good, the best by a long freaking shot. I couldn't get enough of Frey, the more I had the more I wanted, and what was almost better, he definitely couldn't get enough of me. He *really* liked my body and didn't hide it, and he also *really* liked my touch (however that came about), and he didn't hide that either. Not even a little, either of them. And knowing both felt freaking great.

All the rumors were beyond correct. His skills were varied, they were vigorous, and the man had *stamina*.

And it was worth it, yes, even worth the risk of pregnancy. Not only because it was fan-freaking-tastic but mostly because it was with Frey.

And, by the by, right then, I wasn't going to go there. Not then. Not until later.

Probably much later. Definitely stupid later.

But as I stared out the window unseeing at Fyngaard, I thought that my parents had taught me to throw caution to the wind. Life was meant to be lived, every breath was a gift, every risk was worth taking.

But I had a feeling they weren't thinking of something like this.

"Finnie." I heard, and coming out of my reverie, my body gave a small start.

I turned to see Frey was awake, he'd rolled toward me, his dark hair still on his forehead, his massive chest on display, his green-brown eyes were sexy-drowsy, and he was up on a forearm in bed.

"Come here," he ordered.

My feet moved even before my mind made the decision to go and this was no surprise. A man looked like that, he was looking at you like Frey was right then looking at me and he told you to come there, you went there.

I dropped Penelope in the chair as I went, and she instantly collapsed irately onto a haunch and started licking her foot.

I didn't pay attention. My attention was elsewhere. When I got close, I watched Frey push up, twist and reach out to me. He caught my hips and guided me into the bed. When I climbed in on my knees, he pulled me to straddling him and dropped to his back. Then his big hands went under his sweater and up, gliding light and gentle over my hips then around to cup my ass.

My lids lowered and I licked my lips.

"My wife likes my hands on her arse," Frey muttered, his fingertips stroking.

I did. You bet I did. I liked it a lot.

"Mm," was all I could mumble.

Frey grinned and his hands moved up. "Come here, love."

I bent toward him and got close, resting my arms on his chest as he pulled the sweater up with his hands then they drifted lazily along the skin of my back.

"What takes you from our bed?" he asked quietly.

"I ordered us some food," I answered quietly, staring into his somnolent green-brown eyes.

"This is good," he muttered, his full lips curved slightly.

I liked that so much I lifted my hand and held it against his face as my thumb moved out to touch his lower lip.

I barely touched it before he rolled me to my back then he shifted both of his arms so the backs of my knees were hooked in the crooks of his elbows, my legs spread wide, his hands in the bed. He loomed over me, and I sucked in breath as my eyes took in all the power and beauty of him between my legs and I felt my exposed sex quiver.

His eyes held mine and kept hold as my breath started coming faster and my legs tensed against his arms in anticipation. Then his eyes dropped to look at me and I held my breath in reaction to the beauty I saw as hunger consumed his face. He shifted his hips and then he was inside me.

Oh God.

"Frey," I breathed.

His head lifted and I had the burn of his gaze as he moved slow. God, so slow. And gentle, unbelievably gentle. And deep, so, *fucking* deep.

I tensed my legs and clenched my sex tight around his cock.

He growled low in his throat, his face growing dark, and he rumbled, "And I like my wife's caress."

I lifted both hands to trail my fingers on his chest.

"Good," I whispered then urged, "Faster, honey."

He kept thrusting slow and sweet and whispered back, "No, wee one."

"Please."

In then out, taking his sweet time, then, "No."

He held my eyes and moved inside me as my fingers drifted wherever they could reach across his massive chest and tight abs. I did this awhile, his eyes locked with mine as he slowly filled me then glided away and back and back. It started building, unhurried, soft, then more and more until I couldn't take it. It felt so good, he looked so good, I needed more and not having it was like torture. My fingers drifted down his abs, separating to curl around his sides to hold on as he kept driving slow, gentle and sweet.

God, he felt great. So freaking great.

"Please, Frey, faster," I whimpered, my legs beginning to clutch his arms, my sex clenching around his cock.

"No, Finnie."

Pleasure rolled leisurely through me, burning a path so deep, my neck and back arched with it.

With effort, I righted myself, caught his now hungrier eyes and whispered, "You're killing me, baby."

"No, I'm not, wee one," he whispered back. "Just feel me."

"I feel you," I promised, and I did. Oh yeah, I did.

"Watch me take you," he ordered quietly, still going slow, deep, so, so sweet.

"I'm watching, Frey."

I was and it was spectacular.

His eyes moved from my face down my body to our connection then slowly up again and by the time they made it back to my face, my back arched, my legs hooked tight around his arms and my sex started spasming.

God, I was going to come. Just with this. I was going to come.

Oh God, so close.

"You're beautiful, Finnie, but by the gods you have never been more beautiful than you are right now, spread before me, wrapped in my wool and filled with me," he murmured and that was it.

My hips jerked violently, my neck arched back, and a slow, low, sweet whimper escaped me as a slow, deep, unbelievably sweet orgasm swept through me.

I hadn't finished before he moved his arms. Unhooking my legs, he dropped to a forearm on one side of me. His other arm wrapping around my back, he drove me down as he drove up, finally faster, harder, shifting his hips back and forth as he memorized every inch of the heart of me. He did this while I watched in deep fascination, holding him tight to me with all four limbs until his jaw clenched and a low, slow, sweet rumble tore out of his chest as he poured into me.

I loved it, every second of it from start to finish.

See? Totally screwed.

Again. Sex. Again. No birth control.

Okay, no. Again, fantastic sex. But, again. No birth control!

He stayed inside me and took my mouth in a kiss as slow, sweet, deep and wet as how he just made love to me then he released my mouth but stayed close and slid his nose along mine.

God, I'd missed that too.

His head moved back an inch and he caught my eyes. His were languid but they were also serious.

Hmm.

Taking in that look, I was thinking it was uh-oh time.

"I'm best pleased to have you back, my Finnie," he said gently. "*Best pleased*," he repeated, and my limbs got tighter then even tighter when he whispered, "I missed you too, wee one."

"Frey—" I whispered, but he cut me off.

"But mark this, I'll not tolerate you going away again. It's important you understand me. We are new, you and I. You needed time to come to terms with all you had learned. Time, I will add, that I gave you and time that you took. But I will tell you that you took too much of it."

Hmm.

I couldn't say he was wrong about that.

He finished with, "But I won't allow it again. Is this understood?"

I stared up at him.

He said he'd not tolerate me going away again.

He'd not tolerate me going away.

And, in about ten months, I was definitely going to go away.

Shit, I had to tell him.

Shit. Somehow, someway, I had to figure out how to explain what this was, who I was, where I was from and get him to believe me. Then explain to him we could have all of this, and we could enjoy it, we had time, a lot of it.

But then that time would end, and I would go home.

198

I held his gaze as fear started to rise inside me, panic, anxiety and something else. Something far more painful. Something I refused, at that point when I was hanging on to bliss, to understand.

Then I started, "Frey—"

"Don't," he growled harshly, and I blinked at his sudden fierce tone.

I had to so I whispered, "But you have to know something about—"

"I know, Finnie."

I blinked again as my heart skipped a beat.

Frey kept talking. "I know how you've come to me."

I felt my lips part in shock. His eyes dropped to them then they came back to mine, warm and sweet.

"I know who you are, my love. I know how you've come to me. I know you are *Finnie*."

Oh. My. *God*!

He knew I was Finnie!

"How—?"

"That doesn't matter. Just know I know, and we don't need to speak of it. We never need to speak of it. This is the now and you have no choice but to live in the now. You never have a choice but to live in the now. And this, my wee Finnie, *this* is where we will live. We will always live in our now."

I felt my eyes start to fill with tears (yes! again!) because he knew, and he understood and it felt like a weight had lifted from me. He knew about me, who I was and how I came to him, and he apparently understood the way it was between us and that it would end and therefore we had to live in the now.

But even as that weight lifted and I started to feel light, immediately something else started to drag me down, and I whispered, "Frey—"

He interrupted me by touching his mouth to mine.

When he lifted his head, his eyes held mine and he whispered, "You are not in the now, Finnie."

I wasn't. I was thinking about the future and leaving him.

Shit.

"Come to the now, wee one," he urged, and I nodded.

The now.

That sounded like something Dad would say. Live in the now.

And I would live in the now with Frey. And I'd enjoy every second of it while I had it.

A knock came at the door.

I held his eyes.

Forcing myself into the now, I joked, "The now, apparently, means food."

He grinned before he said, "This is good since I'm starved. My wife worked all my energy out of me."

"Don't pretend you didn't like it," I teased.

"I am not," he stated with all seriousness and the weight of those three words made me go still under him as he continued, "It was beyond anything I could have wished it to be. You are, my wee Finnie, beyond my wildest dreams."

Oh my God.

Did he just say that?

I stared at him, and it hit me, not only did he just say that, he meant it.

My eyes flooded with tears, and I whispered, "Oh shit," lifted my face and shoved it in his throat as I burst into tears and I did this *loudly*.

Another knock came at the door.

Frey gently pulled out of me, rolled to his back and settled me into his side. He hauled up the covers and held me close as he shouted, "Enter!"

I tensed but that didn't keep me from continuing to sob into his skin.

The door opened. I shoved closer to Frey and held on tighter.

As did he.

Then I heard him order, "Leave it and us. Quickly."

I smelled food and heard clinking and clunking. Shortly after that stopped, a door closed.

Frey held me tightly long after the door closed, and I kept sobbing not realizing how badly I needed to do it. But I'd apparently bottled a lot in because there was a lot coming out, and in the safety of his strong arms, I let it go.

Once the sobs started to subside, one of Frey's hands moved under his sweater and up to stroke the skin of my back as I snuffled and lifted a hand to wipe my face.

"All right, wee one?" he asked softly.

"Mm-hmm," I mumbled, nodding my head, resting my cheek on his shoulder and wrapping my arm around him again.

Frey kept stroking my back.

It felt really nice.

And it was then I thought of when we were riding to Fyngaard and Frey telling me about the villages, their names and their gods and what the rivers and forests were called.

He knew then. He knew.

It all came to me in a rush, his gentle explanations, his patience, those weird times when I'd watch him come to some understanding. Times that were now not so weird.

He *knew*. And he'd known for a while.

"When did you know?" I whispered to his chest.

"Finnie—"

I gave him a squeeze and repeated, "Tell me. When did you know?"

Frey was quiet a second before he sighed.

"In my gut," he began, "when you kissed me back as I kissed you in the Dwelling of the Gods after we were wed. And every second I spent with you after I returned to the cabin. I knew you were not who you appeared to be. You are not a thing like her, yet you look exactly the same. I knew something was not right with you. The elves verified it and shared with me that you are not of this world."

I pulled in a quiet breath.

"Their message," I guessed.

"Yes," Frey confirmed.

I nodded and thought that was kind of cool that they knew. And hopefully, the next time Frey spoke to them, he would take me with him, and I could ask them how they knew.

I got back to the now.

"Why didn't you tell me?" I asked softly.

His hand stilled at my back for a second then started stroking again when he answered, "Partly, it was because there was much you were taking in and I was concerned about you. But I will admit, my wee one, mostly it was because I enjoyed your response to my world, your blunders, your cover ups. They amused me." I lifted my head, and he looked right in my eyes. "*Greatly.*" He stressed then grinned before he said, "It was very endearing."

I grinned back and stated, "You know, I should be pissed at you for keeping it from me."

His grin got bigger.

His arm curving around me and holding tight, he stated back, "I know."

I started laughing softly and informed him, "It's good you're hot, Frey Drakkar, and good in bed *and* command elves and dragons or you'd seriously be in trouble."

He kept smiling but his brows drew together. "Hot?"

I nodded. "Hot. Handsome. Good-looking. Pleasing to the eye." I leaned into him. "*Hot.*"

He tipped his chin back and laughed.

Still laughing, he rolled me to my back, his arm around my belly tucking my side into his front, he looked down at me and quit laughing.

"And it is good you are beautiful, Finnie Drakkar, or you would have a very pink arse for risking such a venture."

I blinked at him.

Finnie Drakkar.

Shit, but that had a nice ring to it.

Suddenly all his words hit me, and I felt *my* brows draw together. "A pink arse for risking such a venture?"

He nodded and his face again grew serious. "This..." he hesitated, "travel to another world. It was foolhardy."

What?

"What?" I asked.

"You had no idea what you would encounter, and I know when you arrived, wife. I know you encountered a situation that was beyond your means to control. As you know, I do not care for the other you."

Boy, I knew *that*.

Frey kept talking. "I do not like to think of how I behaved with you, thinking you were her." His face grew darker when he stated, "And I do not like to think of what could go wrong with this magic. Where you could have been sent. What could have befallen you. It was reckless, my wee one, and you should not have done it."

I stared up at him.

He was worried about me.

That was sweet *and* hot.

I didn't tell him that.

Instead, I pointed out, "Frey, honey, I'm a princess. I live in a freaking *palace*. My mom and dad are king and queen, and I'm married to a hot guy who is the rightful ruler of the land and commands elves and dragons. I *totally* did all right."

"This is pure chance," he stated firmly, and I smiled.

"Adventure always is," I pushed against him, taking him to his back. Resting my torso on his, I dipped my face close as I wrapped my fingers around the side of his neck. Then I said quietly, "That's the best part, baby."

"Fin—" he started.

But I lifted my hand, touched my fingers to his mouth and got serious.

"My mom and dad, my real ones, back home." I watched his eyes grow intense, which I thought was weird, but I kept talking. "They lived every minute like it was their last." I slid my fingers across his cheek and down to his jaw before I whispered, "And this was good, for their lives didn't last long. They left me behind, Frey, and I miss them. But I like knowing they packed as much as they could get in before they left me. And before they left me, they taught me not just to exist, not just to breathe in and breathe out, but to *live*. And I like knowing they're smiling, wherever they are, knowing that I listened and learned and I'm living my life like they taught me how. Making every single breath I take count."

He held my gaze even as he lifted a hand, sifted it into the hair behind my ear then glided it down through my hair to hold it bunched at the side of my neck.

"I would like to know about them, Finnie," he said softly.

"And I'll enjoy telling you about them, Frey," I replied softly.

His thumb stroked my throat, his gaze still locked with mine, and he muttered, "By the gods, you suit me. This craving for life. Your thirst for venture."

I grinned at him because I liked that he thought that. I liked it a lot.

"Can I tell you something?" I asked.

"Anything, wee one," he answered.

I moved closer and had no idea my eyes got bright and my cheeks turned pink with excitement before I whispered breathlessly, "I cannot *wait* to get on your ship."

He held my gaze for a second before his roamed my face. Then both his arms locked around me and held me tight as he burst out laughing.

I watched him laugh and I liked that too.

I liked it a lot.

When he finished laughing, I tilted my head to the side and again had no idea my eyes were bright and my cheeks were pink with excitement when I asked, "Wanna hear about my world?"

His big hand cupped my jaw and he answered, "Absolutely. But go, wife, and get our food. You can talk while we eat."

I grinned at him and whispered, "Right."

I dropped my mouth to his, kissed him lightly and scurried off the bed. I quickly closed the curtain to shut out the draft and rushed across the room. I grabbed the tray that had been set on a dresser and took it to bed.

Then I climbed in bed with my husband, ate dinner and shared my world with him.

~

"Finnie?" Frey called into the darkness.

"Mm?" I mumbled sleepily, about five seconds away from slumberland.

"You're too tense with your bow."

My eyes opened.

"What?" I whispered.

"You're too tense with your bow," he repeated. "You're concentrating too much. You're letting your brain muddle your aim. You desire so badly to do well, your entire body is locking just prior to release, this jerks your aim off."

Oh my God.

He'd been watching me at archery. When I thought he'd been keeping his distance, Frey had been watching, apparently closely.

I said nothing but my heart again swelled.

Frey spoke again. "If you relax, concentrate on your target, what your arms are doing, your fingers, your shoulders, your spine, focus instead on your body, your bow, the arrow, your target and not on what Atticus will think, you will see improvement."

Oh my *God*.

He knew what I was thinking, what I wanted, why I was out there with Father.

He knew what was in my heart.

I remained quiet.

His arm gave me a squeeze.

"Do not worry, wee one," he whispered. "Atticus will like you, whether your arrow can find the target or not. He won't be able to help it."

I closed my eyes as his words rushed through me and with them my mother's from earlier that day. Not only her giving them but how she gave them, what that said about her, how she felt about me and last, but by no means least, what they said about how Frey felt about me.

Tension I didn't know I'd been holding in my shoulders and neck released, I snuggled closer to Frey and tightened my arm around him.

Then I whispered, "Okay."

His fingers slid up my side and curled in.

"Okay," he whispered back.

My body melted into the warm hardness of Frey's, and seconds later, I was asleep.

17

ANYTHING SO EXQUISITE

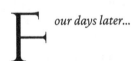 *our days later...*

I BURST out of the house and ran down the stone steps as the mass of riders, led by Frey and King Atticus, charged into the clearing in front of the Palace.

Frey swung Tyr around and reined him in as I got close. I put my hands on his thigh, tipping my head way back to look up at him.

"Did you win?" I asked with a smile, and he smiled down at me.

Then he leaned far down to the side in his saddle, his hand hooking me at the back of my neck and pulling me up to my toes so our faces were close.

"You don't win a hunt, wife," he said quietly. "The only way to lose is if you don't bag a deer, or at least a hare."

"Okay then," I replied. "Did you bag at least a hare?"

"Four," he stated. "And three deer."

I scrunched my nose.

Frey took in my face and his smile got bigger before he asked, "Why is it you burst forth from the Palace with excitement for news about the hunt and now you look as if I told you I scored through a village cutting down every breathing being with my sword?"

I didn't "burst forth from the Palace" because I wanted news of the

205

hunt. I burst forth from the Palace because my hot guy husband rode up to the Palace on his beautiful steed looking...well, *hot*. And he'd been gone since the wee hours of the morning. And therefore I "burst forth from the Palace" because I was excited to see *him*.

I did not tell him this.

Instead, I explained, "Because before, I thought it was a competition you could win. And now it's just a bunch of guys going out and killing things. Competition is exciting. Killing things just to kill things..." I shook my head and finished, "Not so much."

Frey kept smiling as he bent even further and touched his mouth to mine before he ordered softly, "Step back, wee wife, so I can dismount."

He let me go and I stepped back to see Father moving toward us. I turned to him and smiled.

"How did you do?" I asked.

"Not as well as The Drakkar, a hare and two deer," he answered, arriving at me while speaking through a returned smile and bending to kiss my cheek after he spoke. When he straightened, Frey was there, and Atticus looked to my husband. "As usual, not anyone did as well as The Drakkar."

I turned to look up at Frey. "So you *did* win."

Frey looked down at me, eyes smiling. "If it pleases you, my princess, you can think of it this way."

"Okay, I'll think of it this way," I decided.

Frey's mouth twitched and his eyes went to Atticus who was noting, "Plenty of fresh meat for the feast tonight."

I made a gaggy face that Frey caught and I knew this because he burst out laughing. It also made him hook an arm around my shoulders and pull me into his side. And last, and best, it made him kiss the top of my hair after he quit laughing.

When he was done kissing me, I tipped my head back to see he was looking down at me.

When he caught my eyes, he stated, "You eat pork."

I had a feeling I knew where this was going.

"Yes," I confirmed. "But—"

Frey cut me off. "And beef."

"Yes, husband, but—"

"And chicken, pheasant and lamb," he went on.

"I don't eat lamb," I protested.

"Of course, I forgot." Frey looked at Father and informed him, "Finnie doesn't eat baby animals. It's a rule."

This *was* a rule and this rule Frey learned when our trays were brought up two nights ago so we could (again) eat in bed. Lamb was served and I pitched a mini-fit and, like I was a real princess, sent it back.

Frey thought this was hilarious during my fit *and* after it when I explained my reasons for having said fit. I knew he thought this was hilarious because first, he laughed about it a lot at the time, second, he laughed about it a lot afterward whenever he remembered it, and last, because he teased me about it frequently.

He could think it was hilariously funny and tease me about it. I still was not eating baby animals. No way.

I looked at Father, nodded and affirmed, "Totally."

Father grinned at me, and Frey looked back down at me. "You *do* know where all that comes from, Finnie."

"Of course. I just don't wish to discuss it or think of my husband and father riding off into the forest and hunting it down," I returned then continued, "And, by the way, along with baby animals, I don't eat hare, nor do I eat venison."

Actually, to be honest, I didn't know exactly what a hare was except that it looked like a rabbit and there was no way in hell I was eating a rabbit.

I was an adventurer, but you had to draw the line somewhere.

"You'll eat it tonight," Father put in. "For there'll be a great deal of it and I promise you, daughter, you'll think it's delicious."

"I think I'll stick with the canapés," I replied. Father's head tilted to the side in confusion and Frey gave me a squeeze, which meant they had no clue what I was talking about. "Hors d'oeuvres?" I tried. Father's brows drew together, and Frey started chuckling. "Finger food. Like vol-au-vents, miniature quiches, meatballs on toothpicks and such," I explained.

Father closed in our huddle, and he said quietly, "I think, my other world daughter, we do not have the same foods."

By the way, Father and Mother, I now knew, had been told by Frey who I was and where I'd come from. This had made things better for it meant I could be me around both of them. I was obviously way better at being me and that seemed to be working, especially with Father.

Still, I went out with him every day (except today since he was with the hunt) and practiced with my bow and arrow.

And Frey was right. I was worrying too much about disappointing Atticus. Once I started to focus on what I was doing, and not on making Father happy (not to mention, doing that every day, my arms and shoulders were getting stronger and thus I gained more control), I got loads better. I wasn't hitting bullseyes, but the last two days I was out, not one arrow went astray and some of them actually hit the circles in the target.

Father was pleased with my progress and so was I.

"We'll see," I whispered back. "We probably just don't call them the same things."

"Probably not," Father stated then looked beyond me and smiled so I turned to see Mother approaching, also wearing a slight (as was her way) smile.

"And how did you do, my husband?" she asked on arrival and after leaning up to give him a kiss.

When she did, I sighed and pressed into Frey's side as his arm tightened around me.

"A hare and two deer," Atticus replied.

"It's good to know, even if we didn't have royal game hunters, my husband could provide meat for our table," she returned softly.

Father grinned proudly and she turned to me, her face growing serious.

"I'm relatively certain, my Finnie, that you should be at your bath," she stated bizarrely, and I blinked at her.

"I should?" I asked.

"The Gales ball commences in four hours," she informed me of something I knew.

Therefore, I told her I knew.

"I know, but it won't take four hours to get ready."

Her lips tipped up before she returned, "Dear, trust me, your maidservants are upstairs fretting that you've spent the last half hour pacing the windows while looking out, anticipating your husband's return. Now you're out here *with* your husband and didn't, upon his safe return, retire to your rooms to begin preparations where your maids expected you to be at least an hour ago."

I felt Frey's arm tense around my shoulders, indicating he now knew the reason I "burst forth from the Palace," but I ignored that because I was busy blinking again.

"Seriously?" I asked.

She nodded firmly. "Seriously, my daughter."

Wow. Five hours to prepare for a ball? Jeez, I wondered what would take so long.

Looking at my mother, I decided I'd better find out and probably not do that by wasting time with asking.

"I'll go up right away," I told her.

"This would be wise," she replied, her eyes getting soft as I'd noticed they had been doing a lot more these last four days.

I had to say, I liked that.

Then I thought of our morning in town, why I asked her to go with me and what was waiting upstairs. Therefore, I pressed my lips together and bugged my eyes out at her. She nodded her head slightly toward the house then just as slightly jerked out her chin in the same direction just in case I didn't catch her first hint. I bit my lip nervously. Her eyes narrowed on my mouth, she again jerked her chin to the Palace and blinked meaningfully.

I took her meaning and that was when I tipped my head back to look at Frey.

"Can you come up with me? Just for a minute," I asked shyly.

And I didn't know why I was being shy. It was silly. He was, of course, my husband. I did, of course, know him in a biblical sense. I had been getting to know him very, *very* well in that biblical sense for the last five days. In other words, outside of archery, eating, sleeping and afternoon dancing lessons with the girls (for there were a number of dances they danced at the Gales and Princess Sjofn knew them all, and I, of course, did not, so I had to learn them *tout de suite*), that was pretty much *all* I'd been doing. Not to mention, I'd spent a great deal of time with him. Why I was shy now, I had no clue.

But I was.

And Frey, being Frey, and missing less than Mother did (which was to say, not very much), caught it.

And therefore Frey, being Frey, gave me a squeeze and murmured gently, "Of course, my wee Finnie."

I smiled at him then we exchanged farewells with my parents, and he led me up the steps to the Palace.

We were inside and heading to the stairwell when his arm, still around my shoulders, curled me closer into him.

"Is everything all right, wee one?" he asked.

I nodded, my eyes on my feet.

"You've had your maids pack your trunks?" he went on, and I nodded again.

We were leaving tomorrow to go to his ship.

I was looking forward to wearing my fabulous dress that night. I was looking forward to seeing what everyone else would be wearing. I was looking forward to finding out what we'd be eating (though, if it was only hare and venison, I was planning another mini-princess-fit). And I was looking forward to trying out my newly learned dance moves.

But most of all, I was looking forward to going with Frey tomorrow and finally seeing his ship then being on it and being with him out at sea.

And I was looking forward to that *a lot*.

"They're packed. They were loaded on the sleigh two hours ago and they're on their way to Sudvic," I told him.

"Excellent," he muttered, guiding me up the stairs.

"Um...if we get to our rooms and the girls are there, just to give you a heads up," I warned, looking up at his profile. "They're not really happy you won't let me have at least *one* of them along when we set sail."

Frey looked down at me. "I understand you've grown close to them, Finnie, and I'm pleased you have. But a ship is no place for a woman."

"I'll be there," I pointed out.

"And *you'll* be warming *my* bed in *my* cabin and my men will know this and will know they will earn my displeasure and how that displeasure will be communicated if they do not train their attention to other things when you're amongst them. Your girls would be distracting. And when we are at sail my men do not need distractions."

"Actually," I whispered, leaning in even closer to him as we walked. "I think that's why they're all pouty that at least one of them doesn't get to go. Your men have been around quite a bit and the girls have noticed this..." I hesitated as Frey stopped us outside the door to our rooms, curled me into his front, and I emphasized, "*A lot*. I think they're hoping to get lucky."

Frey's lips twitched and he asked, "Get lucky?"

I nodded. "Get laid. Get tagged. Get hit. Get their skirts tossed up." I put my hands on his chest, got to my toes and finished, "*Get lucky*."

Frey threw his head back and burst out laughing as his arms came around me and he gave me a big squeeze.

Then he tipped his head down to look at me. "Even so, my wee one, my ships aren't manned by a few men. They might not want to get *that* lucky and a month or more away, most of that at sea, they would court that possibility."

I shook my head and replied, "I don't know. Every day each has a new favorite. Yesterday, Bess's was Max, but she's switched to Lund today. Orion was Alyssa's favorite yesterday, but she swears she's in love with Annar today. We had a situation yesterday with both Jocelyn *and* Esther carrying a torch for Thad, but luckily today Esther has switched to Stephan.

Jocelyn is still hooked on Thad. In fact, if memory serves, she was hooked on Thad the day before that too."

Hmm, and she was hooked on Thad the day before *that* too.

Interesting.

I forced myself to focus on our conversation and not my possible future matchmaking efforts, and finished, "I'm not certain they'd mind a smorgasbord."

Frey grinned but asked, "Is Jocelyn the dark one with the green eyes and the extremely large—"

"Yes," I cut him off before he could finish, for to say Jocelyn was busty was a serious understatement. And to say Jocelyn didn't mind displaying these attributes was another serious understatement.

I watched his grin turn into a wicked smile.

"Then, we shall inform Thad of this after we return so that he can keep his mind on the matters at hand. It's safe to say he's noticed your maid's rather..." he paused then went on, "*significant* charms and would not mind making her feel lucky."

I leaned deeper into him and whispered, "Excellent." Then I went on to advise, "Though, when he makes his move, you might tell him he should comment on her eyes, not on her rather..." I paused, "*significant* charms."

Frey chuckled, gave me a nod and another squeeze then let me go, turned and opened the door.

We barely got two feet in before all four of my girls fell on me.

"Finnie!" Alyssa cried. "Where on earth have you been?"

"We're never going to have time for her hair to dry in order that we can fashion it," Bess announced in a dire tone as if this possible occurrence would mark the end of the world as we knew it. "*Never,*" she finished on a muted, despairing cry.

"Disrobe! Bath! Immediately!" Esther snapped. "Before the water gets cold."

"It already must be cold," Jocelyn predicted. "It's been sitting there half an hour. We'll have to order more brought up."

"I'll do it!" Bess cried and then ran, actually *ran* from the room.

"Uh...can you gals give me ten minutes with Frey?" I asked hesitantly, for it was clear this request was not going to go down well, and I was right. Esther, Alyssa and Jocelyn all reared back in horror.

"Ten minutes?" Jocelyn asked on a dismayed whisper.

"I know what 'ten minutes with Frey' means," Esther muttered under her breath to Alyssa. "It means another *entire* afternoon of bedplay, and we'll *never* have time to get her hair dry to fashion it for the Gales."

I couldn't hold back the quick, shocked giggle or the heat that hit my cheeks.

"Esther!" I snapped, but teasingly, still feeling the blush.

"Well, he *is* The Drakkar and he's barely let you up for air for *five days!*" Esther returned and I felt my cheeks get hotter.

"Finally," Alyssa muttered to Jocelyn, and I heard Frey start chuckling.

Okay, time to put an end to *this*.

"Right, well, this isn't about that. It's about something else and I need ten minutes," I stated. When all three opened their mouth to speak, I promised quickly, "Just ten minutes." I lifted my hand, palm out to them. "You have my word."

They all looked at me, before they looked at Frey then back at me.

Finally, Jocelyn started tugging the other two out saying, "Ten minutes, Finnie."

"Make it good," Alyssa called back as Jocelyn shoved her out the door. "It'll have to hold you over until after the Gales."

Frey chuckled again and I stared at the door shaking my head.

The door closed and it was just him and me.

That was when I got shy again so, for some lame reason, I kept staring at the door.

"Finnie, love, whatever this is, you've got ten minutes," Frey reminded me.

My body jerked and I turned to him.

His arms were crossed on his chest and his eyes were on me. His beautiful, gentle green-brown eyes.

Shit.

I sucked in breath.

All right, I did it. What I did wasn't a bad thing to do, not by any stretch of the imagination. Thus, I had to get over this ridiculous shyness and just get on with it.

So I told him, "While you were at the hunt, Mother and I went into Fyngaard. We went shopping."

Frey didn't speak but I could tell by the look on his face he was wondering why I imparted this not very interesting news on him for he was a man, not to mention a super-cool action hero Raider who commanded dragons. His expression made it clear both types of men, no matter what world they lived on (not that we had Raiders in my world), didn't care about shopping.

I bit my lip, sucked in another breath and moved to the wardrobe. Opening a door, I disappeared behind it and pulled out the big wooden box I'd put there a few hours ago.

I juggled it as I turned back to him and closed the door. He was standing where he was before, and he was still watching me. He continued to watch me, his eyes flicking to the box twice as I moved to the bed, set the box on it and opened the top.

I reached in and whispered, "While we were there, I bought you something."

Carefully, I grasped the beautiful large dragon fashioned out of delicate spun glass in brilliant colors of gold (neck and feet), vermillion (head and body), violet and a deep sapphire blue that had gold flecks in it (both colors making up the wings) with the tips of its talons, horns, wings, tail and its eyes all painted a glossy onyx.

I shifted to face him.

Frey had turned his body toward me as I walked through the room, but now he did not move, he did not speak, and his eyes did not leave the delicate piece held out in my hands for him to see.

When he continued to stare at it, face expressionless, body unmoving, I rushed to explain, "I, uh...saw it as we rode into Fyngaard, um...when we came back. It was in the window of one of the shops. I thought it was beautiful and wanted to go back and check it out, but, uh...when you, um... explained you are who you are and that you can, uh...do what you can do, well..."

His eyes came to mine, and I stopped talking when I saw not one thing in them. Nothing. Not happiness, not confusion, not an indication he was humoring his idiot wife. Nothing.

So I whispered, "I guess I thought, you being you, you needed to have this."

I thought more than that. It was a dragon. It was beautiful. It was majestic. Even in its delicacy it depicted the fierce power of the beasts. Beasts he controlled. And I thought he needed to own it because, in its beauty and fierce power, it personified him.

But it was more. When I left, I wanted him to have something of me. Something exquisite. Something beautiful. Something to remember the times we shared that already, even though I'd been with him a short while, were both of those. Definitely.

And now I was seeing this idea was totally lame.

"It's...I'm sorry Frey," I whispered. "Thinking about it now, it's pretty stupid. You hunt and ride horses and sail ships. A delicate, glass dragon—"

He cut me off to order tersely, "Lay it in its box."

I blinked at his tone and at the harsh look now on his face.

It wasn't totally lame. He hated it.

He actually hated it.

God.

"Right." I was still whispering, but it had to be said, my heart hurt. I mean, Frey could be severe and even callous, but most of the time he was gentle. It was a gift. Even if he hated it, I was surprised he wasn't even *trying* to be gentle.

I laid it in its box, but I no sooner had it resting in its bed of vermillion silk then Frey was at my side, flipping the lid to it.

Eek.

He *totally* hated it.

I watched as he took the box off the bed, moved it to the dresser and set it on it, so deep in my dejection I didn't notice the care he took. Then I watched in vague confusion that coated my disappointment as he walked to the door and not only turned the skeleton key in the lock, but also shoved one of the wooden bolts home.

And *then* I watched in sharper confusion, some surprise and still with disappointment as he stalked to me.

Okay, um...was he pissed?

It was just a present. A lame one, sure, but that was nothing to be angry about.

Was it?

"Frey," I said quietly, lifting a hand as if to fend him off and stepping back only to hit bed.

I no sooner hit the bed when Frey's body hit mine.

And we were down on the bed with him on top of me and his fingers in my gown, pulling it up.

Ho boy.

Maybe I read him wrong.

"If needs be," he growled, "you'll go to the Gales with wet hair."

Ho boy!

He lifted his hips to move his weight from me, yanked the dress up to my waist then he arched his back and yanked the dress off, forcing my arms up with it.

Ho boy!

"Frey," I whispered as one of his hands trailed down my side then in and swiftly up to slide over my breast, up my neck to cup my jaw.

And now his eyes weren't blank. They were fiery and that fire was in no way bad.

Okay, I read him wrong. He *definitely* liked it.

"No one," he was still growling, his chest rumbling with it. A rumble so deep, it shook mine and there was a fierce expression on his face, a face that dipped to within an inch of mine. "*No one*, since my grandmother died when I was aged thirteen, has bought me a present. Not one gods-damned person has, since her death, given one single thing to me."

Oh my God.

That couldn't be true.

Please God, don't let that be true.

"Honey," I breathed, wrapping an arm around him as my other hand came up to hold him tight at his neck and I thought we really needed to stop having (fabulous) sex and start to talk. Or, more to the point, he needed to stop listening to me jabbering on about everything under the sun when we weren't having sex and I needed to start drawing things out of my husband.

"And never have I received anything so exquisite," he went on. "Save the wedding kiss you bestowed on me."

Oh my *God*.

He said that. I didn't miss it. He actually *said* that.

Shit, he was going to make me cry again.

"Frey," I whispered, fighting back the tears.

His hand moved from my jaw, around my back and down over my ass where it pulled me up so my soft hips were snug to his hard ones.

Then he declared in a thick voice, "I'm bloody well taking my time thanking my wife and your maids will have to wait."

Yes, he liked it.

"Okay," I breathed.

He studied me, his gaze intense, as if he was memorizing every centimeter of my face.

Finally, his head slanted, and he kissed me.

Then he took his time thanking his wife.

And when Frey Drakkar took his time, he did it right.

∽

"I'M GIVING you a present every day," I muttered to the mattress, heard my husband's chuckle then I felt his hand glide light over the curve of my behind.

I felt his lips brush the skin of my hip. They disappeared and I felt them touch my neck and, in my ear, he whispered, "Thank you, my wee Finnie. I'll treasure him."

He would treasure his dragon.

I closed my eyes, felt happiness wash through me, turned my head, opened my eyes and smiled at my husband.

"You're welcome, my handsome husband," I whispered back.

His eyes went soft, and he smiled back, sweet and gentle, leaned in, kissed my temple then moved from the bed, throwing the covers over me.

He'd already dressed and come back to kiss me before he went to his own bath, and now I watched him walk to the door. He unbolted it, unlocked it and threw it open while I sighed contentedly.

All four of my girls were standing outside.

"Have a courier deliver the box on the dresser to my ship in Sudvic without delay. Its contents are fragile so tell him if I see even the barest crack in the glass, he'll answer to me. Also tell him to instruct Skylar that I want it mounted in my cabin before Finnie and I arrive tomorrow," Frey commanded.

All four of them stared up at him with mouths open but Esther finally nodded, peeled off and disappeared.

I smiled yet again.

He so *totally* treasured his dragon.

Frey turned back to me.

"I'll be back to escort you to the Gales, wife," he called.

I pushed lethargically up on both forearms and called back, "Awesome, husband."

He shook his head and grinned before he disappeared.

My girls rushed in with Bess closing the door.

They all stopped four feet from the bed and stared at me.

"Hey, ladies," I greeted, totally not caring I was naked and in bed and had obviously been thoroughly and vigorously laid by my hot virile husband who *seriously* liked my present.

They all kept staring at me.

Finally, Jocelyn stated, "Balls to ten minutes."

She was right. Ten minutes were over about an hour ago.

I burst out laughing.

216

As I knew they would, they joined me.

Still laughing, Alyssa rushed to my dressing room and came back with my robe. I struggled to put it on under the covers as I heard water sloshing next door.

Time for a bath.

Then the Gales.

Then, tomorrow, adventure.

18

BITTER GALES

"Hurry, Esther, The Drakkar has been waiting in the bedroom for twenty minutes," Bess hissed urgently at Esther, who was twisting, curling and pinning up my hair. "I just walked through and there's no mistaking he's getting impatient."

That probably wasn't good.

"How much time do you need, Esther?" I asked.

"Ten to do your hair and ten to get you dressed," Esther answered.

"Can we cut that in half?" I requested thinking of a Frey who was not hiding his impatience, which could mean bad things.

"We'll do our best," Jocelyn decided. "Here, lift your foot. We'll put your shoes and jewelry on and then, when Esther's done, we can just add the dress."

I nodded to Jocelyn and lifted my foot as she kneeled on the floor in front me.

"Tell him ten more minutes," I said to Bess.

She looked like she wanted to tell Frey he had to wait ten more minutes like she wanted her fingernails to be pulled out at the roots.

So I said gently, "Tell him *I* said that, honey."

She nodded and took off. Jocelyn shoved on the other shoe while Alyssa came forward with my necklace.

It was crazy and at first I thought way over the top, but honestly, being a princess, you totally needed four maidservants.

"I can't *wait* to see The Drakkar's expression when he gets a look at you," Alyssa breathed as she carefully dodged Esther and put on my necklace.

"Me either," Esther muttered.

"When he sees you, I hope he actually takes you to the Gales and not back to bed, like he did when he saw your underwear," Jocelyn remarked, moving away to get my earrings. "It would be a pity we spent all that time teaching you and you didn't get to dance."

This would be true. The dances were fun.

Though dancing with Frey was a lot more fun.

Bess came hustling in the room, eyes wide, expression slightly pale.

"He says we've got five minutes," she announced.

I started softly giggling because I reckoned this was Frey being generous. He didn't strike me as a man who liked to wait.

A few minutes later, when I'd been perfumed, my gloves smoothed on and the final touches of jewelry added, I heard Esther announce, "I'm done," and felt her hands move away from me.

"I'll get the dress," Bess declared and hurried to the shimmering bolt of blood-red satin scattered with jet beads that was resting over the lounge.

"Get yourself up, my princess," Alyssa ordered, and I got up and walked to the mirror.

In short order, they had my ensemble complete. And it was so awesome, even if Frey was waiting, I took a moment to examine myself in the mirror and take it all in as Bess did some final spritzing with perfume behind my ears and at my cleavage (yes, royalty didn't even spritz).

The girls had told me that any member of the aristocracy would be wearing the colors of their House. And it was Mother's idea that I would not wear the deep red color of the House of Wilde, the gold that denoted the crown of Lunwyn, or my own color (as Winter Princess) of ice blue.

Instead, I would wear the color of the House of Drakkar.

Blood red.

And that I was. A blood-red satin gown that hugged my body tight from ample cleavage to hips then flowed to my feet with a small train at the back. It was liberally and artistically decorated with hundreds of thousands of polished jet beads, heavy around the bodice but lightening as it skimmed my body and becoming only a sprinkle at the hem.

The gown didn't have long sleeves but was off the shoulder with short, thin straps that made the bodice a sweep across my exposed cleavage and shoulders.

I had on long, black silk gloves that went up high on my triceps. Over the gloves at each wrist was a tangle of strand after strand of jet beads. At my neck was a choker of more strands of beads, the same dangling from my ears. My makeup was done in deep colors, charcoal grays and blacks at the eyes and raspberry at the lips and cheeks. And my hair was swept up elegantly but softly in curls and twists.

But the best of all was the headpiece.

Mother had told me when a Drakkar queen sat the throne, she didn't wear a crown. She wore something like what I was wearing.

A headpiece made of woven and dangling jet beads that covered my forehead from hairline to nearly eyebrow with dips of it coming to the bridge of my nose and down my temples. This disappeared into my hair at the sides but was woven through the curls and twists.

It...was...*awesome.*

The whole thing was.

Though, it had to be said, the dress was super tight and weighed a ton and that headpiece thing, albeit cool-as-shit, was kind of annoying. However, I figured I'd get used to it and hopefully be having so much fun, I wouldn't even notice it.

"Oh, Finnie, you look *beautiful,*" Bess breathed.

I smiled because, silently, I agreed.

Usually, I could take my looks or leave them. Mom had taught me how to play to my strengths, thick hair, unusual eyes, burgeoning curves (before she left me, they'd burgeoned since), and I did it without thought.

Truthfully, I would never have guessed that red would look good on me, but with the dark makeup and the jet beads, my hair seemed shiny white, and the blue of my eyes was stark.

So now I thought I looked *fabulous.*

I took another moment before joining Frey to embrace each of my girls and say quick, heartfelt words of thanks before I rushed (trying not to look like I was rushing) out of the dressing room and into the bedroom while taking in a soft breath.

I was looking forward to Frey's reaction because it was safe to say my husband thought I was beautiful (since he'd told me this more than once) and I couldn't wait to see what he thought of *this.*

I got three feet into the room when I stopped. Vaguely, I noticed his attention come to me and he did what he often did when he first saw me. His body arrested and his eyes locked on me.

But I was too busy taking him in to note his reaction.

Holy moly.

I'd never seen him in anything but his so dark brown it was nearly black clothing.

But now he wore *all* black. Black breeches, polished black boots and a black shirt with puffy sleeves and a high collar that covered his neck nearly to his earlobes, tied with a cravat.

This old-fashioned getup might look ridiculous on any other man but absolutely did *not* on him.

He had a shined, black leather strap on a slant across his chest to which was attached not to a rough hide but instead a length of high-quality black wool that hung at a slant on the back, and where it ended at the backs of his calves there was a short edge of glossy black fur.

His thick, dark hair had been swept back, his strong jaw was shaved, and he looked so beyond handsome, for a second, I couldn't breathe.

When I could, I whispered, "Hi," and he blinked.

Then he moved to me, leaned in, grabbed my hand, tucked it in his elbow and muttered, "We're late. We mustn't delay."

I felt the air in the room change and could almost swear I heard the whoosh of five balloons of deflated excitement whizzing around the room like they'd just been struck by a pin.

"Right," I whispered as Frey led me swiftly to the door. I turned my head and aimed a smile at my girls. "Thanks, ladies, see you in the morning before we go."

"Right, Finnie, see you," Alyssa called, looking almost, but not quite, as disappointed as I felt.

"Have fun," Esther called.

"I will," I assured her.

Jocelyn and Bess both waved, Jocelyn's disappointed eyes on me, Bess's on Frey.

Out the door we went, and Frey moved us quickly down the hall toward the stairs.

We were headed to the third floor.

The Palace was enormous, the first floor filled with official function rooms in one wing such as drawing rooms, a study, a formal dining room, a formal morning room and the like.

In the other wing, places where family gathered such as a less formal dining room, a billiards room, a library and a conservatory.

The first floor also had the kitchens and laundry. The second floor was filled with living space for family and guests, bedrooms, dressing rooms, personal sitting rooms, sewing rooms and such. The fourth floor held the servants' quarters.

But the third floor was where the function rooms were and there were only three.

The middle where the stairs led was a huge hall. Down the center of which were five, large, gleaming dark wood tables, which for the party would hold massive displays of blooms from the Palace's greenhouses.

And there were four gargantuan greenhouses where the Palace gardeners grew everything from flowers and plants to adorn the house, to vegetables and fruits forced to grow out of season in order to feed its occupants and guests. They even had apple, pear, plum and peach trees in one, lime, lemon, grapefruit and orange in another and tangles of blackberry and raspberry vines in yet another.

Off the function hall to one side was a ballroom that was a wide-open space lined with chairs intermixed with small tables and a rise for an orchestra at one end.

Off the hall to the other side was a long open gallery that had walls covered with portraits of past kings and queens of Lunwyn, but mostly Winter Princes or Princesses. In other words, those who inhabited the Palace prior to assuming the throne, and their wives or husbands and children.

This floor was where we were heading now.

I saw two liveried footmen wearing deep red sweaters, dark brown leather shorts, high boots, brown mantles at a slant across their backs and brown leather gloves standing at the landing from the second to third floor. They were guiding people up and down and cutting off access to the living quarters.

As I saw the brilliant-colored gowns and curious faces peeking around the footmen toward Frey and myself, I looked away and up at my husband to see his jaw was hard.

I stared at his jaw, realizing something had pissed him off.

Shit. He was angry about the wait.

Shit! I didn't want to go to the Gales with a pissed-off Frey. I didn't want to go anywhere with a pissed-off Frey.

Before we made it to the footmen, I pulled back slightly on his elbow and slowed my step. He looked down at me, brows drawn, and I saw on Frey's scale of one to ten of how angry he could be, he was resting, my guess, at around a two.

This was good.

"Can I have a second?" I asked softly.

He stopped us, looked to the stairs then back at me before he turned toward me.

"Finnie, the Gales started nearly two hours ago," he reminded me.

"I know but..." I moved closer to him and tipped my head back further. "I just wanted to apologize before we got there for being late and making you wait and—"

I stopped talking when his hand lifted and curled around my neck and his expression instantly changed to show that my apology made him totally drop off the angry scale.

Phew.

This was also good.

"Wee one, it was *me* who made us late. Why are *you* apologizing?"

"You seem angry," I told him.

"I'm not angry about waiting," he told me.

"Are you angry at all?" I asked.

"No," Frey answered.

I peered closer at him and saw this was true.

Still, I could have sworn I saw it earlier.

Therefore, I informed him, "You looked angry a second ago."

"I wasn't angry," he replied.

Well, he was something, and by the by, he hadn't commented on my fabulous dress and that was *not* Frey. Three days ago, when I'd walked up to him talking with Thad and Oleg while wearing a silvery-white wool gown that was sweet, but wasn't close to my best, he'd told me right in front of his men that I looked lovely. He then swiftly finished his talk with the guys, took me to our rooms and took it off me.

Therefore, I stated, "You were *something*."

He sighed then said, "Finnie, we must—"

My eyes narrowed on his, which I could see—just barely—were hiding something.

I leaned closer, cutting him off as it hit me. "You're hiding something."

"Finnie—"

"What?"

"Fin—"

I put a hand on his chest, got up on the toes of my red satin, jet-beaded-pointed-toed slippers and asked, "What's upset you, Frey?"

He kept hold of my eyes before he dipped his face closer to me.

Then he said, "You wear the colors of Drakkar."

I blinked and asked, "What?"

He didn't repeat himself.

Instead, he replied, "I was wrong when I told you I didn't have a favorite color. My favorite colors are *your* colors." I blinked as my heart skipped a beat and Frey continued, "I prefer you in your whites, your silvers, your grays and definitely your blues."

I stared, thinking he really paid attention at the same time my belly got really warm at his words, and he kept talking.

"What I do not like to see you in is the red of Drakkar."

My belly grew instantly cold. I rolled back to the soles of my feet, surprised, and I had to admit, dejected.

"I wore this for you," I whispered. "Mother said—"

His hand at my neck squeezed lightly and he whispered back, "I know, wee one, and I appreciate the gesture. But that does not change the fact that I dislike you in the color of my House."

Oh God.

Of course not. Why was I so stupid? I knew he had nothing to do with his House. I should never have listened to Mother.

I turned my eyes away and muttered, "Hells bells, I screwed up."

"Finnie, look at me, love," he called with another squeeze of his hand and my attention returned to him. "I do not associate with my House."

I nodded and admitted, "I know. I heard. That's how I screwed up." I leaned further into him. "I'm so sorry, Frey."

He shook his head. "Don't be sorry. Your gesture is touching, and your mother knows what she's doing. This does not mean I like it."

I blinked and asked, "My mother knows what she's doing?"

He nodded and then imparted information on me that made my lungs seize.

"There will be members of my House up there. My parents, assuredly. My cousin Franka, considering the level and nature of her curiosity, almost definitely. Perhaps even my brothers, though I have not heard word they're attending."

The news of his cousin was alarming. The news of his brothers also.

But I was frozen at news of his parents.

"Your parents are upstairs?" I breathed.

"Undoubtedly," he confirmed.

"Your parents are upstairs," I repeated on a breath.

"Finnie—"

I pulled away from his hand at my neck, grabbed it and tugged him five feet back down the hall. Then I stood with my back to the landing and hissed, "Why didn't you tell me?"

God.

His parents. I would soon be meeting Frey's parents!

God!

I looked freaking great, but I wasn't ready for *this*.

"Finnie—"

I interrupted him. "You can't...you can't just...just...*spring* this on a girl five minutes before she meets your parents!"

His hands, both of them this time, curled around my neck and he bent so his face was close when he said gently, "Wee one, calm down."

"Calm is not an option, Frey," I told him, panic clear in my voice. "Your parents are upstairs!"

"They are," he confirmed again.

"And your cousin!" I went on.

"Finnie, my love—"

"And, possibly, *your brothers*!" Now I was working myself up into a state.

"Fin—"

"Why didn't you tell me?" I semi-shrieked, the words coming out slightly shrill, slightly loud and definitely panicked.

Therefore, Frey let me go but grabbed my hand and pulled me back down the hall another five feet.

He stopped and resumed our positions, this time turning me, so *his* back was to the stairwell.

"I didn't tell you, my wee Finnie, for this exact reason. I knew you'd react this way. You care. You want to make a good impression. You twist yourself into knots to make your father proud of you. You sit with your mother while she embroiders when I know you'd rather be anywhere but there, doing something, meeting people, gaming, shopping, eating, chatting. Now, you're anxious and I'd rather you be anxious for the second it takes you to control your emotions and move forward being charming the moment you meet them than tell you days ago so you could work yourself up and spend that time in this state."

I glared at him as it hit me this was kind of nice and definitely thoughtful.

"You know, it's annoying when you're thoughtful and I'm geared up to be pissed at you," I snapped.

The unsettled look went out of Frey's eyes, and he grinned.

Then he bent closer and touched his lips to my nose and moved back.

That was also thoughtful because it was soothing and sweet.

Damn the man.

"Since you now know, I'll brief you further," he offered.

"That'd be nice, Frey," I said on a sigh, trying to keep up the glare and failing.

He grinned again, totally seeing I was failing at my endeavors to remain pissed, and his hands dropped from my neck to rest at my waist.

His face got serious, and I braced.

"If you know I have nothing to do with my House then you likely know I do not care for my parents. Therefore, I do not care what they think of you. I know how *I* think of you and their thoughts matter nothing to me."

Well, this was good.

"Okay," I replied.

His fingers gave me a squeeze and he went on.

"But the House of Drakkar holds wealth and wealth means power. Their influence has dwindled over the years, but money can buy nearly anything. Your mother arranging that you wear their colors is a statement that says, upon our marriage, it was not simply me accepted into the House of Wilde, but you also entered the House of Drakkar. She is saying you are one of them. She is attempting to make that point clear."

I felt my brows knit and I asked, "Why would she do that?"

"Because she wishes to build an alliance. Power is power no matter who wields it. The members of the House of Drakkar spend a great deal of time and effort fighting amongst themselves. But the way they are, that does not mean they do not have plenty of time to devote to engaging in hostility to others. You wearing the colors of my House is not only an homage to my House, it is also publicly stating to *all* Houses that you are now a Drakkar. It's a clever ploy. She's reminding them that Drakkars have a member of their House, no matter how distant he is with his brethren, who will eventually be father to the next king of Lunwyn. With you wearing their colors, your mother is also reminding them that his bride, a Wilde and now a Drakkar, will be the mother of our future king and should be treated with the respect she deserves for *all* those reasons."

I stared up at him in mild surprise and asked, "They wouldn't treat me with respect?"

"My wee one," Frey said gently. "With my family, there is no telling what they will do."

Hmm.

Well, the good news was, Mother wasn't stupid, though I'd already pretty much sussed that.

"As clever as it was of your mother and as fetching as that dress is on you, I still don't like you wearing Drakkar red," he muttered, his gaze having drifted down to my middle.

"Frey, honey," I called, and his gaze moved back to mine, "I'm sorry it bothers you, so I suggest you don't think of me wearing this color and instead," I leaned into him, smiled and whispered, "think of taking it off later."

Frey's arms wrapped around my back, and he bent his neck deep to reply low through his own smile, "This is an excellent idea."

I pressed into him. He got my hint and touched his mouth to mine. Though, clearly he didn't read the hint correctly because it was only a touch and not more.

When he lifted his head, he sighed and murmured, "Let us face the Gales."

"Okay," I murmured back.

He smiled again, let me go, grabbed my hand and led me back to the staircase.

We moved up the stairs, and as we did, I caught eyes and gave smiles. When Frey caught eyes, he gave chin lifts.

People had been arriving for the Gales for days, and normally, Sjofn would be amongst them as a number were guests at the Palace. For the past three days, Mother and Father had both been attending large breakfasts, luncheons and dinners with Father taking meetings in between.

But to protect me, Frey had made the decision I would not be involved in these, and further, stringently kept separate from the guests primarily because most of the people I was supposed to know but I didn't. He didn't want to be away from my side when these things happened, and he had no intention of attending engagement after engagement. And since Father and Mother's attention would be turned to hosting their guests, it was without a doubt I'd flub up, repeatedly.

Therefore, guests were informed (not untruthfully) that Frey and I were otherwise engaged (the inference not lost on anyone, I was sure). Thus, not participating in these events, but we would attend the Gales.

It wasn't the most comfortable thing in the world, having smiling and knowing glances coming my way from every direction as my husband and I made our way to the hall on the third floor. Especially since we were two hours late, something which spoke volumes but...whatever. It would have been worse having to pretend I knew people and fumbling through conversations with old friends and acquaintances that were nothing of the sort.

As we ascended the stairs, I saw I was not wrong about the tables in the hall.

Huge, round vases stuffed full of spiked white gladiolas festooned the center of each table, all of which were laid with silver trays covered in food.

They did not have vol-au-vents, mini-quiches and meatballs on a stick.

They had (amongst many other things) what looked like puff pastry stuffed with melted cheese, massive tiger prawns baked with slivers of prosciutto rolled around them, corners of thin toast covered thick in pâté and gherkins sliced lengthwise, crackers covered in what looked like cream cheese and caviar and hunks of meat and fish with small crystal glasses filled with tiny silver, two-pronged forks set beside them. And this didn't even get into the trays of bite-size pastries and cakes on offer.

So, Atticus was right, the same foods but theirs were posher.

Everything looked so delicious, seeing it, I was suddenly ravenous.

Frey, however, must have had a snack for he didn't even pause at a table, nor did he glance at one.

He made a beeline straight to Mother and Father.

Upon approach, I saw Father was wearing much what he wore to my wedding but without the sweater and instead a shirt in deep red with a cravat like Frey's. Mother was wearing a long, deep-red dress but the red of the material melted into gold at her hem. Her wrists, neck, fingers and ears were dripping with gold and rubies, not to mention the ruby-crusted gold clips in the shapes of dragonflies holding up her elegant hairstyle.

Taking them in, tall, lean and regal, I noted not for the first time that they both still had it, and I knew without a doubt if my parents had lived to their age, they would too.

This felt nice.

When Frey and I arrived at them, cheek touches were exchanged. Before I knew what she was about, Mother installed me firmly at her side. That was to say firmly and *closely* to her side.

Frey took his place by Father.

At first, this surprised me that I was not standing with Frey. However, for the next hour, I would get it.

This was because we were almost immediately descended upon by a wave of people. And as these people approached, chatted then moved on, Mother monopolized any conversation that involved me. If a question was directed to me, she answered it. If a comment was required of me, she prompted it. She interspersed names liberally while she spoke as well as deftly adding personal pieces of information or things such as, "Oh, Sjofn, you remember when..." And any time we had a lull in the action, she'd whisper in my ear, giving me tidbits about people coming or going so if I did speak, I wouldn't open my mouth and insert my foot.

Seriously, she was good.

And seriously, it felt nice to know that she and Frey (and maybe Father) arranged this to take care of me.

After a while, I started having fun. A maid brought us flat-bowled, etched crystal glasses of cold, dry, refreshing, delicious champagne and others moved around us offering trays of food.

I partook of both freely (avoiding unidentifiable meat, of course) and started to pay attention to the color of dresses or cravats and linking them with Houses. The clothing was opulent, the jewels even more so, hairstyles and makeup elaborate, men's mantles were everything from leather to full-on fur, and the Gales were obviously a place to see, be seen, and show right the hell off.

It was freaking awesome.

Mother, Father, Frey and I didn't move for an hour and by this time I had two glasses of champagne, had stuffed myself with every piece of food I could get my mitts on and was feeling it was high time to dance when it happened.

And luckily, I had a chance to prepare when Aurora's fingers tensed into the inside of my elbow.

I glanced at her face, then to where she was looking and saw a dark-haired woman wearing a phenomenal blood-red gown on her voluptuous, immaculately-cared-for body. Her eyes were a familiar brown-green, and at her side was a tall, dark-haired man who once was probably very hand-some but who now had a serious gut. The skin of his face showed he either drank too much, smoked too much, didn't eat the right foods or all three... in abundance.

Frey's parents.

Shit.

"Eirik and Valeria Drakkar, Frey's parents," Aurora whispered quickly in my ear, confirming my guess. "You've met them several times in your life, including twice while you were betrothed to The Drakkar. The other times at the Bitter or Solar Gales. They attended your wedding, but you did not converse with them prior to Drakkar taking you away."

"Well!" Valeria Drakkar exclaimed upon arrival, which was approximately a millisecond later. Not hesitating a millisecond longer, she grasped both my upper arms and pulled me away from Aurora to her to touch her cheek in turn to each of mine. She leaned away, pushing me back, and took me in without removing her hold on me. "She wears the color of Drakkar! Excellent!"

"Move aside, move aside," Eirik Drakkar shoved in and did the same, except (gross!) he kissed my *neck* on each side. Then he shoved me back and took me in, and the way he did made my stomach roil and my eyes slide to the side.

I saw Frey had moved to stand facing the huddle rather than at my father's side and not only was his jaw hard, his eyes were too. If that wasn't enough, a muscle ticked in his cheek.

Ho boy.

It appeared that not only did Frey not care for his parents, he actively didn't like them.

It also appeared, since neither Eirik nor Valeria had greeted him nor even looked at him, neither had an ounce of interest in their son.

"Look at my new daughter!" Eirik stated loudly, taking my attention back to him.

He leaned into me and proved that firstly, he'd partaken much of the food and whatever he'd eaten had an abundance of onion, or, more likely, he'd eaten an abundance of something with onion. Secondly, this was mixed with an alcohol smell that was *not* champagne. And thirdly, this mingling of smells was vastly unappealing.

"I must tell you, my lovely, lovely girl, I do not blame my son for dragging the likes of *you* through the Dwelling of the Gods and being away into the night. I cheered with the rest when I saw it, for, if I was twenty years younger, I would do the same, or better yet, take you to the Vallee's study and have you on his desk!"

Uh...did he just say that?

Major *ick*!

Not to mention major *rude*.

Before I could say a word, not that I had a word to say to *that*, Frey spoke.

"I'll thank you to unhand my bride." His voice was low and unhappy, but he didn't wait for his father to comply. He moved in front of his mother, Atticus and Aurora, and with an arm around my waist, he pulled me firmly out of his father's grasp.

Thank God.

"Ah, my Frey," Valeria said softly. "Always so prickly, especially when it came to his belongings." She leaned into me and wagged a finger in my direction. "Never shared with his brothers, our Frey. Always so possessive."

I will note at this point that she *still* hadn't greeted her son.

"It's repulsive, with your words, that you'd insinuate that I should share *my wife* with my father, Valeria," Frey remarked, still in his low, unhappy voice.

"All in the family," she replied, smiling a smile that not only didn't reach her eyes but was cold as Christmas.

Uh...ick again.

Already, I did *not* like these people more than I suspected I wouldn't like them knowing that Frey didn't. Not to mention the not insignificant fact that they'd never given him any presents.

Eirik, unfortunately, butted in, indicating he had a one-track mind, and it wasn't a nice track. "My boy, in dragging her out of the Dwelling, you robbed me of every father-in-law's right to his dance with his new daughter-in-law at the celebration. Which, I might add, includes a kiss at the end. This," he leered at me, "I'll be taking tonight at my earliest opportunity."

Okay, it was safe to say I was not looking forward to *that*.

"You'll not dance with my princess, and you've already touched your mouth to her two more times than I find comfortable," Frey stated, staring down his nose at his father.

I leaned into Frey, pleased beyond reason that he helped me dodge *that* bullet.

"Killjoy," Eirik muttered. He focused again on me in order to comment. "I was surprised you weren't with us today, Sjofn. In the past, you've more than enjoyed participating in the royal hunts."

"Well—" I started but Mother got there before me.

"Sjofn and I had an important errand to run in town. She and Frey are traveling so she was busy preparing to take her leave on the morrow," Aurora neatly entered the conversation to explain.

"Hmm," Valeria murmured, her familiar but nowhere near as warm eyes on me. "Rumor has it she's lost her touch with her bow." At these words, my body got tight. Frey's got tight against me, and I felt Aurora and Atticus get tense too. "I thought that might be it," she finished, watching me so closely, kid you not, I started to squirm.

Then Eirik bizarrely and *unbelievably* coarsely put in, "It's the talk of the Gales, so everyone knows he's been doing naught much else but thrusting between her legs for days, wife. And this undoubtedly means *my* son has

231

been going at her *for weeks*. Drakkar seed, always powerful, stuffed full of it, it causes even our princess, a skilled huntress, to lose her touch with her bow."

At these words, words which should not be spoken at an elegant ball, or, perhaps, *ever*, I gasped. And I knew my guess was accurate for Mother also gasped, Father, jaw clenched and eyes hard, moved forward but Frey had had enough.

I knew this when his hand shot up and fisted tightly in his father's cravat. He yanked his father toward him and up to his toes. Bending his neck only slightly, he got nose to nose with him.

Then he growled, "Thus ends the family reunion."

He let his now red-faced father loose with a rough push and Eirik stumbled back two steps, running into a young woman in a lovely kelly-green gown before he righted himself.

But I had little opportunity to watch. Frey had his hand on my elbow, and he was moving me away.

And he did so while muttering acerbically to his mother, "As ever, a unique pleasure."

Without a backward glance at his father but a tip of his head to Aurora and Atticus, he led me firmly to the ballroom then equally firmly off to the side where there was a small patch of free space. There he stopped us, drew me close and looked down at me.

I looked up at him and saw on the scale of how angry Frey could be he looked to be at around twelve.

"Are you all right?" he asked.

Shaken by what had just happened, I replied honestly if not helpfully, "Your dad's kind of a dick."

"And a 'dick' would be?" Frey queried tersely.

"An asshole. A fuckwad. A douchebag. A screaming jerk," I explained, and Frey scowled a ferocious scowl I could take because it wasn't directed at me.

Then he stated, "You do know I don't know what any of those are either except, possibly, the first."

"None of them are good," I clarified then stressed, "*At all.*"

Frey kept scowling at me and that was when I tardily realized I should do something to make him feel better instead of what I was doing, fueling the fire. So I moved in close and circled his middle with my arms. I leaned back as his arms curved around me and looked up at him.

"That said, I'm fine," I whispered.

I saw his anger ratchet down to about a five before he whispered back, "Good."

"Though," I said, cautiously sharing, "your mom kind of scares me."

Frey's eyes didn't leave mine when he replied, "She should. Where your mother acts first for her husband, then her family, then her realm, my mother acts first for herself. Then she acts on every opportunity presented to behave with malice or cruelty. Next, if it serves her purpose, for the House of Drakkar. But never does she act for the good of her sons, her husband or Lunwyn."

Yep, I didn't like either of them, especially not Valeria Drakkar.

"Malice and cruelty?" I prompted, still treading cautiously.

He sighed, looked over my head, and then back down at me.

"Malice and cruelty," he affirmed.

I got up on my toes.

Frey dipped closer, and when he did, I whispered, "She knows about my archery practice."

He nodded. "This is not a surprise. She has spies and this is what she wants you to know. This, my wee Finnie, is what she does. It's doubtful she's generous enough with any of them to pay for anything she could use, for she's as stingy as she is heartless, unless, of course, it's coin used for another gown or necklace for herself. However, she wanted you to know this in hopes you'd worry about the information she held, planting it in your mind so it could fester as you wondered at her intent and the extent of her knowledge."

Wow.

Wow.

I hated this, like, a lot. So much, it felt like acid at the back of my throat.

And I didn't hate it for me. I hated it for Frey.

I hated it so much I couldn't stop myself from pressing closer, lifting a hand to wrap around the side of his neck and asking softly, "Where on earth did you come from, baby?"

Frey's brows drew together, and he asked softly back, "Pardon?"

My thumb stroked his jaw before I whispered, "My handsome husband is gentle, thoughtful and kind. He laughs and smiles easily, and he makes me feel safe. I was with your folks for about five minutes, and they were so far from any of that, it is not funny. So," I squeezed his neck, "where did you come from?"

I belatedly noticed that my gentle, thoughtful, kind husband was staring down at me with that fiery look in his eyes. The same look he had after I gave him his spun glass dragon. And looking at it, his fire melted my heart, a heart that was already far from frozen.

Before I could say anything, not that I hadn't already said too much, his arms about me tightened and his face dipped super close to mine when he said quietly, "I do not know, my wee Finnie, where I came from. But I'm beginning to know why I'm here."

And that was when stupid, stupid, stupidly, I asked, "And why are you here, honey?"

"I don't need to say aloud what I know you also are beginning to understand, wee one," he answered, and I pressed my lips together because he was not wrong, and I was still not going there. His eyes held mine as his mouth murmured, "She waits for me at windows and buys me dragons. There are reasons we walk this earth. I'm coming to realize mine."

"Frey," I whispered and said no more. I couldn't. I was too moved, and I felt strangely like I was standing in quicksand, sinking fast.

The problem was, I had no will whatsoever to find a vine and pull myself out.

His head dipped further, and he pressed his lips hard to mine.

He broke his sweet touch and moved back an inch to say, "My grandmother."

My head tipped to the side. "Your grandmother?"

"If there is anything gentle and kind in me, my love, she put it there. My father's mother had a light shining from her soul." His lips tipped up and he continued, "Because of that, you remind me in some ways of her. But she lived in a den of vipers and knew how to take care of herself, moving cautiously ahead while keeping an eye to her back lest someone be preparing to bury a dagger in it. Even so, with those she cared about, she displayed great humor, generosity and thoughtfulness."

I studied him and it hit me he'd said she'd died when he was thirteen.

Therefore, I asked, "So, when she passed, is that why you left your family and never went back?"

His lips tipped up further to a grin.

"Someone has been talking," he guessed.

I grinned back and relaxed deeper into him, my hand sliding down to rest on his chest. "Four someones, to be precise, and they had one avid listener."

He chuckled then confirmed, "Yes, wee one, when she died, living amongst them became too much to bear. So I left and never went back."

"What was her name?" I asked.

"Eugenie," he answered.

"I wish I'd known her," I whispered.

"As do I," Frey concurred.

I kept going. "I'm sorry your family sucks, baby."

He chuckled again but concurred with that too. "I am as well, my wee Finnie."

I stared up at a magnificent man who was magnificent against some pretty big odds.

And as I did, I knew I had two choices. Struggle against the quicksand only to have it slurp me up to bury me straight to the throat. Or move the fuck on and have some fun, fun which would undoubtedly suck me deeper anyway, but again, I wasn't all fired up to save myself from going down.

I picked door number two.

And to do it, I tilted my head to the side and smiled brightly at my husband before I asked, "Wanna dance?"

His eyes roamed my face before they locked on my mouth.

Still looking there, he answered, "Absolutely."

Then he bent and kissed my nose yet again before he let me go and led me to the dance floor.

He did this holding my hand.

I let him do it and I did it smiling.

NEARLY EVERY EYE in the room watched The Drakkar lead his princess to the dance.

As they had been watching The Drakkar and his Winter Princess in their intimate, cozy huddle from the moment they entered the ballroom.

And as many had watched from horses, windows or fire drums as that afternoon, the Winter Princess burst forth from her Palace to meet her imposing husband with a bright smile. And that imposing husband smiled back then gave his new wife a gentle touch, soft words and, finally, a light kiss.

And as The Drakkar whirled, twirled and lifted his new bride through the next four dances, all the while he smiled warmly at her or laughed out loud at something she said or at an unusual inexpert stumble in her step (which always made her laugh out loud too, through the smiles she was returning to her husband, of course), they kept watching.

~

"PLEASE, MY PRINCESS, THE NEXT DANCE," the young man begged.

I smiled and shook my head, trying to recall the name he gave me but unable to do so since so many were swimming in my head.

I'd been dancing flat out for what felt like hours and I loved doing it. It was a freaking *blast*. But the dances in Lunwyn were mostly energetic (there were a few slow ones and all of those I'd danced with Frey). They were also complicated with a lot of lifts that included the man lifting you straight up into the air or whirling you at his side while you held your legs out like a ballerina leaping across the stage. Not to mention the footwork, twirls, bobs and dips.

It was a blast, but it was exhausting, and I needed a drink.

When I processed his dejected look, I relented, slightly. "Just a wee rest, the next song after this, we'll dance. I promise."

He grinned and bowed smartly before he straightened and stated, "I'll be there to take your hand the moment the orchestra delivers its first note."

"Wonderful," I murmured on a small smile, and he moved away.

I did too and I did it while scanning the room. I marked Frey across the vast expanse, standing with a formally attired (and hot looking) Thad and Max.

His eyes were on me, and I smiled, watched his mouth get soft then he turned his attention back to his men.

I kept scanning and saw Aurora dancing with a very fat man who was having trouble lifting her, but she didn't give the slightest indication she feared he was going to drop her to the ground.

I kept up my scan and saw Atticus laughing with two men, one in a royal-blue shirt, one in a moss-green one, a woman wearing the same green at his side. I'd danced twice with my father of this world, and I could say two things. One, he was a great dancer, and two, I'd never forget either.

I also noted, as I had since we left Houllebec, that Frey's men were very visible and very close. Orion, Gunner and Lund were all not five feet away from me in different huddles of people, and Annar and Stephan were not much farther.

I found a pocket of space in a corner and dragged my carcass to it while I stopped scanning for the familiar people who made me feel rooted and safe and started scanning for a maid who could get me some much-needed champagne.

Therefore, I had my head turned away when I heard a feminine purr from beside me.

"She wears the blood."

My head jerked around to see an extortionately beautiful, dark-haired, blue-eyed woman standing beside me who was taller than me by at least three inches and she was wearing a blood-red gown that made my cleavage look demure (and mine was nowhere near demure but, honest to God, I saw the edges of the aureoles of her nipples peeping through hers).

"This pleases me," she finished, and my eyes snapped from her shocking décolletage to her face.

Oh shit.

She was clearly of the House of Drakkar, and I saw my mistake immediately. I should have gone to Frey or Father. Princess Sjofn probably knew her, and she was a Drakkar. This meant I had to tread carefully because the usual field of landmines around me just tripled.

I checked myself from sending a panicked look to Frey or Father that would expose too much and swiftly pulled it together.

"Hello." I thought it safe to say.

She turned to me and leaned her long elegant neck in to touch her cheek to mine before moving back.

"We've not met," she purred, and I felt relief flood through me at this news. "I'm Frey's cousin, Franka."

"Lovely to meet you, Franka," I said softly.

She smiled lazily and I felt the relief disappear as I took in her smile, which was not only lazy but weirdly sexual.

Oh shit.

"Lovely to meet you too, my Winter Princess." She kept purring then her eyes dropped to my cleavage and her look at mine was *way* different than the way I looked at hers.

Oh *shit*.

Okay, I had to be polite, have a short conversation, not say anything stupid and then get the fuck out of there.

God, I hoped this song didn't last very long so my eager dance partner would show up and quick.

"Are you enjoying the Gales?" I asked and watched her lip slightly curl up as her eyes moved from my chest to my face.

"I spend as much time as possible in Fleuridia," she informed me, "where they understand the exacting standards of elegance and panache so..." She hesitated then concluded scornfully, "No."

I decided not to reply mostly because she was being rude and I was a princess so I didn't think returning her rudeness, which was what I wanted to do, would be appropriate.

"However, seeing as my dear cousin Frey has bound himself to our lovely princess, I couldn't stay away." She leaned slightly into me and informed me, "Rumors of your beauty run wide, Princess Sjofn. Even down in Fleuridia they speak of it."

"That's nice," I muttered, leaning slightly back to make a point.

She caught it and moved away.

"Though, her interest in swordplay and the hunt and penchant for wearing breeches is also spoken of quite widely." Her eyes swept me slowly before she concluded, "I see Frey put an end to that."

"Not exactly," I looked away. "Although I will say he's introduced me to more enjoyable pastimes."

I looked back at her when she laughed with obvious delight, the sound beautiful, even enthralling, and strangely terrifying.

Then she murmured, looking under her lashes at me, "She enjoys connubial bliss."

I studied her and knew without any doubt she was playing with me.

And that was when I decided that being a princess sometimes could be set aside. Especially with people I knew my husband did not care for (in the slightest), and I doubted my parents did either.

Thus, I stated, "Actually, what *she* enjoys is keeping private matters *private.*"

"You brought it up," she informed me smoothly.

"Actually, no. You read into what I said," I returned.

"Was my reading wrong?" she asked.

No, it wasn't. What she was wrong about was continuing to talk about it when I asked her not to do so. And after what Valeria and Eirik had treated Frey and I to I'd suddenly had enough of the Drakkars.

So I turned to her and said, "If you're curious about your cousin, which would be repulsive, but..." I hesitated. "To each their own. Then yes. I *greatly* enjoy connubial bliss, frequently and *vigorously.*"

I knew my mistake at falling to her level when she smiled with sheer pleasure.

Damn, I'd given her exactly what she wanted.

She turned her head, her eyes moving as if she was looking for something, she found it and tipped up her chin.

"Champagne," she muttered. Her eyes still aimed elsewhere, I looked where they were aimed, and my stomach clutched when I saw Viola nodding her head then moving swiftly toward us with a tray holding two champagne glasses. "We'll toast your marriage," Franka suggested.

I did not want to toast my marriage with Franka Drakkar, and I did not want to be confronted with Viola, who had not, since that first night, attended our table. What she did, I didn't know. I didn't let her go because it wasn't her fault Frey had enjoyed her. Unlike me (in both worlds), she had to earn a living. But I did have a quiet word with Jocelyn, who had one with the housekeeper, and I saw Viola no more.

Until now.

I tried not to look at her as she approached then I couldn't tear my eyes away for she was aiming a look of pure venom at me, hatred clear and openly read in her eyes.

That was when I decided, perhaps upon my return, I would have a word myself with the housekeeper to see about Viola moving on to other employment or perhaps being reassigned to do the laundry.

She bobbed a curtsy and held up the tray.

I wanted champagne and that was the only reason I took a glass after Franka took hers, and without a backward glance, Viola expertly and swiftly melted into the crowd.

"To marriage," Franka lifted her glass and, eyes on me over the rim, she took a sip.

I wanted a sip, actually, I wanted to down the whole glass, but instead I studied her and didn't take one.

I asked straight out, "Tell me, Franka, are you genuinely pleased your cousin has found someone who makes him happy or are you just having some fun?"

She tipped her head to the side and asked back, "*Has* my handsome cousin found someone who makes him happy?"

Actually, it hit me right then, he had. And he made no bones about it.

And that someone was me.

And at that thought, that quicksand slurped up another foot.

"Yes," I whispered. "We're both very happy," I told her honestly and *slurp!* up another foot I went.

Franka didn't speak. She inspected my face, and she did it closely.

"Gods, you don't jest," she whispered back.

"And why would I jest?" I returned.

She took another sip of champagne. Then she moved slightly closer, and I stiffened but held my ground.

She spoke. "I am not of that bent, my princess, although I must admit I've dabbled, and since I've dabbled, and enjoyed it when I did, you must know there are those *of that bent* who feel quite certain you are too. And, I must say, my curiosity for coming here was to gaze upon your beauty, and perhaps see about, as you put it, *having some fun.*"

I stared at her a second before it hit me.

Hells bells, she thought I was a lesbian.

Shit.

"Of course," she said quietly, her eyes warming, her face showing hunger. "If Frey is dipping into that honey, I know him enough to know he'll not share, so alas, although you are everything they say you are, I will stand down."

Seriously, the Drakkars. I had never, in all my travels, met anyone like them. Not even close. No wonder Frey got the hell out of there as soon as he could.

"That would please me," I told her firmly then stressed, "*Tremendously.* But I will say that it is unfortunate for those who are *of that bent,* as you put it, that you cast your lures as you do. I don't wish to be offensive, but you must know it's inelegant and lacks panache."

She blinked at me, her chin jerking back as my hit scored, and I heard the orchestra stop playing as, out of the corner of my eye, as promised, I saw my eager dance partner approaching.

I turned to a table beside me and set my glass next to another resting there before I turned back to Franka.

"A unique pleasure," I muttered to her acidly, using Frey's words as I tipped my chin.

I turned my head and smiled at my partner who already had his hand extended to me.

I took it and also took another cue from Frey and didn't look back.

Luckily, that unpleasant meeting was forced from my brain since I had to concentrate on the dance, which was one of the more complicated ones.

And since I was concentrating, it wasn't until after a woman bumped into me and my partner clutched my hand, stopped dancing and pulled me close that I quit concentrating. I looked up at him to see his face pale, eyes wide, and he was peering toward the corner I had not long ago fled.

I turned that way, and as I did, I saw all the people on the dance floor had their eyes riveted in that direction too. I also heard the coughing, which was uncontrollable. As my eyes moved to the corner where I'd been standing not three minutes ago, I saw an elderly woman in a deep purple gown start retching violently.

But there was blood already dribbling from her lip.

She had one hand to her throat, her eyes were wide with terror and her other hand held a champagne glass, the contents of which sloshed out as she coughed so deeply, it hurt to hear.

There was a low murmur running through the crowd as she struggled, and a man in a deep purple shirt had his hand on her back and looked to be trying to guide her to a chair when it happened.

A profuse gurgle of blood poured out of her mouth.

I took a horrified step back and sucked in a shocked breath as small screams and more gasps were heard. But still more blood rushed forth from the poor woman's throat as her skin turned livid, her eyes bugged out hideously and then she collapsed to the floor.

It was at that exact moment a hand curled around to cover my eyes. I was turned until I felt my front pressed into Frey's.

"Find Franka. Find that *bloody* maid. And get your hands on that gods-damned glass," he growled, his voice a fearsome rumble.

I tipped back my head and his hand slid away. One glance up at his face set in granite told me he'd busted the scales and he was in the Anger Danger Zone.

I looked over my shoulder and saw Max start winding urgently toward the crowd that had closed around the woman. But Orion, Gunner and Lund were already there.

Before I could say a word, Frey shifted me into the waiting Thad's arms and grunted, "Her room. Now. No one attends her. *No one.*"

Frey turned the opposite direction and moved into the ballroom in a direction I noted took him to Franka in her blood-red dress. But Thad was pulling me through the shoving, slightly frightened, slightly curious crowd, and I lost sight of my husband.

I saw Atticus pushing his way toward me, his face pale, his frightened eyes locked on me.

"Finnie," he said when he got close, but Thad positioned himself between me and Father and kept pulling me toward the hall.

"Stand back, your grace," Thad warned as Father kept moving toward us.

Atticus's eyes shot to Thad and the fear left them as anger, shock and royal affront filled them.

"I beg your pardon?" he clipped.

"Orders of The Drakkar," Thad stated.

Atticus's mouth dropped open and Thad yanked me through a bunch of people who were streaming into the ballroom to see what all the commotion was about and then we were in the hall.

He didn't waste any time pulling me through the hall, down the stairs and to my rooms. Once there he didn't waste any time ascertaining they were empty.

He took hold of both my arms and bent so his face was close to mine.

"Bolt the door behind me. I need to see what's happening and I, or another of Frey's men, will be back to guard your door. Do not open it to anyone, Princess Finnie. I don't care who they are, and I don't care if you trust them. You open this door to Frey and me. Only Frey and me. Am I understood?" he asked.

"What's happening?" I whispered.

"Am I understood, Finnie?" he repeated.

"Thad, what's happening?" I repeated too, but louder.

Thad stared at me a second as if trying to decide something.

Then he decided. "That glass was served to you by a maid known to Frey. Frey marked it when you put it down and he marked it when that woman accidentally picked it up. Tonight, my princess, someone tried to poison you."

My mind filled with that woman pouring forth blood and my head got light.

"Gods, don't go down. I don't have time to revive you," Thad muttered, giving me a gentle shake.

"I'm not going to go down," I whispered.

"Your eyes, princess, focus on me," he urged.

I focused on him.

Then I asked, "But, my father—?"

He got closer and his fingers gave me a slight squeeze before he reminded me softly, giving me the knowledge that he held information I was surprised he had, "Finnie, your father isn't your father. Any child you put on the throne will not be his blood. I'm sorry, your grace, but in this land and every other, you have one ally and that is The Drakkar."

I blinked at him as my heart twisted. It did this in a quick wrench that hurt so badly, it was a wonder I didn't pass out.

"Bolt the door, a man you can trust will be here shortly," he muttered.

I nodded. He gave my arms another squeeze and took off.

After he left, I went directly to the door, locked it and threw all three bolts home.

I turned my back to it, covered my mouth with my hand and stared at my beautiful room.

I sucked in a deep breath, pushed away, walked to the bed where Penelope had lifted her head at the commotion and was yawning huge.

I scooped her up. She protested.

I shushed her and held her tight as I waited for the return of The Drakkar.

19

LACK OF VIGILANCE

"By the gods." Frey Drakkar heard muttered in horror behind him. He turned from the broken, bleeding woman at his feet and saw King Atticus and Queen Aurora had entered the room.

Atticus was the one who muttered and he, indeed, looked horrified as his eyes stayed glued to the woman on the floor. Aurora looked pale, but her eyes, also on the woman bleeding and curled into herself, were shielded.

"Your daughter has a traitor on her staff," Drakkar growled, his gut tight, his neck tight, bile in his throat at the thought he'd actually had his cock in the bitch who'd schemed to murder his Finnie, delivering the poison her gods-damned self. "She's confessed. A physician should attend her once my men have transferred her to jail."

Both Atticus and Aurora's eyes shot to him, and Drakkar forced himself from his thoughts in order to remain focused and take in every infinitesimal nuance of both king and queen.

"This maid poisoned Finnie?" Atticus whispered, still horrified and that was all Drakkar read on the king's face.

He read something else on Aurora's. A flash of anger mixed with more than a little bit of accusation.

An interesting reaction and an uncomfortable one.

Drakkar lifted his chin to Oleg who moved to Viola, hefting her over his shoulder with complete immunity to her whimpers and cries as he carried her out, exactly as he'd been immune to the same as he'd extracted her confession.

Drakkar's eyes slid through his cousin who was standing against the wall, arms crossed on her chest, eyes revoltingly excited.

She'd enjoyed watching Oleg obtain information from Viola.

A mistake. He'd thought it would bring forth fear.

But she was a Drakkar. He should have known better.

He looked to Aurora and stated, "Yes. Viola accepted payment to prepare and deliver a poisoned glass to Finnie." Atticus and Aurora stared at him, and he continued, "She's also given us another name to add to Berg Enger's. Hernod Grieg, they're associates."

He continued to regard the king and queen closely. Atticus already knew that Berg Enger was the Lunwynian who had paid for the assassination attempt that had failed in Houllebec. Enger had been found by Drakkar's man Quincy and had not yet provided them with further information. And considering their tactics, it was highly likely he didn't know much more than he'd already told them.

What they knew was that Enger was a malcontent, this starting at his displeasure of losing some land as penance from his liege lord for a string of petty crimes. This was appealed to the king and the king held his liege lord's ruling. Because of this, Enger had no love for the crown, but he also had no money.

What he did have was an association with a network of men who considered they had been wronged by Atticus in some way.

What they did not know was who was financing Enger.

Until now.

Hernod Grieg was a merchant who traded out of Sudvic, as Drakkar did. Drakkar knew of him, had met him and didn't like him. Grieg didn't consider himself wronged by the crown in so much as he disliked paying taxes to it, for he preferred his coin in his coffers.

Why he would participate in a treasonous plot, Drakkar did not know. But both Quincy and Balthazar were already riding to Sudvic to find out.

With Viola out of the room, Atticus pulled himself together and not for the first time, Drakkar thought this was one characteristic every king should have that Atticus of the House of Wilde did not.

He didn't have the stomach for the dirty work of politics.

It was a weakness.

"I've heard of this Grieg," Atticus stated.

"And what do you know?" Drakkar asked.

"Not much." Atticus shook his head. "He's a merchant in Sudvic. He attended the Solar Hunt last year, invited by a member of a House, but he did not go to the Gales. I met him very briefly. I can't even say for certain I recall what he looked like," Atticus answered.

"Which House?" Drakkar pushed.

Atticus shook his head again. "That, as well, I can't recall."

Drakkar studied his king then he whispered, "Try."

Atticus held his eyes and replied, "Ravenscroft or Lazarus, maybe Sinclair or Njord. But saying any at this juncture is slander for, indeed, Drakkar, this meeting was insignificant, and I truly cannot recall."

Drakkar's eyes went to Annar who was standing, hands on hips, in the corner. "Get to Ravenscroft, Lazarus, Njord and Sinclair. They're all here. I'll need to speak to them before I go."

Annar lifted a chin and left the room.

Drakkar looked to Aurora.

"And you?" he queried.

"I've never heard of him before," she replied instantly, her eyes blank but active. Though not, Drakkar sensed, from an attempt to hide something.

Drakkar turned his head to Franka. "And you?"

She lifted a fluttering hand to her wide, garish expanse of cleavage.

"Me?" she drawled.

Drakkar turned his whole body to face his cousin.

Facing her, he said softly, "I know you fancy yourself a cat who isn't content unless she's got herself a mouse to play with, but do not mistake me for a mouse, Franka. A mouse cannot yank a cat's throat out with his fist."

He knew she knew his threat was not idle when she lost some color in her face.

"What do you know of Hernod Grieg?" Drakkar pressed.

"I live in Fleuridia, Frey, as you know. And even there, I don't consort with *merchants*," she said her last with disdain and not a small amount of folly for she was speaking to one.

Drakkar moved to stand two feet in front of her.

"You called the maid to you, Franka. I noted it. There were two glasses of champagne on that tray, I noted that too. You took your glass first," Drakkar remarked.

"It's touching to see how much attention you pay your new bride, Drakkar," she purred.

Frey didn't allow his expression to change but he lifted his hand and touched his index finger lightly on her throat, watching her body tense as she pulled in a breath.

"You cannot forget mere seconds ago, Franka, when I told you I was no mouse," he whispered.

She looked deep in his eyes, read them correctly, and swallowed.

Drakkar dropped his hand.

Franka spoke.

"I cannot say I recall how the tray was offered, Frey. But I simply took the glass closest to me. And your unfortunate wench," she waved a hand low to where Viola had been lying, "left quickly therefore did not wait to see if her endeavors were successful. What I can say was that the girl was hovering, that I noted prior to arriving at your fair princess. But that is all I can say."

"Is it possible for you to assure me in a way that would actually convince me you've had no hand in tonight's events?" Drakkar asked, and Franka's eyes narrowed.

"Now why, my brawny, handsome cousin, would I, Franka Drakkar of the House of Drakkar, poison our beautiful Winter Princess when she'd just been telling me how happy she was with you, and all your nuptial activities. Activities that would seat a Drakkar on the throne of Lunwyn for the first time in seven hundred and fifty years?" Franka asked back.

"Why does a Drakkar do anything?" Drakkar returned.

"Indeed," she replied, slightly inclining her head to accede the point. "However, *this* Drakkar quite likes the idea of the House being restored to its former glory. So, *this* Drakkar would do naught to stop that from happening. Further, *this* Drakkar would not be so stupid as to stand next to her victim whilst she was being poisoned. And lastly, *this* Drakkar, unfortunately, has to rely on her House to keep herself in her apartments in Fleuridia that she greatly enjoys, her Fleuridian gowns she also enjoys. And if she would participate in such foolhardiness, other Drakkars, of which there are many, my cousin, including *you*, who wish to see our House again rule Lunwyn, would not be too happy if she were to scheme against that future event. Therefore, *this* Drakkar is not likely to do something so foolhardy as to lose her the lifestyle she enjoys. Not to mention..." she paused and held his eyes, "a throat she likes perfectly well right where it is."

Drakkar returned her gaze and also sensed she was not hiding anything.

"This is good," Drakkar said quietly. "But I suggest you guard that throat, Franka."

"I always do," she returned smoothly.

Drakkar wasn't finished.

"And, if you enjoy your lifestyle, as you advance through Lunwyn or Fleuridia in your constant play, you'll be certain to inform me should you hear anything I may wish to learn."

Her face grew smug before she asked, "Are you suggesting you can sway my brother into severing my funds?"

When the gods dispensed attributes between Franka and her brother Kristian, unfortunately, Franka received more than her fair share of them including looks and wits. That said, Kristian, being the male child, inherited their dead father's fortune so he held the family purse.

Nevertheless, Kristian was Franka's favorite mouse and she played with him often.

"I'm not suggesting anything, Franka. If I discover you know something you didn't share, Kristian will be given his own choice about the state of his throat. He may be a puppet on your strings, cousin, but one thing I'm certain he was born with and that is a sense of self-preservation."

Her mouth got tight, but Drakkar wasn't finished.

"And something else he has born. A son who would inherit his purse should something befall him, a son whose age would mean his mother would control his funds for some years. In your vicious play, have you been clever enough to spare his wife?"

He knew the answer to that as well because she lost her poise and glared at her cousin.

Instead of answering his question, she asked sharply, "Am I free to leave or will I be treated to some of the same I witnessed your man meting out to that poor woman?"

"That poor woman was a traitor and nearly murdered my wife, Franka, so she's lucky to leave here breathing, if not fully intact. But *you* will not be treated to the same for *you* would enjoy it," Drakkar retorted.

Her glare melted away, her eyes heated, and she smiled languorously at the thought.

"Too true," she murmured.

Drakkar stared at his cousin with disgust wondering if he *did* actually have Drakkar blood in his veins or if he was a changeling.

"You may leave," he muttered, dismissing her by turning away and back to Atticus and Aurora who both had been watching.

Atticus again didn't hide his reaction to Franka and stared after her with distaste as she exited. Aurora didn't move her attention from Drakkar.

Max walked in, and Drakkar looked to his man.

"The princess," Max said, and Drakkar lifted his chin.

"Find Thad, send him to her. Have him tell her she needs to change. Then have Tyr brought around. Finnie and I leave for Sudvic tonight," Drakkar commanded.

Max nodded and left.

"Tonight?" Aurora asked, and Drakkar shifted his regard to her.

"Immediately after I speak with Ravenscroft, Njord, Sinclair and Lazarus," Drakkar answered.

"But it's late. It's night—" Aurora started.

"She's slept on Tyr with me before. She can do it again," Drakkar returned.

"She must be in a state," Atticus put in and turned to Aurora. "We'll be away to her now. See to it she's all right and—"

"You'll get nowhere near my wife," Drakkar cut in, and both Atticus and Aurora looked to him.

"I beg your pardon?" Atticus asked softly.

"I'm certain you heard me," Drakkar replied.

"But..." Atticus began, faltered, his eyes uncomprehending, and he finished incredulously, "By the gods, why?"

"Because Finnie was nearly poisoned tonight," Drakkar explained shortly.

"We know. We were both there," Atticus shot back. "And our daughter was there too. She saw that woman collapse. I saw her face right after it happened. She was in a state. You can't toss her up on a horse and—"

Drakkar cut him off. "I can and this is what I'm going to do, Atticus."

Atticus opened his mouth to protest but Aurora got there before him.

"Drakkar, I understand your wish to be away. But my husband and I would like a moment with our daughter to ascertain that she is well after the events of tonight."

"And your daughter is in another world and has no idea that her selfish actions have put my Finnie in such peril," Drakkar retorted and was mildly surprised to see Aurora rear slightly back.

He was far more than mildly surprised to hear her whisper, "That peril, Drakkar, came at the hands of a woman you tossed aside."

This was exactly what he didn't need and precisely what he was attempting not to think about.

Therefore, Drakkar clenched his teeth before he returned, "A woman who was paid by a conspirator."

"A woman who was open to payment because she'd been bedded by you. She liked it. She wanted it to repeat when you returned, and you gave her hope by requesting she attend the table where your new wife sat. Then you dashed those hopes because you were enjoying yourself elsewhere," Aurora shot back. "I know women, Drakkar, being one, and that woman acted out of jealousy."

Drakkar felt his temper fray as her words made the guilt he'd been controlling rise, and he leaned slightly toward his queen before he replied, "That may be but she also acted out the paid request of a conspirator I can assure you I have *not* bedded."

"I think you understand my point," she said softly.

"No, actually, I think I'd like you to make it clearer," Drakkar retorted also softly, but his was deadly.

Aurora crossed her arms on her chest and bravely ignored his tone. "Atticus told me your man kept him from our daughter."

"Again, she is not your daughter," Drakkar gritted through his teeth, and Aurora's back went straight.

"No, you are right. And, perhaps, not being in my head, or Atticus's, you cannot know that we have found you were right about something else. So as you stand there, certain in nothing but the fact that no one can be trusted, I'll explain something important to you before you whisk *our daughter* into the night," Aurora stated.

Drakkar crossed his arms on his chest and scowled at her.

She lifted her chin and continued.

"You were right. We grieve the loss of our Sjofn, but we have both come to know why *you* came to care about Finnie in such a short time."

Drakkar's body got tight, but she wasn't finished.

"As for me," she said quietly. "I would give my crown to see my daughter again. She vexed me, everyone knows, but I loved her straight to my soul and I'd hand over my crown without that first thought for the chance to see her again. What I *wouldn't* do is harm Finnie."

She pulled in a breath and kept her eyes on Drakkar likely so she would not see her husband's response to her next words.

"It pains me to say, but Finnie is the daughter I didn't have. My husband, I am pleased to know, had the daughter he wanted, one who enjoyed his pursuits. For thirty years, I did not have that. But, for the last two weeks, I did."

With years borne of practice, Drakkar managed to keep his reaction in check and didn't show his surprise.

Queen Aurora would likely not have seen it. She was focused on her message and kept speaking.

"As you have said, my Sjofn is not here, and I do not go a day without thinking dozens of times of what she has done. I think of what she's done to my king and my country. But I also think of me. She left *me* behind, Drakkar, and her father. And it does not escape either of us that your Finnie, *our* Finnie, did the exact opposite. She did not escape her parents. She risked a great deal to *find* them again. You are not a parent yet so you cannot know, but I will tell you, knowing the difference of their two motives twists a knife already imbedded deep even deeper. At the same time, knowing Finnie and seeing her joy at being with those who remind her of the parents she loved soothes a considerable balm over that wound."

Drakkar held her eyes, heard her words, knew they were not false, but sensed she was not quite finished.

He was not wrong.

Aurora continued, "I cannot say at this moment that I would drink that poison for her or give my crown for her return as I would my own daughter. I can say that I would do nothing to harm her, and to those who already have tried, I do not recoil that they find justice."

She inclined her head to where Viola had lain to make her point but didn't take her attention from Drakkar.

She also didn't stop talking.

But she said her next quietly with astonishing emotion trembling in her voice and her eyes were not blank. They were alight with passion.

"You soon talk to the heads of the two Houses whose blood flows in my veins. I am a Ravenscroft, I am a Lazarus, and those two Houses, if they are anything, they are *Lunwynians*. They would no sooner betray their king, their country, their niece," she leaned forward, "*or me*, than they would fly to a dragon's cave and invite his fire."

She straightened again and kept speaking quietly.

"You are The Drakkar, The Frey, and Finnie is your destiny. Legend tells that all the Houses were touched by the elves that have frosted our country to such beauty yet have provided abundance, and they did so that the Houses would lead Lunwyn to prosperity. The Frey and The Drakkar have been born in one man, which means the gods have called upon you, and our cherished elves leave their realm at long last to serve you."

251

She drew in a shallow, almost imperceptible deep breath and continued speaking.

"Although the heads of those Houses do not hold the knowledge of Finnie being your destiny, they, like me, would do nothing to stand in the way of the decisions you make, the commands you give or the actions you take for Lunwyn, because you have been chosen by the gods and Finnie has been chosen by them for you. And with respect, I ask you to remember that, Drakkar, in your fire to avenge what's happened tonight under your nose, a glass delivered to your new bride by the hand of a woman who warmed your bed, when you speak to the heads of those Houses."

"Aurora, my beloved," Atticus whispered, reaching out and clutching his wife's hand in concern at her show of insolence.

But Aurora held his gaze, not looking at her husband, and Drakkar noted her chest rising and falling with her emotion.

He'd seen that before more than once.

"I've noted," Drakkar said softly, "many occasions that Finnie reminds me of you. She has your grace in her bearing, and I didn't know it until now, but she also has your passion of emotion." Atticus sucked in a hopeful breath as his wife visibly worked to calm herself. "The elves told me the twins of the two worlds are different people and this is true of your daughter and Finnie. It is strange and fantastical you share these attributes with Finnie as if you passed them down through your womb. But it is nevertheless true."

The king and queen remained silent.

Drakkar finished.

"It pleases me to know as this plot unfolds and uncovers Lunwynians behind it, that Finnie can trust her parents."

Atticus's shoulders slumped with visible relief.

Aurora lifted her chin and asked instantly, "Does this mean we can see her prior to you both being away into the cold, dark night?"

Drakkar nearly smiled at her motherly dramatics.

She was going to miss his Finnie and she was worried about her.

However, he did not smile.

Instead, he looked to Lund who had been standing quiet, shoulders to the wall, and ordered, "Take them to Finnie."

Lund nodded and moved but when they were at the door, Drakkar called out, "One thing." They stopped and looked back at him. "I'll remind you we're uncovering Lunwynians at every turn."

"I'll see to it my best men—" Atticus started but Drakkar interrupted him.

"That's precisely what you won't do. I've chosen the men I trust and right now Finnie has them, me, the both of you, and if my instincts are correct, her maidservants. You, as I, will treat anyone else as suspect." His attention moved to Aurora. "Even the heads of Houses who were heretofore above suspicion. You will do this until I am assured of their loyalty, and you have my leave to trust them. Is that understood?"

"Understood, Drakkar," Atticus muttered.

Aurora paused only a moment before she lifted her chin.

"Bid farewell to your daughter," Drakkar murmured, and they moved without hesitation behind Lund.

Drakkar stared at the door as it closed behind them, leaving him alone in the room.

An image of the woman spewing blood projected on the wood and this transformed into an image of Finnie doing the same. It was an image so heinous he closed his eyes to shut it out.

He could not blame himself for a woman's ludicrous infatuation or the actions this caused.

He *could* blame himself for lack of vigilance.

Aurora had said, *In your fire to avenge what's happened tonight under your nose...*

And she was not wrong.

Bloody hell, she was not wrong.

Drakkar put a fist to his hip and a hand to the back of his neck, dropped his head and studied his boots.

He should have seen it coming, this was painfully true.

But he would not make that same mistake again.

The door opened. Drakkar lifted his head and saw that Annar stood in its frame.

"I have the heads. Do you want them brought here?"

Drakkar glanced behind him at the blood on the stone floor of the buttery.

Then he looked at his man. "No. Take Ravenscroft to the library, Lazarus to the study, Njord to the drawing room and Sinclair I'll speak to in the sitting room. Then get a maid to fetch my clothes. I'll want our guard prepared to leave within the hour."

Annar lifted a chin and closed the door on his way out.

Drakkar took a few moments to rub the tension out of his neck.

Then he dropped his hand and walked to the library.

20

THE FINNIE

The riders on their mounts moved through the frozen forest swiftly, and throughout the journey they did not relent in their pace for the sake of their steeds.

Before we left, Frey had suggested I try to sleep, but we were going at a fast canter and the jarring pace alone would have kept me awake.

But it was the events of that night that actually kept me awake.

Unlike our last, during this journey, Frey did not talk. He did not share tidbits of information. He simply held me close and leaned into me as Tyr took us through the moonlit forest.

Leaving me to my thoughts.

And I took his silence as indication he wished to be left to his.

I was told that Sudvic was a six-hour sleigh ride if the conditions were right. Considering the not-so-good company of my thoughts, I was glad that it didn't take us that long. I had no idea how long it actually took, but we were not on a road. We were off track, in the forest proper, and likely taking a more direct route.

The entire time we rode, my mind was awash with images and memories of that night, the last two weeks, and everyone in the Palace and at the Gales that I'd come into contact with.

None of them seemed like assassins to me. But I wouldn't know, and assassins, I would guess, didn't have identifying characteristics. Or, at least, not good ones.

My parents had come to visit me prior to Frey and I leaving, and I deduced this meant Frey trusted them enough to allow it. As they looked like my real parents and I'd grown to know them, not to mention the fact that both were openly concerned for me (yes, even Mother), I couldn't believe they would have anything to do with a plot to murder me. And in the end, I had no choice but to act exactly what I was, and that was terrified, so I welcomed their reassuring presence.

Then we were away in the cold dead of the night, Frey and I and my guard, and I had nothing but the moonlight, the snow, the trees, and my thoughts to occupy me for hours.

And therefore, I was beside myself with relief when we suddenly came out of the never-ending forest.

Then, as what lay before me shoved out the dark thoughts and registered in my brain, I sucked in breath.

We had emerged on a high rise and spread before us was a city, and not a small one for its sprawl stretched far.

But this wasn't what made me pull in breath.

The twinkling lights of the city covered the valley and to the left blinked partially up a rise that was not a mountain in comparison to those around Fyngaard. But it was a very tall hill.

However, to the right there was a bay, its dark, night water so calm it was glassy, and its surface was dotted with huge, awe-inspiring three and four-mast galleons that were at anchor. More still were docked at the wharf. Considering the hour, they were lit with few lanterns (though those closer to the wharf had more illuminated) and all these cast long reflections across the bay.

It was freaking *spectacular*.

Although they'd run for hours, it was as if the horses sensed their journey was coming to an end. They wanted it to be done and their pace picked up as the riders in our party forged across the snow toward a well-trod road, down the road to the valley and into the city.

When we hit it, glancing around and taking it in, I saw immediately that Sudvic couldn't be any more different from Fyngaard.

The streets were cobbled, not paths of snow-packed trails. The snow had been cleared and piled high into lots between the buildings that seemed to be there for that sole purpose. And the sound of the horses' hooves pounding against the stone, something I'd never heard in real life, was *way* cool.

The buildings weren't quaint and homey. Even so, they were cool in an olde-worlde, higgledy-piggledy way. They were narrow and tall, one built right against the next with the roads winding through them showing there was no city planning whatsoever.

Some of the buildings were four stories tall, others two or three. Some had peaked roofs, others slanted or dormered. All had square-paned windows and there were a number of windows I saw shuttered against the night chill.

It was clear this city was highly populated, not simply from the dense pack of the buildings but also since it was the wee hours of the morning and there were people out bustling along the wood-plank, snow-cleared sidewalks or standing at the fire drums that were lit on street corners.

Another difference was that they didn't have torches but tall black streetlamps that looked to be fueled. Their lights shone through glass-sided boxes that hung on hooks that alternately curved over the streets or side-walks, cutting through the night and casting illumination on both.

I also noted Sudvic did not appear refined and cosmopolitan. There were a vast number of businesses and shops, but no cafés with sidewalk seating, no fancy restaurants, and from what I could see in shop windows, the wares were utilitarian, not elegant, expensive or sophisticated. There were definitely no fur shops here...or spun glass. There were also shingles suspended above doors advertising solicitors, accountants, merchants and even insurance brokers.

And further, the few women I saw were dressed differently. They did not have the smooth, flowing gowns of wool or long cloaks I saw in Fyngaard and Houllebec. They had full skirts with a mass of petticoats and shorter cloaks that came down only to their waists.

Looking around, it seemed we'd ridden three or four hours from Fyngaard and gone to a whole other world.

Our party took a right and rode on. When we did, I could see the bay coming toward us and I forgot all about nearly being poisoned and people all around me wanting me dead.

All I could think was that I couldn't wait to get there.

But once we arrived, I knew I could have waited a year and it would have been worth it.

When we hit the end of the street, Frey and his men veered their horses left, and we were there, on the wharf, the galleons rising high into the sky to our right, the dock lined by buildings on the left.

There were huge wooden posts ascending from the water with thick ropes twined around fastening the ships to the dock, or thinner ropes securing smaller vessels to the posts or to hooks screwed into the wood of the quay. All along the wharf there were piles and stacks of wooden barrels and crates, beds of tangled nets, messes of fish traps, and enormous coils of bulky rope.

And the dock was waking up. Or, perhaps, it never went to sleep. Men were at work lugging, pulling, pushing, rolling, lifting and shouting.

To the left, there were a great many pubs, all brightly lit, all clearly never closed, and lastly, obviously very popular.

Outside, there were men standing around carrying or glugging from horns or pewter tankards and smoking fat cigars (not the thin ones of Fyngaard).

They were also talking to, making out with or openly fondling women with great masses of hair, heavy hands at makeup and décolletage that rivaled Franka's, but this spilling out of flimsy (sometimes not-so-clean) tops that were gathered (or not, as the case may be) at the neckline with drawstrings. Their breasts were made more prominent by wide belts cinched tight that covered their midriffs and laced up the center. Their full skirts didn't sweep the ground, but the hem fell several inches above their ankle. And they were apparently immune to the cold, or drunk off their asses, because none of them were wearing cloaks (though some wore fingerless gloves).

Doxies. They had to be.

Awesome!

The sounds of men at work, the cry of gulls, the creak of the ships, and the smell of salt and fish filled the air. It was fabulous, every inch of it. And as we swiftly rode through, I saw avid eyes turn our direction, but I didn't really notice. I was busy trying to take it all in.

Frey pulled back on Tyr's reins and tugged him to the right. Tyr veered that direction and we stopped, facing a ship at the dock.

Frey straightened and I came up with him, looking left then right then up, up and *up*.

It was by far the biggest ship I'd seen and absolutely, completely, *definitely* the coolest.

This was all I was able to process as I heard running feet and Frey dismounted, instantly reaching up to pull me down.

I had my feet beneath me, and I saw a young man, perhaps twelve or thirteen who had hold of Tyr's reins. He was blond, very slight and had on breeches, ankle boots, thick wool socks and a thick brown sweater. His head was tipped back, eyes aimed at Frey.

"Take care of Tyr and then attend your lady in my cabin," Frey ordered shortly while taking my hand and then we were on the move.

We headed straight toward a steep gangplank that had slats nailed across as footholds, and a rough rope railing that connected to the ship at the top and a wood pole with an iron hoop at the bottom. I'd faced scarier ascents but not in a long dress and heavy fur cloak.

Before I could get my wits about me and concentrate on climbing that gangway without toppling over into the water, Frey used his hand to maneuver me in front of him. With one hand in the small of my back, the other steadying me at my waist, he pushed me up it. I trailed my gloved hand along the rope as Frey's big bulk right behind me propelled me straight up, through some short railings, two steps down, and I was on his ship.

On his ship!

Woo hoo!

I had approximately one-point-seven-five seconds to look around and see that he wasn't lying. There were men everywhere, lots of them, all of them busy.

I was seeing he was correct about my girls being there. They might like a smorgasbord, and even though every man looked fit to full-on brawny and not one was less than at the very least cute, even my girls who, if their stories were true enjoyed their dalliances tremendously, might find this a bit much.

I did lock eyes (very briefly) with a man that had a shock of white hair that was fashioned in an experimental hairstyle that he'd not been attending, and it had gone awry. He also had a full, thick white beard, deep crinkles at the corners of his eyes, craggy wrinkles everywhere else and an extremely tanned face. He was wearing a sweater, leather shorts and tall boots that all had seen better days and those days were about two decades ago. He was this world's version of a salty sea dog, no doubt about it, and he was squinting at me with an expression that said he wanted to grab hold of me and throw me overboard.

He didn't get this chance.

Frey took my hand and led me up a narrow gangway at the side of the ship. I was watching where my feet were hitting the wood deck so it was only at the last minute when I lifted my head that I saw the steps that led to the elevated deck that had, smack dab in the middle of it, a massive, circular, wooden helm, its handles spiking out. And it was so big it had to be as tall as me.

Freaking *awesome*!

I was hoping we were going there (I wanted to get a closer look at that wheel), but we didn't.

Frey turned me right and led me along another passage for a few feet then he turned me left toward some steps going down. I had no choice but to take them (mainly because Frey wasn't giving me one). Frey let my hand go, pushed me in that direction and put his hand to my head, pressing down so I didn't bonk myself on the low overhang. Three steps down then under the overhang, five more and in through an open door. I walked a few feet into a room and stopped dead.

Frey's cabin.

At what I saw, my eyes went huge, my heart started pumping, and I was so excited I could barely breathe. I wanted to jump around or at least clap and shout "woo hoo!" but before I could do either of these, Frey got in my space and tipped my head up with a hand under my chin.

"I have to see to a few things, my Finnie," he murmured. "If Skylar arrives before me, order some water to wash up, if you wish it, and let him know if you need food or wine."

After delivering that, he bent, touched his lips to my forehead, and without another word or look, he was gone.

I stared after him a few seconds before I slowly turned and took in the space.

"Holy moly," I whispered.

It was *everything* I thought it would be, *wanted* it to be, and *more*.

Directly ahead was the stern of the ship. I knew this because nearly the entire length of it was square-paneled glass where I could see some of the bay and the ship docked behind us. Under the window was a deep bench on which was a cushion covered in battered, dark-brown leather and a tumbled line of dark-brown, dark-green and wine-colored toss pillows.

Suspended in the middle of the window, how I did not know for it seemed to be in midair, was the spun glass dragon I'd given to Frey.

It looked freaking fantastic there. So fantastic, it was like it was *made* to be there.

I tore my eyes from the dragon and saw, sitting a bit of a ways in front of the window, was a desk, massive and well-used. It was covered in papers, some flat, others scrolled, as well as fascinating objects I couldn't wait to peruse. Some of them instruments, others clearly weights to hold things down. Behind it was a heavily carved, just plain heavy looking chair.

To the left there was another vast table on which there appeared to be huge paper charts and maps, again some flat, some scrolled, some partly scrolled and more instruments and paperweights.

At the end of that side of the cabin by the door there was a small table with a copper bowl on top and a copper pitcher on a shelf under it, a wash basin. Over this hung an oval mirror framed in carved wood.

In the middle of the cabin there was a battered oval table surrounded by eight chairs.

To the right off the corner of the desk there was a seating area. One big, comfy-looking chair with an ottoman, a heavy table at its side, a lantern attached to the wall hanging over it to use to read by. Next to that was a divan style bed that was double wide at a stretch but very long (meaning, with Frey's big body and mine, sleeping arrangements would be cozy). This was not covered in sheets, but a scattering of hides as well as a mess of wool and velvet blankets and an abundance of velvet covered, tasseled, square toss pillows. All the velvets were rich colors like wine, chocolate brown, midnight blue and pine green.

There were portholes all around intermingled with some gauges and dials surrounded by brass, some weapons mounted in racks, hanging lanterns (all lit) and a few small paintings of seascapes.

On the floor there were also two crude space heaters that appeared to be portable. They looked like they were made of iron and there were fires lit in them in an effort to ward off the chill, which somewhat succeeded and somewhat failed.

I also saw trunks, most of them I recognized as mine, lining the cabin behind the chart table.

In the back by the desk on the opposite side to the seating area there was a huge, standing globe. For some reason that was where I moved first.

When I got there, I slowly turned the intricately painted globe with the tips of my fingers and, fascinated, I saw the map depicted on it showed that this world was not identical to my world. Not even close. There were no Americas, no Europe, Asia, Africa or Australia. There were Poles at top and bottom but that was the only thing that was the same.

I twirled the globe to find Lunwyn and noted, not surprisingly, it was at the top, nearly to a Pole. The wide Winter Sea was north of it, the icy Pole beyond. The Green Sea, painted emerald on the map, was to the west of Lunwyn and it was more like an ocean, incredibly vast. I saw Middleland, painted in dark greens and blacks, and Hawkvale and Fleuridia, both depicted in deep greens with Fleuridia having a few light greens. And below the equator, there were countries, all painted in browns and creams, called Korwahk, Keenhak and Maroo.

I was turning the globe to see what lay beyond when I heard, "Milady?" and my head came up.

The boy was standing in the doorway.

He was looking uncomfortable and uncertain as well as impatient. I guessed that he had things to do and those didn't include waiting on a woman in his captain's quarters.

I moved away from the globe and toward the boy, saying, "Hello there. You're Skylar?"

He nodded, watching as I approached him and shifting his body in a way that made him look strangely like he wanted to turn around and run.

"I'm Finnie," I introduced myself before stopping several feet away.

He nodded but didn't speak.

"And what do you do here, Skylar?" I asked.

"Captain's boy, milady," he answered.

I nodded, thinking he was kind of young, but what did I know? He was the only captain's boy I'd ever met.

He asked on a prompt, "Aught I can get you, milady?"

I smiled. "Two things, some water so Frey and I can wash up after that ride, and also not to call me your lady. Instead, I'd like you to call me Finnie."

He peered up at me then swallowed what appeared to be nervously before he nodded again.

He stood there staring at me.

When he didn't say anything, I asked, "Is there something you wish to say?"

He shook his head and his body shifted again before he stated, "You haven't dismissed me."

Oh. Right.

I smiled again before telling him, "You can see to that water now, Skylar."

He nodded again, once, quickly, and raced out.

Well, that was a little weird but...whatever.

Determining to ask Frey later, I finally set about having a good look around.

I'd had the opportunity to take off my cloak, hat and gloves, nose through Frey's stuff on his desk and wash up when Skylar brought some warmed water to pour in the copper pitcher. I had a brass spyglass to one eye and was on my knees in the bench at the back, peering out at pretty much nothing (because it was still dark and there was a huge-ass ship behind us that was in my way) when Frey came back.

I turned my head to watch him walk in and saw him stop and stare at me with unconcealed puzzlement.

"What are you gazing at, wife?"

I grinned at him, moved off the bench and put the spyglass on his desk while I walked to him and answered, "Seeing as it's night, a whole lot of nothing. Still, that spyglass is cool. That bench is cool. That window is cool. And this whole freaking cabin," I stopped in front of him and slapped my hands lightly on his chest, tipping my head way back to look up at him, "*is cool*."

His eyes moved over my face before he lifted a hand to cup my cheek, his thumb sweeping out to stroke my cheekbone.

What he didn't do was smile back and I saw he looked distracted.

I leaned in closer and asked, "Is everything okay?"

He didn't answer.

Instead, he informed me, "We're away soon."

I smiled again and whispered, "Awesome." Then I asked, "Can I come up on deck and watch while we set sail?"

He shook his head. "You need to sleep, wee one."

I shook my head too.

"Frey, I'm totally not tired." And this was true. I was wired, not tired.

"All right," he replied. "Then I need to concentrate on navigating my ship out of the bay. My men need to concentrate on setting sail. And while we do that none of us need to concentrate on my curious wife finding trouble as she wanders around discovering. So I'll ask you to stay in our cabin and stare through your scope at a lot of nothing."

Hmm.

Bummer.

Though I could understand why he wanted that. I could also do that for him.

"Okay," I gave in. "But can I get a tour later?" I pushed, and he again shook his head, not in the negative but as an indication he was used to me not giving up.

I knew this didn't annoy him when I saw his eyes warm, but his mouth still did not curve into a smile.

"Skylar will take you around once we're away."

"Cool," I said softly, studying him and sensing his thoughts were elsewhere.

But I wasn't certain they were on navigating the bay.

He nodded and his hand dropped from my face, but I caught it before he moved away.

"Frey," I called. He stilled and his eyebrows went up. "Is everything okay?" I repeated my earlier question.

This time, he answered instantly, "Everything will be okay when we're at sea and you're surrounded by men I trust not to poison you or sink a dagger in your flesh."

Ho boy.

Clearly someone had not had his mind taken off the events of the night by an awesome new city, doxies, galleons, and a cool-as-shit captain's cabin, all of it straight out of a movie.

Therefore, I moved into him and circled him with my arms.

Pressing close and tilting my head way back, I whispered, "Honey, I'm okay."

"Indeed," he replied, curving his arms around me.

I tipped my head to the side and smiled big at him. "And we're off on an adventure."

His eyes again roamed my face before he murmured, "That we are, my Finnie."

"So it's all good," I concluded and watched a darkness settle in his eyes.

Hmm.

Maybe all was not good.

I gave him a squeeze and prompted, "Frey."

"I bedded her," he said quietly.

I felt my brows draw together as my body tensed at his words.

"What?" I asked.

"I bedded her," he repeated. One of his hands coming up to curl around my neck, he bent slightly so his face was closer to me. "I bedded her," he said yet again and went on, "And asked her to attend the table the first night I returned with my new bride. Your mother shared, in doing this, I gave her hope that she would again warm my bed, which, Finnie, I vow to you now, no matter what I said when I was angry with you, she did not."

He was talking about Viola.

I nodded at this news that was not news to me and Frey kept talking.

"I'd no idea she was of weak character. I'd no idea her time with me led to an infatuation that was unhealthy. I'd no idea she would be open not only to conspiring to harm you but actually moving personally to carry out a plot to murder my wife."

Ho boy.

"Frey—" I tried to break in on another squeeze of my arms, but he bent deeper, got closer and kept talking.

"But she did, and I knew the dangers you faced. It wasn't my hand that tipped the vial of poison in the glass delivered to you, but it was my actions that tipped *her* actions. Which means events unfolded, a woman lost her life, and another woman narrowly avoided losing hers, and that woman is my wife. So no, wee one, everything is *not* okay."

All righty, this was a leap he was clearly determined to make. A leap that really made no sense. But a leap founded in deep feelings of guilt, and those *never* made any kind of sense.

And lastly, it was a leap from which I had to reel him back.

In an effort to do that, both my hands slid up his chest and came to rest on either side of his neck as I whispered, "What happened was not your fault."

"I disagree, Finnie."

I gave him a squeeze and a gentle shake. "Frey, you're wrong."

"Change places with me, my love, and tell me," his hand gave me a squeeze too and he continued, "even if it was anyone but especially that it was this woman. A woman we argued over. An argument that spurred me to do something unwise, which caused a rift between us. A woman you could only be sensitive about, and perhaps not now but possibly later, think about her. Think about my thoughtless actions and what they led to and then let that fester. Knowing what already happened and what could happen as your mind invariably turns over the events of last night, how would you feel right now?"

Okay, he had a point there.

"Okay," I said softly. "You have a point but think about it. Firstly, if we were to change places and I was in your arms, feeling like shit that all this went down, in an effort to make me feel better and to understand it was really, truly *not* my fault, wouldn't you explain that the actions of others are the actions *of others*? We had an argument and people do crazy things when they're pissed. You were pissed and you acted on that. Everyone does stuff like that. You asked her to wait on a table, that's it. You didn't make any promises to her. *She* twisted that in *her* head, and she did what she did. But *she* did it. You can't help it that you're great in bed."

He did a slow blink at my words, but I kept talking.

"Well, I guess you could. If you wanted to be bad in bed, you could do that, I suppose. Though I'd ask you don't start doing that *now*."

"Finnie—"

"Because that would suck...*for me*."

"Finnie—"

"And *I* didn't try to poison anyone so I don't think *I* should be punished."

His hand at my neck gave me another squeeze. I focused more closely on him and saw that his lips were tipped up.

"Are you finished?" he asked.

"Do you feel better?" I asked back.

"Yes," Frey answered, and I pressed closer to him.

"Then yes," I said softly.

Finally, he smiled fully at me. One of his hands slid down to wrap around me while the other hand slid up into the back of my hair so he could turn my head and press my cheek against his chest.

And, at that point, *I* felt better.

I felt his chest expand and contract as he let out a big breath before he whispered, "Thank you, wife."

With both my arms around him, I gave him a squeeze and whispered back, "You're welcome, husband."

He held me close for several seconds. I returned the gesture and when his hold loosened slightly, I tipped my head back to see he was looking down at me.

"As you peruse my cabin, try not to move anything so I can't find it."

Weird. He so *totally* knew me.

I laughed softly and nodded. "Okay, I'll try."

He grinned before he dipped his head and touched his mouth to mine. Then he said quietly, "We need to be away."

I stared in his beautiful eyes and nodded.

He held my stare a second then let me go.

He was almost at the door when I called his name. He turned and looked at me, waiting.

"What's your ship called?" I asked.

"*The Finnie*," he answered casually, and I felt every inch of my body lock.

My jaw released so I could ask on a breath, "What?"

Without hesitation, Frey replied, "When I decided you'd be traveling with me, and you demonstrated much excitement for this eventuality, I changed the registers, had her name sanded away, her new one painted on and rechristened her *The Finnie*."

Oh.

My.

God.

He did *not* do that.

I looked at my husband standing patiently but obviously wishing to be away as the realization washed through me that he *did* do that.

I was stunned, my entire body felt warm, my heart felt light, and I knew that quicksand was closing in on my chin.

And I had absolutely no intention of making the slightest effort to pull myself out.

"What was she named before?" I whispered.

"The Skadi," he answered, then, even ready to leave, he took the time to explain. "Ancient lore told that Skadi was brave, but it also said that she preferred the mountains. There was a time when she needed to be called Skadi. That time is past for my Finnie makes the most of everywhere she happens to be, including, I'm sure I will find, the sea."

Yes, he so totally knew me.

"I'll make the most of it," I promised quietly.

"I know you will, love," Frey replied quietly then continued just as quietly but also gently, "Though, you keep talking, there won't be anything to make."

I smiled at him. "We could delay a bit, go out to one of those wharf-side pubs, have a drink, and I could chat to some doxies."

He started chuckling and shook his head. "I see this would intrigue you, my wee one, but I must inform you now so when we return you won't have your heart set on it, you will *never* be going to those pubs, having a drink and chatting to doxies."

I grinned at him.

We'd see about that.

I decided not to say that and instead ordered, "Go, navigate your ship, my handsome husband. I have poking around to do and important papers and instruments to misplace."

He grinned as he walked back to me, cupped my jaw with his hand and again touched his lips to mine. This time harder and longer, but not hard or long enough for me.

His fingers drifting gently along my jaw as he released me, Frey smiled into my eyes, turned and walked out of the cabin.

I stared at the door for a while after he'd gone, thinking I was standing on a beautiful ship a beautiful man named after me.

Yes, I was standing on a beautiful ship a beautiful man *named after me*.

I bit my lip, but even so, I was biting it while smiling.

Then I turned my attention to poking around and misplacing his papers and instruments.

21

ADELA TEA

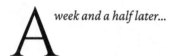

A week and a half later...

MY EYES FLUTTERED OPEN, and I saw velvet, I felt weight and warmth except on my leg, which was partially exposed and wrapped around a tangle of hides and blankets.

I was in bed in Frey's cabin, and I was alone.

I heard papers rustling. I pulled in a soft breath and lifted up on a forearm to look toward the desk.

My handsome husband with a week and a half of beard growth (making him, arguably, more handsome) was sifting through papers on his desk.

"Hey," I called.

His head came up and his green-brown eyes found me.

And his face got lazy. That lazy communicated itself to a variety of places in my body, and he said not a word but straightened in his chair and shifted it slightly to the side.

He didn't have to say a word. I knew what that meant.

I untangled myself from the covers, grabbed my long, soft wool robe that was lying across the bottom of the divan and my cashmere-socked feet hit wood floor. I pulled the robe on over my satin nightgown as I wandered across the cabin to him, tying the belt tight just as I made it to his chair. His arm hooked me around the waist, and he gently guided me into his lap.

When I settled, both his arms wrapped around me, his head bent toward mine, and he murmured, "I'll take my morning kiss now, wee Finnie."

I grinned up at him, placed my hands on the hard wall of his chest and leaned in, tipping my head back, offering him my mouth.

He took his morning kiss. This wasn't the first time he got it with me in his lap in his chair behind his desk in the cabin. Other times he got it when he woke me in his bed when he was still in it. There were a few times he got it when he woke me after coming back from doing something. But there were no other times. He came to me or was with me every morning.

Every single one.

I was clutching his sweater and a bit more than mildly heated by his embrace when he lifted his head and muttered, "Will I ever tire of the taste of you?"

God, I hoped not.

Of course, I didn't say that.

Instead, I smiled at him and stated, "No way. I'm yummy."

He smiled back and his arms pulled me closer as he asked, "Yummy?"

"I'm delicious," I explained.

His smile turned into a grin before he agreed, "That you are, my wee one."

I leaned in deeper, lifted my hand to stroke his rough jaw and my eyes dropped to his mouth before I whispered, "You're yummy too."

I watched his mouth mutter, "Gods," before it was on mine, and he took another morning kiss. This one longer, deeper, wetter and lots better.

Mm. Definitely yummy.

I was clinging to him, one arm wrapped around his shoulders, the other hand in his thick hair when he tore his mouth from mine and slid his lips down my cheek to my ear where he spoke quietly.

"Sadly, I have no time to play this morning, wife. I'm to meet Thad and Kell in five minutes. We make land the day after tomorrow and from there we must make haste. This morning, we finalize plans." His head lifted and his eyes caught mine. "But after that, I'm free. I'll hand the wheel to Thad, meet you here, and we'll lock the door."

I knew what locking the door meant. So did his men.

Awesome. Something to look forward to.

"But now, I must be away," Frey went on. "Would you like me to tell Skylar to bring you breakfast?"

At the mention of Skylar, my good morning mood experienced a hiccup.

In the time I was on the ship, Skylar had not gotten used to me. Frey had explained this was because Skylar was the son of one of his men, a man who had unfortunately died during a mission (this, Frey assured me—probably because I sucked in every molecule of oxygen in the cabin and actually felt my face go pale—was a *very* rare happenstance) which meant Skylar was being raised solely by that man's wife.

She was not a good woman, a kind one, a fair one, a patient one, or, from some of the stories he relayed to me (stories that made my heart hurt), a sane one.

Frey had learned that things were going badly for the boy and he'd taken him (yes, taken him, giving his mother no choice, and honestly, I was glad of it). Now Skylar served Frey and would do so until he was old enough to make his own decisions.

Therefore, Skylar was gun shy with women, and it was no surprise. Also, this meant Frey usually did my talking with Skylar. This was at my request, mainly because Skylar wasn't getting used to me no matter how kind or soft-spoken I was with him. I could tell I caused him discomfort, so I decided to avoid doing that by avoiding him and Frey had agreed to my request.

I wasn't sure an abused boy should be serving on a ship with a bunch of macho men I had noted treated him like, well, a bunch of macho men, and further without the kindness of a woman.

What I was sure of was that, if even half the stories were true, he was better off on Frey's ship with a bunch of brusque men than he was with his mother.

I was also sure I liked Frey even more because he went out of his way to take care of the boy. His care might not be nurturing, but it couldn't be denied it was care.

"Yes," I nodded, answering his question. "And water to wash."

"All right," Frey murmured, leaned in to touch his lips to my forehead then stood, taking me with him and setting me on my feet. He looked down at me. "Your plans for the day?"

"Archery practice with Annar then knife work with Lund."

He shook his head and started chuckling.

I had found my girls had packed some of Princess Sjofn's shirts, sweaters and breeches, and being me, I tried them out. The first time I had appeared in these garments, I caused quite a stir. This stir caused Frey, standing at the helm, to look to the heavens as if seeking deliverance from his gods. But he didn't say a word (this, I also liked).

I also heard from Annar that they'd packed my bow and arrow and they did this by giving it to him to pack with his own as it didn't fit in my trunks. He offered to work with me, and I took him up on it.

While practicing with the bow one day, Lund showed and offered to teach me how to handle a knife. I took him up on that. I thought both were important to know, considering Sjofn knew them, and even though I would probably never be as good as her considering the amount of practice she'd had, at least it would provide some cover, for I wouldn't appear a complete amateur should spies be paying attention (and, obviously, they were).

Not to mention, I wanted to learn.

Orion had offered to teach me swordplay and I took him up on that, but found I could barely lift a sword, they were so freaking heavy. No one onboard had one I could wield so we decided to leave it at knife play until they could find a sword I could use.

Thus, while Frey spent his days captaining his ship, planning raids and communing with his brethren (when he wasn't locked in his cabin with me), I spent my time shooting arrows, dancing around the deck while Lund tried to stab me and playing multiple games of tuble and meerkin while all the men taught me how to cheat (when I wasn't locked in Frey's cabin with him, where, if Frey and I weren't doing other highly pleasant things, Frey also spent time teaching me how to cheat).

In other words, I was having the time of my life.

"Right, wee one," Frey spoke, his deep voice light with amusement, taking my attention back to him. "After you get finished prancing around on deck with your lovely arse on display in your tight breeches, making certain every single one of my men is lying abed in their hammocks at night with their fists wrapped around their cocks and their thoughts on your arse, we'll meet back here this afternoon."

I blinked up at him and whispered, "They are not doing that."

"They are," Frey returned.

"No they aren't." I was still whispering.

"Finnie, am I a man?" Frey asked.

"Yes." I gave the obvious answer.

"Then I know they're doing that."

"But," I protested, "I'm your wife and you said they wouldn't—"

Frey cut me off. "They won't stare, and they won't make their interest obvious for this would cause my displeasure. But I do not control their thoughts. They see. What they see is a pleasing image that is burned behind their eyes, so they don't forget."

Oh God.

"Maybe I should quit wearing breeches," I suggested but Frey grinned wickedly and dipped his face to mine.

"You do, my love, then *I* won't get to watch you prance around on deck with your lovely arse on display. And, fortunately, when I'm abed at night, *I* have a wife who gladly wraps a number of things around my cock that are far, far better than my fist."

Hmm.

This was true.

It also explained why Frey had not said a word against me wearing breeches.

And lastly, it made me warm in a variety of places.

"This is true," I muttered, and Frey threw back his head and laughed.

When he tipped it back down, he lifted his hand, wrapped it around my head and pulled me in and up for another touch of his lips on my forehead.

When he let me go, he caught my eyes and said softly, "Until later, my love."

"Later, baby," I said softly back.

He smiled at me, and I watched him walk out of the cabin.

I went to my trunks, got down on my knees in front of one, opened it and started sorting through in order to decide what I was going to wear that day.

While I was at the trunks, my mind went over the last week and a half and the things I had learned.

One of them was the story of Kell, who was the salty sea dog I'd seen my first night on the ship.

Back in the day, Kell had been first mate on the first ship where Frey worked. Frey had followed Kell when Kell had briefly captained a vessel for a merchant. Kell then had followed Frey when he'd used the inheritance his Grandmother Eugenie left him to order his first galleon to be built and it was put to sea.

And Kell had been with Frey ever since.

Kell and Frey were tight, I could tell (though Frey also told me). It wasn't like they did man hugs or bumped fists all the time, but there was no doubt about it. That closeness was there. It ran deep and Frey had explained Kell taught him everything he knew. And when Frey struck out on his own, Frey had earned Kell's respect because Frey lived his life in a way that he kept learning.

Luckily, Frey told me Kell hadn't been looking at me like he wanted to throw me overboard that first night because he was mentally plotting my murder. Unluckily, Frey told me Kell was looking at me like he wanted to throw me overboard because he did not (at all) like women on board ships and further thought they served one purpose and one purpose only. Therefore, although he'd known his fair share of them, all of them practiced the same profession.

By the way, even though most people liked me right off the bat because I was open, warm and friendly, or I could get through to them being open, warm and friendly, Kell had not thawed even a little bit.

The other thing I had learned was that the purpose of this mission was to recover an elfin relic of great importance. Many Lunwynians had been searching for it literally for centuries. There had been many rumors of it surfacing, which meant equally numerous operations were launched, but in the end these were fruitless. Frey himself had planned and executed three such maneuvers since he started raiding, all ending in disappointment.

He told me he did not hold high hopes for this one either. That said, he also told me that his informant this time was far more reliable than the last three.

Regardless, the relic, a petrified branch of an adela tree, or *the* adela tree, the first one the goddess Adele created, was important enough to make an attempt. So that was what he was doing.

We were now out of Lunwynian waters and in those of Middleland. The relic, Frey's informant told him, was in the possession of Phobin, who happened to be the lover of Princess Sjofn's cousin, Broderick, who was King Baldur's son.

Frey didn't have a lot to say about Broderick, but reading between the lines, I got the sense he didn't like him much. He had less to say about Phobin. But what he did say you didn't have to read between the lines. He disliked Phobin flat out. And I got the feeling he would have probably liked Broderick more if he hadn't chosen Phobin as partner.

Frey had also cautiously informed me that this mission was complicated. And it was complicated because Frey had been to Middleland recently and his last mission there had been dangerous. It had also been secret. Further, it had been politically sensitive. And lastly, my father didn't know about it nor, incidentally, the one Frey was currently planning.

This was because Frey tended to tell Atticus about these missions *after* they were successful for if things went awry (eek!), Atticus could honestly claim no knowledge of them. Unless, of course, it was my father who asked Frey to accomplish them.

Though, that said, the last one was *so* sensitive, Father still didn't know about it.

King Baldur also hadn't known about Frey's previous mission. Frey wasn't fired up for either brother to know and he was intent upon entering Middleland, hopefully retrieving the relic and exiting without anyone being the wiser about this mission, and with any luck, they were still no wiser about the last.

As the story goes, Thad had a communication from a woman he had once had a somewhat long affair with and still held in high regard. This communication was an urgent request to aid in the escape of another woman as she was desperate to flee her captor.

Thad, still carrying feelings for his ex-lover and therefore trusting her, agreed to assist without actually getting all the information. Frey had not meant to go, seeing as he was getting married, though he did offer Thad one of his vessels. But, once married and deciding he'd rather be at sea doing dangerous deeds with his men than hanging with a lesbian (in all fairness, I could see this) at his wedding celebration to her and after, he'd changed his mind, deposited me at his hunting cabin, and gone.

Once they arrived, they found that Thad's friend was actually the maid to King Baldur's personal sorceress, a woman with great power. But even so, she was controlled by Baldur.

It was a sad story, actually, because Frey and Thad had learned from the maid that this sorceress, named Circe (totally kickass name, by the by) had displayed she held magic from practically birth. In order to control her power, Baldur had kidnapped her when she was very young. And to make certain to keep her with no attempts made to gain her return, he'd executed both of her parents.

Yes, executed two people in order to steal their daughter.

It seemed my uncle was a true peach.

Unfortunately for her, not only did she hold a great deal of magic, she also grew into great beauty. So my lovely uncle (*not*), had started forcing himself on her when she was fourteen. She was still known to be his mistress, even though she was more than double that age now.

That was to say, Circe was his *unwilling* mistress.

Nevertheless, she was a prized possession of King Baldur's for more reasons than one and assisting her to escape was, as Frey phrased it, "politically sensitive." But what he meant was politically explosive, thus Father still being none the wiser.

However, two things happened.

One, Frey was Frey and Thad told me that, upon learning her story, he didn't hesitate to agree to help her escape. Two, the sorceress's maid had relayed that Circe had information about the elfin relic everyone was seeking, and she would pay for their efforts by providing this information to Frey.

Therefore, Circe was Frey's source, and although centuries of experience with disappointment made him keep his expectations in check, as the days went by and launching the operation came closer, I could feel the men's restless excitement.

Expectations might be in check, but there was still hope.

Yes, this was how important the relic was.

Thinking of all this, I pushed deeper into my trunk to find a clean pair of breeches to wear and pulled some out. When I did, a small pouch dropped out of a fold and with it a piece of paper fluttered.

I stared at the tiny purple satin pouch on the floor by my knee then reached down to pick up the folded piece of paper.

I opened it and read:

Sweet Finnie,

We hope you find this sooner rather than later.

We've packed some adela tea for you to use with your husband.

We don't know if you've read about this in your books, but in case you haven't, we'll explain.

Harvesting anything from adela trees, which grow very slowly and are very susceptible to disease, is strictly controlled. Any adela tree is sacred for they are created by the goddess, but also, they are the entry point of the elves from their realm into ours. If anything were to happen to the adelas, the elves would be trapped under the earth for eternity and no one wants that, so they are handled carefully.

Adela tree branches can be gathered only for wedding bundles and their bark is harvested cautiously and used for a special tea. Adela tea is quite expensive, very rare, and not used widely.

We were not able to purchase more than just enough for you to make one cup. But one cup, shared by lovers, is just enough.

You see, the tea serves to heighten your senses, touch, taste, smell, sight, hearing, and also it significantly heightens arousal. Alyssa has an ongoing dalliance with the head of the Ulfr House. She is a particular favorite of his and she visits him every time he comes to Fyngaard. Once, he had some tea that he shared with her, and she said it was marvelous (underlined twice).

Please do not worry. The effects are not debilitating nor are they lasting. Alyssa says that half a cup each for her and her gentleman lasted several hours. They slept well and woke up refreshed.

With your spirit, we thought this was an adventure you had (underlined three times) to take.

So this is our gift to you and The Drakkar.

Enjoy, sweet Finnie, and we look forward to seeing you upon your return and hearing all (underlined four times) about it.

With love,

Jocelyn, Alyssa, Esther and Bess

I picked up the pouch and fingered the soft parcel.

Then I grinned.

My girls were the...absolute...best.

And this was one reason of many, including the fact that they'd procured and provided me with a powder they promised (because they all used it) that I could sprinkle just a touch into water or coffee, and it would keep me from getting pregnant. I had to do it every day and luckily it tasted pretty good, though weird, like a minty orange. Although it hadn't been very long, so far, so good (since, unfortunately and fortunately, considering it was unfun having your period in this world and I knew that because I'd already experienced it twice—not to mention doing it on a ship with a bunch of guys—but two days into the voyage, I had it and luckily, four days later I was done and this meant I was free and clear...for now).

The door opened.

I jumped and looked that way to see Skylar standing in it, keeping well away from me.

"Eggs, bacon and toast, milady?" he asked like he asked every morning for reasons I didn't know because I'd learned from Frey that unless I picked just eggs and toast or just bacon and toast, or I wanted lunch for breakfast, that was my only choice for the ship's cook was nearly as cranky as Kell. He wasn't hot on personal orders and didn't do anything "girlie" such as pancakes apparently were.

I smiled gently at the boy and said softly, "Yes, Skylar, that would be lovely. Thank you."

He nodded once and moved quickly out of the room.

I stared at the closed door wondering what, if anything, I could do about that.

Then I decided to talk to Frey about it later.

My eyes drifted down to the pouch in my hand and again my mouth curled into a smile.

Yes, I'd talk to him about it.

Much later.

~

I WATCHED my dagger skitter across the deck and come to a stop against some rope.

I bit my lip and ignored Stephan, Max and Gunner, who I knew would be grinning, thinking this was hilarious. And Kell, who would be scowling, thinking I should be hiding in Frey's cabin for the duration of the trip repeating to myself that I would never again set foot on the ship that was named after me...or any ship for that matter.

Then I looked at Lund as he pulled out of the lunge he'd used to knock my dagger away and sheathed his own. He planted his hands on his hips and glowered at me.

"Finnie, I've told you, you have inexperience and lack of strength as formidable weaknesses, but quickness, surprise and..." he paused and leaned slightly toward me, "*concentration* can be used as your strengths. To have quickness and provide surprise, you need to..." he paused again, leaned back and crossed his arms on his chest, "*concentrate.*"

He was not wrong. My mind was not on learning how to wield a dagger. It was afternoon. My mind was in the cabin where the adela tea pouch was and where, I hoped, Skylar had left a boiled kettle for me (a request, since I was thinking to surprise Frey, I had actually made myself).

"I'm sorry, Lund. My mind is elsewhere," I admitted.

"If this is so, then you should not be working with a dagger. What just happened, happened because I am good, and I don't wish you harm. In a true fight, a man could take your hand with that maneuver, had he the strength and sharpness of blade. At the very least, he could cut your wrist where blood flows freely. Then you'd be significantly weakened and even face death."

Ho boy. Death was never good.

"Right," I said softly.

He uncrossed his arms, got closer to me and I looked up into his gray eyes, which I noted had stopped glowering and had warmed. I had also long since noted that this was Lund's way. He could lose his patience in our practice, but only when I did really stupid shit he'd told me time and again not to do. But he didn't lose it for long.

"I enjoy our sessions, my princess, but I equally enjoy teaching you how to cut a deck false. If you wish to skip your lesson, we can sit down to cards. All you need do is say."

God, seriously, he was a nice guy, and spending time with all Frey's men, I'd found they all were.

Except Kell, who disliked me. And Oleg, who was kind of monosyllabic and a little scary, but mostly he was okay too.

"Thanks," I replied quietly, and Lund grinned at me.

"Wife." I heard and since it was Frey's voice, and that could only be me, I turned to see him striding toward me.

My knees wobbled and not only because he, as ever, looked hot.

"We'll leave it at that for the day," Lund muttered.

I looked from Frey to him, nodded and smiled. He moved away to collect my lost dagger.

I turned back to Frey who was now very close. He didn't touch me, but he was way in my space.

Hmm.

I knew what that meant and that meant firstly, he did not want us to be overheard and secondly, he actually *did* want to touch me, but this was something he avoided doing too much in front of his men. There were times he did, of course, but in broad daylight in the middle of the waist deck with us having a large audience was not one of those times.

"We have plans, wee one," he reminded me of something he so *totally* didn't need to remind me of. "I need words with Kell. I see your lesson is finished?"

I nodded.

"Good," he muttered. "I'll meet you in our cabin."

My knees wobbled again, and my nipples tingled. But my head nodded.

He grinned like he knew what was happening in my head *and* under my sweater and that grin was so good, my nipples got hard, and I felt a really nice spasm.

"See you there, honey," I whispered.

His eyes flared and he whispered back, "Indeed."

I decided to get to the cabin first, to make the tea and second, before I melted into a puddle on the deck in front of everyone at just thinking about what would happen after I made the tea.

So I did that, smiling at Frey, then turning my head as I walked toward the bridge deck and calling, "Later boys!"

I got some chin lifts and Max called back, "Until later, Finnie."

I hightailed it out of there.

When I got to the cabin, I saw the good news was Skylar was a really good cabin boy. He didn't make the bed because there was pretty much no point. But he delivered water for washing, took it away, cleaned out the basin, brought food, took away the dishes, cleaned clothes, and spent not a small amount of time shining brass.

He also made sure I had a kettle of boiling water, a cup and tea infuser.

The bad news was, by the time I made it to the cabin, I'd begun to get nervous.

What if it didn't work or it went wonky? What if Frey wasn't into this kind of thing? What if we got a bad batch and not-so-good things happened?

I stood by the boiled kettle that, in the not even close to warm cabin was cooling fast and worried my lip. I heard a noise outside and jumped, thinking it was Frey. I looked to the closed door. It didn't open so I looked back to the kettle.

I did not partake of drugs. This was an adventure Mom and Dad warned me (repeatedly) was not worth risking.

But this was the bark of a beautiful tree. It was natural. It wasn't drugs...*exactly*.

Shit!

There was another thump outside and I jumped yet again, looking to the door. After several moments with no Frey, I decided to suck it up.

It was now or never.

And I lived in the now...with Frey.

I grabbed the infuser, poured the tiny, glittery, gorgeous pieces of bark into it, shaking the pouch to make sure they were all out. I screwed the infuser closed, dropped it into the cup and poured over the steaming water. Then I waited, staring at it wondering how long it should infuse. Then wondering if I should wait for Frey before I tried it.

I took hold of the little chain, dunked the infuser several times and watched with fascination as glitter flowed out, permeating the liquid and making the water in the cup actually glow.

Yes...*glow*.

Totally *freaking* cool.

I pulled the infuser out, set it aside, and after taking a deep breath, before I lost my nerve, I lifted the cup to my lips and took a sip.

Holy moly!

I stared into the glowing cup.

Heaven. Absolutely divine.

I took another sip tasting licorice and peppermint with hints of vanilla.

God, celestial.

Taking another sip, I decided that the gods of this world *had* to exist. No other being could create something so heavenly.

On sip four, I felt it start and on sip five it grew stronger. I knew it because I was no longer *tasting* the tea. I was *feeling* it. The flavor had intensified to such an extent it was a thrill simply experiencing it.

Sip six brought more, the coolness of the air in the cabin started stinging my skin, the drafts gliding across were almost physical. The shine on the brass on the instruments on the walls had grown so bright, it was nearly blinding. I could feel every centimeter of the handle of the cup weighing on my fingers. I could hear the men moving about on deck above me.

Wow. This stuff worked fast, and it was *awesome*.

Sip seven and I'd had half the cup. I wanted more, it was delicious, divine, freaking bliss in liquid form, but I forced myself to set the cup down to save the second half for Frey.

The warmth slid through me, starting right in my sex and slinking up, down, and out until it heated me from top to toe. Every inch of my skin, every centimeter of my innards. The warmth was so intense, I had to put my hand to the table to hold myself steady because I thought my legs might buckle from under me.

It didn't freak me out because the sensation was nowhere near scary.

It was *beautiful*.

So beautiful, so intense, so pervasive, I felt like I was going to overheat.

God, if Frey didn't get to the cabin soon, I was going to have to take care of myself.

And I knew I'd enjoy every...*freaking*...second.

I heard his boots on the steps outside and my feet moved me directly to the door. They did this because suddenly my hands itched to touch him. My tongue was dry with the need to taste him. My stomach was hollow with hunger for him. And my sex ached for his to fill it.

And because of this, he barely closed the door when I was all over him, pressing close, my hands gliding up his chest to curl around the back of his neck. In position, I insistently pulled his mouth down to mine.

"Fin—" he got out, which was good, perfect, his mouth was open, and since my lips were there, my tongue slid inside.

Oh yes. Ho boy. *Yes.*

I had my answer. I'd never tire of the taste of him, *ever.*

I felt his hands on my hips and the touch was light, but it burned into me and felt so freaking good I moaned into his mouth.

That mouth tore from mine as he shuffled me in a few steps. I pulled on his neck to bring him back.

"Wee one, what on—?" he asked, but something caught his attention.

He glanced beyond me briefly then did a double take, his head jerking to look back at the table.

He looked down at me, his eyes locked on mine, and he studied me intensely as his arms glided around me, pulling me close.

I bit my lip at the touch of his hard body against mine and wondered if he'd be put off if I started tearing off my clothes (and his) when his head bent, and his face got close.

His voice was a low rumble that reverberated through me, causing my knees to go weak (and a variety of other things, all so fabulous they were nearly tortuous), when he asked, "That cup, Finnie, it glows. Have you drunk of the adela?"

I pressed closer. My lids had lowered, I was trying to focus on not pressing my mouth to his (or pressing it other places), but instead answering his question and also assessing his reaction to this idea, and I whispered, "The girls gave it to me. Uh...to us."

He stared at me for a second that seemed to last five hours then both his hands were suddenly on either side of my head, he tipped it back and thank God, thank God, thank God, God, *God*, he was kissing me, hard, deep, with lots and *lots* of tongue.

I shivered against him and held on tight.

Oh man. I was going to come just from kissing.

His mouth tore from mine, the heat in my body was communicated in the heat in his eyes and he growled, "By the gods, wife, you suit me."

After declaring that wonderfulness, he whisked me up in his arms, carried me to the table, planted my ass on it and curled a hand around my neck as he curved the fingers of his other through the handle of the cup. He picked it up, and I held my breath as he held my eyes while he brought it to his lips. I lost his eyes as his neck bent back and he downed the whole thing in one gulp.

Okay, evidence was clearly suggesting Frey was really, *really* into this.

His head righted, he set the mug aside and he grabbed my legs behind the knees, opened them and moved between.

Oh yeah. Now we were talking.

My hands slid up his chest to latch on to his neck and my legs lifted up, knees bent, to press against his hips as he leaned into me.

"They explained what the adela does?" he asked as he braced one hand on the table while the other arm curled around me.

"Unh-hunh," I mumbled, staring at his mouth and wishing it wasn't so damned far away.

"And you want this, Finnie?"

I forced my eyes up to his and my mind to concentrate. "Is it bad?"

"No," he replied, his arm lifting me up from the table and pressing my body into his as I watched his heated eyes start to scorch. "But it's power-ful, wee one. You do not share the adela cup with someone you don't trust with every inch of you."

Oh yes. Every inch of me.

I liked that. I wanted to get to the every inch of me part.

"But you drank it," I whispered instead of whined because he *still* wasn't kissing me. But he'd bent lower, his arm curling around and cush-ioning the back if my neck, his body leaned deep into mine, pressing it into the table even as he pulled it up and into him.

He grinned and his grin was so damned wicked it was physical.

I trembled in a really, *really* good way, and he whispered, "You're in no state to change your mind."

He was right about that.

"And, my Finnie, I trust you with every inch of me," he went on, and I felt that too, all through me, and that was in a really, *really* good way too.

So good, my lids lowered, and I pressed my hips into his.

"Finnie, love, look at me," he growled.

I opened my eyes and saw his were so damned hot, they were fevered.

It was a *seriously* good look, the best *ever*.

"It is strong, but I will walk out that door. Finnie, look in my eyes, focus and tell me, are you ready for this?"

I looked in his eyes. I focused for a nanosecond and then I told him the truth that would be the truth if I'd drunk from a glowing cup, just woke up in the morning, was eating lunch or was about to fall asleep at night.

"Frey Drakkar, I trust you with every inch of me."

I barely got out the "e" in "me" when his mouth was on mine. He ground his hips into me at the same time his arm drove me down into his hips and I groaned deep into his throat.

Oh God, it was too much, too big. I tore my mouth away, shoved my face in his neck at the same time my hands, acting on their own, yanked up his sweater so they could get to the sleek, muscled, unbelievably brilliant to the touch skin of his back.

"Too much, Frey," I whimpered against his neck as I felt his lips and tongue at mine and his hips kept grinding into me. "God, baby," my head arched back, "I'm going to come with just this."

His arm moved from my neck so his hand could cup my head and he positioned it to facing him as he kept pushing his hips deep into mine.

"Oh yes, my love, prepare," he warned on a low growl. "You're going to climax over a lot of 'just this.'"

Then his mouth took mine, his tongue invaded, hungry, devouring, his hips pressed in hard, and I came, fast, deep and *hot*.

It was excruciatingly beautiful.

I was still climaxing as he yanked off my sweater, my boots, my socks and breeches, taking my underwear with them. My eyes somnolently focusing, I watched him pull off his sweater.

At the mere sight of his chest, I did a full body tremble.

Then he disappeared as he dropped to his knees between my legs. I sucked in a breath of anticipation, he tossed my legs over his shoulders and his mouth was on me.

Oh my God. He was good at this normally, *really* good.

Hungry and fevered, both him and me, it was off the charts.

No, there was no chart. It was indescribable.

My heels dug into his back, my hips lifted to rub against his mouth as his big hands cupped my ass to pull me to him. He took and took and took, and I came again and again and again, crying out at first then whimpering, my fingers in his hair, holding him tight to me.

"Frey," I gasped, suddenly needing him. "My turn, baby."

He didn't need to be asked twice. He sucked deep one, last, gorgeous time then his mouth went away, and I sat up, jumped off the table and was on my knees in front of him before he'd got the first button opened on his breeches.

I took over unbuttoning his fly then I *took over*, taking him in my mouth.

This was something I liked to do, but now it was something I *adored*.

The noises Frey was making, noises coming deep from his chest, his big hands cupping either side of my head lightly, his hips thrusting gently into my mouth, it was *fantastic*.

Oh God, I was close again.

Before I could let go, he pulled out and his hands were in my armpits, yanking me straight up. My arms went around his shoulders, my legs around his hips. He strode swiftly to the bed. By the time we got there, I had one arm down, my hand at his cock wrapped around, guiding him to me so when he dropped me to my back on the bed with him on top of me, I had him right there.

Then he was inside me.

My body arched and I came instantly. It took Frey about half a minute longer.

And thus it began. It was about touch, taste, scent, sight, sound...and trust.

Every moan, groan, grunt and whimper was a caress. Every inch of his skin that caught my eye was a lazy, effective stroke. The smell of his hair was a tight embrace. And actual touches and the flavor of him took me almost instantly to orgasm.

I thought I had Frey memorized, but that afternoon every nuance of him was burned so deep in my brain I'd never forget it. Not a second, not a touch, not a taste, not a vision, not an aroma, not the barest whisper.

It was the most intense, profound, agonizingly beautiful thing I ever experienced.

Every second sheer perfection.

And after hours, when we came down, when the strokes became more languorous, the whimpers more subdued, the groans turned to growls, and our eyes grew less fevered, I knew I was in love.

Not with a man who would share this with me and give me multiple orgasms multiple times. But with the man I would choose to share this with, trusting him enough to open myself so completely. I was fully exposed, and instead of taking everything, he handed me the world.

He handed me the world.

And I was going to take it.

I wasn't going anywhere. I wasn't going home except to tie up my life, explain, and say good-bye to people I loved.

I was going to embark on the ultimate adventure.

Somehow, someway, I had to figure out how to talk my husband (and the king and queen) into accepting me as a replacement for good and communicate with Sjofn that her hopes for Lunwyn had come true.

I was going to stay with the man I loved in this fabulous world that had elves and dragons (and people who wanted to kill me, but I decided not to think of that).

And I was going to do it forever.

~

"Do you suppose we should eat, wee one?" Frey murmured.

Frey was on his back, his arm around me, his fingers drawing lazy patterns on my hip. I was pressed to his side, cheek on his shoulder, my leg over his, my fingertips floating absently across the skin of his wide chest. But at his question, I dropped my hand to that chest, pressed in and curled my body deeper into him.

Truth be told, I was absolutely famished. I'd learned having hours of very energetic sex and countless orgasms did that to you.

But right then it was just Frey and I tangled in each other and velvet blankets on a divan in a cabin on a fabulous ship with nothing but the dark cut minimally by moonlight coming in his windows and the fact that I'd come to the realization I was in love for the first time in my life. And I liked all of it just like that and I didn't want to lose any of it.

To communicate all this, I mumbled, "Mm."

His body shook with his inaudible chuckle, and he rolled into me so we were both on our sides, face to face.

I could barely make him out in the moonlight, but I didn't need to. I'd remember his face and every inch of his skin until my dying breath.

His hands drifted up and down my back and his voice was soft when he asked, "Do you want to doze while I find food?"

My arm around him got tighter and I blurted, "I don't want you to go anywhere."

His hands stopped drifting and he held tight before he whispered, "All right, my Finnie. I'll not go anywhere."

I nodded and dipped my chin, pressing my face in his chest and his hands started drifting again, one gliding up to play with my hair.

I didn't stroke. I just held on.

And both of us did this for a while.

Finally, I broke the silence to ask quietly, "How do people go back to normal sex after that?"

Frey answered just as quietly, "If they do it with their partner, they don't."

I blinked at his chest then my head tipped back. I heard his move on the pillow and I knew he was looking down at me.

"They don't?" I queried.

"Never."

Ho boy.

"Frey," I whispered. "That was...it was...well, *freaking awesome*. But we can't do it like that *every time*. It would kill us."

His chuckle was audible this time and he gave me a slight squeeze before he explained, "No, my love, the adela tea isn't meant to be used every time, not even sometimes. It is meant to be used carefully. It is meant to be used as a means to deepen something that is already deep, to heighten awareness of things that are already there. There are those who use it simply for pleasure. But when a husband and wife who care about each other use it, the goddess Adele's intent for her gift is much more meaningful."

Both his arms got tight around me, and he gently pulled me up so my head was on a pillow by his.

Then he said softly, "I know things about you now, things you like, sounds you make, expressions on your face that I may not have understood or would have missed before. I would assume you now hold the same knowledge about me."

He would assume correct in a *big* way.

"Yes," I whispered.

His head bent so his forehead was touching mine and he was whispering too when he replied, "It will never be the same between us because we hold that knowledge. We're more in tune. We better understand not only what brings pleasure to each other but also to ourselves. We won't miss those things as we might have done before, wee one. We'll know how to take advantage of them. It will not be the same as we just had but it won't need to be, and it will make something that was already splendid *much* better."

Wow. That was actually kind of beautiful.

"Boy," I breathed. "That Adele knows what she's doing."

Frey gathered me closer and tipped his mouth so his lips touched mine.

I felt his were smiling.

"She *is* a goddess, Finnie," he said quietly.

"Right," I whispered.

He chuckled and moved his head slightly back.

I asked the question no girl should ask, no time, no place, no reason, no matter what.

But I asked it.

"Have you done that with other women?"

His big, relaxed body grew stiff, and I closed my eyes tight, opened them and tried to repair the damage.

"I'm sorry, Frey. So, so sorry. It's none of my—"

He cut me off to say, "Two."

I blinked at him in the dark then asked, "What?"

"Two," he repeated and continued. "A courtesan in Fleuridia, and that time it was not about a deeper meaning but an intense experience. It had no meaning. I don't even recall her name."

Hmm.

"And a woman in Sudvic," he went on. "A widow who I visited frequently when I was in the city and this acquaintance lasted some time. She introduced it in an attempt to get me to feel more about what we shared than was there. But if it isn't there, you can't make it be there. Her attempt backfired for she exposed how she felt about me, feelings I knew I couldn't return. I came to understand it was unfair to give her hope by continuing our liaison and shortly after, I stopped visiting her." His arms gave me another squeeze and he explained, "Adele rules passion, but she holds no sway over love."

I was pleased he was honest and trusted me without hesitation with stories of his past. That felt nice and said a lot of good things about him.

But at his mention of love, I held my breath hoping he wouldn't notice I was holding my breath. And also hoping that maybe he was about to share something so I could share something, both of which were crucially important.

I quietly let my breath out when he didn't.

I hid my disappointment with another question. "So the Lunwynians don't actually have a goddess of love, just passion and motherhood?"

"For the ancients, when the dragons flew freely, they did," Frey answered. He gave me another squeeze and whispered, "Her name was Sjofn."

I held my breath again, and after a while let it out when he said no more.

"My parents named me after a Norse goddess of love," I shared. "She was an ancient goddess too. They did this because I was born with my hair.

They thought it looked like snow. There's a lot of snow in Scandinavia so that's why they decided on that. They were going to name me Tabitha."

His body shook with a brief chuckle before he stated, "You are not a Tabitha."

No, this was true.

"It's spelled differently," I informed him. "No one would get it the way it was spelled, and they didn't want people to mess it up so they spelled it S...e...o...a...f...i...n."

He pressed closer to me, indicating, like he always did in some sweet, gentle way when I shared something he liked learning, that he liked learning the spelling of my name before he muttered, "This was probably wise."

"They were very wise," I concurred then I said as if to myself, "I wonder if it's the same goddess in both worlds."

"This, my wee one, we will probably never know."

Probably not.

"Though," Frey went on, "I find, if you pay attention, there are curious links to your world and mine. For instance, the Aurora of this world could clearly be your mother in both."

This was also true. I'd noticed that too.

I sighed and muttered, "I wonder what the you of my world is like."

His arms got tight, and he said gently but firmly, "This, my Finnie, you will *definitely* never know."

I had to admit, his firm response was a tad surprising, but the words he said were undoubtedly true.

I brought the conversation around full circle and said softly, "You're hungry."

His arms relaxed and he murmured, "Indeed."

"One of us should rustle up some food, and since I haven't decided how to get Skylar not to be terrified of me, that person should be you."

"Indeed," he repeated, again on a murmur, but this one held humor.

"We need to eat and then we need to talk about Skylar," I said softly.

Frey sighed before he murmured, "I had wondered when you'd get to that."

My head tilted into the pillow. "Get to what?"

"You have been very patient, wife, but I knew eventually you would make your play to win Skylar. I see your face when you note someone is troubled. Atticus is an example. You felt his disappointment keenly, allowing it to settle in your heart, determined to do something about it. It is almost as if you experience other's discomfort as your own and cannot abide it. Naturally, you bring light into every situation with a smile, an understanding look or a laugh, helping others to be instantly comfortable when they're in your presence. If you don't find this reaction, you set about doing something about it."

God, what a nice thing to say.

And, incidentally, yes, I was *so totally* in love with this man.

"But I fear Skylar will be a challenge, even for you," he finished.

"You'll help me," I guessed.

"I will, my winter bride, but he was gravely mishandled and the way he was, those wounds run deep in very dark places even your light might not penetrate."

"Can it hurt to try?" I asked.

"Absolutely not," he answered.

Oh yeah. I loved my husband.

Therefore, I melted into him and declared, "So tomorrow, Operation Skylar commences."

His arms convulsed and he laughed straight out. Then he bent in to kiss my forehead.

He left his lips there when he murmured, "I'll see about food."

He kissed me again and slid away but he pulled the velvet and hides over me until I was cocooned in warmth. In the dark, I heard him dress and then he lit the lantern by the door before I watched him pass through it.

And it felt wrong, his leaving the bed after what we'd shared and me not whispering "I love you," and also Frey not returning the sentiment.

I pulled a pillow to my front, held on tight and tilted my head to look out the window at the back of the ship.

I sighed deeply.

I forced my thoughts to food and Skylar.

There would be a time to discuss what I wanted to discuss but that time wasn't right before Frey intended to enter a country in secret, penetrate the prince's lover's home and steal a priceless, ancient relic.

But there would be a time and it would be the right time.

And I'd find it.

22

KING TO PRINCESS

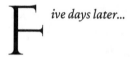ive days later...

I SAT CURLED in the corner of the bench in front of the window and studied Skylar, who looked very small sitting behind Frey's desk.

The tip of Skylar's tongue was poking out of the side of his mouth as he concentrated on some addition and subtraction questions I'd written on a piece of paper.

He looked cute, very boyish and even younger than his eleven (I'd learned) years.

I was giving him distance and time so he could concentrate.

I was also trying not to think of my husband and his men off on their adventure. Something I didn't even try to talk Frey into allowing me to participate in. I was okay on a horse and now wasn't a total amateur with a bow and knife. But I'd had not that first lesson in being stealthy or participating in a raid and was in no way experienced enough with the limited skills I had to try them out on a mission as important as this.

So, three nights ago we set anchor, and without delay, under the moonlight, the men lowered a boat into the water and rowed ashore.

Frey said the operation, if it went well, would take five or six days. One would be spent on travel, three or four would be spent on gathering updated intel and reconnaissance, then they'd do the deed (hopefully), and it would take a day to come back.

After that we were again away, back to Lunwyn so that Frey could meet with Ruben to hear his report on how his business went. And after that, Frey gave me the choice of seeing his lodge, his chalet, his fishing cottage, traveling to one of his foreign properties, or returning to his hunting cabin.

I was still considering this choice and about every other minute I settled on a different location.

But I had time to think about it.

And hopefully I would have a lifetime to experience them all.

Before he left, Frey had decided how I would work through Skylar's discomfort, and I thought his decision was excellent.

That was for me to teach Skylar reading and math.

Kell had taken an interest in the boy. But Kell, being Kell, had not devoted his days to these endeavors. Therefore, whenever the fancy struck him, he would work with Skylar.

I had learned in short order after Frey called Skylar to his cabin and told him he would begin tutorials with me that the fancy hadn't struck Kell often.

I also learned that if Skylar was uncomfortable around me normally, the thought of me teaching him anything terrified him, and even though he fought to hide it, especially in front of Frey, he didn't succeed.

Lastly, upon gently instigating some simple exercises, I found his skills were rudimentary at best. But at least we weren't starting from the drawing board.

The first two tutorials began with Frey in attendance, but he didn't stay long, leaving the boy with me after Skylar's attention was turned from his fear to his work. The ensuing days without Frey, it took me longer to settle him in. But today he was settled, and I was giving him space to work through his assignment without me hovering.

And I was thinking about Frey, where he was, what he was doing, if he was safe and lastly, the two days we shared before he and his men rowed away.

To say the adela tea heightened our awareness of each other was a vast understatement.

And it didn't only succeed in this sexually, but in every way.

In our short time together, I'd attuned to Frey's moods, tones and learned his expressions. Now I read him easily just with a glance at the line of his frame, the set of his jaw, or the look in his eye.

And there was something so superbly intimate about this, it was hard to take in the immense beauty of it, the intense feeling of connection with the man you loved. Not only being so attuned to Frey but knowing he was just that attuned to me. It did not make me feel exposed. It made me feel safe, protected, like I belonged somewhere and to someone, and since my parents died, throughout all my roaming, I had not felt either.

It was a beautiful thing to have back, a treasure, the best gift I'd ever received.

For Frey, post-adela tea meant something more.

He was the kind of man who was not afraid of showing gentleness and affection. He was also the kind of man who had things to do, and he did them. But after our afternoon in his cabin, more often than not he wanted to do these things with me close.

Therefore, his last day aboard, as we stood behind the wheel on the bridge deck, his hands on the spiked handles, me in front of him, we sailed the emerald waters of the Green Sea, our eyes on the horizon. As we did, Frey often bent to speak to me, his mouth at my ear. Or, if I had something to say, I turned to him, my mouth at his, and we whispered to each other for hours.

It was magnificent, not what we said so much as how we did it.

And I'd learned why he received his salutes from men of fist to chin and from women of chin to neck. The fist to chin was the salute of The Drakkar, a manly salute. The chin to neck was the salute of The Frey, considered a feminine salute. These were his due, as if he was king, and if anyone caught his eye, they were obligated to give it to him.

I'd also learned that he didn't get these salutes from the people of Houllebec, because the first adela tree, the most sacred one in all of Lunwyn, was in the forest close to the village and thus why he had his hunting cabin there and often where he met with the elves. He was there regularly, if not often. Because of this, most of his men had cottages there. And he had long since communicated to the villagers that they did not have to salute. This was something he found tedious, for if they saluted, he'd have to return a nod and he did not enjoy walking through the village or having a horn of ale at a pub and constantly needing to meet eyes and tip his chin.

I could totally see that. At the Winter Palace, practically everyone bobbed a curtsy to me. I was cool with smiling and saying "hi," but those curtsies felt weird, seeing as I was not born a princess and did not grow up being entitled to them. And acknowledging required more effort than a smile or a passing "hello." It didn't actually require it, but it seemed to, and I guessed (and shared this with Frey, who concurred) that it was the constant reminder of my responsibilities as princess and the fact that their show of respect was required, not earned, that made it so.

During our talk Frey had asked (and I'd answered) about what Princess Sjofn had shared with me in her letter. We'd also discussed why she did not relate the information that he was The Frey or The Drakkar or various other tidbits that would have been extremely helpful to know such as, say, someone had tried to assassinate her.

Although we discussed this (at length), neither of us came up with an answer, and eventually I gently closed the conversation. This was because it was clear Sjofn was not Frey's favorite person. It was not that he wasn't pleased with the outcome of her play, but because he was seriously displeased that in making it, she committed what was considered an act of treason against the realm *and* he was not a big fan of how and when she'd maneuvered my entry into their world.

Although it wasn't for Sjofn, I took this as good news that Frey, Atticus and Aurora all considered Sjofn's actions an act of treason.

First, knowing this, she wouldn't want to return (for the punishment for treason was hanging, which obviously anyone would wish to avoid).

Second, for this reason, Atticus and Aurora would not want her return.

If she faced that, what it would mean for Lunwyn as a whole, for, if hung by the neck until dead, obviously, she could not bear a child who would sit on the throne and assure peace for the land. But instead, political maneuvering (already unpleasant, to say the least, what with daggers and poison involved) would careen out of control.

So I took this as good news (for me) because, with all of that, they all would be less likely to want me to go home and more likely to wish me to stay.

Discussing Sjofn led me to thinking (and sharing with Frey) that there were a number of questions and contradictions about her behavior. There were things she did that were thoughtless and selfish and others that were neither.

I couldn't help but think that Frey was wrong about her, and this was because she had the devotion of all her maidservants. It was clear Sjofn didn't think like Frey did about the different classes. They were not her maidservants. They were her friends, her confidants, and she was theirs.

293

And I couldn't imagine my girls caring for a woman who did not deserve their emotion.

I also couldn't imagine carrying the burden of Sjofn's responsibility to her country that forced her to hide her sexuality, something innate and so crucial to not only who she was but her happiness.

I could not say I agreed with everything she did, but I was not her. I'd never had to hide who I was, so didn't understand these feelings and how she had to be torn between happiness and duty. And not knowing, I could not make a judgment.

When I quietly shared this with Frey, he disagreed. It was clear he felt quite comfortable making a judgment, and he did. I left him to his thoughts, for, obviously, he was entitled to them.

But I couldn't help but think, hopefully in the end, both Sjofn and I would find ourselves high on Valentine's line of happiness in our different adventures.

"I'm finished, milady," Skylar called.

My thoughts moved back into the room, and I turned my head his way.

I smiled, uncurled from my corner and walked slowly to him.

As I did, Skylar shrank slightly back in the big chair and didn't quite meet my eyes, something he did normally but something I noticed intensified when he had completed his work and it was time for me to look over it. Therefore, when I arrived, I reached in carefully, took hold of the corner of the paper and moved slowly away, again giving him space.

I scanned the paper. In the twenty questions, he'd crossed out two answers, but in the end, got them right. In fact, he got all the answers right.

I took another small step back because I intended to speak to him, and he seemed more comfortable with distance when I did.

"Not a single mistake, Skylar," I said gently. "You're learning this extremely quickly. Tomorrow, I'll have to make them a bit more difficult."

I had hoped he would blossom under the quiet praise, but the mention of the questions becoming more difficult made a flash of fear fire in his eyes.

Therefore, I rushed to assure him, "Not that much more difficult, honey. We'll take it slow. No worries."

He bit his lip and nodded, looking no less worried.

I pulled in a breath. Frey had advised me not to give into my instinct to protect him by responding to his uneasiness and fear by releasing him from the cause, namely me. Frey had said that Skylar couldn't get used to me if I let him scurry away, but that I would need to be around for him actually to get used to me.

This was, of course, wise.

It was also really hard.

So instead of seeing that fear in his eyes, his teeth sinking into his lip anxiously and giving into my instinct of cutting our lesson short and letting him off the hook, I decided to move forward and work with him on his letters.

"All right, Skylar," I said softly, taking a step toward him. "We're going to move on. You've got the alphabet down pat so now we'll work on putting it together to make some—"

I stopped speaking when the door opened suddenly.

Skylar's eyes shot to it and so did mine.

And when they did, I saw Kell barging in.

He looked to Skylar at Frey's desk then me and he announced in his gruff voice, "We got a problem."

My heart skipped.

He didn't look happy, as in, way more than his usual unhappy when he was looking at me, so I was thinking this problem was a *problem*.

"Out, boy," Kell barked at Skylar.

Skylar jumped up and took off.

He closed the door behind him and Kell's gaze came to me.

My eyes had not left him, and my fingertips were on the desk, pressing in, seeking support hopefully without looking like I was.

"Frey?" I asked quietly, and Kell's bushy white brows shot together.

"*What?*" he barked.

"Frey," I repeated, turning more fully to him and stiffening my spine. "Have you heard some word? Are Frey and the men all right?"

"Gods, woman, a' course they are. Stealin' a branch from a poof? Bloody hell," he replied, and I decided that I would not share my thoughts on him calling homosexuals "poofs." But even if I wished to do so, I didn't get the chance because Kell kept speaking. "We got riders at the shore. They hold Baldur banners."

Oh shit.

Kell went on, "They're flashin' a sun message. Bloody Baldur knows you're here. He's camped close and he wants you and Frey to attend him."

Oh shit!

"A sun message?" I asked.

"Sun," he grunted. "Mirror. Message."

That was all he said, but I put two and two together and figured that the riders were flashing a mirror at the sun in some way that the men on the ship could read.

And that message was, my uncle—who was not my uncle—wanted me and my husband— who was not here but instead on a clandestine mission to steal property from Middleland soil some weeks after, of course, he and his men had helped the king's captive sorceress (and forced mistress) to escape—to come and see him.

This was not good.

"I'm guessin' from that look on yer face you're readin' this situation as *not good*," Kell accurately deduced and without a breath continued, "We're exposed. Until nightfall, without them seein', we can't get a man to shore to get a message to Frey. And we got a command from a king on our hands. One we cannot defy without good reason, and we got ourselves a couple a' those, but none of 'em are ones we can share. And Baldur is not the kind a' king who's big on bein' defied. Not to mention, we send you in, you got no idea who this blighter is."

By the way, Kell, like all of Frey's closest men, knew who I was and where I'd come from.

"Thanks for summing that up, Kell," I said softly, and his eyes narrowed.

Then he stated, "I ain't here to sum it up, princess. I'm here 'cause I'm plum outta ideas and wondered if *you* got some. The king's men cannot board this ship."

"Why?" I asked and he gave me a look I couldn't quite decipher because I didn't know Kell all that well, but I had a feeling there was something on the ship the king's men couldn't see.

Shit!

Thinking fast, I suggested, "Can you send a message that I'm indisposed, um...not well and ask the king to wait until tomorrow when I'll hopefully feel better? That way we'll have time to make up a story and form a plan."

He crossed his arms on his chest and his irritated impatient look got more irritated and impatient.

"Tried that. They told us to send a boat ashore anyway as the king's concerned about his niece and wants to send his men across to board in order to ascertain she's all right."

I blinked then asked, "How long have they been out there?"

"Over an hour."

I blinked again and asked, "Why didn't you tell me earlier?"

He uncrossed his arms and planted his fists on his hips and asked back, "And why would I do that?"

I put my hands to my hips too and shot back, "Oh, I don't know, Kell. Probably so I'd have more time to consider this dilemma and maybe come up with an answer. Rather than receiving the news there *was* a dilemma at the last possible moment so my only choice is to freak out and make a rushed decision about what the heck we're going to do. Jeez, two heads are better than one," I ended on an annoyed snap.

"Not when one a' those heads belongs to a woman," Kell fired back.

Oh no he did *not*.

I glared at him.

Then I ordered, "Prepare a boat and pick men you trust to accompany me, but the party must include Gunner and Stephan."

It was his turn to blink before he breathed out a, "What?" that clearly stated he thought I was insane.

"Prepare a boat and pick men you trust to accompany me," I repeated.

"Woman—" Kell started but I interrupted him.

"Kell, we have a demand from a king. We're in his waters and my husband is in his country doing something he will probably not like. Frey is not set to return for days." I leaned forward and reminded him, "We need to *buy time* and the only one who can do that is *me*."

"Princess, that man has known the other you since she was a baby and *you* have never seen him in your life," he reminded me back.

I threw out a hand and declared, "I'll wing it."

His brows shot together again, and he grunted, "Wing it?"

"Make it up as I go along. Wing it. Now send a message that I'm rousing myself for the journey, prepare a boat and select men you trust to accompany me."

He didn't move. He scowled.

Then he announced, "Drakkar is *not* gonna like this, woman."

I didn't figure he would. Then again, I figured he'd come to understand I had no choice.

With any luck.

"I'll deal with that later."

"Hopefully it won't be *much* later, say, Baldur already knows what's happenin'. He's makin' his play and that play is abducting you, incarceratin' your rounded arse in one a' his castles and sendin' word to your father that he ain't real happy his niece and nephew-in-law are runnin' amok in his kingdom. Somethin', by the by, your papa don't know balls about."

Hmm.

"We'll cross that bridge if we come to it," I decided.

Kell scowled at me some more but still didn't move.

"Kell, time is wasting," I reminded him.

He ignored me and continued to scowl at me. Finally, something shifted on his face, the scowl was still there, just not as severe, and something had lit in his eyes.

I didn't have time to decipher it. I had no time at all, and I needed to get changed before all this went down. I wasn't wearing breeches to this meeting. I was meeting my uncle, king to princess, and I needed an outfit that would remind him of that.

So I prompted, somewhat loudly, "Kell!"

That was when he muttered, "He said you had the spirit."

"What?" I asked impatiently, and Kell's unfocused eyes focused on me.

"Nothin'," he grunted. "I'll send the message, prepare the boat and gather the men." He lifted a finger and jabbed it at me. "But, woman, *I'm* gonna be one a' those men. You stay close to me, you pay attention to me, and you learn real quick to *read me*. We got no choice, you and me, but to get through this bloody mess together. Don't go goin' princess on me and don't go goin' cockamamie on me. Yeah?"

My shoulders straightened in umbrage, and I declared, "I'm never cockamamie."

"Woman, you transported yourself to a whole 'nother world not knowin' where your arse would land or what it would land *in*. Most women got at least some cockamamie in 'em, but *you* are head-to-toe cockamamie," he returned.

That was arguable, but I didn't have time to argue it now.

"Kell, time is wasting," I reminded him, and the scowl shot back to severe.

Then he burst out, "Balls, I see it in yer eyes. You're gonna go cockamamie on me."

"Kell!" I snapped loudly.

"All right, all right. Smooth your knickers, princess," he said, hands up but pressing down. "You got an hour then your arse is on deck."

"Right," I replied.

He sucked in breath and seared me with another scowl. Then he shook his head and exited the cabin, slamming the door behind him simply, I guessed, because he was a curmudgeon and didn't want me to forget it.

I stared at the door, and with that confrontation over, the coming one loomed in front of me.

I had two choices, freak out or get my shit sorted.

I rushed to my trunks to get my shit sorted.

FIRST OFF, it was clear we'd traveled far enough south that Middleland, unlike Lunwyn, was not charmingly crusted with ice and snow. I'd noticed that from viewing shore from the ship and I'd definitely noticed the air was warmer, not well above freezing, but not below it.

As Kell, myself, Gunner, Stephan and three of Frey's crew acting as impromptu royal guards made our way to my uncle's camp on horses provided for us, I also noticed that Middleland wasn't that charming at all.

It wasn't exactly barren, but it also wasn't colorful or overly fertile. It seemed bleak, craggy and dark, and although the days were longer, that wasn't exactly a boon because Middleland would probably look better in the moonlight.

Seeing it, I thought that perhaps Sjofn's grandfather had a favorite son after all for Atticus definitely got the better deal when his father was doling out kingdoms.

Once we'd navigated the dark rocks that made up the shore and spread inland, it didn't take long for the tents to come into view.

The sun was beginning to set, but I could see they were striped wide in red and black. They were large. There were several of them. They each had a number of peaks and all of these peaks had red and black checked pennants flying.

We were escorted by the king's men, of which there were twelve (my opinion only, but I thought this was overkill). They all were wearing amour breastplates with black and red dragons painted on them, high black boots that came up to their thighs, poofy black shorts and they also had red and black striped poofs of material around their shoulders. But their biceps and forearms were covered solely in black. On their heads they had gleaming helmets with a Mohawk arrangement of stiff black and red feathers. All their weapons (swords on scabbards attached to their saddles and a knife at their belts) shone as if they'd never been used.

I read from their number and attire that Baldur liked pomp and circumstance.

Frey's men wore what they wore. There was no uniform of The Drakkar or even of his merchant ships. My father's men wore a uniform, but it was warm, sturdy, comfortable and utilitarian. All the heads of the Houses I'd met at the Gales had worn their colors proudly, but they let their wives display the finery that indicated their wealth. The men's clothes were excellent quality and there were touches that indicated affluence. But none of them were overt about it.

This pageantry to meet your niece in a tent on a desolate plain seemed a bit much and said a great deal about my uncle.

His men led us straight to the biggest tent, and when I say that I mean it was the biggest tent by far, at least double the size of any other, maybe more, and as large as a small house. The entryway had a ten-foot-long awning stretching out from it, along which four guards stood. It was clear these guards were more important for their feathers in their helmets were bigger and each had a ruby in the hilt of the daggers on their belts.

Immediately upon arrival, there was a wee situation when we stopped and Gunner (most of the men I knew well were with Frey, however he'd left Gunner and Stephan behind, likely in case something like this occurred) dismounted instantly and came to help me off my horse. Unfortunately, one of Baldur's men did the same and Gunner didn't take kindly to this.

As glowers were exchanged and chests puffed up, an idea hit me, and I was both thankful that it did because I'd been wracking my brain since Kell left the cabin as to what I intended to do (to no avail). Also, I hoped I could pull it off.

"Please," I fake rasped, and it sounded so good even I was surprised at how real it sounded.

I saw instantly so was Gunner who knew I didn't have a sore throat. It also surprised the guard *and* Kell who'd stopped his horse close to mine and I felt his eyes come to me.

"I am comfortable with my guard. If you will allow…" I kept rasping then trailed off, grimaced in fake pain and wrapped one of my hands daintily around my throat as if those mere words had caused me more than mild suffering.

The guard looked at me and his face softened. I smiled what I hoped was a benevolent princess smile on him. His lips tipped up and I figured I'd pulled off the princess smile. He gave a small bow and stepped back gallantly. Gunner reached up and pulled me down, but he did it so my face stayed parallel to his for the barest second and I saw his blue eyes smile.

I didn't smile back because his back was to the guard and mine wasn't, but I rolled my eyes the barest bit.

He set me on my feet, and I leaned into him like I didn't have the strength to hold myself up. He took his cue and hooked my arm firmly in the crook of his elbow before he escorted me to the awning where Kell joined me on my other side. I grabbed on to him too (might as well go for the gusto). They led me through the awning and inside the tent.

If I thought the tents, pennants and uniformed soldiers were a spectacle, they were nothing compared to the opulence I encountered inside. I tried not to look as surprised as I was at the overabundance of fur (the ground was covered in it, yes, *covered*), sheets of red and black silk draping the walls, the ornate, heavily carved, shining wood furniture, the gleaming silver candelabrum all over the place, and the two, large, overdone thrones (yes, *thrones*) sitting smack in the middle of the tent on a fur-covered rise.

Holy moly.

One could say I was not averse to luxury and indulged in it frequently. But this was way over the top.

There were more guards inside (eight to be exact) and the feathers in their helmets were even bigger, and they had elaborate jaw and chin guards wrapped around the lower half of their faces.

And sitting on the thrones (one much grander than the other) were two men.

On the bigger one was a graying, jowly man with a large belly and a larger gold crown on his head. This was decorated with black fur and inset with rubies and diamonds. He wore his own poofy shorts, these striped in black and red. He also had a breastplate painted with a dragon, but it looked funny considering it had to be made with a bulge to cover his big belly.

Hilariously (I thought), at his booted foot there was a helmet with a huge spray of red and black feathers shooting straight out of the top. This I read as his indication that he was battle ready at all times when he was, clearly, *not*.

But as amusing as this was, I didn't find him humorous because his eyes were directed right at me, and I saw at once they were mean.

At his side sat a very handsome, much younger man not wearing a breastplate, poofy shorts or even a crown. But black breeches, shined black boots, a red poofy-sleeved shirt with laces at the collar and a black, brocade vest. His ensemble, even with the red poofy shirt, was understated but elegant.

My uncle and cousin.

And, by the way, my uncle clearly was *not* an identical twin with Father.

There was a man standing to the right and behind Prince Broderick's chair and he, too, was dressed like Broderick but his shirt was pristine white, and he had a thin scarf with a silk fringe wrapped jauntily around his neck.

A not-so-wild guess (considering the scarf), the lover, Phobin.

I let Kell and Gunner go and dropped to a low, formal curtsy, which was my guess at what he would expect regardless that he thought we shared blood and royal status.

"Rise, my niece." I heard him command in a voice as pompous as his surroundings, and I did what I was told.

Then I hoped to all that was holy that I read even the slightest hint of Sjofn's feelings for these two in her letters and I smiled dutifully at her uncle but far more warmly at her cousin.

Baldur inclined his head.

Broderick smiled warmly back.

Okay.

Phew.

That seemed to go well.

"Come, my dear, embrace your brethren," Baldur ordered.

I looked back at him, saw he had his hands to the arms of his throne, appearing like he was preparing to shift his bulk from the chair, and I lifted a fluttering hand to my throat.

"If it pleases you, your grace," I rasped harshly and saw Baldur blink before his brows drew together and he sat back. "For your welfare, I will not." I pushed out, moved my hand from my throat to my mouth, coughed roughly yet delicately (yep, I pulled that off and was pretty freaking proud of myself doing it), dropped my hand and finished, "I've caught a chill in my throat, and I do not wish you to catch it."

"Yer grace," Kell cut in. I turned to him to see he was still bent low, eyes to the furs at our feet. "If we could have your leave to get our princess a chair. She's unwell and don't have a lot a' energy."

"See to a chair for Princess Sjofn, Phobin," Baldur ordered.

The face of the man behind Broderick grew slightly hard at being ordered about, but he moved off toward some furniture sitting at the side of the tent.

The good news was, Phobin and Broderick were here so they weren't wherever Frey was.

The other good news was, so far, I was pulling this off and Kell had fallen in with the plan.

And luckily, there was no bad news.

Yet.

"Guard of Sjofn, you may also rise," Baldur muttered distractedly.

I looked to my left to see Gunner had, as well, been bowed to this king all this time.

What a dick, leaving them like that. It wasn't like it was hours, but still.

I shook off this irritation as Phobin brought me a chair. I smiled at him then collapsed in it pretending to pretend I was not actually collapsing in it but regally taking a very needed load off my princess feet.

When I was settled, Gunner and Kell took their places, Gunner at my left back and Kell at the right.

"If you are so unwell, niece, why did you make the journey? My men could easily have attended you on your husband's vessel," Baldur made a good point, and I looked at him.

Shit. This was true.

I thought fast.

Then I rasped, "You are my father's brother, but you are also king." He winced at my voice with the addition of a curled lip to show his distaste, the latter of which I didn't like all that much. I mean, I wasn't actually sick, but *he* didn't know that, and no one could help being sick. "It is my duty to attend you," I concluded.

"That is my sweet Sjofn," Broderick said softly in a lovely, deep, gentle voice, and my eyes went to him to see his were soft and warm on me. "Always putting duty above self."

Well, not always.

I obviously didn't mention this but tipped my head to the side and smiled at him.

"And your new husband?" Baldur asked, I looked back at him and opened my mouth to speak.

"Inland," Kell grunted before I could say anything. Baldur's eyes narrowed in annoyance, and they shot to Kell.

"Did I give you leave to speak for my niece?" he demanded to know.

"You didn't, Father, but you should," Broderick stated firmly but softly. "It's clear Sjofn experiences pain every time she does."

Baldur sniffed to communicate he acceded this point then addressed Kell. "And what does your master do inland?"

Ho boy. I wasn't certain Kell would like Frey being referred to as his master.

Kell, however, didn't miss a beat, but he also didn't share masses of information.

"His wife is unwell."

"I can *hear* that. And?" Baldur demanded.

"She caught a chill not long after we set sail. Not bad at first but it got worse. Laid up in bed, soundin' funny and sick as a dog. None of the medicine we got onboard was doin' her any good. The Drakkar set anchor and came ashore to go inland, find a doctor, get her somethin' to help her so we can be on our way, and she'll quit sufferin'."

"And you're on your way to where?" Baldur asked.

"Chateau in Hawkvale. They got a baby to make," Kell answered. "The Drakkar likes seein' to that particular duty and didn't want any distractions."

I sighed heavily mainly because I would normally sigh heavily at Kell's highly personal answer but also because I figured Sjofn would sigh heavily at Kell's highly personal answer.

Baldur stared at Kell with distaste. My eyes slid to Broderick to see his on me and they were twinkling. He thought that was funny and I could tell by the way he was looking at me Sjofn would share in his humor, so I gave him a little shrug and a small smile, and his twinkle got brighter.

"Seems to me The Drakkar could send a man inland to find medicine for his wife so he could stay aboard and tend her," Baldur noted, and my eyes went back to him.

"And seems to me you don't know my master much, I'm guessin'. Errand's important, he don't send no one to do it. The man does it himself," Kell replied.

Baldur straightened in his chair, obviously not liking Kell's tone.

"Indeed," Baldur murmured, scowling at Kell.

"He's being very kind," I put in, still rasping. I lifted my hand delicately to my throat as Baldur's attention went from his angry contemplation of Kell to me. "I told him I would be all right, given time. But he's concerned."

"Taken with her, he is," Kell added. "Don't like to see her sufferin' and also don't like not gettin' his husbandly privileges 'cause she's sufferin', if you take my meanin', yer grace."

"I do, indeed," Baldur sniffed through a lip curl, which, as much as I didn't like this guy, I had to admit was pretty good, "*take your meaning*, my dear sir."

"I'm pleased to hear this, Sjofn," Broderick said quietly, and I looked to him. "That The Drakkar has taken to you. This is lovely news."

I smiled at him. He smiled back and it wasn't understanding, like he knew Sjofn's secret and felt for her. It was genuine, like he was truly pleased her arranged marriage was working out.

"We suit," I whispered, taking the rasp down a notch because I was whispering but also saying it with feeling because it was true.

"I'm pleased to hear this too, cousin," Broderick replied on another sincere smile, and I smiled back.

"Well, I cannot say this comes as a surprise," Baldur declared, and I looked to him. "He practically dragged you from the Dwelling of the Gods. Vulgar, most assuredly, but telling." He smiled at me, it was definitely *not* genuine, and finished, "But who would not be taken with Lunwyn's Winter Princess, far and away the fairest beauty in that frigid land?"

I wasn't all that hot on him calling Lunwyn frigid. It was, of course, frigid, strictly speaking, but there were nicer words to use.

It was then there seemed to be some commotion outside. The guards inside went on alert, four closing in on their king and two immediately going out the tent opening.

I turned in my chair, peering around Kell to see what was happening and didn't have to wait long when one of the guards rushed back in, bowed and said to the furs, "The Drakkar is here."

Uh-oh.

My eyes shot upwards, caught Kell's and I saw his mouth surrounded by his bushy, white beard was tight.

Shit.

I leaned around again to look beyond Kell to see Frey, followed by Thad, Orion, Max, Annar, Lund and Oleg striding purposefully into the tent, and Frey was looking pretty freaking displeased.

Uh-oh again.

"What's the meaning of this?" he demanded to know before he got five feet into the huge tent.

I rose quickly, intent to move to him and find some way to give him a heads up regarding what was afoot.

"You don't bow to the king of the land whose soil your boots tread upon?" Baldur asked, and he sounded pissed too, pissed and full of outraged affront.

Frey halted beside Kell, bowed shallow and swift, not bothering to wait for his command to rise. I got close to him, putting my hands on his chest. I pressed in as hard as I could and tipped my head back.

Then I rasped, deeper and far more harshly, "Husband, it is my duty to attend a king when called upon to do so."

Frey's brows shot together, and his head jerked down to look at me the instant the first word came from my throat.

"You get that medicine you were after, *master*?" Kell asked casually, and Frey tore his eyes from me to look at Kell.

Then, cottoning on quickly, as was his way, he clipped, "No. I heard word the king's men were at shore, and hearing that, I was certain he would call on my bride so I abandoned the search and returned instantly." His eyes moved to Baldur as his arm moved to circle my waist and he pulled my front close to his. "And I was not wrong. The king called upon my bride."

"Of course," Baldur stated. "She is my niece, which means you are now my nephew and the moment I heard your ship was anchored offshore, we rode to extend familial greetings."

Frey's jaw went hard.

Then he returned, "That is kind, your grace, but if we were in Middle-land for an official visit, rather than to run a swift errand, we would have sent word and come to you to extend *our* familial greetings. Now my wife, who should be abed, is out in the cold." He looked at Kell. "Did you not inform his grace that Finnie was ill?"

"Finnie?" Broderick whispered, but Kell spoke over him.

"Sure did, *master*," Kell answered, and I pressed my lips together to stop myself from laughing. "He said he'd send men aboard to attend her, but she wasn't hearin' none of it. Said it was her duty and so on." He flipped out a hand that eloquently (or as eloquent as Kell could be) said what he felt about royal duty. "So she dragged her carcass outta bed, got all tarted up, and here we are."

At that, I had to press my lips together harder. I caught a look at Thad as he was standing at Frey's back right and I saw his jaw clench. It made him look annoyed, but my guess was Thad thought Kell was pretty amusing too.

"My wife informed you she was ill, and you sent word you intended to disturb her in her rest by sending men to my ship if she didn't attend you?" Frey asked, his voice low and rumbling and unmistakably infuriated.

"It didn't happen exactly like that, Drakkar," Baldur stated.

306

"Then maybe you'll explain *exactly* how it happened," Frey mock suggested. That was to say, it wasn't a suggestion at all.

"It hardly takes two days to seek medicine, which is at least the amount of time you've been anchored off Middlelandian shore," Baldur shot back, and I tensed as he shared this information.

"Perhaps you don't know your niece very well, your grace. She dislikes being ill, refused to admit she was and has an aversion to being tended. It took me that long to convince her I should go," Frey totally lied.

"This is true, Father. Sjofn has always been a poor patient, as you know when she caught flu during that visit when she was sixteen," Broderick put in smoothly then smiled at me. "Remember, cousin, I had to resort to sneaking medicine in your tea."

"I remember," I rasped softly on a returned smile, thinking I quite liked Broderick. He seemed very sweet.

Baldur puffed his chest up and ignored our exchange. "Well then, seeing your proximity to our shore, you were here two days, you should have sent a missive. It is, as you well know, my due as king."

"My apologies, your grace, and I hope you don't find it offensive when I remind you we did not expect to be at your shore this long and I was dealing with a headstrong, unwell bride. My attention was taken by her, not sending a meaningless message, the effort of which would be a ridiculous waste of time for one of my men," Frey returned.

"See here," Baldur said quietly, now *his* voice was rumbling. "I'll remind you again whose soil your boots rest on."

"And I'll remind you that my wife is clearly not well, and the curiosity and mistrust, the latter of which is unearned, I will add," Frey impressively lied through his teeth, "that were the true reasons you are here with tents and *thrones*," he said this with disgust, "has delayed me on the errand of seeing to her health."

"Careful, Drakkar, you don't have leave to speak to this king the way you do my brother. The elves don't leave the snow and you can't call the dragons from this far," Baldur retorted.

"Care to test that?" Frey returned.

Ho boy.

Time to intervene.

Pronto.

"Oh dear," I whispered on my rasp and lifted a hand to my head, turning in the circle of Frey's arm toward Sjofn's uncle. "Do you, in all these tents, have someplace I can lie down, uncle? I'm feeling lightheaded."

At my words, I was instantly swept up in Frey's arms and held close to his chest.

"You'll rest in our cabin," Frey gritted then his eyes snapped to Baldur. "If I may have your leave to see to my wife?"

"Of course," Broderick answered for his father. "And to save you the trouble, I'll send to my personal physician for some medicine. It may take until morning, but we'll message you the moment it arrives so you can send a boat to retrieve it. That way, you can attend your..." he hesitated. His eyes came to me, and they were warm because he clearly mistook the reason Frey had used the name he called me, and liked it, before he finished, "*Finnie*."

"My thanks, Broderick, but do not go to that trouble. We'll be on our way," Frey stated, jerked his head at Baldur, turned on his boot and stalked out of the tent.

For my part, I'd wrapped my arms around Frey's shoulders, and I looked over the right one and smiled regally (I hoped) at father and son, seeing the king looked fit to be tied but Broderick was smiling so big he looked like he was trying hard not to laugh.

Yeah, I definitely liked Broderick.

Then I saw them no more as we were out of the tent, I was on a horse, Frey swung up behind me, leaned into me, dug his heels into the horse's flanks and barked, "*Yah!*" and we were galloping away.

After a few minutes, I felt it was safe to speak.

So I did, starting with, "Frey—"

I was wrong about it being safe to speak.

I knew this when Frey growled, "Quiet, Finnie. We'll wait until I have you *and* Kell sitting down so you can explain to me which one of you had the spectacularly *stupid* idea to go it alone with minimal guard, only two of whom are trained, and without *me*, to attend a man who might want you dead."

Ho boy.

I got quiet as ordered, thinking it was my best bet at that juncture and watched the sea, Frey's beautiful galleon drifting on it with the sun setting behind it, coming closer.

23

MARRIAGE IS MARRIAGE

"Please tell me you're not back early 'cause that sorry excuse for a king set up his throne in a bloody tent of all places."

Kell chose this perhaps not very wise opener to our conversation as he strode into Frey's cabin looking more than his usual grumpy.

We were all around the table. Frey seated at the head by his desk, me to his left, Thad to his right and Orion, Max, Lund, Oleg, Annar, Gunner and Stephan rounded out the mix with Oleg standing behind the empty chair at the foot, beefy legs planted apart, arms crossed on his chest. Orion and Stephan were also standing because we didn't have enough chairs and I made a mental note to visit the galleon furniture store the next time I was in Sudvic.

Skylar was squeezing between the big men setting trays of cheese, meat, crackers and pickles on the table. He'd already seen to making sure all the men had horns of ale, save Frey, who'd ordered and received a glass and a bottle of whisky, from which he partook immediately, and I did not think this boded as a good sign.

As was apparent since refreshments had been readied and served by an eleven-year-old boy, Kell took his time showing up at our party, which made me, as the seconds ticked to minutes then those minutes ticked to more minutes (and not a few of them), very uncomfortable. The men didn't seem to mind it, although they kept their silence as Frey's seething anger filled the space.

"We are not, old man, we're back early because Broderick and Phobin were both with Baldur and we discovered Phobin is not nearly as clever as he thinks. We arrived, surveyed the situation and were in and out in a day," Frey returned.

Kell's brows shot up as he planted his ass in a chair and immediately reached for a hunk of cheese.

"You get the branch?" he asked.

"Yes," Frey bit off, my heart jumped, and I turned to look at him.

"You did?" I breathed.

Frey's angry eyes sliced to me.

I pressed my lips together and he growled, "We did."

I decided, considering his expression, now was not the time to jump up and give him a sloppy kiss in an effort to reward him for succeeding in a quest where others, for centuries, had failed.

"So, we're celebratin'," Kell stated then looked to Skylar. "Boy, get me a horn."

"Kell, we are not celebrating," Frey ground out, his infuriated eyes locked on his friend. He stated angrily, "By the gods, you walked my wife into the tent of a man who may be plotting her murder."

Kell sat back and agreed, "Yup." Then he popped the hunk of cheese into his mouth.

Ho boy.

The fury rolling off Frey increased about seven levels. I felt it, fancied its heat burned my skin, bit my lip and avoided looking at him.

"Gun, Steph, would you like to explain why you not only didn't stop this venture but participated in it?" Frey asked, obviously giving up on Kell.

I watched Gunner look at Stephan and Stephan looked at Gunner then they both looked to Frey.

"You left Kell in charge, Frey, and you were pretty clear about that," Gunner answered.

"Indeed. And this will be a mistake I do not make again," Frey stated low, and I watched Kell roll his eyes, but other than that, he didn't seem too upset.

There was more silence, more fury waves from Frey and then Frey called, "Wife."

Ho boy.

I gave Kell a raised-brow look indicating I could use his assistance. Kell's response was to grab another hunk of cheese and pop it into his mouth. My look became a death glare when I realized Kell was throwing me right under the bus.

I sucked in breath, rearranged my features and turned to my husband.

When he had my eyes, he asked in a soft voice that was not his gentle soft but an altogether different kind of soft, "Would you like to tell me, when I believe while you were trembling in my arms after seeing three men die, that I informed you specifically your uncle is a threat, why you would board a boat, sit in it while it was rowed ashore and attend a man who, it is highly likely whether he's acted on it or not, wishes you dead?"

Actually, no I wouldn't like to tell him. Though I didn't think I had a choice.

"Um..." I started.

Frey's eyes narrowed and I clamped my mouth shut.

Then he clipped, "Finnie, you saw a woman spewing blood and that woman was supposed to be *you*."

I got my wits together and began, "I know, Frey. But—"

"You had entirely no idea what you would be walking into when you walked into that tent," Frey cut me off to say.

"Listen, I—"

Frey interrupted me again and I could tell by his eyes, his tone and the way he held his body that he was getting angrier, and I didn't need our afternoon with the adela cup to read it.

"I could have come back with a bloody branch to find myself without a bloody *wife*."

I leaned toward him and said, "Frey, listen—" but I was interrupted again.

This time by Kell.

"Got a sharp wit, that one," he stated, and Frey's eyes cut to him, so mine did too. "We were in a bad position, Frey, you off doin' what you were doin', Baldur suspicious. Got nerve, your woman does." He jerked a head my way. "Got smarts too. Was her idea to fake bein' sick and how she did it. We'd already used that ploy to call 'em off. They weren't fallin' for it. But her act was so good, man, even I thought our lie was true. And the way she faked bein' sick meant she didn't have to talk much so I could do the talkin' for her, which helped hide who she is. In the end, she made a show of takin' pains in payin' her respect to a man who don't deserve it but sure as hell demands it, and he came off lookin' like an arse. Quite a play, all 'n all, and worked out fine. So calm, man, pull up anchor and let's get outta here."

311

I thought this was an excellent suggestion, not to mention I was pleased that I'd impressed Kell.

Frey did not agree.

"It worked out well by pure chance," he growled and when I turned to him and opened my mouth to speak, his eyes cut to me, and he kept growling. "And don't, Finnie, don't you tell me it was a risk worth taking. Three times," he held up three fingers, "fortune has smiled on you, and, wife, if you keep riding that particular blade of luck, you're going to get sliced wide open."

Eek!

All righty, clearly it was time to soothe the pissed-off Raider.

"Honey," I whispered, hoping my tone would calm him. "What did you expect us to do?"

"Not bloody walk into a tent with only two trained guards when Baldur had twenty-four and sit down for a bloody *chat*," Frey returned, not soothed even a little bit by my soft tone.

Hmm.

Unfortunately, it seemed I was getting mad.

"We needed to buy time," I informed him.

"As it works out, love, you didn't," he informed me.

"Well, we didn't know that!" I shot back.

"You waited an hour, you would," he retorted.

I glared at him and then scooted my chair around to face him.

"Listen, Frey, we were in a situation. They weren't falling in with our efforts to stall. And you were out there," I swung out an arm, "doing something *I* didn't want *you* to get caught doing. We thought you wouldn't return for days, not hours. For God's sake, I couldn't huddle in your cabin biting my nails and hoping for a miracle rescue!"

"Finnie—" he started, but I talked over him, leaning toward him to do it.

"You know, marriage is marriage, a partnership. You aren't the only one who needs to step up and keep one of us safe. It's my job as your *wife* to do the same if a time comes when I have to and it's my job to do it however that might need to come about. We were exposed and I didn't want *you* to be exposed. So I did what I did in an effort to keep you safe. It was dangerous, yes, I'll grant that. But we had *no choice*."

"Fin—" he tried to get my name out, but I kept right on going.

"You're angry because I was in danger, *again*. Well, you were in danger too! You rode right up to those tents and came charging in to

312

keep me safe. What? I don't get to do what I have to do to return the favor?"

"Love—" Frey began, but yep, I kept right on talking.

"I get you're angry because it was dangerous, and you're concerned. I'm sorry about that. But I'll tell you this, given the chance, I'd do it again. No joke. I'd do it in a heartbeat."

Frey was silent after that, and I was too, but I was communicating through my angry glare. Frey, on the other hand, was not communicating. He was simply holding my glare.

Then he asked, "Are you finished?"

"I don't know. Do I need to go on?" I asked back.

His tone was quiet when he said, "I think you've stated your case, wee one."

"Told you she had a sharp wit," Kell put in, and Frey and I looked at him to see him gnaw a piece of meat in half and start chewing. With mouth full, he went on, "And she's got nerve, head-to-head with you?" He shook his head and shoved the rest of the meat in his mouth even though he wasn't done with the last. Then, still with mouth full, but his voice was different, he said, "But you know that, don't you? Was you told me she had the spirit and, by the gods, man, we learned today you were *not* wrong."

I was interested in this spirit business, and I was feeling all warm inside because I'd obviously earned Kell's respect and equally obviously Frey had been talking me up. But, as nice as they were, both of these things made me feel slightly embarrassed.

Therefore, I admonished, "Kell, there's a lady at the table. Don't talk with your mouth full."

His eyes came to me then he smiled huge exposing meat in his teeth.

I shook my head and couldn't stop my quiet laughter that mingled with the same coming from Frey's men around the table.

Kell reached out for another hunk of meat while barking, "*Boy!* Where's my horn?"

My eyes moved to Skylar who I was stunned to see was looking at me, and as he did it, he was clearly in another world. His boyish face was soft, his eyes active and wheels were turning in his mind.

"*Boy!*" Kell barked again, and Skylar jumped then dashed to the chart table where he'd put the pitcher of ale and the horns.

I looked to Frey to see he was also studying Skylar and I called, "Husband." He turned to me. "Are you still angry?" I asked.

He shook his head and lifted his hand to trail his fingers along my jaw while his eyes roamed my face and he muttered, "No, as all is well." He dropped his hand, faced the table, his gaze circled the men and stopped on Gunner. "Not that this will happen again. But if it does, Finnie goes nowhere without heavy guard. I don't care if you have to arm half the crew and take them ashore."

"That was my idea, Frey," Stephan put in and I looked to him. "Gunner, Kell and I discussed it and we thought, considering it was simply a visit with her uncle, if we went in with three boatloads of men, it would expose too much. A visit of niece and uncle wouldn't normally require that precaution. We decided it was likely he was there because he was suspicious about your ship anchored offshore and what you were doing and wasn't there to take action against Finnie. And we hoped that she and Kell could pull off something to provide you cover. With that, we didn't think you'd wish to tip the fact you consider him a threat by making that show."

"It was an understandable risk you took, Steph," Frey conceded. "But it is likely, if he's not behind them, that by now news has traveled to Baldur that at least one attempt has been made on Finnie's life. Therefore, he would understand, because of this, even on a visit to her uncle, her guard would be intensified."

Stephan inclined his head. Frey nodded to him, and I watched in fascination mainly because Frey thought Stephan, Gunner and Kell had fucked up and that fuck up could have been huge. Frey was angry about it, but he didn't blister them with his wrath or order them tied to a mast and flogged. He listened, disagreed, explained why and made his wishes known.

It was a cool way to command, and I liked it.

"Uh...you think we could quit gabbin' like a bunch a' women, pull anchor and get the bloody hell outta this place?" Kell asked, grumpy eyes on Frey.

"Yes," Frey agreed and turned to Thad. "Take the helm, Thad. We're away home to Lunwyn."

"Uh...don't think that's such a good idea," Kell stated quickly, and Frey and I looked back to him. "We kinda told the king we were on our way to Hawkvale. It probably ain't a leap to think he's already dispatched boys to the shoreline to watch where we're goin' if he hasn't set sail to ships to follow us. Best we head in that direction."

Frey studied Kell then he sighed and looked at me.

"Fancy a stay in my chateau?" he asked, and I grinned...*big*.

Frey's eyes dropped to my mouth, his lips twitched then he turned to Thad.

"Pull anchor and make way to Hawkvale. The minute we're out of Middlelandian waters, send a man ashore to head up to Lunwyn to meet with Ruben. He's to tell Ruben to make haste to my chateau. Yes?"

"Right, Frey," Thad muttered. He sucked back what was left in his horn, set it on the table, got up and left the room.

The rest of the men fell on the food.

Suddenly starving, I did too.

"Sky, refill your lady's horn," Frey ordered, and I looked to my husband, a cracker with cheese on it in my hand.

His eyes came to me, then his hand came to me, curling around the back of my neck. He pulled me to him as he leaned into me and touched his mouth to mine.

When he pulled away slightly, I smiled at him, and I knew my face was soft because I saw his eyes move over it and his got soft too.

"That, wife," he whispered, "is the welcome back I'd prefer in the future."

"No way," I whispered back. "As soon as I get good with my bow and daggers and learn some stealth tactics, I'm totally going with you..." I paused then finished, "In the future."

Frey stared at me.

Then he pulled me super close, so close, I nearly came out of my chair. When he had me where he wanted me, he shoved my face in his neck and burst out laughing.

∽

THE MEN WERE GONE, including Frey, to check with Thad at the helm.

I was curled under a blanket in the chair reading by lantern light a book that my girls had packed for me.

Skylar was tidying the table and I was pretending he wasn't there so he could do it comfortably.

Therefore, when Skylar called, "Er...milady?" I was surprised.

I looked from my book to him to see he had a stack of dirty but devoid of the barest hint of food trays in his hands and his eyes were on me.

"Yes, Skylar?" I responded quietly.

He licked his lips then worried them by pressing and rolling them together.

I waited.

315

Eventually he said, "You coulda died today? Uh...makin' that journey to the king an' all."

Even more surprised at his question and that he'd ask it, I quickly assured him, "It turned out not to be that dangerous."

"But..." he hesitated, "you didn't know that."

"No," I said softly, studying him and taking care with the first conversation he'd instigated between us. "I didn't know that."

"And you did it for the captain?" he asked.

"Yes, I did it for the captain," I answered.

He nodded and worried his lips again.

Suddenly he whispered, "And you'd do it again? Like you said, in a heartbeat?"

"Yes, honey," I whispered back. "For my husband, I'd do it again." I paused then finished, "In a heartbeat."

He worried his lips again and his face went from cautious curiosity to fear, and I felt my heart hurt because I thought we were making some headway.

He took a step forward before he immediately retreated and took a step back.

Then he blurted, "Mama used to try an' teach me."

I blinked and asked, "What?"

He didn't repeat himself. Instead, he said, "She got real mad when I got things wrong."

I felt the backs of my eyes start stinging and I held his gaze as I felt them get wet but didn't say anything.

"Tried real hard," he whispered, "to make certain sure I got nothin' wrong."

I bet he did.

I didn't respond.

"Always got somethin' wrong," he murmured, his voice aching from old wounds that in no way were healed, and I felt them score at my own insides.

"This is life," I whispered as I steadily held his gaze. "Skylar, know that. It is life to get things wrong. It happens all the time to everyone. We make mistakes, all of us. There is no shame in that. None at all. The thing that's important to understand is, if you make a mistake, you try and learn from it. But honey, you will make mistakes and that's okay. One thing I can promise, and you can take your time to trust me, is that if you do make mistakes with me or with Frey, we won't get mad like your mama. We might get upset or disappointed, but we won't get mad at you like her. You don't have to believe me now, Sky, but I hope, someday, you do."

He stared at me while worrying his lips and I held his stare.

When he screwed up the courage to go on, he said quietly, "I like it here on the ship with Captain Drakkar."

"I'm glad, Sky," I said quietly back.

"Wouldn't want nothin' to happen to him," he went on.

"Me either," I agreed.

"You faced bad things to make certain that didn't happen," Skylar kept going.

"Yes," I said softly.

He bit his lip. Then he whispered quickly, "Thanks," and before I could say a word, he dashed out of the room.

I stared at the door after he'd gone. After a while, I put the ribbon in my book, closed it and set it on the table before I bent my neck, lifted both hands to my face and pressed my fingertips into my forehead.

"Finnie?" Frey called, and I dropped my hands and looked to the door to see my husband striding toward me. "Gods, love, what on—?"

"I want," I started, my voice trembling, "you to take..." I paused in order to gain control, "me to that woman..." I paused again to suck in a breath. "So I can tear her *fucking* hair out at the roots."

Frey had made it to me and stood by the chair looking down at me.

"What woman?" he asked quietly.

"Skylar's *mother*," I hissed.

He studied me for a moment then I found myself plucked out of the chair only to be settled in his lap when he sat in it.

His arms wrapped around me as I tipped my head to look at him and put my hands on his chest.

"I'm being very serious, Frey," I whispered.

"I know you are, wee one," Frey whispered back, watching me closely and one of his hands started stroking my back.

"He just opened up to me," I informed him.

"I guessed that," Frey muttered, still watching me.

"I'm angry," I announced.

"I guessed that too," Frey replied.

I glared at him then suddenly my eyes filled with stupid, *stupid* tears and about a nanosecond later my face was in Frey's neck because he tucked it there and his arms were tight around me.

"I...I don't like c-c-crying," I cried into his neck.

317

I heard his sigh and felt his chest rise and fall with it before he murmured, "My wee Finnie has had a trying day."

He had *that* right.

I pulled in a deep, shuddering breath that fortunately controlled my tears, but I didn't move my face from his neck. Instead, I lay cradled in Frey's lap, held in his arms and I let his strength envelope me.

When I had myself together, I informed him, "Baldur, by the way, is a *jerk*."

"This I know," Frey muttered.

I pulled in another breath, lifted my hand to wipe my face and pulled up to look at him.

"Sorry," I whispered and Frey grinned.

Then he said softly, "I prefer your smiles and laughter, wife. But there are far worse things than your tears wetting my skin."

I stared at his handsome, bearded face thinking, *God, I really*, freaking *love this man*.

Then I smiled at him, slid a hand up to curl around his neck, leaned in close and decided a change of subject was in order, therefore I asked, "Any chance you'll tell me why Kell was all fired up *not* to let Baldur's men board your ship?"

Frey's lips twitched and he hesitated only a moment before he answered, "While we were rescuing the sorceress Circe, some of the men *might* have nicked a few things that it's highly likely were important enough for some to notice are missing and want them back badly. And some of those things *might* still be aboard *The Finnie*."

I felt my lips twitch too, before I asked, "What's this spirit Kell's talking about?"

Frey lifted a hand to my temple and trailed it along my hairline as he tucked the hair back behind my ear before pushing a mass of it that was at my neck over my shoulder, his eyes watching the movements of his hand.

Finally, they came back to me.

"I told him you have the spirit of the sea, the spirit of a Raider," he answered. "I told him you're a Voyager like him and like me. The Voyager doesn't settle, his feet itch to move, be it on ship, on land, in stirrups. The Voyager acts fast and thinks faster. He has courage. He doesn't wait to face the risks that come his way, instead, he rushes to greet them." He paused and his eyes held mine before he finished softly, "Before, Kell didn't believe me, but today, he believes me."

Oh my God.

Oh my *God*.

I felt tears well in my eyes as warmth swelled in my heart.

Then I accused, "You're going to make me cry again."

Frey grinned and noted, "Finnie, I think I may not have made this clear, but this does not bother me."

"I bet a Voyager doesn't burst into tears at the drop of a hat," I returned in between deep breaths I was taking to control my emotion.

"I wouldn't know, wee one. I've never met a beautiful one with white-blonde hair and soft curves. But I'm learning those kind do a lot of things differently."

His words made me laugh softly and the tears melted away, then I slid my arms around his neck and pressed close to whisper the God's honest truth in his ear, "I'm pleased you're home, husband."

His arms gave me a squeeze, and in my ear, he asked, "How pleased?"

I held on tighter and answered with feeling, "*Very*."

His hand drifted up my back to curl around my neck and he replied, "If this is so, wee wife, right now, I wish you to show me how much."

I lifted my head and looked down at him to see his beautiful green-brown eyes had changed in a way I liked a whole lot.

"Okay," I breathed.

He smiled his wicked smile then he got out of the chair, taking me with him and he carried me to the divan where I did not delay in setting about showing him just how happy I was he was back.

Suffice it to say I was *super* happy and suffice it to say I took great pains to convince Frey of that fact.

And I was even more pleased to note my efforts succeeded.

24

FIRE AND BLOOD

T *wo months later...*

"Frey," Finnie breathed into his mouth and gods, *gods*, every time she said his name like that, from the very first time she did it when he felt the unreal softness of her hair in his loft in his cabin, Frey Drakkar felt the whisper of his wife's voice saying his name right in his cock.

Then she gave him her neck as her head arched back, her fingers fisted in his hair, her other arm clutched him tight, and she rammed herself down on his shaft as she climaxed.

Frey spun her to her back. Her long hair splashed across their bed, her four limbs held tight even as she continued gasping through her orgasm and his hips pumped between her legs.

He fought the climax that threatened to explode so he could take in her beautiful face awash with pleasure. The vision of her hair all over the sheets. The feel of her arms and legs gripping him tight. The brilliant torture of her sex spasming around his driving cock. Then he couldn't fight it anymore, and through five, deep, hard strokes he poured his seed inside his wife.

Frey dropped his forehead to the bed beside her and focused on her soft body under him, her wet tightness enveloping his cock, her hands drifting light along his back, the smell of her skin, and he rethought their plans to leave Hawkvale on the morrow to return to Lunwyn.

He liked right where he was.

"Are you sure you want to go home, wife?"

"No," she whispered. He lifted further up on his forearm to look down at her, his other hand moving to cup the side of her head, his thumb drawing circles at her temple. "But there are places to go, people to meet, things *to do*," she finished on an appealing, sated grin.

That was his Finnie. Her feet itched.

"This bed is very comfortable," he observed, but made his point by shifting his hips between her legs. He watched with satisfaction as her eyelids lowered and her lips parted.

Then she lifted her head to touch her lips to his throat and dropped it back.

"You're right," she agreed. "It is. But so is your bed on your ship." She grinned again. "I like the velvet blankets." Her four limbs gave him a squeeze as did her sex and a short, low rumble slid up his throat, which caused her to smile a *very* appealing, *very* sated smile. "And it's narrow so we have to cuddle," she concluded.

"We cuddle even in this big bed," Frey pointed out.

"Indeed," she whispered, her eyes growing soft and moving over his face before she said quietly, "If you wish to stay, husband, I'm good with staying."

"And if you wish to go, wife, I'm good with going," he replied, and she smiled again.

"Then we'll go," she decided.

Frey smiled back and dropped his head to touch his lips to hers.

"Yes, my wee one," he said softly after he lifted his head, "we'll go."

Her hand drifted up his spine and into his hair as her eyes drifted to his mouth.

She touched her lips to his and repeated quietly, "We'll go."

Then she kissed him, unhooked a leg from his hip, planted her foot in the bed and bucked to roll him to his back.

He allowed this because she went with him.

Then he allowed his wife to make best use of their big soft bed.

Again.

～

FREY MOVED through the bedroom to get his gloves. After her archery lesson with Annar, he was taking her riding through his estate and the village one last time before they left early the next morning.

Absently, his eyes moved through the room that had been the setting for some very happy memories since they arrived nearly six weeks ago. This, after docking the ship in Bellebryn, staying in that small city-state for a week because Finnie was enthralled by its charm, and then making their way into Hawkvale to his chateau.

Finnie had been even more Finnie as she discovered the appeal of Hawkvale (though she surprised him by telling him she favored Lunwyn, felt more at home there and preferred the clothing of Fyngaard). She'd delighted in every second they spent in Bellebryn, traveling to then being at his chateau, and as always with Finnie, she didn't hide it.

And Frey delighted in giving it to her.

Even so, without Finnie in his arms and Frey in hers, he had to admit he was ready to move on. He could not remember the last time he'd stayed in one place for so long. And as enjoyable as it was with Finnie, he was keen to take her on her next adventure.

His step slowed and his brows drew together as he saw one of Finnie's small trunks open on the dresser. Jewelry and hair bobs spilled out, and poking out of the top was the edge of a small envelope used by herbalists to hold tinctures or powders to prepare draughts.

Frey moved to it automatically, feeling mild surprise. Except for the falsehood she told of being unwell when they argued about Viola, Finnie had not ever complained of feeling sick. And he knew the adela tree bark used for tea was always ritually held in a purple pouch as a nod to the goddess, not to mention, she'd told him she only had enough for that one cup.

When he arrived at the dresser, he saw there was more than one of these small envelopes in her trunk. In fact, there were several. He lifted one out, folded open the top, put it to his nose, and he smelled a hint of citrus, rosemary, ginger, all of it nearly overwhelmed by the aroma of mint.

His body froze, but even so, heat burned from his gut upwards, setting fire to his chest.

He knew that smell.

Pennyrium.

Pennyrium.

"Bloody hell," he whispered, that whisper shaking with fury.

322

His wife was dosing with gods-damned *pennyrium* to guard against conceiving his gods-damned *child*.

Without his knowledge.

And without—except for a brief conversation a long bloody time ago that by no means had ended in a definite bloody decision—discussion.

And further, without his permission.

He pulled in a deep breath to calm the fire in his chest.

This did not work.

Then he reminded himself his wife was of another world. Perhaps, in her world, females did this regularly.

But he could not fathom that. He could not fathom any world where such an integral discussion between any wife and her husband, especially considering the bloody conception of a gods-damned child meant the continued peaceful rule of an entire, bloody kingdom, for the gods' sakes, would not only happen between that wife and her gods-damned husband, but would be crucial.

And further, she was the one who introduced the subject in the first damned place. Clearly, in her world, this was discussed amongst partners and decisions made prior to any action.

He stared at the packet in his hand.

Pennyrium.

Taken daily it very rarely failed to prevent a woman getting with child. And the longer it was utilized, the longer it took for its effects to clear after it was ceased. In some instances, when women had recklessly used it for years, it had made them infertile.

She could have chosen differently. But then again, if she had, it would mean contacting a witch to cast a spell or speaking with him to convince him to wear a sheath, something, admittedly, he had no bloody intention of doing with his damned *wife*. Especially since that wife was Finnie and he was not about to shield his sex from hers and thus have a bloody, gods-damned barrier between them, not to mention diminish the pleasure she gave him.

So she had decided on pennyrium.

Bloody hell.

Frey folded over the envelope and tucked it back in her trunk. Then he found his gloves and exited the room.

He did not, however, go outside to watch Finnie finish working with Annar and her bow.

No, he found the first of his men he could find, who was Oleg, and he ordered tersely, "Find Ruben and send him to me in my study immediately."

Oleg grunted, jerked up his chin and moved away.

Frey went to his study, which had a window that faced the back garden where Finnie, looking too tempting by half in her tight breeches with her skin now honeyed by the kiss of Hawkvale's bright sun, was at the bow. Her target was now thirty feet away instead of the twenty where she'd started as she had improved and Annar felt he should increase her challenge.

Annar was standing behind her, Skylar at her side, his own target twenty feet away, his bow shorter and easier for him to wield.

Frey tossed his gloves on his desk and turned back to the window to watch his wife.

She was paying more attention to Skylar than her task, as she always did, and watching it, Frey's mouth grew tight.

She was brilliant with the boy and refused to leave him behind with the crew on his ship as Frey usually did. She had said she wanted his lessons to continue, but this was nonsense. She wanted time to light those dark places the boy had haunting his soul.

And she did.

She didn't work miracles, but she tended him gently, cautiously and regularly, giving him just enough distance and closing in only when Skylar offered her a sign he was comfortable with her doing so.

Then, not long ago, all her careful tending broke through and the boy blossomed.

Hell, Frey heard their laughter while they were in this same bloody room not two bloody hours ago while she was working with him on his letters and numbers.

She'd make a brilliant gods-damned mother.

Why in the bloody hell was she dosing with pennyrium?

"Frey?" Ruben called his name, and Frey turned from the window to see his man walking into the room.

"The door, Ben," Frey ordered.

Ruben halted, gave him a look then turned back and closed the door before he walked into the room and stopped four feet from Frey.

"You don't look happy," Ruben observed.

"This would be because I am *not*," Frey replied.

Ruben said nothing.

Frey did. "Upstairs, in Finnie's trunk on the dresser, you'll find several envelopes of pennyrium."

Ruben blinked and his chest expanded with his big breath.

He crossed his arms over it and Frey kept speaking.

"Count them. Then go to the herbalist in the village. Have her create a powder that very closely resembles the sight, smell and taste of pennyrium but has none of its medicinal properties. Purchase the exact quantity of the exact same number of envelopes and then switch them with what's in Finnie's trunk. Dispose immediately of what's in that trunk."

Ruben didn't move and he still did not speak.

"Ben, this has to happen today. We leave on the morrow," Frey prompted.

"I take it you didn't know Finnie was dosing with pennyrium," Ruben remarked.

"You take that correctly."

Ruben nodded but still didn't move.

"Ruben," Frey growled.

"You remember Olivia," Ruben stated.

Frey did and that was why his jaw got tight and he crossed his arms on his chest as well.

"I did not ask you here for a lecture, Ben. I asked you here to give you an order."

"I am your man, Frey, but I am also your friend," Ruben replied. "And as your friend, I advise you to ask your *wife* here for a discussion rather than switch her draughts on the sly."

The burn in Frey's chest intensified.

"I appreciate you taking the time to give me your opinion regardless that I didn't ask for it," Frey said softly, his tone unmistakable and Ruben wouldn't mistake it. They'd known each other over a decade, and he'd heard it many times.

He still ignored it.

"Frey," Ruben returned softly, "Olivia made this decision for us. Yes, if she hadn't, I would not have Lincoln. And yes, now, seven years later, I could not imagine my life without Linc. What I can tell you is, when I was under the assumption she was taking the pennyrium as this was what I told her to do, and she was not, she made that choice on her own, acted without my knowledge and she told me she was with my child, I was far from happy. You know this. You and Thad were called to pull me out of her cottage when the level of my anger erased my common sense after the news was delivered. I urge you to think about how Finnie would feel if she learns you have essentially done the same."

"I do remember this, Ruben, and you were justifiably angry," Frey returned. "She was your woman, you are a man, and it is your right to make this decision, not hers. You'd informed her of your decision regarding pennyrium, and she did not bow to that decision. Your reaction was not wrong, and your anger *did* erase your common sense at the time, though she did not feel the power of your hand and many of the men thought she should. However, you also did not bring charges as you could. I respected your decision and understood you did not wish your son's mother to spend the duration of her pregnancy in bound service to her realm. Your leniency saved Olivia that sentence but Olivia's decision lost her *you*, for you never went back to her bed and, I have heard, no man does for fear of the same befalling him."

Ruben's chest expanded again as he conceded this point nonverbally.

Frey went on, "*My* wife is a princess whose duty it is to birth the future king of our country. She was not born thus but that does not mean she does not know it. She does. She knows it very well. I am the father of the future king, but even if I was not, I am a man and the decision to wait or not is *mine*. She must understand this because we discussed this very early upon being wed. She was the one who introduced the discussion, but no decision was made. *She* is dosing with pennyrium on the sly for she has never dosed before me, and it is my right to make her desist in doing so and it is my choice how I do that."

He paused and held his friend's gaze before he finished.

"And this is my choice, Ben. Go to the herbalist in the village and see to it that Finnie's pennyrium is destroyed."

"Finnie is of another world, Frey, and although she has been here for some time now, she is still becoming accustomed to ours. She is wrong in her decision, but that decision is understandable." Ruben said quietly and when Frey made no response, he went on quietly, "Mate, I can't help but think this is a bad idea."

"The bad idea was Finnie's," Frey replied. "I'm rectifying it."

Ruben hesitated. Frey lost patience.

Therefore, he commanded, "Ben. *Go*."

Ruben took in another breath, nodded then turned and left the room.

Frey returned to the window and watched his wife pull back on her bow and let fly.

With her near daily practice, not only had her target grown more distant, her aim had grown truer. All her arrows were embedded in the circle just outside the bullseye and the one she just let loose was no different.

He pulled in a calming breath that, with Ruben on his errand, actually calmed him.

His Finnie, he knew, would have some reason she did what she did. It might be a foolhardy reason, but it was likely *she* did not think so.

And he determined to discuss it with her at some later date when his anger was not so close to the surface.

And this later date would be around the time she missed her first cycle, and he knew his seed had found purchase in her womb, she was further bound to him through their child, and the future of the realm was safe.

There came a knock on the door, he turned to it and called, "Enter."

He watched the chateau's housekeeper come in, stop and announce, "There is a woman here who says she urgently needs to speak with your princess."

Frey sighed again.

Of this, he had no doubt. As in Houllebec, Finnie wasted no time befriending nearly everyone in the village. It was not unusual that a woman came calling so she could sit with coffee or wine and his wife, and they could cackle about whatever women cackled about.

The urgency of the message, however, slightly surprised him.

"And she is?" Frey asked although he really did not care.

"Says her name is Agnes. She's of your land, my lord," the housekeeper replied, but at her first five words, the burn in Frey's gut and chest changed as ice encased his innards and then crawled through his veins.

"Bring her to me immediately and she is not seen, nor does she see my princess," Frey ordered.

The housekeeper nodded and swept out.

Frey lifted a hand to his neck and his fingers squeezed. He did not turn back to the window. He waited for the witch to come through the door.

When she did, he dropped his hand and waited for the housekeeper to close it behind her.

"I thought I made myself clear," he stated quietly, his eyes locked with her faded blue ones.

"You did, Drakkar," she replied just as quietly.

"If this is true, you're here because?" he prompted.

"I have an urgent message for your Finnie," she told him.

"And you did the last time we spoke in Lunwyn. And my message to you was that you do not see or speak to my wife," Frey returned.

What was now months ago, just days after Frey and Finnie argued over Viola, Stephan had intercepted the witch Agnes when she visited the Winter Palace and demanded to speak to the princess. For obvious reasons, his men vetted anyone who made such a demand. Upon hearing who she was, Steph wisely brought her to Frey.

It took some doing, but Frey had convinced her to share the message she had for Finnie, and this was a message Frey himself had not, at that time, yet delivered to his wife. The message was that Finnie's witch from her world, a woman called Valentine, had sensed the elves binding spell. She had communicated with this Agnes to warn Finnie this had happened and awaited instruction on what she should be doing in her world to rectify the situation.

Frey had, at the time, lied to Agnes, saying Finnie was well aware this had happened and was happy to remain in his world. And he had paid her to communicate the same to this Valentine.

He had also warned her not to see or try to speak to Finnie without seeing him first. He paid her for that too. He'd also made it very clear what would befall her if she reneged on their deal.

Since then, of course, he and Finnie had spoken of where she came from, and his falsehood had turned true.

Frey knew straight to the depths of his soul, more and more as every moment passed with his wife, that she was pleased she'd risked her venture, and in the end, been bound to him as his wife and thus to his world.

What Agnes would travel to Hawkvale to communicate, and risk communicating it, he could not fathom, nor did he wish to know.

But he had no choice but to find out.

And his concern was that something had befallen one of the friends his wife spoke so lovingly about. This was something that would cause Finnie distress, for she felt deeply, especially when she came to care about someone, but even when she hardly knew them.

And if there were problems, Finnie would feel it. She would feel it worse for she could not return and do anything to help.

And he did not want his wife to feel distress. But if this had happened, he was powerless to help, except offer his neck for her to sob into, and although he knew his presence soothed her, he also knew in such a case this would be no help at all.

"You did, Drakkar, but there is much news," Agnes replied.

"And this news is?" Frey asked.

"Princess Sjofn, of our world..." She paused. "Much is happening."

Frey's body got tight as the jagged shards of the ice slithering through his veins started scoring.

"And what is Princess Sjofn of our world up to?" Frey queried.

The witch took two steps toward him, leaned in and whispered, "Drakkar, the princess is a guenipe."

Frey instantly relaxed.

"I'm aware."

The witch's brows shot up, then she started, "The Princess Finnie—"

He cut her off. "My wife, too, is aware."

She leaned back, visibly surprised at this news, and she surveyed him.

Then she stated, "This may be so, and Valentine reports the dalliances are discreet, but nevertheless, she is living the life of your wife in that other world, and no matter how discreet, word has a way of getting out. Valentine tells me it is there not like it is here. There are people who do not accept the guenipes. There are even those who are violently opposed to them."

Finnie had told him of this curious fact about her world, something not shared with his own. Frey himself had no issue with guenipes, unless, of course, he was pledged to marry one.

"This is true, witch, but as Finnie will never return to that world, it matters not."

"Perhaps she will not agree," Agnes suggested.

"I can assure you she already knows, and she does not care," Frey stated then crossed his arms on his chest and his brows went up. "You traveled all the way from Lunwyn for this?"

She shook her head. "No. This is not the only news. It isn't even half of it."

Gods damn it.

"Spit it out," he clipped.

"There have been many communications back and forth. *Many* communications," she stressed. "And Princess Sjofn is aware of the perils the Princess Finnie is facing, including the assassination attempts."

"And?" Frey prompted.

"And she is feeling great guilt about these perils." Her face went slightly hard before she went on, "As she should. Through our communications both Valentine and I have become aware that the Princess Sjofn has been far from forthright with your Finnie."

After that, the witch said no more.

"And this matters because...?" Frey asked, losing patience.

329

"It matters because her guilt is ascending. She's becoming frantic about these perils she's placed Finnie under. She's gravely concerned something will befall her. Princess Sjofn is highly trained and rightly feels she is better equipped to deal with these threats, as she has proven in the past. And I can assure you, Drakkar, that communication is not easy for me, and it is not cheap for Princess Sjofn. Every time she sends a message through Valentine, she pays dearly for it and the messages are coming one on the heels of another."

When she quit speaking, Frey lifted his brows, not about to prompt her again.

"Drakkar," she snapped. "It is not *her* currency Princess Sjofn is using. It is your Finnie's."

"Again, this matters not," Frey replied. "Finnie has no further use of that currency. She is mine and my coin and property are hers. And, woman, I'll remind you, she has taken over the life of Sjofn and is now a princess with her own funds and property. That property being a bloody palace."

"That may be so, Drakkar, but I'm telling you, Sjofn's guilt is ascending. She is now talking of paying Valentine to send her *back*."

Frey felt the ice disintegrate as the fire came back.

"By the gods, you jest," he whispered.

"No." She shook her head. "Valentine is refusing until she hears word from Finnie. But Princess Sjofn is making refusal difficult, for she's offering three million of what they call 'dollars' and from what I gather from Valentine, this is enough coin to set a single being in a life of relative opulence for *decades*."

"My princess is bound here and Sjofn bound there by the elves," Frey reminded her.

"Valentine is strong, Drakkar. I cannot say for certain if she can circumvent an elfin spell. What I can say is that I feel her power, and if anyone can, *she* can."

Gods *damn it*.

"And if she were to return Sjofn here, would that mean my princess would go there?" Frey asked.

The witch shook her head. "The talk is not of the Princess Finnie returning to her world, but only of Sjofn returning here."

"She cannot return," Frey declared.

"I *know* this, Drakkar, but she is determined."

"Then tell this Valentine to tell Sjofn that if she does, I will see to it that she sits at a secret tribunal to hear testimony of her treason. After which, when judgment is passed, she will face private execution. Her mother and father both agree that her selfish actions brand her traitor to the realm and traitor to the crown. And if they do, any head of a House chosen to be judge at her tribunal will as well. All of this will be done without any but the four people involved knowing it is done, plus, of course, her executioner. Sjofn will be hanged for her crimes, but no one will be the wiser as Finnie carries on as princess then king mother. This news, I would suspect, will likely halt her desperate attempts to return and make amends for her treacherous actions."

"I agree," Agnes said softly, her eyes again surveying him. "But do you not think your wife should have some say in issues of such great import?"

"No," Frey answered shortly.

She surveyed him again closely and he sensed she did not agree.

He did not care.

Wisely moving on, she declared, "There is more you need to know."

Frey waited.

She took in breath and stated, "Valentine is a powerful witch."

"You've explained that," Frey replied, and she had, as did the elves.

Agnes went on, "She is witch not seer." She paused then announced, "But I am both."

At the look on her face, the fire died, and the ice returned.

"Speak," he ordered.

She pulled in breath then let it out on a whispered, "Drakkar, I see fire and blood and I see it around your Finnie."

Frey's body locked so he wouldn't go back on a foot at this news.

"Fire and blood?" he asked softly.

"Dragon fire," she whispered. "The heat so intense, buildings melt. And blood, so much, her boots stand in rivers of it. I dream of it. I dream of it every night. I can't stop dreaming of it."

"I control the dragons," Frey reminded her quietly.

"And in ancient times, when The Drakkar called the dragons to duty, it is told it was not unknown for an innocent to perish in the line of their fire."

Frey was silent as that ice again stole through his veins.

Agnes spoke on.

"It is an awful thought, worse to speak of and worse still for you to make the decision, but I believe you should relent to the return of Sjofn and let it be her that faces this future, not your Finnie."

"You're speaking of murder," Frey replied, his gut twisting with disgust.

"You yourself said if she returned, she'd face certain execution," Agnes retorted.

"Execution, witch, is not murder," Frey clipped.

She lifted her chin to grant his point then said, "I see the vision. I dream the dream. I do not know if it is Sjofn or Finnie who stands in the fire and blood. I also do not know the outcome. The fire surrounds her, the blood flows over her boots. But I do know this will happen, Drakkar. Never, not once since I started dreaming the visions as a wee girl, has one not come true." She pulled in a visible breath and finished, "I am sorry, but this is your choice. If you bar Sjofn's return to this world, you must pray to Keer who holds Princess Finnie's and *your* destinies in his hands, or you make the dreadful choice to stand Sjofn in that fire. But the choice is yours."

Frey studied her.

Then he asked, "You say you do not see the outcome?"

She shook her head and confirmed, "I do not."

"And how does Finnie or Sjofn come to this pass?"

"I do not see that either, Drakkar."

"And is she alone or surrounded by men, guards, soldiers?"

She shook her head again and repeated, "I do not see that either."

Frustration crawled up his throat and he growled, "This vision is not very helpful."

Her back shot straight. "I'm not a fortune teller as they don't exist," she snapped. "I am a seer. I do not control the visions, they come to me. This is what I saw. It was grave, and because of that I have traveled far to inform you. But this was *all* I saw."

At that moment, a loud, feminine cry of delight pierced through the room and Frey turned to the windows.

Finnie was jumping up and down, her arms around Annar's neck with one hand still holding her bow. Her movements were so excited the arrows in the quiver strapped across her back were cascading to the green grass at her feet. Annar was standing feet planted firm to the ground, his hands at her waist but her exuberance was jolting his body. He was in profile, but Frey could see his man's wide smile.

Finnie detached swiftly from Annar, whirled to face an excited Skylar, threw both her arms up in the air, still holding her bow and shrieked her delight again before she bent and caught Skylar up in a tight embrace, shaking him side to side as Frey heard her laugh.

Skylar's boyish laughter mingled with hers.

Frey's eyes moved to Finnie's target, and he saw the arrows had been cleared. Now there were only two.

One in the circle outside the bullseye.

One embedded directly in the middle of it.

He felt his lips curve into a smile.

She'd done it.

Fire and blood.

Frey's smile died.

He turned to the witch.

"Have you eaten?"

She blinked then asked, "What?"

His eyes moved over her dusty, travel-worn gown. "You've traveled far, have you eaten?"

She shook her head and said, "I have made haste, starting on my journey the minute I learned from Finnie's Jocelyn that you were at the chateau. I have ridden hard, consumed little and slept even less due to my haste and that dream. So no, Drakkar, it has been since yesterday I have eaten."

He nodded and stated, "I will order a meal for you. You have three hours to eat it, wash and rest. Then you are away with one of my men. You will ride fast to Bellebryn and board the first vessel bound for Lunwyn. You live in Fyngaard?"

"Just outside it, yes."

Frey nodded again. "You will go home, my man will accompany you, and you will prepare to be away for some time. Finnie and I leave on the morrow, headed back to Lunwyn ourselves. We will first go to the Rimée Keep so she can see her parents. My man will take you there. We will stay there a week, perhaps two, then we will be moving on to my lodge in Kellshorn. You will follow us."

Her brows drew together, "But, I don't under—"

Frey impatiently anticipated her question and therefore answered it before it was fully asked, "So that I will know immediately, I want you close at all times should you receive more communications from the other world, have any dreams that shed further light on the situation you fear will befall my Finnie or any dreams you have about Finnie at all. And I want you to use your powers to protect my wife." He paused and added, "For these endeavors, you will be paid."

"There is no protection against dragon fire, Drakkar. You know that," Agnes stated quietly.

"Finnie faces a variety of dangers, witch, and there *are* protections for those," Frey returned.

The witch nodded.

Then she took a step toward him, her gaze grew cautious, but her mouth opened to speak.

"There are no dragons in the other world, Drakkar."

Frey's body went solid, and it did this because he took her meaning.

"You speak treason," he whispered.

She pressed her lips together, clearly hesitant, but went on.

"I do and I do with purpose. There are few matches like yours with Finnie in this world *or* hers. So few, they are so rare, they are precious and need to be protected at all costs. Valentine may be able to break the binding spell of the elves and she could take your Finnie *and* you to the other world where she'll be safe. If Princess Sjofn doesn't run through it, your princess has the means for you both to live there comfortably for the entirety of your days, and—"

Frey leaned toward her and cut her off.

"Witch," he clipped, his tone fierce, "you...talk...*treason*."

She leaned back slightly and pressed her lips together, but Frey continued.

"And treason is heinous, but what you speak of is worse. If I were to remove Finnie from this world, an elfin, dragonian child will not sit on the Lunwyn throne as our gods' desire, our frosted land would again descend into turmoil, the dragons would lose their Drakkar and would remain at slumber in their caves for the gods know how long. The fact I *am* The Drakkar means there is a threat looming for all of Lunwyn for which the dragons will need to be roused. And lastly, the elves would again be betrayed by The Frey and because of that may retreat for another seven centuries or worse, may never ascend again. And you know that breaking their binding spell would mean sacrifice. The elves will demand it as their due before they withdraw to their realm. I do not know what this sacrifice will be, but I *do* know it will be terrible. The gods have chosen Finnie for me and me for Lunwyn. Our destinies are linked, and this link is for the future of Lunwyn. We cannot desert our land. This *cannot* happen."

She stepped back, her eyes moving to contemplate the rug, and she nodded, but he saw her hands shaking with fear, as they would. It took great courage for her to suggest betraying his country, his responsibilities and the elves.

But she did it to advocate safe harbor for his wife.

"I will forget you suggested it," Frey said quietly.

"Thank you, Drakkar."

Frey continued speaking softly, and when he did, her eyes moved back to him.

"As you can see, we must do all we can to keep my princess safe."

Agnes nodded. "It will be my honor to serve The Drakkar and his Ice Bride."

"My thanks," Frey replied, watched her draw in a breath then he stated, "I will see to your meal and bath. You're away in three hours."

Agnes nodded again.

Frey moved to the door muttering, "Safe journey. I will see you in Snowdon."

He did not await her response.

He went in search of the housekeeper.

Then he went directly to his wife.

25

HIT THE BELL WITH
A LOUD CLANG

*wo days later...*

I STOOD at the railing on the bridge deck at the stern of *The Finnie* and looked at the terracotta tile-roofed, adobe buildings with their brightly colored awnings, pots of profuse flowers, multi-colored lanterns and wrought iron whimsies all stretching up the hill where, at the top, there was an unbelievable fairytale castle.

The city-state of Bellebryn.

And I watched it all slowly get smaller as we sailed away.

The first time I saw it nearly two months ago, and at that moment, it was the most beautiful place I'd ever seen in my life. Nothing like it existed in my world, not even close.

Except in animated children's films.

Yep, seriously, it was a city only the most whimsical, artistic minds could create.

It was amazing.

As amazing as it was, I was pleased we were heading home to Lunwyn, pleased to turn the page to a new adventure, pleased to get back to my parents, but most of all pleased to be setting sail because something was bothering Frey.

I could read him easily, but for some reason his strange, subdued, weighty mood—a mood that had lasted over two days—I could not read. And after asking him (four times) and receiving the response, "Nothing's amiss, my wee one," (when something *was*), my only guess was that my Raider, like me, itched to be on the move.

"Sky," I heard, and I looked down at Skylar who was standing beside me at the railing, his eyes on the fading beauty of Bellebryn. But he, like I, turned to see Orion striding toward us. "Sword, boy, now. The sun will be setting soon, and you've not practiced today. Waist deck, fifteen minutes," Orion ordered.

Sky nodded to him. Orion jerked his chin at Sky, looked to me and smiled, turned on his boot and left the bridge deck.

Skylar looked up at me with bright, excited eyes and asked, "Anything you need in the cabin, Miss Finnie?"

I shook my head and smiled down at him. "No, honey, you go on. I'm good."

He smiled huge then took off on a run.

My smile faded as I watched him go.

Frey had informed me that sword and knife work were going to be added to Skylar's archery lessons and math, writing and reading tutorials. Wooden daggers and swords, which could do little harm should mistakes occur, had been purchased for this very purpose.

I did not like it and told Frey so. Archery was one thing. Sky was too young to be working with weapons, which swords and daggers definitely were, even wooden ones.

To this, Frey informed me in the coming weeks Skylar would turn twelve, and then he went on to inform me this was not too young. I disagreed with that too, thinking such lessons should start when he was fifteen or sixteen.

Or thirty.

When I shared this opinion with him, he'd laughed his ass off. Unfortunately, Thad and Stephan were with him, so they'd laughed their asses off too. I stormed off in a huff after glaring death rays at them which was not a good choice because this made them all *keep* laughing their asses off.

Skylar, however, agreed with Frey and was excited beyond reason to begin his lessons as any boy would be, learning cool-as-shit boy stuff from trained, experienced, skilled, tall, fit, hot, action-hero-type guys.

And thus, I was outvoted.

I heard boots on wood and twisted my neck to see Frey heading my way from the other side of the bridge deck. I smiled at him, and his gaze dropped to my mouth then back to my eyes. I started to turn toward him, but he halted this when he arrived at me, his hands turning me gently back to face the fading beauty of Bellebryn. Then his arms wrapped around me, one across my chest, one at my ribs.

His mouth came to my ear, and I knew he knew my thoughts because he whispered, "As I explained, love, boys of his class sometimes never even learn their letters and numbers. Knowing those, the workings of a ship and being skilled with knives, swords and bows brightens his future. When he's old enough to make decisions on the life path he wishes to follow, these lessons will provide a choice, paths most of the boys of his class could never hope to pursue. It is good the men wish to take this time with him. It is a boon, and he knows it." Frey's arms gave me a squeeze. "And they are skilled. No harm will come to him while he trains."

He *had* explained this. And it did make sense.

I still didn't like it.

And it was more than my opinion that boys Skylar's age were too young to begin serious training with weapons, something else I explained to Frey before.

So, since he repeated himself, I did too.

"He's eleven and he's still vulnerable, Frey," I whispered. "Annar and I have been working with him and he still freaks out when he messes up. He gets so tense at the slightest mistake, it takes days to calm him down."

"This will pass, Finnie," Frey whispered back.

"But—"

His arms squeezing me gently cut me off then his voice sounded in my ear. "This will pass, wee one, and the only way to get it to pass is to work him through it."

I pulled in a deep breath. Then I let it out.

This made sense too, damn it all to hell.

I gave in (again) by whispering, "Okay."

I felt Frey's lips touch light on my neck and in my ear, I heard, "Okay."

I relaxed into his big, powerful frame and ran my hands along his arms until my fingers linked through his. Standing thus with Frey, I watched Bellebryn become tiny as *The Finnie* gained distance.

"I'm glad to be aboard again. It means I get your beard back," I remarked.

I felt Frey's body start behind mine and the amusement in his voice when he asked, "What?"

I kept my eyes on the distance when I repeated, "I get your beard back. I haven't decided if I think you're more handsome with the beard or without it. I'm glad I get it back, so I'll have another opportunity to try and figure it out."

This was true, but it was also a lie because I was never going to figure it out.

This got me another squeeze and a short, low chuckle, then, "Anytime you want it back, my Finnie, you only need say. Shaving is a pain in the arse, and I'm pleased to give it a rest."

"All righty then," I agreed. "I'll give you a heads up when I'm in the mood for whiskers."

"My thanks," he muttered, voice still amused, but something weighed on it. I could hear it. I could even feel it.

I just didn't know what it was.

Except I knew what it was for me.

The last two months had been perfect. Sailing south over the emerald waters of the Green Sea, the days becoming warmer and longer, feeling the sun shining on my skin. Experiencing the fairytale beauty of Bellebryn and the breathtaking fantasyland that was Hawkvale. Making new friends, eating new foods, working with Skylar and seeing progress as his tension ebbed and his personality began to flow.

Not to mention, I'd gotten my first bullseye.

And all of this happened with my gentle, quick to smile, quick to laugh, handsome husband who I knew enjoyed, just like me, the heat of the sun, the longer days, the food, the vistas, the people and being with me.

And he made no bones about that.

As ever, he was often at his own tasks, but these were few when he didn't have me close. And as our days slid by and with it our time, nothing had cooled, nothing had faded, in fact, everything, including the time we spent alone and naked, heated, grew brighter, more intense.

All this, I told myself, meant Frey had to love me.

He had to.

He just hadn't told me.

And therefore, I hadn't told him.

Considering we were again at sea, we were again on the move, we were off to face whatever was next and that weight still pulled at his tone, I wondered if it was because he was waiting for me to say it so he could.

He was a virile, hot, action guy, and although he never shied away from demonstrations of affection, both physical and verbal, maybe declaring his deep, abiding (for mine was both, so his *had* to be too) love was a shade too far and he needed me to assure him that these feelings were mutual.

But I was nervous at the thought of putting that out there even though Frey gave me not one, single indication I should be.

Still, I was.

But I shouldn't be.

Nevertheless, I was.

Shit.

Shit!

I sucked in breath and let the emerald of the sea and the green of the shore fill my vision.

Then I whispered to my husband, "We're breaking the cardinal rule."

"The what?"

"The cardinal rule. The most important rule there is. The one you never, ever break," I explained.

"And what is this important rule we're breaking, wee Finnie?" Frey asked.

I studied the vista as I answered, "Dad always said, never look back. Always look forward. Always look where you're going. Never waste time on where you've been. You've been there so you don't have to take that time, and wasting any time, even a breath, is a mistake. Memories can be shared of the good times, but they need to be shared while your eyes are to the horizon, faced forward. No matter where we went, when we left, he didn't let us look back. When I was young, he made a game of it. By the time I grew older, I did it out of habit, never looking back, not even a glance." I pulled in a soft breath and finished, "And now we're looking back. Dad would be disappointed."

I barely stopped speaking before Frey moved me from the railing, turned me toward the helm, and I heard him say low, "Thad."

Thad was at the huge wooden wheel. He looked over his shoulder at Frey, lifted his chin then looked to me and grinned. I grinned back. He moved away and Frey moved in, positioning me so I was standing with my back leaned into him, his hands were at the wheel and the blue of the cloudless sky meeting the brilliant emerald of the Green Sea with the lushly greened islands rising out of the water *The Finnie* was flowing past were all I could see.

Then Frey's mouth came to my ear. "Better, my wee Finnie?"

I pressed my lips together as my throat clogged because Frey had again, without word, without hesitation, given me exactly what I needed. And receiving it yet again at long last, I made an enormous decision.

I was going to tell my husband I loved him.

I swallowed the lump in my throat, relaxed into him and whispered, "Better, my handsome husband."

Frey's head moved so his lips could touch the hair at the side of mine, then it was gone but he wasn't.

As always, his large, strong frame supported my small one.

And together we stared straight ahead at our future.

"Finnie," Frey called, his voice thick, and I tried to focus on him.

I was on my back on his divan in his cabin, my hands moving feverishly over his skin, my legs spread wide. Frey was thrusting between them, slow, gentle, his hips on a slight slant, my hips slanted with them. He was on a forearm in the mattress beside me, his other hand free to roam the skin of my side, belly, ribs and right then it was cupping my breast.

I was close. So damned close.

"I'm close, baby," I breathed as my gaze locked with his.

"I know, love," he whispered, his neck bending, his mouth touching mine, gentle, light sweet, he pulled back slightly, "Hold on, stay with me."

I lifted my hips. He slid in deeper, that felt so fucking good, I told him the truth.

"I don't know if I can."

His hips rotated as he slowly slid out then rotated again as he slowly slid back in, and I bit my lip, arched my spine and my nails trailed across the skin of his back.

"Stay with me, wee one," he growled low, exposing he liked it too and just how much. "I want us to climax together."

Oh God, yes.

I wanted that too. I wanted it bad.

"Okay," I panted, and his mouth came back to mine, opened, and he touched the tip of his tongue to mine as his thumb slid across my hard, oversensitive nipple.

I whimpered into his mouth.

"Baby," I whispered against his lips, that word trembling with agonized pleasure.

He glided out and glided back in. "Stay with me."

"Frey."

"Watch me," he urged. "Feel me. You'll know when to let go. Wait for it, Finnie."

My hips moved with his and the pleasure rolled through me, then again, and again.

Beautiful.

Torture.

God, he needed to hurry up!

My hand slid around his chest and up to cup his jaw. My thumb moving to slide over his lower lip as he held my eyes, his heated, his hips moving, his cock stroking deep, his hand gliding along the skin of my ribs and all of it was better than anything I'd ever had. *We'd* ever had.

Even with adela tea.

I moved my hips with his, slid my thumb back over his lip, my gaze locked to his as I whispered a thought that came out of my mouth straight from my heart, "God, you're beautiful."

At my words, Frey groaned so deep I felt it straight up to my throat, starting at my sex. He dipped his head, his thrusts going off rhythm, pounding deeper, moving faster, his big hand spanning my hip, manipulating its movements to take him, meet each stroke.

I circled his shoulders, pressed hard against him, wrapped a calf around his thigh, and I felt it in his frame, in his flesh. He was there, I was there, and we were going there together.

And that was when I turned my head and whispered, "I love you, Frey Drakkar."

He buried himself to the root inside me, let go, and I let go too, my back arching, my neck arching, my moan deep and low. His strong teeth sunk into the flesh where my neck met my shoulder, his rumbling growl sounding through his teeth, pounding against my skin, and my moan turned to a whimper as his arm wrapped around me and closed so tight, he squeezed the breath out of my lungs.

Yes, climaxing with Frey was better than anything, even the adela tea. Perfection.

As I came down, I held on to him, fighting for breath, but unusually, Frey's arm didn't loosen.

"Frey—" I breathed.

"Say it again," he growled against my skin, so fierce, my body trembled, but his arm, so tense, stiffened further until it almost caused pain. "Say it again," he repeated, his voice now harsh.

"I love you," I whispered, breathless, but his arm only got tighter, his cock still planted deep, his hips bucked, thrusting it deeper and my body jolted as a residual wave of heat burned through me.

"Again." His voice was now beyond harsh. This demand was abrasive.

"Baby."

Another squeeze, another buck of his hips, and I whimpered.

"Say it, Finnie," he grated.

I closed my eyes tight, fought for air and pushed out, "I love you, Frey. I'm in love with you. So in love, I'll never stop loving you. Not ever. You, everything about you is beyond my wildest dreams."

He pushed his face into my neck as his arm squeezed me even tighter for a second before it released, and his hips pressed mine to the bed as he lifted up on both forearms so his big hands could frame my face on either side. His head came up and he looked down at me, face soft, beloved brown-green eyes active, stare intense.

And he did this for a while. Actually, what felt like years, and he did it without speaking or moving. He just lay with his large body covering and connected to mine and he stared at me.

Um...I wasn't certain that was good.

"Do you...?" I pulled in a breath, and with it, courage. "Uh...do you...um, feel the same...uh, I mean..." I rushed to finish, "Like, not *the same*, the same, but...um, even a little bit?" I asked.

He stared at me another second that led to two, which led to three, which led to four (I counted) before he asked, "Are you mad?"

I didn't know how to take that answer.

"Um...no?" I asked back, because now he was looking at me like he was convinced I was, and his conviction made me question mine.

His face dipped close, his hands put gentle pressure on my head, and he whispered, "Finnie Drakkar, I fell in love with you when you told me you had a rule about dead game on the kitchen table."

I blinked and my body jolted with surprise.

He couldn't...

Could he?

Seriously?

"Seriously?" I whispered.

He didn't answer my question.

Instead, he stated, "No, it was before that. When I walked into the cabin to see my wife in a pink gown with a pink ribbon in her hair looking more beautiful simply stirring batter in a bowl than most women do after their maidservants spend five hours on their appearance."

Oh my God.

Oh my God!

What man remembered pink dresses and pink ribbons?

What man?

No man. None of them. None at all.

Except ones who witnessed these things while falling in love.

Oh. My. God.

"Shut up," I whispered, but I didn't know how I did it since my throat was closing.

Frey grinned and replied, "It's true."

"That's crazy." I was still whispering.

"Indeed, it is, my wee one. But it's still true."

Oh my God.

"I'm going to cry," I announced, my voice trembling with the evidence that proved my statement true.

Frey's grin became a smile and his eyes warmed. "I see that, love."

My breath hitched and a tear slid out the side of my eye before I demanded on a weak shove at his shoulder, "You have to quit making me cry."

He dropped his head and slid his nose along mine as he muttered, "I'll work on that."

I looked at his olive-green eyes close up knowing without a doubt he was so totally not going to work on that.

I held on tight and lifted my head, pressing it into his neck. He rolled, disengaging our bodies but taking me to the top where one of his arms stayed closed around me and his other hand stroked my back as I wept softly in his neck.

I didn't cry long because I thought of something, pulled myself together, lifted up on a forearm in his chest and looked down at him.

"Why didn't you tell me?" I asked.

"You did not know?" Frey asked back, and I blinked.

"What?"

His brows drew together, and he studied me. "Wee one, how could you not know?"

"I—" I started.

"It was clear as day," he declared, and I had to admit, that was true.

Mostly.

"You still could have told me," I informed him.

"Indeed," he stated, and his arm gave me a squeeze. "As *you* could have done. Why didn't *you* tell *me* you cared so deeply for me?"

Shit. He knew I'd been holding back.

"Well," I began. "It was clear as day."

He grinned and muttered, "Right."

"Well it was!" I snapped, because, truthfully, it *was*.

His grin turned to body rocking laughter as he rolled me again so I was on my back and he was pressed to my side looking down at me.

When he controlled his hilarity, he remarked, "Well, it is said now, thank the gods."

"Yes," I bit my lip and stared up at his handsome face. "It is," I continued on a whisper. "And it's funny because the first moment I saw you, you terrified me." I watched a shadow pass over his face and instantly lifted my hand to rest against his cheek and went on, "But looking at you now I cannot for the life of me understand why." I slid my thumb along his cheekbone, pulled in a light breath, and said it again, "I love you, Frey Drakkar."

His eyes closed and his forehead dropped to rest against mine before he opened them again, stared into mine, and replied, "And I you, Finnie Drakkar."

I circled him with my arms and rolled into him so we were on our sides, face to face. Then I held him tight as he returned the favor.

"So much," he murmured belatedly, "I'll never stop loving you, my winter bride. Not ever. You, everything about you, is beyond my wildest dreams."

I closed my eyes hard as those words settled around my heart. I shoved my face in his throat and pressed my body deep, held on tighter and my strong husband absorbed my fierce embrace.

Then I smiled against his skin because at that moment, I rocketed straight up and hit the bell with a loud clang at the bliss end of the happiness scale, embedding myself in a way I knew would be forever.

~

VALENTINE ROUSSEAU'S EYES OPENED, and she stared at the dark ceiling.

Then she slid out of bed, leaving the young, slumbering, firm, naked male form in it.

345

Bending gracefully, her red-tipped fingers tagged the slip of green silk and lace off the floor. She pulled it over her head and the soft material slithered down her body.

She moved out of her bedroom, down the hall and to the room with the salmon-colored walls. She did not bother herself with turning on a light but glided across the room and stood at the small, round table on which the large, clear, smooth, round crystal sat on top of a bed of jade-green silk.

The tips of her fingers skimmed the ball and instantly a wisp of jade smoke curled inside the crystal.

She stared at its glow through the dark and felt her mouth grow tight.

Just as she thought.

What she didn't understand was why she cared. Cared so much it woke her.

"Annoying," she murmured as the smoke twisted, coiled and curved. "Why are lovers so...very...*obtuse?*" she asked the ball, it had no answer, so she went on, "Especially *men.*"

Valentine took in a delicate, displeased breath.

Always misunderstandings, never enough communication, expectation, pride, blind faith.

Not to mention, making life-altering decisions without even considering whose life it would be altering.

It was ridiculous.

Valentine studied the smoke, sighed and thought of Seoafin, her goddess of love.

Really, she should simply let it play out, wash her hands of it. There was nothing she could do. The magic binding Seoafin there was so strong, even Valentine couldn't break it, and unusually, she expended some effort to find an answer to this dilemma, though, admittedly, not much. Valentine Rousseau rarely expended effort on anything someone didn't compensate her for, except, of course, one of her toys.

She *definitely* expended effort on her toys.

And anyway, Seoafin Wilde meant nothing to her.

She meant nothing to her.

And yet, not once but too many times these past nearly five months, Seoafin Wilde's adventures reached across the worlds and tugged Valentine from her slumber.

She stared at the smoke, and while doing so, it came to her that it had been quite some time since she herself had an adventure.

And even longer since she'd delighted in the pleasurable pastime of meddling.

And truthfully, this Raider, Valentine thought, had it coming.

Though she had to admit, she did wish such a specimen would be open to her penchants. A toy such as him would be—she drew in a wistful breath —*delicious.*

Alas, such as him, she had found, didn't tend to like the way Valentine played.

She stared at her crystal ball deliberating.

Then she decided she'd give him time, not much but perhaps enough to rectify his mistakes. She did this having little doubt that gorgeous creature could do it.

If he didn't...

Well, Valentine would.

Every girl deserved true bliss.

No, this was not true. Many of today's tedious girls did not. The mere existence of boy bands proved this fact irrefutably.

But girls like Seoafin Wilde did.

Valentine sighed as she shook off her uncharacteristically soft, romantic thoughts.

She was losing her touch.

She needed to find it again.

Her thoughts moved to the young, naked, firm, male form asleep in her bed, and in the dark, Valentine smiled her cat's smile.

Then her fingertips skimmed the cold crystal again and the smoke vanished.

26

THE MEASURE OF A PRINCESS

T*hree weeks later...*

WITH OUR USUAL posse of Frey's men, Tyr galloped through Snowdon as I sat on the steed held tight to my husband's front, watched the city go by and realized I was wrong.

Bellebryn was not the most beautiful place I'd ever seen.

Snowdon was.

Snowdon, the capital of Lunwyn and where my mother and father lived, was a city like Sudvic, huge and sprawling. But it was not skirting a bay and nestled in hills.

It spread across a valley and up the sides of white, snowy mountains. Its tall, densely built buildings were made of white stone capped with snow-covered roofs dripping sparkling icicles, their doors painted in dove grays, creams or the lightest blues or lilacs. Its winding roads were cobbled in creamy stones that, like Sudvic, had been cleared of snow.

And as we rode through the city, we passed many snow-blanketed parks from large and rambling, to small and square in which there were twinkling fountains, white monuments, grand cream-colored statues of the gods, dragons or past kings, queens, Drakkars or Freys.

In one I even saw an iced-over pond where people were skating.

Frey told me (and I noted he was right as we rode over four bridges) there were three rivers snaking through the city. And as we rode over them or beside them, I saw their water was glistening and clear, their banks shimmering with ice, their rock beds glittering as if covered in fairy dust.

Over these rivers were arched, ornate, cream-colored bridges with tall, white-painted streetlamps rising from the balustrades. One river was much larger than the other two and flowed from a valley between two mountains fed from, Frey also told me, the Winter Sea.

Unlike Sudvic, which seemed working class from what I had seen, and Fyngaard, which was entirely cosmopolitan, Snowdon had working class areas and the pubs, shops and businesses that tended to those classes as well as posh areas with the cafés, restaurants and shops that catered to the more affluent.

You could easily assess the status of those who lived in the dwellings in the different areas, the tall, narrow buildings that were likely apartments or row houses of the lower classes. And then, as we rode from the outskirts to the more elite inner city, the stately, extensive homes and even mansions with the crystalline frost on their windows and window boxes filled with carefully tended miniature evergreens.

And best of all, built into the side of the mountain and overlooking the entirety of the city, was Rimée Keep, a frost-colored castle that somehow shimmered in the sun.

It had an abundance of conical roofs that had long, thin, red and gold diamond-patterned pennants drifting across the sky attached to short flag-poles. These were over circular turrets of which there was also an abundance.

The façade had stone balustrade balconies and blinking, diamond-paned windows with shutters painted a gray so light it was almost indecipherable from white.

The front of the Keep was landscaped with tall, white painted lanterns and taller, lush, long-needled fir trees.

Leading up to what had to be three-story, arched, double doors was a sweeping staircase that looked to be carved from ice and up both sides were green, tapered miniature pine trees.

And at the front of it all, even from far away I could see the massive, twinkling, five-tiered fountain with flowing, crystal-clear waters.

The whole city with its white and cream stone, muted colors and evergreens all coated with glimmering snow and dripping with icicles looked like it had sprung up magically from the snow.

It was bloody *fantastic*.

We made it to the Keep (me, with my lips parted in shock at its beauty, Frey, probably not noticing it) and Frey led Tyr around the fountain as his men on their horses positioned themselves around the drive.

It was then I stopped looking at the Keep and instead saw Mother and Father emerging from the double doors followed by my girls.

My heart squeezed and my mouth smiled huge.

Frey stopped Tyr and dismounted. Reaching up to grab hold of my waist, he pulled me down.

The minute my feet touched the ground I dashed up the icy steps (which were not, by the way, ice, I just didn't know what they were).

Two steps down from my parents, I dropped into a full-on curtsy and waited to hear my father mutter, "Rise, daughter." I then shot to my feet, ran up the last two steps and threw my arms around him.

On impact, he rocked back on a foot, and I knew he was surprised because he hesitated before his arms closed around me. But when they did, they did it tight.

"Missed you," I whispered into his neck, holding on just as tight.

"And I you, my Finnie," he whispered back on a light squeeze.

Still whispering, I told him, "I got a bullseye."

His body stilled for a moment before he pulled back slightly. I did too and I looked up in his surprised but delighted eyes and felt my belly warm.

"Indeed?" he asked.

I nodded, leaned in and said quietly, "From thirty feet." His eyes widened and I grinned and went on, "I only got the one but I'm definitely better. I can't wait to show you."

I saw a shadow pass over his face before he hid it.

I felt a corresponding shadow pass through my mind, but he quickly said, "And I cannot wait to see, daughter."

Before I could ask after the shadow, I heard, "Finnie," and turned my head to Mother who was watching us with an expressionless face but soft eyes.

I moved from Atticus's arms to Aurora's as I heard the murmured greetings between Frey and Father.

Mother's hug was not as tight, but it was just as warm. I couldn't say how she pulled that off. I could just say that she did.

"From what I could tell riding in," I whispered in her ear, "we've got *tons* of shopping to do."

Her arms went from around me, but she didn't let me go. Holding my biceps in a firm grip, she caught my eyes, her lips tipped up and her fingers squeezed.

"There is much I wish to show you," she said softly. "And I look forward to doing it."

I grinned at her, her lips tipped up more, then her eyes flitted to Atticus and Frey. I saw a shadow pass over her face too as she let me go.

I moved out of the way for Frey to lean in and touch her cheek with his bearded lips.

"We must go in, get you warm," Father muttered.

Mother nodded and they wasted no time turning and heading up the steps. And when I say wasted no time, I mean they looked to be hurrying.

Frey slid an arm along my shoulders and guided me up the steps. I glanced at his profile and saw his gaze was locked on the king and queen's backs, and I knew he, too, thought something was up. I looked away as we ascended the top of the steps because Jocelyn, Bess, Alyssa and Esther were all standing to the side of the two, tall double doors and they were all grinning at me.

I smiled back, gave them a low wave and whispered, "Hey, ladies," as we approached, and their grins got broader. They dropped down in curtsies as we walked past.

We made it through the double doors, which were closed by a footman against the cold the minute my girls swept through. I took a look around and tried not to react to the beauty of the inside of Rimée Keep that impossibly rivaled the outside.

There was no dark wood here.

There was no darkness at all.

There were tons of windows through which the sun shone through. The walls and floors of the inside were made of the same frosted stone that strangely and magnificently glittered, but inside there were carvings of pine boughs and cones in the stone. These could be seen around arched beams and at the casements of the windows.

The vast slabs of stone that made up the floors were cut with thick pile carpets in mellow, muted colors all of which had a low sheen that I knew meant they were made of silk.

Many of the walls were covered in enormous, intricate tapestries depicting mountain scenes or views of Snowdon or the Keep.

The furniture was not heavy and dark like at the Palace, but it was lacquered in an eggshell white, dripping carved lacework, looking elegant and refined.

And there was a wide stone staircase with a muted carpet runner and a carved stone balustrade, all of it curving up the side of a circular turret that rose right in the middle of the Keep.

I didn't get a chance to take much in, however, for Atticus and Aurora were walking swiftly through the vast entry hall that seemed to sweep the Keep from side to side (and I was right about the front doors—the ceiling was at least three stories tall and vaulted with carved arches and lattice-work that were extraordinary, even at a glance).

At the end of the hall, my parents turned and walked through another set of double doors.

Frey and I followed, and then we were in a massive, elegant sitting room decorated in whites, creams and the palest of pale yellows.

There was a fireplace with an elaborately carved exterior that was so big that I could lie inside with arms stretched over my head and toes pointed and my fingertips nor toes would touch the walls. And I could surely stand in it without my head brushing the top. An enormous fire roared there as well as three space heaters having been dotted around the room, these made of iron like the ones in Frey's cabin on *The Finnie*. Except they were enameled in cream, they were bigger, and they were far more ornate.

Between the heaters and the fireplace, the entire room was cozy warm.

People entered with us, and Mother and Father's cloaks were taken by servants. Jocelyn and Bess had followed me to take my wool cloak, hat and gloves. The gentleman who took Atticus's cloak waited beside Frey as he unstrapped the one he didn't need to ward off the chill and handed it to the man.

"Coffee, please, and cakes," Mother ordered. Her servant nodded and she went on, "Close the door as you leave."

I looked from a grinning Jocelyn and Bess who heard this, and their smiles faltered. They started to back out of the room, and I turned my attention to Atticus and Aurora who both appeared tense.

I shifted my attention to Frey, who I felt had tensed at my side. Then I felt his hand in the small of my back propelling me toward the two sweep-lined, graceful sofas upholstered in pale-yellow damask that faced each other but ran perpendicular to the fireplace. They were separated by a low, gleaming eggshell lacquered oval table.

"Is something amiss?" Frey asked quietly after we heard the doors close.

"Please, sit," Father muttered, and I looked back up to Frey who was studying my father.

He guided me to a sofa, and we sat close together, Frey's arm around my shoulders pulling me even closer and tucking me to his side. I leaned into him as he sat back and crossed one booted ankle on the other knee.

Mother and Father sank into the sofa opposite us. But even close to my husband's solid warmth, my parents' behavior was beginning to freak me out.

"You're anxious, Atticus," Frey stated the obvious. "And your unease is causing the same in my bride. Tell us what's happening."

"You made haste from Sudvic," Father replied strangely, and Frey nodded.

"Indeed," he confirmed. "We docked just late yesterday afternoon and rode swiftly, spending the night in Dalehavre and leaving early. Finnie was keen to see her parents."

Father's eyes moved to me so he could give me a warm smile before they went back to Frey.

The warmth fled and he studied him a moment before he said, "We received word only this morning from the messenger you sent ahead that you were to arrive in Snowdon imminently. As you have actually arrived, I can see our return messenger did not meet you."

Frey's body got tighter when he returned, "We took the forest trails. They're swifter."

This was true. Frey, I was getting, didn't bother with roads. He was not a man to waste time that didn't need to be wasted, and unless there were sleighs involved, he always took the more direct routes. And our journey didn't involve sleighs. Frey and my belongings would follow and likely not arrive for hours if not take until the next morning. Though Kell had charge of the sleighs so I figured, that man on land, anything went.

"This is unfortunate," Aurora murmured.

I felt Frey's impatience mount and my anxiety increased.

"Perhaps we can dispense with the mystery, and you can explain why," Frey suggested in his way where it was clear his suggestion was not a suggestion, as such.

Father looked Frey directly in the eyes and he did it in a manner where I could tell he was avoiding mine, which obviously made my anxiety increase even more.

Then he announced, "The executions commence at nightfall."

I blinked and Frey's body went solid before he muttered, "Bloody hell."

"Executions?" I whispered and felt Aurora's gaze on me, so I turned to her.

"The traitors, my dear," she said softly. "Berg Enger, Hernod Greig and Viola Milstrom. In your absence, they were tried, found guilty and are sentenced to hang this eve."

Oh *shit*.

"Our messenger rode out to warn you this was imminent and suggest you delay your arrival for a few days," she went on. "It is unfortunate he did not succeed in this task."

Unfortunate was not exactly the word I'd use. Still, I wasn't quite certain why this was such dire news. Of course, executions were dire news seeing as they were executions. But considering I wasn't scheduled for the noose, I was a little concerned why they were being so careful with me.

"You rode through the city, I assume?" Atticus asked, and to this, Frey grunted, "Of course," which caused Father to pull in a breath and let it out in his own curse of, "Bloody hell."

"What?" I asked, but no one seemed to want to answer, even Frey, which I did not take as good. Mother and Father were avoiding my eyes, and when I glanced up at Frey, I saw his jaw was tight like he was clenching his teeth. So I repeated, "What?"

Father finally looked at me and his face went soft before he lowered the boom. "It is our responsibility, my daughter, as sovereigns, to attend the executions of traitors to the crown."

It was my turn to suck in breath and go solid as I stared at the king.

One could say this was not, in any way, the next adventure I had hoped for.

Shopping with Mother in a new city, yes. Attending a play in one of the acclaimed theaters Snowdon had that Frey told me about, certainly. Taking Gunner up on his offer to teach me advanced maneuvers on a horse, definitely. And skating on that pond in that park was one I'd just added.

Witnessing an execution?

Uh...*no*.

"They conspired against the crown," Mother put in gently, and my horrified eyes slid to her. "We wear those crowns, Finnie, and every breath we take is a breath taken for Lunwyn. They collaborated against you, which means they collaborated against their country. The crown survived and it is our duty to sit and watch as a symbol of their failure and the strength of Lunwyn as they hang."

Oh God.

I did not like this.

"If you had been away with your husband, this would have been excuse for you not to attend," Father stated at this point, his eyes on Frey. "But you are now here, and as you rode through the city, it is without doubt that news is spreading like fire. With the people knowing Finnie is here, she will be expected to attend. Indeed, many will assume that she's here just in order to do so."

Frey's arm squeezed my shoulders as he muttered, "Gods damn it."

"There is more you must know," Aurora said quietly.

Frey and I both got still again, and the door opened. A servant bustled forward with an ornate silver coffee service, exquisite china and a plate of beautifully decorated delicious-looking petite fours. These I would have tucked into without delay at any other time but, obviously, not after I'd received the news that I'd have to watch three people hung from their necks until dead.

We all waited for the coffee and cakes to be arranged on the table and the servant to move out of the room and shut the door before Aurora leaned forward and started pouring at the same time talking.

"In your absence, especially considering that absence was just after a heinous plot unfolded that caused a woman to lose her life rather grue-somely, and that woman was supposed to be Finnie, talk has been sweeping all of Lunwyn."

"What talk?" Frey asked, and Aurora lifted her eyes to him as she handed him a cup and saucer.

"You and Finnie," she answered, went back to pouring but said no more.

"Aurora," Frey growled, clearly not happy to need to prompt her.

She sighed then replied, "As you know, Drakkar, it started with your wedding kiss then you dragging Finnie away only to disappear for weeks. Then, your reappearance for the Gales and your behavior there."

Her eyes moved to me as she started listing examples.

"Finnie greeting you with such open enthusiasm after the hunt."

Her eyes moved back to Frey.

"Your closeness at the Gales. And you disappearing again after the attempt was made on Finnie's life. A clear indication you care deeply for her and will not hesitate to ensure her safety. All of this, every moment you both were together with an audience, was noted avidly and passed on to any ear that would hear it even more avidly."

"It is not unheard of for such gossip to spread about the royals," Frey noted. "Indeed, it's commonplace for such talk."

"You are correct," she nodded and handed my cup to me after pouring in a splash of milk. "But considering the dramatics of assassination attempts and your forthrightness about your regard for one another, this talk has become extreme."

"Extreme how?" I asked.

Mother handed Atticus his coffee then turned back to pouring and answering.

"Minstrels sing of you, storytellers weave tales. It is not just the talk that is sweeping the land. This is all building to extremes, creating legend."

Ho boy.

"I do not understand why this would cause you both alarm," Frey remarked. "This, too, is not unusual."

Mother sat back with her coffee and Father took it from there.

"You are correct, Drakkar," he stated. "But you are The Frey, The Drakkar, and therefore revered. Your union with Finnie heralds continued peace and prosperity for Lunwyn and was already anticipated greatly. The fact that your match appears a splendid one founded in deep affection has served in a short time to romanticize your story to extremes. And..." he paused and held Frey's gaze, "it makes those who would conspire against you and Finnie, not so much Lunwyn, but instead a love match that is already, even after only a few short months of you being wed, nearing legend, it makes those condemned individuals that inspire more than disgust and anger...but extreme loathing."

"The inns are full," Aurora put in, and I focus turned to her. "Those citizens with empty rooms have let them out. And it is reported there's a large camp that has formed around the gallows just outside Snowdon filled with people who have traveled far but who could not find accommodation within the city."

"Bloody hell," Frey growled, taking his arm from around me, his ankle from his knee and leaning forward to set his cup and saucer down with a clatter.

"I don't get it," I said quietly, and Father looked to me.

"Executions are public, daughter," he replied just as quietly.

I stared at him as I got it.

"Ho boy," I whispered.

"Indeed," Aurora stated, lifted her cup and took a sip, her eyes on me over the rim. She dropped her hand and kept hold of my gaze. "Your father has called in extra guard. There are concerns that things will get out of hand. And, my dear, you will be on display to a great number of people." She hesitated then went on gently as *she* lowered the boom. "It is estimated to be thousands."

Great.

Just great.

"Finnie won't go," Frey stated, and both Aurora and Atticus looked at him.

"I'm sorry, Drakkar, but she must go," Atticus replied.

Frey shook his head and returned, "Make an announcement that she's indisposed."

"Unfortunately, when royal duty calls, indisposed is not an excuse. She's not missing a state breakfast or a royal hunt but an execution of traitors," Atticus said quietly.

His gaze came to me, and he continued to speak quietly.

"I'm sorry, Finnie, but as princess of this land, future mother of the king and the target of these plots, now that people know you're here, you will be expected to attend. There is no way around it. It is a show of the strength of the crown." As I held his gaze and held my breath, he continued, "We had hoped to waylay you, but since this has not happened, it is your duty to attend." He pulled in breath and finished, "I'm so sorry, my daughter."

I sat back, looked at the fire, took a sip of my coffee and tried to pull my shit together.

Okay, well, I was princess now and maybe forever. This was the gig. It was a shitty gig, but it was the gig.

Apparently, being princess wasn't all about beautiful palaces, fantastic castles, shopping, archery lessons, wearing awesome crowns and kickass underwear and being married to a hot guy who named his ship after you.

Apparently, there were drawbacks.

And this was a big one.

Hells bells.

Aurora spoke and my eyes went to her as she did.

"You will need to be strong, my dear. If she were here, Sjofn would not blink. You will need to look on, show strength and no reaction." She paused and her eyes got soft before she finished, "It does not take long, and we will soon be away."

"Right," I whispered.

Frey's arm again slid around my shoulders, and he pulled me into his side.

Then he somewhat changed the subject.

"Explain why Grieg is amongst today's condemned," Frey demanded, and I knew who Hernod Grieg was and Berg Enger. Frey had filled me in.

Atticus's eyes moved between Frey and me swiftly, clearly catching on that Frey had shared before he asked, "The messenger did not reach you in Hawkvale?" At Frey's shaking head, Father went on, "And, at your return, you did not receive a briefing?"

Frey kept shaking his head. "Ruben arrived in Hawkvale with the news Grieg had been incarcerated and was being interrogated, but not tried and condemned. And, as I explained, we made haste to Snowdon, news of this did not reach us prior to our leaving The Vale and no one met *The Finnie* with a report."

Father's lips tightened before he replied, "Your men picked him up, worked with him and he has confessed to being the man behind the plots."

"Simple as that?" Frey asked, sounding disbelieving.

"Apparently," Father answered cautiously, communicating to Frey with his eyes something I could not read but I could tell he didn't believe it either.

"I'll want to speak to Balthazar and Quincy," Frey stated.

"Quincy is not far," Father told him. "Once we received your message, I sent word to both of them you would be arriving and learned your man Balthazar is away. I do not know where. When the messenger arrived, I had assumed he'd heard word you were back in Lunwyn and rode to you. But Quincy is close. I'll have him brought to you." He paused a moment before continuing, "But, Drakkar, Grieg's name is on the proclamation. The people will expect him to be there. There is no circumventing that. He will be hanged tonight." Atticus leaned forward slightly, his eyes intense, and said quietly, "Therefore, if you wish to have a word, your time is short."

I had a feeling something was going on here I didn't get, but I also didn't get the opportunity to ask.

Frey didn't hesitate to stand, saying, "Then I have little time so I should make haste."

Father nodded and stood too, setting down his coffee before he straightened. It was then I heard my cup clatter in its saucer, and I looked down at my hand to see it shaking.

At about the same time, my cup and saucer were swept away by Frey. I watched vaguely as he set it on the table and then I saw nothing but his face for he had bent close to me and lifted his hand to my jaw.

"I will be with you," he whispered. I nodded, knowing he meant at the executions and his gaze moved over my face before he noted, "They do not do this in your world."

I shook my head and said softly, "They do. It's just not public and criminals aren't hanged. They're injected with poison and, well...whatever, but it's private, and it happening at all is controversial. Many of my world do not believe in the death penalty and some are vehemently opposed to it."

"And your opinion on that?" he prompted, and I bit my lip.

Then I replied, "I'm not a big fan."

Frey's eyes softened before he assured me, "It is rare here, my love, and the only times this sentence is carried out is for traitors, rapists and murderers. And your attendance would only be expected at the executions of traitors."

Well, this was good news. Except for the fact that there just happened to be three traitors who needed hanging.

"Fabulous," I muttered.

"That is rarer still, my Finnie," Frey whispered, his fingers tensing at my jaw briefly. "I only remember one other in my lifetime and that was decades ago."

I nodded and that made me feel better, just not much.

Frey leaned in, touched his mouth to mine and that made me feel better too. This time a lot more.

"It will be swift, and we will be away," he said gently.

I nodded again and he again tensed his fingers on my jaw as he said, "I must make haste to talk to the conspirator."

I nodded yet again.

Frey went on, "I will return as soon as I can."

That was when I realized that he was keen to get away, but he was worried about me and staying to make sure I was okay before he went.

So that was when I lifted my hand, curled my fingers around his wrist, squeezed and gave him a small smile.

"I'll be all right," I assured him.

He still didn't move as he replied, "I do not like the light I see in your eyes."

"Well, honey, you probably won't for a while because this is an adventure, if given the choice, I would say a big fat no to. But I'll get through it then I'll get over it." I gave his wrist another squeeze and finished, "Promise."

His thumb stroked my cheekbone then he leaned in and slid his nose along mine as I pulled in a fortifying breath.

359

He must have been assured I wasn't going to fall apart for he straightened, nodded at Mother and jerked his chin at Father. Father smiled his approval at me briefly (and that made me feel better too), and they moved out of the be room.

Mother regarded me over the rim of her coffee cup through another sip before we heard the doors close behind Father and Frey.

She dropped the cup again and drily observed, "It upsets me to note that it appears your husband doesn't like you much at all, my daughter."

I blinked at her but saw her mouth twitch as I watched her eyes light.

I leaned forward, nabbed my own cup, sat back and remarked, "It's terrible. We simply do not get along," then I took a sip.

"I see this," Aurora murmured.

"He's insufferable," I added.

"Mm." This she murmured into her cup while her eyes danced.

"And he thinks I'm a shrew," I informed her.

"He made that quite clear," she replied.

"The last few months have been a nightmare," I shared.

She lifted her chin slightly. "My profound sympathy, my dear, that you are suffering so greatly," she returned, and I couldn't help it, I smiled.

That smile grew to a grin then I burst out laughing.

Aurora of the House of Wilde did not laugh with me, but she did smile.

And when I stopped laughing, she leaned forward, picked up the delicate, china plate of petite fours and extended it to me while inviting, "Tell me all about your adventures with your Raider, my Finnie."

And therefore, Mother deftly took my mind off the coming events and to better places. Something I not only let her do but was extremely grateful for, and we sat, drank coffee, ate cakes and had a long, fabulous mother-daughter chat in a beautiful room next to a roaring fire.

I would have preferred our welcome home not to include news of my required presence at a triple execution.

But it ended up great.

And, by the way, the petite fours tasted even better than they looked.

"Don't be cross, Penelope," I whispered as I cuddled my cat who I'd been reunited with a few hours earlier, and who, I had found, was holding a pretty mean grudge for being left behind.

She stretched her neck over my arm and looked to the side, clearly wishing to be put down and not receive snuggles and soft words from her momma who she considered abandoned her.

"You told me you didn't want to go on a ship," I reminded her.

"Mrrrr that was before you, mrrr went away for, mrrr *ages*," she retorted.

"Next time, I'll take you with us," I promised.

"Mrrr, let me down," she demanded.

"You cannot tell me my girls didn't take care of you," I stated.

"Mrrr, they didn't let me go, mrrr outside," she replied.

"No, you mean they didn't let you go outside every ten minutes and then jump to let you back in ten minutes after," I amended.

She blinked at the distance, granting this point with ill-grace by repeating, "Mrrrr, let me *down*."

"Just give Momma a cuddle before I do," I urged.

She turned her head and blinked at me then she turned it away again to look over my arm.

She was being ornery, and I knew she wasn't going to give in (just yet) so I moved her to the bed and dropped her on it. She waddled to the pillows throwing a disdainful look down her chunky body at me. She then collapsed on the comforter at the edge of the pillows and glared at me a second before she curled into herself and started to clean her big belly.

I sighed. Then I looked around the room, which was more elegant furniture, tapestries, glittery stone walls and floors, but it was decorated in whites and the palest of pale greens and lavenders. It was fantastic.

The other thing that was fantastic was that the sleighs with our things, as driven by Kell, arrived about an hour ago. They included our trunks and much more precious cargo, Skylar.

And lastly Skylar had taken Frey's spun glass dragon down and now it was sitting on its feet, its wings spread wide, on a bed of silk on a dresser.

My girls had been called close after the message was received that Frey and I would be arriving. They'd packed for themselves and me and made haste from the Winter Palace to Rimée Keep, arriving, Alyssa told me, just twenty minutes before Frey and I did. Therefore, next to the dragon, Esther had set my wedding bundle in a beautiful, crystal vase.

I studied the beauty of the adela twigs and Frey's glass beast and decided in that moment that wherever we went, those two things would be with us. No matter where we were, they would always be with us.

Always.

The door opened and Frey walked through followed by Alyssa and Bess.

The girls went to the wardrobe, Frey came to me, and I could tell by the look on his face it was time.

He stopped close, both his hands came to my neck, and he bent so his face was near mine before he whispered, "We must be away."

I knew it, therefore I nodded.

He pulled in breath and stated, "Finnie, the last traitor to be hanged was hanged when Sjofn was a young lass. She did not attend due to her youth. Although you are princess and the people think you have been trained thus since birth and much is known about Sjofn, no one can know how anyone would react to what you will see this eve." His fingers gave me a squeeze before he whispered, "It will be difficult, love, and therefore you must not add to that difficulty by feeling the responsibility of guarding your reaction and displaying one that is not your own."

Uh...what?

"Sorry?" I asked.

"What I'm telling you is not to worry about what people see, Finnie," he said softly. "Just be yourself."

I closed my eyes because I loved that he knew me so well and therefore knew that would be weighing on my mind (or, one of the things).

I opened them, looked in his eyes and shared, "I don't want to disappoint Mother and Father."

"I know you don't, but I'm also not certain you could do that," Frey replied.

I closed my eyes again because his words felt nice. I felt his lips on my forehead, which felt nicer, so I opened my eyes, and he looked back down at me.

"We must be away," he repeated on a whisper.

I nodded.

Alyssa and Bess were waiting outside the door holding a pair of dove-gray, suede gloves and a fur cloak made of fluffy white pelts dusted in dove-gray hairs. They gave me understanding glances before Frey led me down the hall, down the curving stairs and into the great hall where Aurora and Atticus were having their outer garments arranged on their shoulders.

Both of them were wearing crowns and I saw Jocelyn and Esther rush to me as we made it to Mother and Father, Jocelyn carrying a sleek wooden box. Bess and Alyssa settled my cloak on my shoulders and shoved the gloves on my hands as Jocelyn unveiled my fabulous icicle crown in its bed of ice-blue silk that Esther took out and brought forward, settling it low on my forehead.

"You are ready, Finnie," she whispered before she stepped back.

I nodded and Bess squeezed my hand before all four girls stepped away.

Frey put his hand in my back, and we followed Mother and Father out the front doors.

Once outside, at the foot of the steps I saw two sleighs, each one fronted by teams of four horses. Around the fountain there were a number of royal guards and what seemed like all of Frey's men on mounts and this included Kell and Skylar.

The minute I saw Skylar, my step faltered, and my head shot back to look at Frey. "Honey, Sky...I don't—"

Frey cut me off with a muttered, "He asked to come."

I shook my head and grabbed his arm, dragging my feet and whispering, "He could ask to wrestle a rattlesnake for the fun of it, but we wouldn't let him do it."

Frey looked down at me, brows raised, "A rattlesnake?"

"You don't have those?" I asked back as he stopped us at the last step.

"We do, but why on earth would he ask to wrestle a rattlesnake?"

"Exactly!" I cried, my voice rising.

"Finnie—"

"I don't wish him to go."

"Wee one—"

"Frey, tell him he can't go. It's macabre, this interest in death. It's unhealthy. It's even wrong. In my world we had public executions, but they stopped ages ago. I mean, I think some lands may still do it but most of them don't because it isn't humane. And I feel Sky should learn he shouldn't be that way."

Frey got close as his brows knit and he bent his neck so he could hold my eyes, "My wee Finnie, he does not wish to go to see the condemned hanged. He wishes to be a part of your guard."

I blinked up at him as my heart jolted.

"What?"

"All my men are here as your personal guard and Skylar requested to be amongst them. For this, their presence will be ceremonial only, therefore I agreed."

At this, my heart jumped.

"He wanted—?"

"Yes."

I blinked then whispered, "Really?"

"I would ask why you find that so intensely surprising, my love, considering the fact he thinks the sun shines through you, and you hang the moon. But the longer we delay, the longer it takes for this to be done, for you *and* for them."

Ho boy.

He was *so* right.

Still, it was totally awesome Frey thought Skylar thought the sun shone through me and I hung the moon.

"Right," I said on a nod, taking myself back to the (not so great) task at hand.

Frey returned my nod then looked over my head and nodded to someone else.

Tyr was brought to him. Frey lifted me up in the saddle and mounted behind me.

"Drakkar," Atticus called from the back of a sleigh. "A sleigh has been prepared for you and Finnie."

"She rides with me," Frey called back.

"But, she's the Winter—" Father started, but Frey interrupted him.

"She is indeed. She is also my wife whose life is in danger. She rides close to my protection and on transport that will provide a much quicker getaway should it be required," Frey returned, and I sighed deeply at the reminder of another of the many things that had been weighing my thoughts since I left Mother to go with my girls and be prepared for this grisly event.

Father considered this before he nodded.

And I reconsidered Frey's long-ago suggestion that we not leave his big soft bed in his big fancy-ass chateau in the sun-drenched fantasyland of Hawkvale.

But, alas, it was *way* too late for that.

Father commanded his driver, "Onward," and their sleigh moved forward.

Frey steered Tyr behind it and the guard and Frey's men surrounded us.

This, I found shortly after we rounded the fountain, was not going to be a stately, sedate royal procession. All the horses were prompted to a fast canter, and it would become apparent why. This was because where we were going was not close to the city, but far away.

At our pace, Snowdon was quickly left behind. We climbed and rounded the low swell of a mountain and came out on another valley, this one dotted liberally with dark tents that had open fires.

But the tent city was a ghost town, for beyond that there was a sea of people edged by horses and sleighs all spread in front of a wooden plat-form. This was all lit against the falling night by an abundance of torches, especially around the platform.

As we drew nearer then started to ride through an avenue of onlookers that was being forged by Father's guard as well as members of the guard who met them who had already been there patrolling the crowds on horse-back, I saw the platform was a scaffold. Behind it was an elevated dais on which there were three thrones that were only mildly ornate compared to King Baldur's.

If the events that were going to occur weren't going to occur, I would have thought they were way cool. Obviously, dreading what was to come, I didn't give it a thought.

My thoughts were turned from the thrones (but mostly the scaffold with its three, dangling nooses) as a cheer started to ring the air that esca-lated to a shout which heightened to a deafening chant of, "The Dragon and The Ice!"

I started to look around as we rode through the mass of people.

I saw a great number of salutes aimed Frey's way, arms thrown in the air, huge beaming smiles and bigger shouting mouths as eyes stayed glued to Frey and I, and the chant kept rising as we rode.

It was like we were rock stars arriving at a concert, and it would be, I suspected, disconcerting normally.

Considering that evening's events, it was ghoulish.

To take my mind off of it, I twisted, looked up to Frey and asked, "The Ice?"

His eyes, which were pointed over my head, alert and scanning, came down to me. "I do not know, wee one. I've never heard it before, but it would seem you've earned a nickname."

"Great," I muttered, looking ahead again.

I mean, "The Ice" was pretty cool, I supposed. I just didn't feel it was fitting.

I didn't have a chance to consider my new handle because it didn't take long to make it to the platform. No one hesitated to move swiftly to it including Atticus and Aurora, who exited their sleigh almost the instant it stopped, Father not even waiting for someone to approach to open the little sleigh door.

Frey swung down nearly before Tyr came to a halt, then immediately reached up to pull me down.

What made me feel a whole lot better was when the entirety of his men, including Kell and Skylar, also dismounted and ascended the platform with us to line up at the back of our thrones with Frey standing at my right side, Thad at my left, Skylar in front of Thad and Kell at my back.

Truth be told, it didn't make me feel better. It made me feel great, their show of support was awesome.

That was until the crowd took this in, The Drakkar and his men flanking his bride, and they went totally freaking berserk.

Shit.

Sitting in my throne, I reached out to grab Frey's hand, tugged on it, and he bent so his ear was at my mouth, which also caused a crushing wave of sound.

"Maybe the guys being here—" I started, and Frey turned his head to catch my eyes.

"They stand with you," he stated implacably.

"But, all those people are—" I began again, and Frey cut me off again.

"All those people are a mob of unknowns with unknown intents. You are exposed. My men stand with you."

Oh. Right. That made sense.

So it wasn't a show of support so much as protection.

That worked too.

"Okay," I whispered.

Frey's lips twitched as he straightened, faced the crowd, squeezed my hand reassuringly once then let it go to cross his arms on his chest.

I took the hint.

Time to be a princess.

I put both hands in my lap, clutching them tight.

It was then a ripple filtered through the crowd, changing the euphoric excitement to something else that didn't feel very good.

My eyes shifted to the back of the sea of people.

There I saw a black, covered sleigh led by four black horses that had entered the avenue we'd left behind and this was guarded by a large phalanx of my father's armed soldiers.

The condemned had arrived and almost immediately the crowd, already having started to whip themselves into a frenzy at seeing Frey and I, didn't delay in shouting jeers and throwing snowballs that hit the side of the covered sleigh, the horses and even the guard who, luckily, carried large shields at their sides.

"Oh no," I whispered as my body tensed, and I felt, in two places, reassuring squeezes. One was my right shoulder and that was from Frey. The other was my left and that, to my surprise, was Kell reaching over the back of my throne to do it swiftly then removing his hand.

Father stood and strode purposefully across the platform and down the steps to the scaffold where he spoke with a guard there.

He strode back, face stony, the guard peeling off, and I understood his intent, but it was too late. The sleigh was now being rocked back and forth by the number of snowballs hitting it and the jeers had escalated to the point the air felt laced with acid.

Once the sleigh stopped at the gallows, more guards rode forward to form a shield of horses around it as well as further guards on foot marching down to stand in front of the horses, the men unsheathing their swords in warning.

But it was too late.

Much too late.

And the guards knew it, so they wasted even less time.

The prisoners were led out of the sleigh and quickly moved across the scaffold to stand at their noose. The two men first with Viola, looking thin, pale and terrified, bringing up the rear.

It was Viola, and perhaps the violent and public way her scheme had been carried out, that caught the sheer force of the biting fervor of the crowd. The minute she became visible to onlookers, snowballs were hurled with such violence and quantity, her frame jerked with every missile that landed. It became clear very quickly that these projectiles had been prepared in advance and embedded with rocks or maybe worse as only snow would not rip through her coarse clothing or tear open her skin.

And it was when she slipped on the snow at her feet and fell to her hands and knees, her hair sodden and dripping, her clothing in tatters within seconds, the icy missiles coming fast even as guards stood in front of her, holding up shields attempting to shelter her and getting pelted in their attempt, the crowd going wild at her fall and a new wave of sound hit me that I lost it.

Without thinking, I shot out of my throne, shrieked, "*Stop!*" and dashed to the stairs that led to the scaffold.

I didn't make it.

Stephan caught me first and then I felt myself transferred to Frey's arms.

But I continued to screech, "*Stop! Stop right now! Stop right now!*" as I struggled against his hold.

"Finnie, wee one," he growled in my ear with a rough squeeze. "Calm yourself."

I totally ignored him, kept struggling and kept shouting, "*Stop right now!*"

And that was when I noticed it.

Frey did as well for he stopped trying to pull me back to my throne. He stood still and stared as those closest to the platform heard me, saw me and stopped throwing their snowballs and started staring up at me in shock.

This, too, shifted through the crowd with amazing speed and they all quickly become motionless and silent as I kept screaming, "*Stop!*"

It took only moments for the entirety of the crowd to stop and stare.

I stood there, in the curve of Frey's arm, my chest rising and falling, and I returned their stare.

Then, I don't know what came over me, I started yelling.

Or, more accurately, lecturing my subjects like I was an honest to God princess.

"It is a measure of a nation their cunning! It is a measure of a nation their strength! And it is a measure of a nation," I leaned forward and screeched, "*their mercy!*"

I leaned back and surveyed the crowd, and for some bizarre reason kept right on shouting.

"The condemned you see before you have been tried justly and meet their sentence fairly. They have done wrong, and they will pay for it. But I am not the Winter Princess of a nation who does not see that even the condemned deserve to be treated with respect as they face death. You may think they do not deserve it, but it is your duty as Lunwynians to rise above their actions, *not* fall to their depths. They will hang for their crimes, and you will watch this sentence carried out. How could that not be enough for you?"

I tore my eyes away from the now whispering crowd as those close sent my words far, feeling Frey's arm still tight around my middle.

But I ignored it and looked down at the scaffold.

"Bring her to her feet," I ordered the guard standing around Viola and they shifted and stared up at me in stupefaction, so I snapped, "*Bring her to her feet!*"

They jumped toward Viola, who I avoided looking at as they helped her up and moved her to her noose.

Instead, I looked back to the crowd and, yep, you guessed it, kept right on shouting.

"Today, you witness something infinitely sad. Three people who have gone wrong somewhere in their lives, done wrong because of it, and therefore are paying the ultimate price. Do not stand there shouting and jeering, demonstrating that they were right to move against this great nation, those fortunate enough to inhabit her ice-bound earth and those privileged to wear her crowns. Stand there, and as the Lunwynians I know you to be, stand strong, stand proud and stand filled with mercy." After delivering that, I turned in Frey's arm, looked up to him and bit off, "I'm done."

He was staring down at me with an expression I wasn't in any mood to read, and luckily, he didn't give me time to do it. Swiftly, he guided me back to my throne, and I went, sat and looked back out at the now silent crowd, hands clasped in my lap, trying to deep breathe.

"Commence without delay," Atticus barked from my left side.

I watched silently (as did the crowd) as each of the condemned were allowed their last words. Berg Enger and Viola Milstrom both declined, Enger clearly shaken by the events and Viola obviously so. Hernod Grieg strangely lifted a fist and shouted, "Unite Lunwyn!" and that was it from him.

Their heads were covered with black cloth sacks. The nooses were pulled over their heads and tightened around their necks. Then a man in a white robe with the band displaying all the gods' colors dangling said a few words in the ancient tongue.

Finally, Father shouted, "Lunwyn!" and the hangman walked down the length of them kicking a high wooden lever behind each of the damned.

Down went Enger. Down went Grieg. And I couldn't help it, I closed my eyes, but it was bad enough just hearing her short, sharp, heartbreaking scream that stilled abruptly when down went Viola.

The hangman turned and shouted, "It is done, my king!" and Frey had me out of my throne so fast, I got lightheaded.

We were down the platform, the soles of his men's boots sounding behind us. Then I was on Tyr, Frey was behind me, his arm tight around my ribs, he leaned us to Tyr's back, dug his heels into Tyr's flank and shouted, "*Yah!*"

There was no avenue anymore and before us the crowd jumped away, parting on their own as Frey, me, Tyr and his men all galloped straight through them and away to Rimée Keep.

∾

It took half the time to get back to the Keep than it did to get to the platform because Frey rode Tyr hard all the way there. Once we arrived, he dismounted, and while doing it, dragged me down right along with him.

Then he dragged me up the steps.

Then he dragged me through the doors that were opened by a footman before we arrived.

Then he dragged me right by my hovering girls who all rushed forward at the sight of me.

Then he dragged me down the hall and into the room we'd been in earlier with my parents.

The girls followed as did, by the sounds of the hustle and bustle, every one of his men as Frey pulled me inside then turned on me.

I took one look at his face, knew he was pissed and did *not* care.

I yanked my hand free, lifted it palm up toward him and shouted, "*Don't start!*"

He looked beyond me (and my hand) and barked, "*Go!*"

I looked over my shoulder and shouted, "*Stay!*"

Both men and women looked between Frey and I, and Frey repeated, "*Go!*"

So I fired out, "*Do not dare go! Stay!*"

"Gods damn it, Finnie," Frey growled, and I looked back at him.

"They were pelting her with snowballs, Frey, *right before she was to hang from the neck until dead!*" I shouted. "She'd done wrong but wasn't her sentence as it stood bad enough? Did she have to endure—?"

I stopped talking because suddenly I was crushed in Frey's arms and his mouth had slammed down on mine whereupon he laid a hot and heavy one on me.

I was clutching his shoulders and blinking up at him dazedly when he lifted his head and started speaking.

"It would have been nice to have privacy when I told you how gods-damned proud I was of my wife this eve, but since you seem to wish a continued audience for your night's performance, so be it."

I blinked again, realizing vaguely that he wasn't pissed. The intensity of emotion I read on his face was something else altogether.

He gave me a squeeze and stated, "I'm proud of you, Finnie Drakkar. What you did took courage and showed compassion, and if your people didn't already love you, witnessing that, they will."

I blinked again then asked, "You think?"

"Absolutely," he answered.

I felt my body melt in his arms.

"What'd she do?" I heard Jocelyn whisper from behind me.

Then I heard Thad answer, "I'll tell you, but I'll do it outside."

After that I heard the shuffling of bodies moving right before both Frey and I were rocked to the side as arms came around both of our thighs.

I looked down to see it was Skylar giving our legs a hug and I melted even deeper in Frey's arm as I moved a hand to touch Skylar's hair. But Skylar, being Skylar, didn't wait around for that. Without a word or look, he let go and raced out of the room. I twisted in Frey's arms to watch him as he did it and saw the only one left was Kell.

He was standing, feet planted, arms crossed on his chest, eyes glued to Frey.

"Don't know if it's the spirit she's got," he remarked. "Don't know what the bloody hell it is. Never seen the like from a woman." His eyes shifted to me before he finished brusquely, "Only know whatever the bloody hell it is, it's good."

Then he uncrossed his arms, stomped out of the room like coming to this conclusion was beyond annoying and indeed rocked his world to its very foundations and he didn't like that all that much, and he slammed the door behind him.

I turned back to Frey feeling warm inside and out.

"I think Kell likes me," I whispered.

"You would think correctly." Frey didn't whisper.

My eyes went to his chest as my fingers went there to fiddle with the strap of his cloak. "So, uh...you're not mad at me for losing it. You're, um... proud of me?"

He gave me a gentle shake and my fingers quit fiddling as my eyes lifted to his.

When he got my gaze, he stated, "You weren't born princess, Finnie Drakkar, but that does not mean you're not one."

I closed my eyes and dropped my forehead to his chest as his words washed over me. And when I did my crown dug into my forehead, so I immediately pulled it right back.

"I need to get rid of my crown," I whispered.

He nodded but didn't move. Instead, he asked, "Are you all right?"

I answered honestly, "No, that was heinous, and I hope no one else tries to kill me because that isn't much fun at all and watching them hang for it isn't much better."

His mouth twitched and he agreed, "I hope so too."

I leaned into him and stated, "Now I need food, and after that I need my husband to take me to bed and hold me so I can forget all this and think about where Mother is going to take me shopping tomorrow."

His arms tightened and he replied, "My wee Finnie, if we're in bed I would hope you're not thinking about where your Mother is going to take you shopping."

I grinned at him then challenged, "Well then, it seems you have your work cut out for you because some of the shops we passed today..." I shrugged and finished, "Just saying."

He grinned back, his body shaking with laughter, and he accepted my challenge by dropping his head and kissing me.

Incidentally, several hours later, after dinner, when I was in Frey's arms in our warm, soft bed in Rimée Keep, not once did I think of shopping.

Or executions.

27

CONJECTURE

T wo weeks later...

FREY DRAKKAR STOOD between Max and Thad and watched Gunner putting Finnie and Sky through their paces, Finnie atop her new mount Caspia.

Drakkar had presented his wife with her horse two days after they arrived in Snowdon. It was a dapple gray. Its dapples an extraordinary shade that bordered on lilac, and when he saw her, Drakkar knew she was Finnie's.

He was correct. Finnie had been entranced the moment she met her, named her within a second and fell in love with her the second after.

As for Drakkar, he'd become entranced the moment his wife did, and he made note to bestow gifts upon her far more often.

Now, every day, as with her archery and knife work, she and Sky spent an hour or more with Gunner learning what Finnie termed, "Raider Horse Maneuvers."

At that very moment she was bent over Caspia's neck, snaking her gray at a gallop closely around obstacles Gun had set out, after which she (and Sky) encountered a fence that they had to jump. Once they achieved that they were to rein their mounts around sharply, re-jump the fence and snake again through the obstacles, this time snatching pennants from the top (Finnie's, blue, Sky's, black) only to end having to jump another fence.

His bride, Drakkar noted, was taking to her Raider Horse Maneuvers far quicker than she had archery or daggers, and he knew why. First, she had experience on a mount. Second, she was fearless. The speed, the maneuvering, her position in the saddle nor the jumps fazed her. She faced it all unblinking and drove herself to excel. Horsemanship was part skill, part finesse and part daring, and she had the latter of those in abundance.

That said, she was beginning to excel at archery, having achieved three more direct bullseyes. Therefore, Annar had advanced her to stalking young, male servants who volunteered to wear padded cloaks and tripled wool caps and were set to skulking through a local forest where Finnie would, if she found them, shoot at them with arrows that had no points but instead pads wadded with cotton. Her volunteers, Annar reported, enjoyed this tremendously, looking on it as a game even when Finnie's arrow found its unharmed target. This was because, Annar told him, Finnie made it a game.

She was, also according to Annar, excelling at that too.

Although proud of his wife, Drakkar couldn't contain a sense of amused disquiet that she seemed so determined to gather all the skills required of a Raider.

It would be good when she fell pregnant with his child. This, he hoped, would turn her mind from adventuring with him and his men, something he was getting the not-so-vague sense she was intent on doing, to caring for herself and their child.

Drakkar watched as Finnie re-jumped the fence and wound through the seven obstacles, missing only two pennants as Sky followed her much slower while missing five of his and one of the ones he'd gained, he dropped.

"Finnie takes to this Frey," Max muttered, his focus on Finnie who had jumped the last fence and reined Caspia in to trot over to where Sky was atop his mount, shoulders slumped having given up in his dejection therefore he pulled back on his horse and did not make the final jump. "Gun will have to increase her challenge soon," Max finished.

"He will," Thad concurred. "But Sky is nowhere near equaling her and she'll not advance until Sky can advance with her."

Drakkar watched as Gun cantered to his wife and the boy, and both started speaking with Sky who was obviously dissatisfied with his performance.

Thad was right. There was no hope of Finnie leaving Sky behind which Drakkar thought was good. She needed to slow. They were leaving for Kellshorn on the morrow but would likely stay there no longer than they had Snowdon. The summer thaw had already begun, and the resulting waters favored by the well-to-do throughout the Northlands would be bottled. And every year at the thaw, all of Drakkar's ships were loaded to capacity with Lunwyn water and then set sail to Middleland, Bellebryn, Hawkvale and Fleuridia where they sold for ridiculous prices and were, by far, his most lucrative payload regardless of the fact they were simply water.

Therefore, he would need to be in Sudvic to assist Kell managing this as well as discuss with his captains what their cargo holds would be filled with on their return. He and Finnie would then board *The Finnie* for Fleuridia, and he didn't want Finnie's head filled with new adventures and training for them when their course was set simply to unload water on Fleuridia.

He wanted Finnie's head filled with what she'd name their child and how they would be raising him.

And as his bride trained to become the Raider Drakkar was never going to permit her to be, Drakkar was putting a fair amount of effort into siring the child that would slow her down.

He heard hoof beats in the snow behind him, turned to see Oleg heading their way and tensed.

Outside the execution, their time in Snowdon had been good. Finnie enjoyed the city even more than Bellebryn or Hawkvale, and when she wasn't with him, training or tutoring Sky, she was holed up with her girls giggling or she was in the city with her mother shopping, eating in restaurants and partaking in copious pastry sampling at cafés.

He had, unfortunately, been called to duty to see two plays with her. One which he fell asleep during only to have Finnie prod him very hard in the ribs waking him in time to hear her burst out laughing which caused the patrons close to the royal box to glare at them. This made Drakkar laugh and Finnie laugh more.

His talk with Hernod Grieg had garnered no more than what Quincy and Balthazar had learned, and he'd unfortunately had no time to get creative. Grieg was adamant he was the man behind the plot and his desire, he said, was to unite Lunwyn and Middleland as they should never have been separated by King Halldor.

Drakkar could not argue with this, though, obviously, he would never consider assassination, which was a coward's play, not to mention in the present circumstances, the target was his wife.

And he knew there was a not small faction of Lunwynians and Middle-landians who agreed that Lunwyn should never have been split. Those in Middleland were not fond of Baldur as their king and those in Lunwyn were displeased with losing the land granted to Baldur. Not to mention citizens of both countries had been parted from family members who were forced to live in different borders by Halldor's decision, which was arguably fair to his sons but not-so-arguably unfair to his people.

Even though Atticus and Baldur had assumed their thrones at very young ages, the decades passing had not changed these sentiments.

Atticus had made two attempts through his reign to affect some kind of compromise with Baldur in an effort to settle this ongoing dissatisfaction. Both attempts were offers to build an alliance between nations including providing all in both countries with dual citizenship and uniting their taxes, treasuries and currency.

But Baldur would not hear of it.

This was likely because his taxes were high, they were expected in gold, silver or copper, but his treasury printed currency he expected his citizens to use on anything not tax-related. He printed this at vast amounts beyond what was held in his country's coffers making the printed tender mostly useless but Baldur extortionately wealthy.

His people were, with reason, restless, and if Atticus, or King Ludlum of Hawkvale and his son Prince Noctorno, who ruled Bellebryn, were different kinds of rulers, this would make Middleland ripe for invasion.

Unfortunately, they were not.

With this, Drakkar knew there was unrest, but Finnie being a target of that made little sense and in fact seemed counterproductive, unless Baldur or the leader of a House wishing to take the throne as his own was really behind the plot.

Further, Grieg was ruled by coin, not patriotism, and would not be moved to act in a manner that courted, and indeed had ended in his execution unless there was something exceptional in it for him.

However, whatever that was he'd gone to his noose without sharing it.

Therefore, Drakkar did not feel Finnie was safe yet.

Quincy and Balthazar agreed with Drakkar, and Quincy remained behind to continue to dig locally because both were suspicious of Grieg's quick trial and his being scheduled to hang with Viola and Enger. Enger and Viola were both only pawns whereas Grieg was clearly a player, and more time should have been allowed to glean information from the man.

Drakkar had learned this push had not been instigated by Atticus but pressed by Frey's father, the head of the Houses of Drakkar (with the excuse that Finnie was a Drakkar and they wanted immediate retribution).

It was backed by the Houses of Lazarus and Ravenscroft (who also both claimed Finnie as their own, for their blood, they thought, flowed in her veins and this was true with Sjofn as Aurora was of both Houses).

But it was also pressed by Apollo, the young head of the House of Ulfr and Drakkar's cousin, for Ulfr was his grandmother, Eugenie's House. Apollo's reasoning was that he felt Baldur was clearly behind the plot and their act of reprisal should be swift in order to deter future attempts on Finnie's life.

This was not surprising.

Drakkar knew Apollo well, liked and respected him and he knew his cousin returned these sentiments.

But he also knew his cousin was most assuredly not a man to cross, and for Lunwyn, and his cousin, Apollo would demand vengeance and would be immensely displeased and not afraid to show it in ways no one wished to court should his demand go unheeded. Considering the power, influence and wealth of the House of Ulfr was only rivaled by the House of Wilde and Drakkar's personal wealth and influence, Atticus bowed to Apollo, and the pressures of the further familial Houses of Lazarus, Ravenscroft and Drakkar.

It was annoying but it was understandable, and Quincy, so far, had not uncovered any nefarious reasons behind Grieg's swift dispatch.

Balthazar had not remained behind but gone forth to see if further information could be gathered to refute Grieg's claims that he was the mastermind. However, the three messages he'd sent Drakkar since his and Finnie's return to Lunwyn had shared that Balthazar's endeavors had not yet borne fruit.

And now, taking in Oleg's expression as he reined in his horse next to their grouping, Drakkar did not think it boded well. Oleg had few expressions and this one was not one of the even fewer good ones.

Oleg did not hesitate to share his news and announced on a grunt, "Valeria and Franka Drakkar are at the Keep awaiting you to attend them."

Instantly, Drakkar's mouth got tight.

He'd been informed his mother had arrived at her mansion in Snowdon two days earlier. He did not visit her, and she did not send official word she was in the city. He was hoping she was there to shop. Now he knew she was awaiting Franka, as this was the first word he'd received that his cousin was close and it was highly likely she'd just arrived.

He nodded, jerked his chin to Thad and Max, walked to Tyr and mounted. He raised his hand to Finnie who was watching his movements. She waved in return, her smile for him sunny even though he knew she was distracted, and he knew this because she almost immediately tilted her head back to Skylar after she waved. Then he and Oleg galloped into Snowdon, through the city and to the Keep. He dismounted at the fountain, tossed Tyr's reins to a waiting boy and walked swiftly up the ice marble steps and into the castle.

A servant girl was hovering and approached him the moment he entered.

"Queen Aurora is entertaining the Ladies Drakkar in the state drawing room," she informed him, and Frey nodded.

Aurora had intervened and Drakkar found, as he had been discovering more and more every day the last two weeks as he watched her with his wife, that he quite liked his mother-in-law.

He moved away from the girl and walked to the state drawing room, an official room that was elegant but large, cold and never used when it was simply family.

A statement.

Aurora didn't like the surprise visit and was not afraid to let that be known. She was also happy for Finnie to show allegiance to the Drakkars by encouraging her to wear their House red. But she was not happy with how Finnie was treated by his father and mother at the Gales. Her stamping this visit as official and not familial was her way of showing that.

Yes, he was definitely coming to like his mother-in-law.

He opened the door and walked through to see both his mother and cousin outfitted resplendently, Franka's layering of jewels bordering on ostentatious, his mother's well past that. Aurora, her clothing stylish and refined, her manner graceful, next to the displays of the two other women still looked a pauper.

All of the women's heads turned to him the moment he arrived, Valeria's face lighting with faux delight, Franka's lips curling for reasons unknown and Aurora's expression benign but unreadable.

"Son!" Valeria exclaimed while standing and Drakkar closed the door and walked fully into the room.

"Let's dispense with the artificial sincerity," he stated without delay. "And instead let us get to why you both are here."

Darkness instantly swept his mother's features and Drakkar found that much easier to bear for it was nearly all he'd known of her when he was a child.

"Really, Frey," Valeria snapped. "Minstrels are singing and mothers are setting their daughters to bed with stories of The Handsome Drakkar and his deep adoration for his Beautiful Winter Bride. It's been months since I've seen you and your lovely wife, and you do not allow your mother a moment to bask in the glow of her son's extreme happiness?"

Drakkar stopped, crossed his arms on his chest and leveled his gaze on his mother.

"Prior to the Gales, and of course your attendance at my wedding, at which we did not converse, I had not seen you for over a year, and when I did, it was in passing. You made no overtures to me for years prior to that, and the only one I made to you since I was thirteen was inviting you to my marriage ceremony. And it wasn't me who did that but Queen Aurora's secretary. You're not here to bask in the glow of anything. So, let's dispense with this farce and tell me why you actually *are* here."

Valeria glared at her son and then she sat back down.

"Well, for me, though you didn't ask, dear cousin, I'm looking after my throat," Franka put in at this point, and Drakkar's eyes went to her as he steeled himself against showing a reaction to her announcement.

"You have news," he stated blandly.

"Indeed," she inclined her head and leaned forward to the table that held a coffee service, china and a bowl of candies. Controlled and calculated, as was her way, Franka took her time selecting a white candy-coated almond and popped it in her mouth, chewed and swallowed under Drakkar's impatient stare before she spoke again. "Baldur is away to the Southlands with thirty thousand men."

Drakkar noted that Aurora didn't move a muscle at this extraordinary news, though she could not know it for he knew Atticus told her everything and the king also told *him* everything. Drakkar didn't move a muscle either except to raise his brows.

"This interests me because...?" he prompted.

"You may..." she paused, studying him closely, "or may not know that Baldur had a plaything. A delightful specimen called Circe." At these words, Drakkar continued to regard her impassively but fought against clenching his teeth. "A powerful sorceress, but unfortunately for the lovely Circe,

Baldur had found a nearly equally powerful witch to bind her powers so she could not use them to harm him or to escape him. Unfortunately for the revolting Baldur, he wasn't shrewd enough to bind her to him so she could not find *others* to assist her to escape him. And this she did some months ago."

"I was called here for you to tell me tales of King Baldur?" Drakkar asked skeptically.

"No," Franka answered. "You were called here because Circe has been sighted and Baldur is off to collect her."

Again, Drakkar raised his brows instead of clenching his teeth.

He had not spent a great deal of time with the sorceress Circe, but the time he had, he liked her. Baldur had callously mistreated her for years, imprisoned her, used her in a variety of repugnant ways, and through all that, by what had to be a miracle, she'd somehow retained her dignity. Even as four earlier escape attempts were thwarted, and Baldur punished her for each in ways it didn't bear thinking of.

It was not good news she had been sighted and worse news that her sighting had reached Baldur's ears.

Drakkar had a feeling he would not be taking his bride to his lodge in Kellshorn or loading *The Finnie's* cargo holds with Lunwynian water and onward to Fleuridia but instead sailing directly to the Southlands.

But at this point, he had to learn more without letting on he cared.

Therefore, he said with feigned resignation, "Again, Franka, I'm uncertain why you're imparting this information on me."

"The lovely but unlucky Circe has clearly had a misadventure since her escape and it has led to her being included in the Korwahk Wife Hunt," Franka replied.

Drakkar stared indifferently at his cousin.

But he thought, *Bloody hell.*

The Korwahk Wife Hunt was well known, and although it had been happening for centuries in Korwahk, it was considered a savage ritual outside the Southlands.

Local women hunted by the Korwahk warriors felt honored to be chosen for this hunt. But those women not of the Southlands who were scouted, kidnapped and included in the hunt most definitely did not feel the same.

As they wouldn't, considering participation in the hunt meant they were paraded in front of the warriors, let loose, then hunted and "claimed" as wives. In other words, the moment they were captured, they were raped.

After what Circe had already endured, Drakkar was dismayed to hear she'd now endured this.

Franka continued, "And, word is, she caught the eye of their king. He's claimed her and made her his queen. The word is, after doing so, he declared great pride at her courageous nature and immense satisfaction with her astonishing beauty."

At that, Drakkar relaxed.

He had been to the Southlands—to trade not to raid. He knew a number of Korwahk merchants and had met several Korwahk Horde warriors.

He did not know Lahn, the king of Korwahk, but he knew much of him. Although Circe would likely find adjusting to her new life an ordeal, it was not unheard of, in fact it was frequent for women even outside the Southlands to adjust to their lives with their warriors. So far as enjoying them and considering themselves Korwahk.

King Lahn was greatly admired by his people, known to have honor, and any bride he chose would undoubtedly be equally admired.

Not to mention he had great wealth, which it was known warriors showered on their brides. If his people felt him honorable, and he had declared satisfaction with her, Drakkar hoped he would behave as such with his new bride.

And, lastly, there was absolutely no chance Baldur would succeed in retrieving his sorceress. The Korwahk Horde of warriors was renowned for their protection of their people, their nation, its vast wealth, but most especially of their wives. King Lahn being, if word was true, by far the mightiest of a celebrated horde of exceptionally skilled and strong warriors, he would make short work of Baldur if he even tried.

"Franka, I'm losing patience," Drakkar warned.

She examined him a moment, he knew she read nothing, and finally continued, "This makes Middleland vulnerable."

"Yes," Drakkar agreed. "Any ruler foolish enough to leave his land and take thirty thousand of his soldiers with him on a personal errand that has no hope of succeeding would leave that land vulnerable. What I'd like to understand is why you think I'd care?"

"Because," she replied instantly, "leaving his land doesn't only make it vulnerable to others, such as Ludlum and Noctorno, who may still be smarting after Baldur's invasions of years ago, regardless that Noctorno has resecured the lands Baldur wrested from them. But because his leaving his land makes it vulnerable to those *inside* Middleland who may be weary of Baldur's rule and preparing to do something about it."

Aurora entered the conversation at this point with, "Staunch Lunwynians in Middleland moving to reunite our two countries?"

Valeria looked to her queen and answered for Franka. "No, my queen, staunch *Middlelandians* moving to reunite our two countries."

It was at that that Drakkar's body grew tight and he demanded, "Explain."

His mother looked to him. "Who would, my son, outside Baldur, gain the most from your new bride being dead?"

Drakkar held her eyes.

Broderick.

Bloody, *bloody* hell.

Broderick.

Drakkar moved his gaze to Aurora and when he did, he saw her eyes on him and her mouth was tight.

"It is rather unfortunate," Franka noted while sitting back against the couch, "that Prince Broderick and his lover have recently discovered they've been robbed of something they held quite dear. It has come to my attention that the young Phobin is most annoyed he's lost this cherished article, and everyone knows when Phobin is displeased, Broderick is."

Bloody, bloody hell.

"Broderick holds great affection for his cousin. He would never—" Aurora started but Valeria interrupted her.

"Affection gets lost when land, power and coin are in the balance."

His mother spoke the truth as she definitely understood it.

She looked to her son.

"Everyone knows Baldur got the short end of the stick when King Halldor split Lunwyn. Regardless of our ice, the bounty lies within Lunwyn's borders and Middleland is but a bunch of rock and sparse vegetation, none of which is useful except that which butts Hawkvale. It is so desolate, even when the land was Lunwyn, the elves refused to tread there."

"Yes," Drakkar agreed. "But that which butts Hawkvale is exceptionally fertile and the rock you disdain, if forged, makes arrowheads coveted even in the Southlands. And under that rock is an abundance of coal, which, if mined for the country and not to line Baldur's coffers, would make the nation rich. Broderick isn't greedy and reckless as his father is and could easily capitalize on these to bring prosperity to his people rather than increase his personal treasury. If he were to do this, he wouldn't need Lunwyn."

"Perhaps you should petition to be his advisor, dear Frey, rather than

Phobin," Franka suggested on a distastefully catty curve of her lips making her implication clear.

And with that, Drakkar was done and therefore demanded, "Let us dispense with this play and talk straight. Do you know that Broderick is plotting against Seoafin?"

Franka shook her head but responded, "I know that Hernod Grieg, prior to his recent untimely demise, traded exclusively with Middleland. I know he was there almost more than he was here, though I don't know who he consorted with when he was. But one can guess. And I know that his final words were 'Unite Lunwyn,' which could have been called true or could have been a final attempt to cast suspicion off those who truly are behind the schemes to do away with the princess who will birth our future king."

"So you're piecing this together through conjecture?" Drakkar asked and Franka shook her head again.

"The story of Circe and Baldur's departure is true. The information that a valuable asset held by Phobin was purloined is also true, as is the fact they are both angry about it. The rest, indeed, my dear cousin," she inclined her head, "is, as you say, conjecture."

He studied his cousin then his mother.

It was conjecture but good conjecture and important information. If Broderick were to wish to move on his father, now would be the time. And if he would wish to gain momentum for this campaign and earn the loyalty of those who wished to see Middleland reunited with Lunwyn, time would be of the essence.

Without Finnie, Lunwyn would eventually fall in Broderick's hands and that would be far sooner if he only needed to await the death of Atticus, not both brothers, if he were to move on his father's throne now. It would only be a matter of course, and one which would be supported by many in both countries, enough for them to be moved to pick up arms, for Broderick to move against Atticus. In so doing, securing both thrones, reuniting Lunwyn, and with Finnie out of the way, doing so without direct competition for rule. Hell, half of the Houses of Lunwyn would bear arms to unite it again with Middleland.

Bloody *hell*.

Not to mention, Phobin might not be clever, but Broderick was no fool. He would piece together Drakkar and his men being in Middleland at the time the adela bough was stolen and this would only add fuel to their fire.

Bloody *hell*.

He pulled in a breath in an effort to prepare to say something he meant but didn't wish to say and let it out, muttering, "Although conjecture, I am grateful for your time and the information you shared."

Valeria's brows went up, and without hesitation, she inquired, "Grateful enough that, upon return from delivering Lunwyn's waters through the Northlands, you'd share the profits of a galleon? Say..." she hesitated, "half?"

Drakkar stared at his mother before he asked back, "So, you're here for coin and not your concern about your daughter-in-law, a woman your first-born son has come to care for deeply who also happens to be your Winter Princess and the future mother to your king?"

"Well, Frey, if you put it like that it sounds positively dire," Franka murmured through a small smile.

"I apologize. I didn't mean it to sound dire. I meant it to sound disbe-lieving and snide," Drakkar replied, and Franka's smile got bigger, so she pulled in her lips and bit them to hide it, an effort that didn't succeed just as she intended.

His mother's already hard eyes grew harder. "I see, my son, you do not change."

"I am a Drakkar," he retorted. "This cannot be a surprise. Especially considering the fact that you have exposed you have not changed as well as you expect payment *at all* much less the amount you do for aiding my efforts to do something as crucial, not only for our country, but to my happiness, as keeping my wife alive."

Valeria opened her mouth to speak, but Aurora got there before her.

"I see there are family issues here that are unlikely, even with a great deal of discourse, to be resolved at the present time." Drakkar and Valeria looked to their queen as she went on, "Drakkar has expressed his gratitude verbally. I would like to express mine too, and you will both receive a gift selected personally by your queen delivered to Valeria's home on the morrow. You can rest assured, although not the worth of half the profits of a galleon filled with Lunwynian waters, you will not be disappointed, as my gift will indicate just how grateful I feel that, for whatever reasons, you have come forward to aid my daughter, my country's princess and the mother of our future king."

Both women, with nothing for it, shut their mouths and inclined their heads to Aurora.

Yes, it was now certain. Drakkar quite liked his mother-in-law.

"Now," Aurora began while standing, forcing both women to stand too. "My daughter soon will be home. She and Frey leave on the morrow, and she and I have plans this afternoon to go skating in Ulfr Park. I'm keen to spend as much time with her as I can before I again lose her and Frey to their adventures so..." she trailed off, extending her hand to the door.

Valeria and Franka took the hint and started moving that way.

Drakkar stayed where he was as Aurora guided them to and through the door then deposited them in a hovering servant's hands with murmured words of farewell that he was not about to offer. She then moved back into the room, closing the door and coming directly to him.

And he knew he had her trust when she dropped her mask long enough to snap, "I am sorry if you find this offensive, my new son, but your family is repugnant."

Drakkar bit back laughter before he replied, "I don't, Aurora, find that the least offensive for it is unfortunately true."

Her eyes held his, he saw hers light as her lips twitched then she regained control of her features and spoke on.

"Franka knows of the adela branch," she noted.

"This is not surprising. As I told you and Atticus, *The Finnie* was detected, Baldur forced a confrontation and Broderick clearly put two and two together. But either he, or more likely Phobin, was not smart enough to keep his mouth shut about it."

Aurora nodded then she said softly, "I see their point, though it is stolen from Lunwyn and known to be sought after, so they had to know, if they didn't guard it closely, it would be detected and returned to its rightful land." Her eyes on him grew intense. "But, Drakkar, I've known Broderick since he was born. He has far more of his mother in him than he does his father. He adores Finnie. He always has. I can't imagine, even for power and coin—"

Drakkar cut her off. "He was soft with her during our conversation with him and his father and this appeared genuine." Aurora nodded but Drakkar went on, "He was soft with her, Aurora, but I noted as did a number of my men that Phobin couldn't take his eyes off her and we both know he was not admiring her beauty." Aurora eyes flashed quickly before she nodded again. "And Phobin, it is told, has Broderick spellbound. He shows Prince Broderick one face, others an entirely different one."

Aurora nodded again and whispered, "We should look into Phobin."

Drakkar returned her nod and replied, "I will send a message to Balthazar." Then he noted, "However, we may not need to concern ourselves with this. If Ludlum and especially Noctorno hear that Middleland is vulnerable—"

385

Aurora interrupted him. "Word from Bellebryn is that Noctorno has reconciled with his wife."

Drakkar couldn't stop his blink at this news for he knew Tor very well. They were friends, he held him in high regard and Drakkar knew Tor detested his wife regardless of the fact she was destined for him. It had been written in the sky at each of their births by the She-God of their land.

They'd been married for some time, Drakkar was even at their wedding, and Tor's wife was exceptionally beautiful but visibly cold and nothing about her manner would be something that attracted Tor. They had spent just enough time together to consummate the union and lived separate lives since, with Tor not keen to change that.

"We were, as you may not have known," Aurora continued, "scheduled to journey to Hawkvale for Prince Noctorno's brother's wedding, but we had to cancel due to the situation with Finnie and then the imminent executions. We have heard since that, for reasons I do not know, that wedding has been postponed. But in the meantime, Noctorno has reconciled with his wife and installed her in his castle in Bellebryn."

"Interesting," Drakkar muttered.

"Indeed," Aurora replied. "And it is known he is actively working on siring an heir to Bellebryn and Hawkvale."

Drakkar grinned and Aurora's lips again twitched.

Drakkar's grin faded and he asked, "Is it known if he is happy?"

She shook her head but said, "It is known that Princess Cora is much changed, and she is the talk of Bellebryn and Hawkvale. Enough for that talk to make it here. They are calling her Cora, the Gracious."

Drakkar found that difficult to believe. She had been known as Cora, the Exquisite, for her beauty. During his brief meeting with her at her wedding to his friend, however, she was far from gracious.

"So, I suppose the answer to your question is, yes," Aurora carried on. "It is said he is greatly taken with her...finally."

Drakkar nodded.

Aurora kept speaking. "It is also known that *you* are actively working on siring an heir."

Drakkar's grin came back but Aurora simply regarded him closely.

"Is there aught to report with that?" she asked.

"Not yet, but soon, my queen, I hope Finnie and I will have good news."

Her eyes softened and her lips tipped up before she shared on a whisper, "I watch her with your boy, Skylar. She will make a good mother, my new son."

"Yes," Drakkar stated. "She will."

She lifted a hand and touched his arm lightly before dropping it and saying softly, "I await your good news."

"And I look forward to imparting it," Drakkar returned softly and at that, the door flew open, and Finnie rushed in, cheeks flushed, eyes bright, smile firm on her face.

She skidded to a halt several steps in, shared her smile with both of them then her eyes fixed on her mother, and she cried, "Let's...go...*skating!*"

Bloody hell, his bride hadn't even taken off her cloak from riding obstacles on her new horse and she was ready to go off on her next escapade.

He studied her bright eyes and pink cheeks, thinking, *By the gods, I love this woman.*

Then he crossed his arms on his chest and stated, "Before you're off to break your ankle, wife, your husband will take a kiss."

She moved to him swiftly, replying, "I'm not going to break my ankle, Frey."

"Sprain it then," he returned as she made it to him, curled her fingers around his forearm and leaned her body into his.

"Not that either," she retorted.

"Gods, don't give yourself delirium by falling on your head," he implored and she giggled and got up on her toes.

"I'll not be doing that either. I'm a good skater," she informed him.

"And you've done this before?" he asked.

"Yes, twice, with my parents when I was young," she answered.

"You're not young anymore, Finnie," he pointed out.

"Well, I'm not gray, blind, crippled and doddering, either," she shot back and he grinned.

Then he murmured, "Kiss," and bent his head to hers to assist her.

She accepted his offer, pressing her mouth to his and opening hers before they touched tongues, and when they did, Drakkar not only tasted her, he felt the beauty of her taste right down to his blood.

He lifted his head and whispered, "Have fun, wee one."

She smiled up at him and whispered back, "I will, handsome husband. I always do."

Yes, that was his wee Finnie. She always did.

She squeezed his arm, turned to her mother, wrapped her hands around her mother's arm and guided her out of the room, their heads bent together.

Frey looked to Gunner, Max and Thad as they stood just outside the door and jerked his chin to them. They nodded and followed Finnie and Aurora.

He pulled in a deep breath, let it out and went to find Ruben who would procure a trusted messenger to send off to Balthazar with this latest news and further instruction.

28

THE GLOW OF THE ADELA TREE

"Wee one, wake." I heard Frey whisper in my ear, his big hand warm on my hip.

My eyes slowly opened, and I saw darkness cut with only weak candlelight.

I rolled to my back to see he was out of bed but sitting on the side of it fully clothed and I felt my body go instantly tight.

"What's wrong?" I whispered.

"Nothing, my love." His hand, now at my belly, pressed lightly. "I've a message from the Elves. I thought you'd wish to accompany me."

I stared at him only a second before I was out of bed faster than lightning.

I was rummaging through the wardrobe when I heard Frey say, "I'll take this as a yes."

"Totally," I told the wardrobe then felt his hands at my hips, his lips touch my shoulder before they came to my ear.

"I'll saddle Tyr and bring him 'round front. I'll meet you there when you're ready."

I nodded at the wardrobe and pulled out a cream woolen dress.

Frey left the room.

I dressed as fast as I could considering how many clothes I needed to wear and how difficult the underwear was to strap on. Finished with that, I pulled on a cream wool cloak with a curly-furred collar, a cream knit cap that fit snug and bunched all my hair out at the sides and cream leather gloves and dashed out into the hall.

As it was the dead of night and no footmen were around, it took a bit of effort to get the front doors of the Keep opened and then closed again. But when I did, I turned and saw Frey was waiting for me at the foot of the steps with Thad, Orion and Ruben.

I rushed down the steps straight to Frey with only quick smiles at the guys. The moment I was close enough, he bent to the side in the saddle, his arm curved around me, and he lifted me up in front of him. I settled my ass in his groin as his arm tightened around my ribs.

He leaned us both forward, touched his heels to Tyr's flanks and shouted, "*Yah!*"

And off we went to visit the elves.

～

WE RODE WELL out of Snowdon and well into a forest because Frey told me the elfin messengers would come to him but whatever message there was to be delivered would be delivered at an adela tree.

So, bonus, I was going to get to see an adela tree.

As we raced through the forest, I was seeing I needed way more practice on Caspia as Frey and his men snaked at a full gallop through the trees, sometimes coming so close I could feel the wind as we whizzed by them. And all the boys, as far as I could tell, did this without hesitation using nothing but instinct.

It was super cool.

I saw it before we hit it, the opaque mist that looked like dense, glittering fog that shrouded the dark trees, and I noticed we were heading right to it. But as we got close, Ruben, Thad and Orion pulled back. The minute we penetrated the mist, the men were left behind.

"What—?" I started, twisting and looking around Frey to see the hazy figures of the men on their mounts quickly receding.

"The mist is created by the elves, wee one," Frey told me, and I looked up at him. "Only I can penetrate it...and you as you're with me."

Wow. Cool.

I looked forward, my heart beating that familiar excited beat, my blood singing through my veins. This only increased when I saw the beginnings of a golden glow that pierced the fog. It increased further as we rode into a glow that was becoming brighter and more intense until we were suddenly there.

The adela tree.

And it was *magnificent.*

Not tall, its thin, twirly-ended branches rising direct from the earth for the tree had no trunk. Even though it wasn't tall, it was wide, its thousands of thin branches growing up and out. And its bark glittered bright and golden, lighting the large clearing around it almost like it was daylight. Except it was cooler, more fan-freaking-tastic daylight.

And if that wasn't awesome enough, with an ice-blue flash and a bright-white spark, mini elves were appearing from what seemed like straight out of the earth at the base of the tree's stump. Once they formed, they immediately turned, touched a glittering branch and grew to the size of a normal human right...in front...*of my eyes.*

Unbelievably *cool.*

As I watched, Frey halted Tyr at the outer edge of the clearing and dismounted, pulling me down and setting me on my feet beside Tyr.

"Stay here, Finnie, yes?" he said quietly.

I tore my eyes away from the elves, now numbering six with more flashes and sparks coming from the tree, all of the elves regarding us with ice-blue eyes filled with curiosity under their feathered caps. I looked up at him and nodded mutely.

He grinned at me and turned to Tyr.

"Stay with Finnie," he ordered.

Tyr's strong, sleek jaw rose up and he whinnied softly.

Frey moved into the clearing and directly to a male elf who gave Frey the elfin salute of chin bent to the side of his neck. Once he lifted his head, they started talking quietly so I couldn't hear what they were saying, and the flashes and sparks stopped coming. I counted nine elves and none except the male talking to Frey was looking at Frey. They were all looking at me.

I smiled and waved.

When I did, there seemed to be a low, cheerful twitter that filled the air although none of them spoke nor did their lips move. They looked amongst each other and then back at me. That was when I got smiles.

Through this, Frey continued to speak with the male elf, and I saw that the discussion was intense, but I wasn't reading bad vibes from Frey. This reading proved accurate when suddenly they stopped speaking and both Frey and the elf turned to look at me.

And when they did, Frey smiled, broad and white, and my heart stuttered at the sight.

My husband didn't hide his smiles from me, but I'd never seen one like that.

Never like that.

Ever.

It was gorgeous.

He tipped his chin at me and gave me a flick of his hand, which told me I could approach. Without delay, I did, quickly, making it to his side with Tyr at mine in a second.

When I arrived, Frey's arm curled round my waist and he pulled me close to his side before he said softly, "My wee Finnie, it is my honor to present you to Nillen, Speaker of the Elves."

I looked from Frey to Nillen, who was my height, and I smiled before whispering, "And it is my honor to meet you, Nillen, Speaker of the Elves."

Nillen smiled back and replied, "The honor is mine, Seoafin of the other world, bride of our Frey."

I inclined my head like Mother would and told him softly, "Thank you for allowing me to come."

"It was our pleasure, Seoafin, Ice Bride," he returned just as softly and went on, "And we do hope you are present when there are future joyful messages we will share with our lord Frey."

Joyful messages.

Cool.

It was good news.

This pleased me. With all that was going on, we could use good news.

"I do too," I agreed not knowing what the message was but not caring. Anything that made Frey smile like that was totally okay with me.

He inclined his head to me then looked to Frey and stated, "We return to our realm now in order that you can celebrate with your Ice Bride."

Celebrate?

Apparently, whatever the news was, it *was* joyful.

Awesome.

"Of course," Frey murmured.

Nillen gave him another elfin salute. Frey lifted his chin to him then looked around at the other elves all of whom gave him a salute. They then all smiled happily at me before they all slowly drifted back to the tree, bent low to touch its bark where it met the earth and disappeared with an ice-blue flash and a white spark.

When the last disappeared, I stared at the glowing tree and whispered, "That is *so cool.*"

I barely got the words out before I suddenly moved, and it wasn't me who moved me. One of Frey's strong arms came tight around my waist dragging me up his body just like he did during our wedding kiss, but this time higher, so I was head and shoulders over him. His other arm closed around my thighs just below my bottom.

Automatically, I grabbed on to his shoulders and looked down as he twirled us around twice, his head back, his eyes on mine, that broad, gorgeous smile on his face.

"Frey," I said softly, mesmerized by that smile. I moved one hand to his cheek, "What on—?"

But I didn't get the rest out. His arm at my thighs disappeared. He dropped me down a foot and his hand cupped the back of my head, pulling it toward him, crushing my mouth to his, and he kissed me, hard, deep, wet, long and, last but oh so not least...*wonderful.*

When he was done, he moved my head to shove my face in his neck and held me against him, feet dangling in the air, arms tight, and he did this for a while.

My arms had curled around his shoulders, my heart was still beating hard from the kiss, my breath coming harder, but I turned my head so my lips were at his ear and I asked, "Frey, what's going on?"

His head turned too so his mouth was at my ear, and he answered, "The message of the elves, my winter bride, is that you carry my child."

I blinked at his neck as I felt my belly drop.

What?

"What?" I whispered.

The pressure of his hand at my head lightened. I lifted it up and looked at him to see he was still smiling that beautiful, joyous smile.

"You carry my child, Finnie," he whispered in return, pressing my head to his again for a soft touch of lips then he slid me down his body to my feet, but he didn't remove his arms. In fact, they squeezed me hard as I saw by the glow of the adela tree his eyes were warm, soft and lit with a blissful light that, no other way to put it, was utterly enthralling. "You carry my child, and the elves did not tell me but I know down to my blood that if he is boy, we will teach him to be a strong, fair ruler, and if she is girl, she has no hope to have anything other than the tremendous beauty of her mother."

At his words, my belly did a somersault then melted.

Okay, well. Shit.

A lot was happening here. *A lot.*

One was that it was coming to me that I hadn't had a period since Hawkvale and, until that moment, I hadn't even noticed. Now, obviously, I did. So, weirdly, elfin pregnancy detection, it would seem, was accurate.

Two was that powder the girls had given me wasn't as foolproof as they said it was. That was now abundantly clear.

Three was that I did not want to have a baby, not now. Yes, I wanted to have Frey's child, absolutely. In fact, I wanted us to have more than one. But I also wanted to wait awhile, say, after I knew that my future in Lunwyn was secured, I'd traveled back to take care of business at home and after I'd had a few adventures with Frey and his boys.

Obviously, this wasn't going to happen.

Four was, equally obviously, Frey was freaking ecstatic about this news. This meant that he not only loved me, he was happy as all get out I was carrying his child and he couldn't possibly wish to let me go in six months. No way.

Which meant I was staying.

I already knew this, what with him loving me, and the way he did, but it was way nice having this confirmed.

Which led me to five. And that was that if this made Frey this happy, even though it was too early for me, I couldn't help but share his joy.

So we were going to start a family early. Who cared? We were going to start a family. I hadn't had a family in fifteen years, and now I had one, and not only that, it was getting bigger.

And I was staying.

It was clear that I was going nowhere, and if I'd thought about it logically, I knew that already not only with the way Frey was with me but also Aurora and Atticus. The decision had been made by The Drakkar. This was my family. This was my life, my world and looking up at my husband's handsome, ecstatically happy face, I knew I'd shot past bliss and was exploring new heights on that end of the happy scale.

I slid a hand around his neck to his jaw where I glided a thumb out to touch his smiling lips as my eyes watched.

Then I moved my gaze to his and I whispered, "I've never seen you this happy."

Instantly, Frey whispered back, "This is because I've never been this happy."

My body melted into his and I kept whispering. "Really?"

His arms gave me another squeeze and he, too, kept whispering. "Really, my wee Finnie. These past months with you, I have thought there is nothing more beautiful than my wife. Now, I know this is wrong. There is. And that is my wife carrying our child, a child which will herald the beginning of our family."

Family.

Oh yeah. *Family.*

I liked that.

I pressed my lips together to bite back the sting of tears in my eyes and then I pressed my cheek to his chest and my body to his. When I did, Frey held me closer, and I felt his jaw against the top of my knit cap.

"Love you, baby," I said against his chest, got another squeeze of his arms, and he replied, "And I you, my Finnie."

I pulled in a breath and tipped my head back again to look at him.

Then I asked haltingly, "Do you think, um...that Mother and Father will, uh...be happy about this too?"

He smiled that gorgeous smile again, dipped his head to touch his lips to my nose and pulled back an inch before he answered, "Just today Aurora asked how we were getting on with creating the heir to the throne. She awaits good news, and tomorrow, we will delay our departure so we can have a celebratory breakfast with them before we go." He gave me another squeeze as I felt my brows draw together, and he finished, "She and Atticus will be delighted."

Okay, the good news about that was, I was right. Atticus and Aurora were also obviously already on board with me taking their daughter's place.

The bad-ish news was that I didn't think Frey and I had been trying to create the heir to the throne, not yet. But his words would indicate *he* did.

Or maybe just Aurora did.

I had no opportunity to think on this as Frey gave me another squeeze and his head dipped, his lips touched mine then slid down my cheek to my ear where he murmured, "It is now time to get my wife and child home and warm. I could stand in the glow of the adela and the brighter glow of this news for a decade, my wee one, but I must take care of my family."

My belly somersaulted again, and I twisted my neck to look at him.

When I caught his eyes, I smiled and said, "Living in Lunwyn, he or she is going to have to get used to the cold, husband."

To which Frey returned, "As they'll have to get used to their parents' loving care, wife."

Okay, there it was again, another belly somersault and I couldn't stop the huge smile that spread on my face.

When Frey saw it, his hand cupped the back of my head again and he pressed my face in his throat and his other arm held tight for a moment before he let me go, took my hand and walked me the three feet to Tyr.

I was up on Tyr, Frey behind me and wheeling his steed around when I asked dreamily, "I wonder if she'll be an adventurer like her mom and dad."

Frey moved us into the forest, this time much slower, the mist having disappeared, and I watched the moonlight glint on the snow as I listened to him chuckle before he muttered, "If so, gods help me."

I giggled because he was right about that. Then I giggled again just because.

Frey leaned me into Tyr's neck and touched his heels to Tyr's flanks. We shot forward and I giggled again as I watched the trees stream by and felt Frey's command of his beast as they did. The power of the animal under us, the rider and his mount one, and I experienced a late-night, carnival-style ride that was better than any I'd had before.

And although I eventually stopped giggling, I never stopped smiling.

Not once...all the way home.

29

MEDDLING

 *ne week later...*

I had a problem.

We were at Frey's lodge in Kellshorn or, more accurately, outside the large mountain town that catered to vacationing skiers and fishermen who came to fish at the vast lake that Frey's lodge and the town skirted.

My girls hadn't been exactly right. The lodge wasn't fit for a queen as it was no Winter Palace and definitely no Rimée Keep.

But that didn't mean it wasn't cool-as-shit.

First of all, it skirted a vast lake and that would be a *spectacular* vast lake.

Secondly, the lodge was gorgeous. It was made of blond wood and stone. It had a lower level built into the swell of a hill and two upper levels that had wraparound balconies, the lower one wider, all of them with wooden railings made of flat planks that had been stamped through along their lengths with the shape of a pine tree.

Nothing inside or outside of the lodge was graceful, refined or ornate as with the Palace and the Keep. This was not a place for stately affairs or official meetings. This was a place to relax, unwind and be surrounded by nature in all its immense beauty. It was comfy, cozy, welcoming and warm. There were lots of windows, lots of open spaces, lots of beautiful, gleaming wood, lots of gorgeous stone, lots of furniture that invited you to sink into it and lots of fires that seemed to keep every corner warm.

There were also lots of bedrooms, which was lucky because all four of my girls came with me.

This meant the journey included sleighs, which made that journey longer (two days rather than the one Frey told me it would have been if we were able to take the more direct route). As we traveled, Frey's men rode around the two sleighs packed with his, my and the girls' trunks and, for the first time since I arrived in that world, I rode *in* a sleigh with Esther and Bess (the first day) and Jocelyn and Alyssa (the second) because Frey didn't want me on Caspia.

This was my problem.

I was pregnant and Frey, as early signs were indicating, was going to be one of those ultra-careful, concerned, not exactly hovering but nevertheless protective expectant fathers.

Case in point, Frey had put his foot down that, considering my condition, I would not be continuing my lessons on Caspia, and he'd also called a halt to knife work with Lund.

I gave in on quitting working with Gun and Caspia. Frey was ecstatic I was pregnant, and it had to be said (after the initial shock), I was ecstatic too. Therefore, it would not do for me to take a fall off Caspia and harm myself or our child.

And, incidentally, when we told Aurora and Atticus, they were both (even Aurora) beside themselves with glee.

In other words, all was well in my world, and we didn't need me to do anything stupid to change that.

But the knife work wasn't dangerous. Lund knew what he was doing, he never got close to hurting me and we'd been working together for so long, I knew he wouldn't.

And anyway, all that running around, lunging, twirling and squatting would be a good way to keep fit while pregnant.

Frey, however, did not see it this way and also thought I was a little crazy for wishing to keep fit during my pregnancy, stating, "Part of the beauty of a woman with child is her curves, wife, and you'll not deprive me of the ones I bestowed on you by 'keeping fit.'"

Yes, this was what he said.

Further, Frey had allowed me to continue with my bow and arrow but only target practice, not "skulking" (his word) through the woods aiming at human beings.

We'd argued about all of this, our first argument in so long, I didn't remember when we had our last.

I was pregnant, not an invalid, and this I shared with my husband.

I was not going to be on a horse, working with knives or skulking through cold woods and this my husband shared with me.

My problem was, to practice with Lund and skulk with Annar, I needed his men and they listened to Frey and not me.

Therefore, Skylar continued his work with Frey's men, and I did not (except the bow and arrow, but seriously, it was fun skulking through the woods and it was a lot less fun standing there and shooting at a stationary target).

This pissed me off.

And as I nursed my snit, it came to me, if Frey was going to be this cautious with me while I was expecting, then there was no way he was going to let me find a witch, send a message to Valentine, communicate with her what was happening and that I had to go home, talk to Sjofn, sort out my life back home, say good-bye to friends and return.

No way.

And I had to do this. My return journey was scheduled to happen in less than six months' time. I was guessing I was maybe a month pregnant, perhaps a bit more. That would mean I'd be in my third trimester and no way Frey would let me journey back then and I wasn't keen to do it then either. But if I didn't get a message to Valentine, he wouldn't have a choice and nor would I.

Thus, my husband and I needed to have a discussion.

But I was avoiding that discussion because, although my anger had cooled to worry, Frey's had disappeared completely. He was back to my sweet, gentle Frey and held no grudges (then again, he didn't need to since he got his way).

But when we were fighting, I found it upset me (tremendously) when he was angry. We got along so well, fighting with him was no fun. It didn't feel good at all in so far as it didn't even feel right, and I wasn't all fired up to get in another argument with him then. Or ever, really.

Therefore, I needed to find a way to discuss this with my husband without either of us getting upset *and* with Frey agreeing to let me go home.

Something I thought would be impossible.

I was thinking of all this as I was wandering along the upper balcony, taking in the lake, the sea of pine trees rising up all around, the snow-capped mountains rising behind the trees, the pretty village of Kellshorn some ways away and all of this reflected in the calm, clear waters of the lake. And I was doing this hoping for those calm waters to calm me when I saw Bess, Alyssa and Esther at the end of the balcony looking down and whispering to each other.

As I approached, Bess heard me, turned, put her finger to her lips and then she lifted her hand and waved it toward herself urgently, her face smiling.

I smiled back and moved toward them, glad to have something to take me away from my thoughts.

When I arrived at their huddle, I got close to Bess on the end and looked over the railing to see what held their attention. I scanned the somewhat cleared area around the house, saw nothing then I caught it.

Thad had Jocelyn pinned against the side of the stable, her arms were around his shoulders, his hands were at her ass, and they were going at it, hot and heavy.

Whoa.

When did this happen?

"When did this happen?" I whispered to Bess.

"He took her last night," Bess whispered back. "Her room's next to mine. They were noisy." After she imparted this information, she giggled and tried (unsuccessfully) to stifle it as I heard Alyssa giggle and unsuccessfully try to stifle hers too.

"I heard it as well, so I went to Bess's room to listen," Alyssa whispered like Jocelyn and Thad were five feet away rather than yards away.

My eyes went around them to look at Esther at the other end who was looking at me and rolling her eyes. As for me, I couldn't help it, I was smiling.

"He has stamina too," Alyssa finished, and my smile got bigger.

"*Lots* of it," Bess added on a huge grin.

I turned my smile on them both before I teased, "You two need to get yourselves some so you won't be up in Jocelyn's business."

Alyssa's eyes wandered to where Max and Stephan were standing, chatting to each other some ways away from the goings-on with Thad and Jocelyn, and she said wistfully, "You're indeed right about that, Finnie."

"So right," Bess added, also wistfully, her eyes had wandered to where Orion was dismounting his horse close to the lake.

I looked around them again to Esther, who was not looking at me, Bess, Alyssa or any of Frey's hot guys, but at Thad and Jocelyn, and I saw her face was thoughtful.

My head tilted to the side before I looked back at the couple only to see Thad had Jocelyn by the hand and he was leading her into the stables.

"Someone's going to get their skirts tossed in the hayloft," Alyssa muttered then giggled again.

Bess giggled with her then stated, eyes still on Orion, "My turn next," and she moved away from the balcony with a quick wave, a big smile and a, "Farewell, ladies."

Hmm.

It seemed Orion was about to get lucky.

"Not a bad idea," Alyssa murmured, gave me a wicked grin and both Esther and I a wave as she also moved away, saying to me, "Please don't need anything for, say...a few hours."

Her wicked grin got more wicked when I nodded to her request then she sashayed down the balcony and disappeared inside.

Now Max or Stephan was going to get lucky.

Or whichever of Frey's men Alyssa ran into first for I didn't think Alyssa was all that picky. Then again, all of Frey's guys were hot *and* nice.

I grinned to myself even as I wondered if this was all a good idea, for Frey's men were Frey's men, my girls were my girls, it was likely this would always be the way and we didn't need a soap opera unfolding around us. I moved to Esther who, I was thinking as she still looked deep in thought and her eyes were still directed at the stables, agreed.

"You okay?" I asked when we were close.

She started, her eyes came to me, and I watched her force a smile.

"I am fine, Finnie," she answered.

"You don't look fine," I observed. Her fake smile faltered, and her eyes slid back to the stables, so I got closer and inquired gently, "Is this going to be bad, you girls having dalliances with Frey's men?"

Esther's eyes came quickly to me, her brows drawn then her face relaxed and she shook her head. "No. It is usually fun and games, the heart isn't involved. Dalliances occur often and those involved move on with no ill-will, even to friends of the men or women involved." She explained this but hesitated, her gaze drifting back to the stables, and she muttered, "But..." and she trailed off.

"But what?" I prompted.

She looked back at me, got closer and took my hand before saying softly, "But our Jocelyn, she admires The Drakkar's Thad and not just because he is a tall, hearty lad with broad shoulders and pleasing eyes. But because he has a quick wit, an easy smile, and she's noted on more than one occasion, a soft heart. I fear," her eyes went back to the stables, "hers is involved but his," her attention came back to me, "is not."

I bit my lip for this might be true.

While we were in Hawkvale, I wrote to my girls, and they wrote to me. Mail took for freaking ever to get where it was going so there wasn't a lot of communication, but we'd managed to exchange a few letters and Jocelyn's contributions asked after Thad. Her tone was casual but a forced casual that I thought, at the time, was kind of cute.

Now, thinking about it, all the time my girls had been amongst Frey's boys, they switched favorites nearly daily. But Jocelyn's attention had always been taken by Thad and never strayed. Thad, on the other hand, I knew, unlike Ruben, did not have a steady woman, and indeed, like all of Frey's other men, had a steady *stream* of women.

Ho boy.

I squeezed Esther's hand, promising, "I'll have a word with Frey and see if he'll have a word with Thad to, um...assess the situation. If he won't or if he will and the news is not good, then I'll have a word with Jocelyn just to see where she is and give her a little, um...guidance."

Esther's eyes went soft, and she nodded, "This would be good, my princess."

I nodded back.

She squeezed my hand, her eyes going intense. She paused as if uncertain and I waited until she said quietly, "We all, well..." she hesitated. "We miss Sjofn."

We hadn't talked of it, but all my girls knew I was expecting (though they were surprised I was for they said the powder was usually very reliable) and all of them knew what that meant, which was the fact that their friend wasn't coming back. And I knew all of them were sad about this, but I also knew they were trying to hide it from me.

I held her hand tight and whispered, "I know, honey."

"But we're also glad you are so sweet."

I smiled at her, and still whispering, said, "Thank you, Esther. That means a lot."

She returned my smile before her attention wandered back to the landscape, stopped on something and she muttered, "I best move. I don't want to be left out." she squeezed my hand again, let it go and hurried away.

I watched her a second before I looked out to see Oleg striding toward the house while scowling at an Orion who was now smiling down at Bess. He swung his scowl to Max and Stephan who both appeared to be flirting with Alyssa, and I had to admit, I was a little surprised at Esther's choice. Oleg wasn't hard on the eyes, but he also wasn't easygoing and quick to laugh or smile like all of Frey's other men. In fact, he so wasn't any of these, he seemed grumpy a lot of the time.

I waited then watched Esther approach him and then watched him stop and scowl at her, something which I thought was kind of scary but didn't affect her in the slightest. She said something to him, his brows shot together before he jerked up his chin then jerked his whole head to the house. She turned toward it. He followed her and I wondered what she'd said to him.

As she moved, her eyes came up to me and she smiled.

I smiled back.

Oleg, if her smile was anything to go by and he could quit being grumpy long enough to catch a pass, was about to get lucky too.

I left the balcony, in so doing left my girls to it, and headed to Frey and my bedroom to get my book and Penelope.

Instead of thinking about how I was going to get my husband to agree to let me return home for a little while to say good-bye to my old life, I wanted to lose myself in a book while reclining on one of the comfortable, wooden lounge chairs on the deck. These had a big, iron fire pit next to them that put off so much heat, what with that and the summer thaw Frey told me about that was warming the air, making the days longer, the snow melt and the icicles drip, you didn't have to wear a cloak.

I knew this because I'd tested it last night, cuddling with Frey in one of those chairs with a big fire blazing beside us and making out until Frey was done making out and carried me to our bedroom to do a lot more than make out.

But considering the activities of my girls and Frey's men, and the fact that he only had a housekeeper at his lodge, no other servants, and further he likely wouldn't be fired up about me building my own fire considering he thought pregnancy required severely limited physical activity (as in, none at all except to walk, sit, eat and have sex), I decided I'd curl up by the fire in the living room. There were super-soft, comfy couches in there. So comfy, they were a very good second best.

Or at least they would be until Frey returned from whatever he was doing and I could ask him to build me a fire.

I entered our bedroom through the wooden doors that led to the balcony, closed them behind me and started to the nightstand on my side of the bed where my book was, when the hairs at the back of my neck stood up.

I stopped, my breath stopped, and I turned slowly then halted again, going completely still at what I saw.

In the armchair in the corner by the windows sat Valentine wearing a fabulous jade-green wool knit, wraparound dress, equally fabulous spike-heeled charcoal gray boots and her tremendously fabulous red hair was framing the classic features of her alabaster face.

Penelope was curled in her lap purring as Valentine's blood-red finger-nails moved through her thick, ginger fur.

Holy moly.

"Valentine?" I whispered.

"Hello, my goddess of love," she replied quietly.

My eyes got big, and I felt a smile hit my face as I rushed to her.

"Valentine! It is *so* cool you're here!" I cried.

Her head tipped to the side, her lips tipped up slightly and her eyes flashed in a way that made my excitement at what I thought was a very surprising, but also very fortunate turn of events fade to hesitant concern.

She solidified that concern when she said softly, "I fear, my Seoafin, after I say what I've come to say, you will not feel this same way."

I felt my heart squeeze and a million thoughts raced through my head, primarily Sjofn wanting to come back and wanting to do that early.

Okay. Shit.

First things first.

I needed to go get Frey.

"Please sit," Valentine invited, regardless that it was actually my bedroom, and she did this by gracefully throwing out her pale hand to indicate the bed.

"I..." I started, didn't know how to go on then I went on anyway, "A lot has happened Valentine, you can't imagine. A lot. Huge. I need to go get someone so you can meet him and then we need to talk."

"Please, Seoafin, sit," she semi-repeated, and I blinked at her.

"Seriously, I have to—" I started, but she interrupted me.

"Tell me you are married to Frey Drakkar and you are pregnant with his child. This, *ma chérie*, I know," she stated. I sucked in a surprised breath, and she went on, "Now, please, considering you are, indeed, expecting, I would very much prefer it if you were seated when I say what I've come to say."

I stared at her thinking this did not sound good.

Then I moved to the bed and sat.

What I wanted to do, watching her face, was move to the door and run.

Penelope, shockingly, didn't leave Valentine's lap but stayed purring right where she was and while doing it didn't even twitch.

My cat, by the way, was still holding her grudge.

Once I was down, I unhooked my light wool cloak, pulled it off my shoulders and it fell to the bed as I kept my eyes on her.

"How do you know about Frey and me?" I asked.

She tilted her head slightly before answering, "I told you I am not a seer, and this is true. I am not. I do not have visions and I cannot call up scenes from the future. This does not mean I cannot tune into people of our world, or this one, and see what has passed. And this I have been doing with you since you left."

"You've been keeping an eye on me?" I asked, not upset about this, exactly. Just surprised.

"It was not by choice. You call to me, Seoafin, I do not know why. But you do. So, yes, since you do, I have been keeping an eye on you."

It was interesting, this "calling to her" business, but I decided for now that we needed to keep on target.

"So you know when I got here that I—" I started.

"I know everything," she interrupted me.

She took in a delicate breath, her eyes narrowing slightly on me and then she went on, speaking softly, but even so, the words she spoke rocked my world.

"I know that your emotion runs deep for your husband and his for you. However, I feel it is important that *you* know all so the happiness you are experiencing will be true and rich rather than shadowed by misunderstanding. So, I've been watching and waiting for your husband to clear those shadows. Alas, he has not, so, unusually, I feel compelled to do so."

I didn't have anything to say to that, and since I was concentrating on keeping my tightening neck muscles from snapping, I didn't make a peep.

Valentine carried on.

"Therefore, I must inform you that I also know that before you felt this emotion for him, and before he was aware of his depth of feeling for you, in order to bind you to this land and to him for the future of this country and for his own ends as he held extreme distaste for your twin, he ordered the elves of this world to bind you here for the rest of your days. At the same time, he ordered that the other Sjofn be bound to your world...and your life...for the rest of hers."

I blinked but said nothing mostly because I had no air in my lungs and my throat suddenly felt parched.

Valentine kept speaking.

"The power held by these creatures is immense, unbreakable. It is so powerful I have never felt the like of it. Still, I have searched for magic, or some means of thwarting it. But my search was fruitless, and I fear this kind of magic does not exist." She paused, held my gaze and delivered the killing blow. "You are never to go home, Seoafin, ever. And your twin will never come back, ever."

I stared at her, now unblinking.

She held my stare and continued.

"Your husband made this decision without consulting you and he did this on the night you first learned of the existence of elves."

I kept staring as my mind reeled.

That night...that night...

Oh my God.

We barely knew each other back then. He'd just come back from being away with his men. Although he told me he fell in love with me while I was mixing pancake batter, and maybe when he looked back this was the true, but at the time he didn't trust me, and I wasn't even certain he liked me. He didn't even know who I was until the elves told him. In fact, he wouldn't start being really sweet and gentle, becoming my Frey, until *after* that night.

After he'd cut me off from my world—completely and forever.

And he cut me off because the elves had told him who I was. He cut me off because Sjofn was a lesbian, and I was not. He cut me off because he could get from me for the rest of his life what he wouldn't get from her.

And he did all of this without asking me.

He irrevocably changed my life and imprisoned me in this world, cutting me off from people I loved and the world I knew without asking and at a time when I had no intention of staying.

Oh...my...*God*.

"And when," Valentine continued, and my dazed, wounded attention shot back to her, "I sent a message through the witch of this world, Agnes, to inform you this happened, your husband intercepted it. He lied to me through Agnes about your desires to remain, saying you were aware of this situation and had agreed to stay. He then disallowed Agnes any communication with you even though much was happening in this world and your own."

Oh my *God*.

"And now, *ma chérie*," she kept going, her voice gentling, indicating she was not done delivering her death blows, "even though I do sense you are pleased that you are bound to this world and further bound to it through the child you carry, you must know that your husband orchestrated that as well. He did this without your knowledge, and until it came about, and you decided to be pleased mostly because the deed was done and you had no choice, he also did it against your will."

It was then I finally blinked again.

"What?" I whispered.

"This powder you took?" she asked. I nodded slowly and she went on, "It is quite powerful and nearly foolproof. However, you have not been taking it now for some time. He discovered it and switched it with a placebo with the intent to sire a child on you in order to safely deliver an heir to the throne of this nation."

I felt every inch of my body lock.

No.

God. No.

Why would he do that?

"Why would he do that?" I breathed.

"He is a man," Valentine answered gently, studied my face that I could actually feel was pale and continued, "Therefore, my goddess of love, your husband has been very busy. Your parents of this world have known all of this since your return to them after the time you spent in the country. The three of them have known you are bound to this world everlasting and Princess Sjofn would never return. But it is only your husband, and one of his men who procured the placebo for you, that knows he has schemed behind your back to get you with child."

I couldn't believe this.

This was unbelievable.

Why would Frey do this? Any of it.

Why?

Memories clashed in my head. Atticus seeming so despondent when I couldn't hit the target I knew now was not because he was disappointed in his Sjofn but because he was mourning the loss of his daughter. Both his and Aurora's easy acceptance of me, acceptance they had no choice but to have for their Frey, their Drakkar had commanded the elves. All of them, including Frey's quick and unreserved happiness I was pregnant without me having to say a word about remaining in this world, switching places with Sjofn and providing an heir to the throne.

God, I was so stupid, so blind, so involved in falling in love I didn't even notice, didn't think, didn't piece it together—but this was because they all knew I was never leaving way before I did and way before I even knew I *wanted* to stay.

I felt my jaw clench and a red film descended over my eyes.

"That said..." Valentine's voice came to me, but I had stopped hearing her. Nothing was penetrating the injured, infuriated fog filling my head.

I slowly stood and turned to round the bed.

"Seoafin," she called, but I ignored her and moved, my gait slow, my head feeling fuzzy, my eyes still seeing red.

"Seoafin." I heard again and then I heard an angry mew from Penelope, which could only mean that Valentine had stood. But I kept going, my pace quickening. "Seoafin, my goddess of love, I'm not quite—"

But she didn't finish because I was running to the door, out the door, down the hall, down the stairs, down the next flight, out the door and into the snow.

And as I blindly ran, I ran right into Ruben who caught me in his arms.

"Finnie, what are you doing outside without a cloak?" he asked, and my head shot back, my gaze locked with his and his head jerked at what he saw.

"Where's Frey?" I demanded to know.

"Finnie—" Ruben started, his gaze turning guarded as he took in my face, his hands coming to my upper arms, fingers curling around carefully.

"Ben, where...is...*Frey*?" I ended my question on a shriek and Ruben's head jerked again as his fingers tightened.

Then he said gently, "Go inside, my princess, I'll get him."

"Fuck that," I snapped, yanking free of his hold and ignoring his wince at my words. "Tell me where he is."

"Fin—" he began. Something caught his attention, he looked beyond me, his big body went tight, and his eyes narrowed.

"Ben!" I yelled and his attention snapped back to me. "Where the *fuck* is Frey?"

"Right here, wee one, what on earth is amiss?" I heard Frey ask, and the minute I heard his voice, I turned on him.

I took him in as he moved toward me, his boots crunching in the snow and my heart squeezed, hard and tight, staying frozen like it was never going to pump again.

My beautiful husband. My sweet and gentle Frey. The man I loved. The man whose child I was carrying. The man who had lied to me and irrevocably changed the course of my life...*twice*...without bothering to discuss it with me.

"Frey, there's a wo—" Ruben started to say in a low tone, but I cut him off.

"You unbelievable *asshole*!" I shrieked.

Frey's brows shot together over narrowed eyes as he stopped walking about four feet from me and his body went still.

"Finnie, what—?" he started.

"Fuck you!" I spat, leaning forward to do it. "Fuck you, Frey! I cannot fucking *believe* you!"

"Frey—" Ruben said quietly.

Frey's eyes unlocked with mine and he looked around me. He focused on something in the distance, I saw his face go hard but I ignored all of this and kept at it.

"You told the elves to bind me to this world," I accused hotly, and his focus shot back to my face. "You did it a long time ago. You did it without asking me. You did it before you even knew you liked me much less loved me. And you did it so you wouldn't have to be bound to Sjofn for the rest of your days. You did it for completely selfish reasons. You did it without once thinking of me. You did it only thinking of *you*."

I watched as he flinched. I knew that proved Valentine's words true and my heart started pumping so fast, in an instant my blood felt like it was going to boil through my skin, and it pushed me to keep right on going.

"Who could do that and how?" I shouted. "*How?*" I screamed. "*How could you do that?*" I shrieked, arms straight down at my sides, hands in fists, torso leaning toward him.

"Finnie, love, let's go inside," he said gently, moving to me, hand coming toward me, but I took two quick steps back and lifted my hand, palm out to him, and he stopped but only at my next words.

"Don't you dare touch me, Frey. Don't you *fucking* touch me because that was just the worst of it but not all of it. I know...*I fucking know* you switched my powders without talking to me about that either."

I heard Ruben pull in a breath, but it was Frey's face that had my attention because it changed, his eyes flashed and his voice got low when he ordered, "Finnie, we're going inside."

409

"Fuck that and fuck *you!*" I leaned forward to screech. "Who does that? Who does any of this shit?" I yelled, throwing my hands out. "It's *my* body, Frey! *I* get to decide or at the very least *we* talk about when we create a baby, but oh no..." I drew this out sarcastically, shaking my head and taking another step back. "Not The Drakkar. Not The Frey. My life isn't mine. My body isn't mine. Both are clearly yours to do with whatever you wish without *once* consulting me."

"Wife," Frey cut in, "you're distressed and there's a woman I do not know standing behind you. Let us go inside and—"

"Unh-unh," I shook my head. "No way. No fucking, *fucking* way. I'm not going *anywhere* with you. The only thing I know, because Valentine told me, is that wherever I go has to be *here!*" I shouted, pointing to the ground realizing belatedly we had an audience of all my girls (save, probably, Jocelyn, though I was in no state to check) and a number of Frey's men.

But I didn't care.

Not even a little bit.

And that was why I kept yelling.

"I had friends back home, Frey. People I love. And I'll never see them again not even to say good-bye. I didn't have family, but I had a family of friends, and without thinking of me *once* you swept them all away. You swept *my whole world away.* How could you do that? How could my sweet, generous husband *do that to me?*" I ended on a screech.

Frey's face shifted to concern at my rising hysteria, he took two swift steps to me, but I scuttled quickly away, hand back up, palm out, rounding Ruben and retreating while still speaking.

"Don't come near me." I shook my head. "Don't you dare come near me." This I whispered as the despair began to overwhelm me. "You've... you...I can't believe I'm not safe with you. I can't believe I can't trust you and I can't believe I now know I never *fucking could.*"

Frey's body turned with mine and he followed me as I backed through the snow. "My love—" he started but I shook my head hard.

"I'm not that," I told him, tears making my voice hoarse as they shone in my eyes. "I'm not that to you. I'm not your love and I never have been. You don't treat someone you love like this. You don't. Not ever. Not ever."

At my words, I watched the expression on his face shift to ravaged, and he whispered, "My wee Fin—"

But he didn't finish the name I loved him to call me.

This was because I heard a whistle fill the air, a whistle I knew very well.

And then I stood still and horrified as I saw Frey's powerful body wrench forward at the same time, I saw the bloody point of an arrow come out his shoulder.

And at this same time, I heard Bess, Esther and Alyssa scream and their screams mingled with my own.

Then it happened, everywhere, all around me, all around Frey, all around the men, Valentine and my girls. Whistling arrows flying everywhere, landing in the snow, landing in flesh, men's grunts of pain, women's screams, people rushing and horses suddenly galloping through the snow all around. So many of them, it felt like an army had descended on Frey's lodge.

I stood frozen and watched as, injured, Frey started to race toward me, but then I watched in stony shock, horror and with a pain so immense it scored through my insides as two more arrows penetrated my husband's big, beautiful body, and then I watched the powerful Drakkar go down to a knee.

"No!" I shrieked, my body belatedly unlocking, moving to run to him, but I didn't get a step before I was pulled up and planted in front of a man on a horse.

"Get the witch!" I heard my captor order, then he bent into me, drove his heels into his mount's flanks and we galloped into the surrounding forest.

I struggled, pushing and grunting, my vision filled with nothing but Frey's powerful body penetrated by three arrows, the blood soaking his wool and down on a knee and my system knew nothing but the driving need to get back to my husband.

"Spell!" my captor shouted, struggling to contain my thrashing. "Now!"

I bucked back at the same time pushing at his arm at my waist. I felt the back of my head collide with his chin and the piercing pain that caused reverberated through my skull. I heard his grunt, and I felt a tickle hit my chest.

Then I felt nothing at all because I was asleep.

30

UNTIL THE DAY I DIED

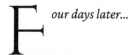*our days later...*

"MY WINTER PRINCESS, WAKE, PLEASE WAKE." I heard a woman call and my eyes slowly opened then fluttered closed again. "Please, my princess, *wake.*"

With effort, I opened my eyes and focused on a blonde woman, blue eyes, not young, not old, maybe late forties, early fifties. She had great hair and a lot of it, and she was very pretty.

"Hey," I whispered, feeling funny, not myself, strangely out of body.

"She needs food, water, immediately. It's been days." I heard from behind her, and I blinked because I knew that voice.

My attention moved from the blonde to the redhead who was now wearing a disheveled, dusty, torn in places, jade-green, wool wraparound dress and scuffed, dirty, charcoal gray suede boots.

And it all came back to me.

I pushed up to sitting, my head swam alarmingly, and my hand went immediately to it. But even so, I didn't stop trying to push up from wherever I was reclining. However, two sets of hands held me down and I didn't have a lot of strength.

And since I didn't, since my head was woozy and there was an emptiness in my stomach that had not one thing to do with hunger and a scary feeling around my heart that I didn't want to think about, I gave in.

But I gave in as I whispered, "Frey."

The blonde glanced at Valentine and I didn't like the look on her face so I grabbed her arm and I did it tight. I also shook it when I had hold and I did this hard.

She looked back at me with sad eyes. Sad eyes that spoke words she really didn't want to say and words I never, never, *never* wanted to hear.

"No," I whispered, bile filling my throat.

She grabbed my hand as Valentine dropped to her knees on the floor beside the blonde.

"I am sorry, my princess," she whispered, squeezing my hand. "He has gone from this world."

He has gone from this world.

Frey has gone from this world.

My sweet, gentle Frey was gone from this world.

Emotion surged through me, so much, none of it good, that I suddenly felt like I was going to explode.

"*No!*" I shrieked, pushing her away.

I gained my feet, rushed several paces across the room and stopped dead when I saw we were in a room made of stone and there was nothing in it but high, barred windows at least two stories up, three dirty pallets on the floor with thin, rough, tattered wool blankets and a wooden table that looked like its legs held it up by a miracle.

We were in a prison cell.

And I didn't care.

No, I didn't care.

"He isn't dead," I told Valentine and the blonde as both slowly stood and turned to face me.

"I'm sorry, my princess," the blonde murmured.

I leaned forward and shrieked, "*He isn't dead!*"

Valentine moved toward me, whispering, "My goddess of love—"

"*He isn't dead! He isn't dead! He isn't dead!*" I screeched then saw even the cool, composed Valentine's face filled with sorrow and my legs collapsed under me as my body started shuddering with sobs.

"He isn't dead," I whispered through my tears as both women made it to me, pulled me to my feet and supported me while they moved me back to the pallet. "He isn't dead," I repeated, my entire body quaking with the force of my grief as they gently pressed me back down to the dirty mattress.

"He isn't dead," I whispered as I curled into a ball, arms around my calves, rocking my body back and forth while one of them, I didn't know who, stroked my hair.

"He isn't dead." These words were hoarse, rough, ugly. My stomach empty, my heart actually felt broken and that hurt. A lot. Too much. So much I couldn't bear it.

It was unbearable.

"Please, God, make him not dead." I whispered then I turned my head, pressed my face into the filthy pallet...

And I sobbed.

I CRIED myself out while Valentine stroked my hair and cooed to me. When I was done and turned my face to stare at the stone wall, she gently forced me to sitting on the pallet so my back was to the wall.

The blonde went to the table and came back with a plate on which were some slices of ham and a battered copper cup filled with water that was luckily clear and clean.

"Eat, *pour votre bébé*," Valentine urged.

I looked at her vaguely, nodded just as vaguely, took the plate, set it on my thighs, took the glass, started eating slowly and chased the salty ham with water.

Pour votre bébé.

Our baby.

Would I live to give Frey that?

I looked around the room and doubted it.

My eyes fell on the blonde.

"Who are you?" I asked.

"I am Lavinia of Lunwyn, servant of Alabasta," she replied softly, and I nodded because I knew who that was. Frey told me stories of Lunwyn's most powerful witch and the goddess Alabasta's servant on this earth.

And Frey told them to me while we were eating dinner in his chateau in Hawkvale.

I felt my throat close, my eyes sting and I looked away, shoving another piece of ham in my mouth and having no clue how I'd get it down.

"Do you think...?" Lavinia of Lunwyn started. My gaze moved to her, and I swallowed the ham with effort before she finished, "That you can hear what is happening?"

To this, I replied, "Considering my husband is dead and that hits the one to ten scale of bad news you could give me at around five hundred and seventy-two, how bad is the rest of the news?"

"It is bad, not as bad as that," Lavinia replied.

Nope. Not as bad as that. Outside of the world coming to an end, there was no news worse than that or even close.

I sucked in breath through my nose and nodded, saying, "Well then, hit me with it."

She nodded in return, then she and Valentine exchanged a glance and both settled on the pallet on either side of me.

"You have been under a sleeping spell for four days," Lavinia stated.

I nodded.

She took in breath and continued, "I was captured and imprisoned here a week ago. You and Valentine arrived yesterday, and when you did, Valentine was bound but awake."

I finished the last piece of ham, set the plate aside, took another drink of water and said, "Okay."

"We are..." She hesitated, looked to Valentine then back at me. "We are both bound still, though we bear no straps. Wherever we are has a powerful spell over it. Neither of us have command of our magic. It is not gone, we both still feel it. We just cannot command it."

My eyes slid away, and I whispered, "Great."

"This is why, I am certain, they have brought me here for I would not stand for what is happening to my Lunwyn," Lavinia told me, and I nodded.

Valentine took it from there. "We both can, however, sense things. This is how we know..." she trailed off and I jerked my chin up so she wouldn't continue.

I didn't want to hear the words again. I got her.

This was how they knew Frey was gone.

Lavinia spoke next. "We also know more, or I do. Valentine senses things, but as she is not of this world most of what she senses, she doesn't understand."

"And what more do you know?" I asked, but I didn't really care.

I wanted to know about my girls and Frey's men. I wanted to know about Aurora and Atticus. I wanted to know about Skylar. And I wanted to have some time to lick my wounds and then figure out how to get the fuck out of there, out of this world and home, home, *home*.

"The adela trees burn," Lavinia whispered, all these thoughts flew from my head, and I felt my mouth drop open as I felt my heart squeeze.

Then I whispered back, horrified, "No."

She nodded, her eyes growing bright. "They do. The trees burn, our glorious, glowing adelas which is bad enough, but this means the elves cannot rise."

I closed my eyes and turned my head away.

The elves could not rise.

And they had no Frey.

I had no Frey.

If I lived to deliver him or her, my son or daughter would have no Frey.

I looked back at Lavinia and said with feeling, "That sucks."

Her head tipped to the side. "Sucks?"

"Sucks, stinks...it's awful." I lifted a hand, and rudely, I had to admit, circled it at her to get on with it, but I didn't have it in me to be polite. "What else?"

"Aurora is taken," Lavinia said gently, and I pulled in breath.

I let it out on a hissed, "Shit."

"She lives and she is held captive, like us. Not here but far away. I cannot sense where. But...I am sorry, my princess, I do not sense your father."

I closed my eyes tight and turned my head again as the hitch in my throat tore out in a wrenching sob.

Through it, I forced out on a stammer, not looking at her, "He's...he's...is he dead?"

"I am sorry," she whispered.

I lifted a hand to my mouth and curled my fingers around.

I'd lost him again. Again.

Fucking hell, once was bad enough.

Tears forced themselves out of my eyes and slid down my face as I fought for control, but my chest heaved with the effort and my throat burned so much I thought it would disintegrate. It took a while and a lot out of me, but I pulled my shit together, wiped my face with my hand and looked back at Lavinia.

"What else? My girls? Frey's men?"

She shook her head, but when she saw my face and understood I misread her, she said quickly, "I do not know. I have not met them and therefore I cannot sense them. I can only sense those I've met or people of prominence, like your husband. I'm sorry. I have no news of them."

I looked to Valentine. "You?"

"I was in their presence, my Seoafin, but I'm sorry, not long enough to know their auras and be able to feel them," she answered.

"All righty," I whispered, sucked in another breath then looked between them both. "Do you know anything else? Who's doing this?"

I asked this as a key scraped the lock. All three of us looked to the door, then it was thrown open and I couldn't believe my eyes or stop my mouth from dropping open when I saw Broderick saunter in followed by his lover Phobin.

No.

It couldn't be.

But it was. He was right there, and he wasn't entering to be imprisoned.

Broderick took one look at me, his face grew hard, my heart started pumping, and he turned on his lover.

"What is the matter with you?" he snapped. "She is of my blood, she is princess and she sits in filth?"

"She is prisoner," Phobin retorted coldly.

"She is *princess*," Broderick shot back then turned to address the two guards that entered with them and stood at the door. "Take the Winter Princess to my quarters. Find women to draw her a bath, find her a decent gown and bring her proper food."

"You cannot do that, Broderick," Phobin stated, and Broderick turned on him.

"I cannot? I'm sorry. I thought it was *me* who just became king of *two* lands. Did I miss something? Was it you?"

"I've told you. She is of the elf, the witch said so," Phobin clipped. "We cannot take the chance she holds any magic and escapes."

"She is my cousin, and she is princess, and she will not sit in filth," Broderick returned.

Phobin's face grew stony, and his eyes became so furious and so cruel, not only I shrunk back, but so did Lavinia and Valentine.

Then, he strangely whispered, "Come to heel, Broderick."

Broderick's head twitched, his expression blanking for a moment, before his eyes flashed, he glared at Phobin and stated firmly, "A king does not heel, Phobin."

Phobin got closer, his voice got lower, and he repeated, "Come to heel."

Broderick smiled, and speaking softly, returned, "You fool. Did you honestly think our play in bed translated to my rule of a vast kingdom?"

Broderick got closer too and his voice got softer, but not so soft we couldn't hear.

"Yes, my lover, I will beg to suck your cock and I will beg you to do other things with it, but outside our bed, Phobin, hear this and know it, *I* rule, and *you* come to heel. Or I'll find a lover who will play like I like in bed *and* know his place out of it."

Phobin's stunned face had paled, but Broderick ignored it and the three of us on the pallet, turned and walked to the guards, stopping in front of them.

Once there, he ordered, "Take my cousin to my chambers. She is princess and treated as such. Keep guards at the door, and for the gods' sakes, give these witches some decent blankets, palatable food, wine, and water to wash up. I do not reign like my father. Learn that now, and part of what you need to learn is that this treatment of women is unacceptable."

With that, he swept through the guards, leaving the cell and leaving behind a still shocked and immobile Phobin.

We heard from the hall, "Phobin! Come!"

Phobin's body jerked, he looked confused for a moment then he rushed out of the cell.

"Come!" one of the guards grunted at me and my eyes shot to him.

"Go, Seofin," Valentine whispered. "We'll be all right."

"Come!" the guard grunted again, starting to move forward.

I quickly glanced at Lavinia who smiled reassuringly at me then Valentine, who did the same and I set the cup I still held aside and started to get to my feet.

Rising, I turned to Valentine and Lavinia and whispered, "I'll be back."

I gained my feet, straightened my shoulders, tossed my hair, nodded regally to the guard and swept out of the room.

I tortured myself.

Throughout my bath, throughout the two silent women assisting me to strap on my underwear, pull the soft, woolen gown over my head, my boots up my calves and doing my hair, throughout my solitary meal, and after, as I was alone in the luxuriously appointed but chilly rooms, I tortured myself.

I tortured myself with memories of the first time I saw my huge, frightening husband at our wedding.

And the first time he kissed me.

I tortured myself with memories of him throwing a dead deer on the kitchen table, pulling me in his lap and telling me I fit there, and bathing with him in a hot spring.

And the first time we made out in bed together and how gentle he was with me.

I was wrong in my anger. He had been my gentle Frey before he knew me.

I tortured myself with that too, that I had forgotten and all I said to him prior to his death.

Then, when I could bear those particular thoughts no longer, I tortured myself with memories of playing cards with Frey's men. Of Father's proud cry the first time he saw me get a bullseye and his tight hug the second time he saw me do it. Of Skylar sitting at a desk, any desk, all of the desks he sat at, his tongue poking out in his concentration, looking so cute and boyish. Of my girls' giggles and gossip and tender care, and how they took me in without reservation. Of Mother's dry wit and small smiles and eyes that told you how she felt about you in a way you would always believe and never forget.

I tortured myself with memories of a ship called *The Finnie* and all that had happened aboard her.

I tortured myself with memories of strong hands guiding me on a dance floor while I wore a blood-red dress at a ball.

I tortured myself with memories of touches, tastes and words whispered in my ear.

I tortured myself with every memory I could pull up of the best by far, the most beautiful by a landslide, the most perfect adventure I'd ever had, and I turned each in my head. I burned them in my brain. And as I did it, as the seconds slid to minutes, minutes to hours and the guard remained outside and I remained alone in the prince's room, I prepared.

Thus, when the door opened, I was ready.

I was ready to do what I had to do for Frey, for Atticus, for Aurora and for Lunwyn, which was rightfully *mine* to give to the child I carried. Frey's child. The Drakkar's child. The elves' child. My child.

Lunwyn's child.

And by my God *and* my husband's gods, I was fucking going to do it.

So, prepared, I watched Broderick walk in and I schooled my face not to show a reaction when his eyes fell gentle on me, and his lover trotted in obediently at his heels.

The guard closed the door and Broderick continued to approach as I sat in my chair, unmoving, my hands hidden in the folds of my skirt, and I watched.

"You look better, Sjofn," he said softly.

"You killed my husband," I replied and watched with morbid fascination as he winced.

Then he whispered, "Sjofn."

"You killed my husband," I repeated, holding his eyes.

He stopped in front of me and looked down at me. "I'm sorry I needed to do that."

"Can you tell me *why* you needed to do that?" I asked, my voice bland, flat.

It was Phobin who answered with an incredulous, "Why?"

My eyes didn't leave Broderick as he turned to his lover and hissed, "Quiet." He turned back to me, and his voice was gentle when he explained, "Sjofn, I could see you were taken with him and he you, but he's The Drakkar, The Frey. He commands the fire of dragons and the magic of elves, and he let it be known very openly that he would not hesitate to call his beasts in defense of you." His voice became even gentler when he finished, "I am sorry, my cousin, but he was too powerful to let live."

"You didn't believe that then," I stated, and he blinked.

"I'm sorry?" he inquired.

In what I hoped was a good impersonation of Aurora, I regally inclined my chin to indicate Phobin and declared, "It was his idea. When we met in Middleland, you were pleased for me."

"I was," he whispered, watching me closely.

"So, tell me, why did you kill my husband?" I asked, and he pulled in a light breath.

"Sjofn—" he started, but I interrupted him with a wave of my hand.

"It matters not now, Broderick. He is dead. And my father is dead, I assume?" I waited for his careful nod. I took the hit of confirmation of this news and the further hit it took forcing myself not to react, and I went on, "But you had different ideas back then, am I wrong?"

"Sjofn, I don't think—" he began, but I interrupted yet again.

And I did this with a soft, "You owe this to me."

Broderick held my eyes. Then he nodded.

"I thought..." he started then concluded, "exile."

"And why didn't you follow through with this thought?" I pressed. "Was it him?" And again, I lifted my chin to Phobin.

"He did, I will admit, point out the errors in my thinking." Suddenly he crouched before me, made as if to reach out for my hand. I pulled back in the chair slightly but not slight enough he didn't notice. He gave up, rested his wrists on his knees and kept speaking. "Phobin knew, *you* know, and I also knew but in seeing you so happy, I was denying it, but I knew that The Drakkar would not stay in exile long, no matter what magic or guard or—"

"The adela branch," I stated, cutting him off again. "You and Phobin, you've been collecting sacred relics, articles of power to wield for this endeavor. It isn't the only thing you had, is it, Broderick?" I guessed a guess that just sprang to my mind.

He smiled a small, actually un-freaking-believably *proud* smile before he whispered, "Always so clever, my Sjofn."

"So you have relics, things with magic?" I pushed.

"Indeed," Broderick replied.

"They would be more powerful if we had the branch," Phobin muttered.

My gaze slid to his angry face and Broderick tilted his head back to look at him. When Broderick did this, he clamped his mouth shut and a muscle ticked in his jaw.

I looked back to Broderick, waited for his attention to come to me, and asked, "You have a witch wielding them?"

"I do," he answered.

I nodded once then stated, "This makes her very powerful."

He inclined his head.

Right.

Well then, I'd have to deal with that later and hope to all that was holy Lavinia and Valentine could beat the bitch.

Moving on.

"Then, since you were considering exile, the attack in Houllebec, the poison at the Gales, this was not you?" I inquired.

He shook his head. "The attack in Houllebec was meant to take the life of The Drakkar but you were to be seized and held for ransom then let go. However, the kidnapping would have been a ruse. If this had been success- ful, it would have meant you were safe with no aspersions cast on us. But there would be no imminent heir to the throne until you or your father could find another suitable candidate as husband for you, and in that time, we would have instigated our campaign to unite Lunwyn and Middleland." At this, his mouth got tight, and his eyes slid briefly to Phobin before coming back to me when he went on, "I left that in other's hands and those chosen for this deed, fortunately for you and The Drakkar, were not very skilled."

Phobin obviously was behind this maneuver and Phobin obviously fucked it up.

Broderick studied me with his gaze back to soft then said, "This was before I saw the two of you together and considered exile."

He paused for me to speak, but I made no reply.

"The poison," he continued, "was not me. I have allies, heads of Houses from both Lunwyn and Middleland. Until our current campaign, there was..." he paused then finished, "some disagreement about what to do with you and how to contend with The Drakkar. There were those who felt his influence, if not his power, would be diminished if he was not to sire a child on you, the heir to the throne. And therefore, they felt, if you no longer lived, obviously, this would not come about. They also felt you were the easier target. And it is known The Drakkar had no ambitions to the throne and it was believed, if you were out of the way, he would continue with his business and, as was his wont, leave the politics to others. During your betrothal he did not show a great deal of interest in you. It was only after, when it became known he..." he paused again, continuing cautiously, "grew to hold a good deal of affection for you that our plans needed to be reconsidered."

Grew to hold a good deal of affection for me. A convenient way to put it, the little, scheming, backstabbing pissant.

I shifted my attention over his shoulder as if taking this all in then looked back at him and nodded.

Then I asked, "Do you love him?"

At my question, Broderick's head jerked.

"I'm sorry?"

"Him." I motioned my chin slightly to Phobin and continued, "Do you love him?" When Broderick looked bemused, I explained, "Earlier, you said you'd replace him and, you see, I loved a man, and I lost him, and I know in my soul where it burns so strong it's a miracle I'm breathing that he will never be replaced." I hesitated, held his gaze and whispered fiercely, "*Never.*" Then I pulled in a delicate breath and noted, "So, you cannot love him."

Broderick's eyes were soft on me, and he whispered, "Sjofn, you are safe. I know you hurt but you are safe. It pains me, seeing the sadness in your eyes, knowing I'm behind it, but you know me, my cousin, you *must* know it *pains* me. But with time, I hope you will understand my actions. With time, you will see my vision for Lunwyn, for Middleland. My people could not go on under my father's rule, you know that. Everyone does. And

Lunwyn should never have been severed. Now it is again intact. I will rule and you will be at my side while I do. You will have my ear. I promise you. You are wise and strong, and I know you will be a trusted advisor to me when your heart mends. And I will listen to you as I always have. And later, I will find a way to sire a child, but if this does not come about, perhaps we can find someone..." he hesitated and cautiously went on, "*appropriate* for you to—"

I interrupted him before he *really* pissed me off. "I asked, Broderick, do you love Phobin?"

He studied me then he replied, "I do not understand why you wish to know this, my cousin."

"It matters not why, it only matters if you do or do not," I returned.

He sighed then he said quietly, "I hold affection for him, but love..."

He trailed off and I nodded again.

Once.

I knew what I needed to know.

It was time.

So I whispered, "Then you will not mind too much when I do this."

With that, I shot out of the chair, catching Broderick on the chin with my knee as I did. He fell back, and instantly I lunged at Phobin with the knife they'd given me to cut my meat at dinner. A knife I'd stolen, and they'd extremely stupidly not checked to see if it was there when they took the tray away. A knife, throughout our conversation, I had hidden in the folds of my gown.

And, as Lund taught me (or told me since this was obviously not demonstrated), I planted that knife in Phobin's jugular and yanked it across his throat, severing his windpipe.

Blood spouted out and he started dropping to his knees, hands to his neck, eyes huge, face going white. But I immediately yanked out the blade on another ghastly spray of blood, twisted, dropped to my own knees and held the knife to a still unrecovered Broderick's neck. And he was unrecovered because he was staring in shock at the dying Phobin whose body was now jerking in death throes behind me on the floor.

"Do not utter a noise," I hissed. His body went still, and his terrified eyes came to me as he nodded, and we listened to Phobin's sickening gurgling as the lifeblood poured out of his neck and he gasped unsuccessfully for air. "Roll to your stomach," I ordered.

"Sjofn—" he started but stopped with a squeak when I pressed the blade deep and blood flowed at its edge.

"I said do...not...*utter a noise*," I hissed again. "Now roll to your gods-damned *stomach*."

He rolled to his stomach. I planted a knee in his back and reached for the ties I took from the curtains and sat on in the chair.

"Hands behind your back," I demanded.

Broderick hesitated and there was nothing for it. I further had to demonstrate my resolve.

Therefore, I plunged the knife in his side, and he groaned with pain, hopefully not loud enough for the guards to hear.

"Hands behind your back!" I hissed.

He put his hands behind his back.

I pulled the knife out, wiped it on my gown, put the hilt between my teeth, tied his hands then moved down and bound his feet.

I moved back to my chair and grabbed the handkerchief I'd purloined from a trunk with one of Phobin's scarves. I rolled Broderick to his back, and he groaned in pain as I did it. I quickly shoved the handkerchief in his mouth and secured it by tying the scarf tight around his head.

That done, I wasted precious time, and I did this not for Frey, not for our child, my father, mother or Lunwyn.

I did it for me.

I took the knife from my teeth, got in Broderick's face and whispered, "You know, cousin, it pained me to do that," I jerked my head at the now dead body of Phobin. "You know me. It *pained* me to do that. But you see, I could not fight you both and bind you both so one of you had to be neutralized. Hopefully, you will not bleed out before someone knows aught is amiss." I got closer and my voice dropped lower as I held his eyes and whispered, "Thank you for uniting Lunwyn for the child of Frey's I already carry inside me. He will be most appreciative."

With that, I pushed away from him and hurried to the door, hoping there were only two guards. One was one too many, two, God only knew. I'd probably fall at the first hurdle.

But I wasn't going to give up.

I was three feet away when I heard grunts, steel clashing and then bodies thudding on stone.

I blinked at the door.

Oh shit.

I quickly put both hands behind my back.

The door flew open, and I stared at two big, brawny, exceedingly handsome men.

And they stared at me.

Both their gazes flicked to the room behind me then back to me.

And, to my shock, they smiled.

One turned to the other and, to my shocked *delight*, stated, "Lund appears to be a good teacher."

They were Frey's.

"You are Frey's," I whispered.

"Balthazar," the dark one said.

"Quincy," the fair one said.

I'd heard of both though never met them.

"Hey, I'm Finnie." I was still whispering.

"We know," Quincy said while still smiling.

I smiled back.

"So, Finnie, you think we could rescue you rather than loiter chatting in a wounded king's room with his murdered lover still bleeding on the carpet?" Balthazar asked.

"That's probably a good idea," I answered then thought quickly and told them, "But before we do the whole, um...rescue thing there are a couple other things we need to do."

They looked at each other.

They looked at me.

Then my heart flew to the sky when Oleg stomped through the door and grunted, "Yup, and I know one of them."

"Oleg!" I cried, never in my life thinking I'd feel complete and utter joy at the sight of Oleg, but I did in that moment, I *totally* did.

But Oleg, being Oleg, didn't even look at me.

He walked by me. Unsheathing the sword from his back, he walked to Broderick, stood over him, and right in front of my eyes, he ran Broderick through with his sword, straight through the belly, yanking up.

Broderick's body jerked, what I had to admit was sadly, on the floor as his cries of pain were muffled by his gag, and Oleg pulled out his sword, sheathed it and walked to me, stopping in front of me and meeting my wide eyes.

"Raider rule, my princess, do not leave a job undone," he grunted then grunted again, "Lunwyn."

"Lunwyn," I whispered then felt a hand on my arm and that hand was pulling me to the door.

"Let's go," Balthazar, who had hold of me, said, and we went.

But at the door, I turned back and took in the carnage. Phobin motionless and dead at my hand, Broderick's head turned, his face pale and awful in his pain, eyes on me.

And I knew in that moment I would remember that scene, the blood, the gore of exposed wounds, the look on Broderick's face, and I would do it until the day I died.

But for the life of me, I couldn't find it in me to care.

Then I hurried out with my men and whispered, "Okay boys, somewhere close, there are two women..."

31

DRAGONS

ne month later...

"FINNIE, APOLLO REQUESTS YOUR ATTENDANCE."

I looked from cleaning the wound to Lund and nodded. "Let me finish here, Lund, and I'll go directly to him."

Lund looked at the man I was working on then at me. His eyes soft as all Frey's men's eyes were soft when they encountered the shadow of mourning drifting steady and unrelenting in mine, he nodded and left.

I looked at the man in the cot. "Am I hurting you?"

He shook his head then lied through his teeth (literally, because he was clenching them), "No, my Winter Princess."

I smiled at him. I knew it was a sad rather than reassuring smile, but I had to try and I didn't have any smiles that weren't.

He didn't smile back mostly because he was clenching his teeth and I decided to finish quickly so he could relax. I tipped my head and read-dressed his thigh, cleaning it with spirits, biting back the impulse to blow away the burn as I heard him suck in breath then I dabbed it with clean cotton, spread a healing salve on it and redressed it.

Once done, I curled my fingers around his ankle, gave him a squeeze

427

and caught his eyes. "It's beginning to heal, Joshua," I said softly. "I shouldn't have to do this again for a while."

To that, he nodded, and I finally saw relief on his face.

I gave him another small smile, got up from the edge of his cot and looked to Lavinia and Valentine, who were both seeing to other wounded. I caught their eyes, indicated the flaps to the tent, waited for their nods and walked out.

To get you up to date—Lunwyn was at war, and if that wasn't bad enough, one faction was at war with itself.

With the fall of Broderick, the conspirators, which did indeed include the heads of Houses of both nations, were fighting amongst themselves as to who would take the throne of the united land at the same time fighting against my men who were intent to regain control of the throne in order to keep it and Lunwyn safe until Frey and my child could assume his rule.

My notable Houses included Ravenscroft, Lazarus, Sinclair, Drakkar and Ulfr. The outside factions of note included Njord, Roar, Andreas and Viggo. These were of Lunwyn and didn't include the Middlelandian crew, all of the heads I had met at the Gales (and all of them had feigned respect and friendliness while they were plotting my and/or my husband's deaths). And all of whom felt their head should now assume the "throne of the united Lunwyn."

The good news was, with Baldur still in Korwahk with a good deal of the country's soldiers, the Middleland Houses were weak, and the Lunwyn Houses were not the most powerful of the northern land.

The other good news was the infighting was causing disarray, and skirmishes against my men were diminishing as they skirmished against each other.

The further good news was, when rescued and taken from the highly fortified castle of the House of Roar that Broderick had chosen as his stronghold in Lunwyn, Lavinia and Valentine had regained their magic, which they were using for healing as well as protection, cloaking of our troops and gathering (or "sensing") information about our enemy.

And the last good news was Oleg, Lund, Ruben, Max and Skylar had emerged unscathed from the attack on Frey's lodge. Stephan was wounded superficially and had already recovered enough to join the rest of us. And Bess and Jocelyn had also not been wounded.

The bad news was Orion, Gunner, Annar and Thad had all taken arrows as had Esther and Alyssa.

In rating the news, Orion, Gunner, Annar and Esther also had relatively superficial wounds, and it was reported they would eventually recover, though it would take longer than Stephan, so I was considering this good-*ish* news.

The definitely bad news was that Alyssa had sustained critical injuries, and I was informed, Thad had moved to protect Jocelyn (and succeeded in this) and also sustained multiple injuries of which not one, but two were critical. When Stephan arrived, he explained that Bess and Jocelyn were staying behind to assist the physicians, healers and witches in Kellshorn who were seeing to them as well as taking care of Skylar. But it did not look good for either Thad or Alyssa.

Further, Ruben informed me, unbeknownst to me but another indication my husband would do all he could for my safety, Frey had hired a woman named Agnes, the witch I met the first night I arrived, and charged her with protecting me with her magic.

This failed and the attack on Frey's lodge could go ahead because Broderick's men found her and killed her, thus her protection magic died with her.

Therefore, the woman with the cranberry cloak who could jump from the second story of a building and had a face lined in a way where I knew she laughed much through her life was also no longer of this world.

Although my mind often moved to what occurred in the prince's quarters and the blood on my hands, and my heart turned over at the memories as my mouth filled with saliva when these memories reminded me I was a woman capable of those actions, receiving all this news made this phenomenon much less distressing.

The other bad news was that Aurora remained captive in the stronghold of Njord and the witch that wielded the sacred relics and magical implements had not been found by soldiers or through Lavinia trying to sense her. Although, now that they were no longer in Broderick's clutch and she no longer had hold over Lavinia and Valentine, her being at large was not a good thing for my side or the other, who spies informed us, were also scurrying to find her so they could attempt to control her.

And last, the wildcard news was that Kell had disappeared. No one knew where he was, no word, no sighting. He had gone to Sudvic to prepare for Frey's fleet to leave, but he had not been seen or heard from since the rebellion started and Balthazar and Quincy had both ridden to Sudvic and various other places in search of him. Balthazar had returned two days ago with zero information and Quincy just that morning with the same.

Valentine, with her magic back in her control, could have returned home, but surprisingly, she didn't. She also didn't share why she didn't. Although she worked with me, Lavinia, the physicians and healers who saw to our wounded, and she did this with her usual calm, cool composure that bordered on indifference, I knew she felt remorse for meddling between Frey and me.

I would need to discuss this with her and let her off the hook. I just had not had the time, and on the infrequent occasion I did, she was not exactly approachable.

She shouldn't have done what she did, this was true. But it was me who said the things I said, so that was on me. It was on me that the final words Frey heard from me were shrieked accusations and the absolute last thing he ever heard from my mouth was me telling him he didn't love me.

That was on me.

All of it on me.

These were my thoughts as I walked through the busy camp of tents staked into the melting snow and men moved past me, dipping their chins or giving me a shallow bow, horses rode by, and I lifted my chin to others standing by fires or exiting tents.

I made my way thus to Apollo's tent and entered it.

Inside I saw all the heads of my noted Houses including Eirik, Frey's father, who was flanked by his two surviving sons, Calder and Garik. Both men I had met, both men who looked too much like Frey (though not nearly as handsome), therefore setting eyes on them even for a moment wounded my soul. Thus, both men I avoided.

Because of this, I did not know them very well, but what I did know was they were not repugnant like their father, malicious like their mother or wicked like their cousin. But even so, since they were Drakkars, I remained wary.

My attention went directly to Apollo and my feet went to him too, for he dipped his head to a chair indicating I should sit.

In that tent, the only one I completely trusted was Apollo. This was because I knew Frey had trusted him because Frey had told me about him. He told me he liked his cousin, he respected him, and I'd learned since from Apollo that sentiment was returned.

Also, I knew if I birthed a daughter, the rest of them would easily be at each other's throats to control Lunwyn just as our enemy was. But I understood innately, rather than Apollo telling me, that if Frey and I had boy *or* girl, Apollo would always have my back.

And I trusted Apollo because he looked at me with a look that I knew was mirrored in my eyes.

Frey had told me he had lost his wife, but the minute I met Apollo, I read in his eyes that he had loved her, he had not recovered, and I knew, reading the look, he never would.

Ever.

I nodded to him as I moved across the tent, sat in the chair and looked around.

Calder, Frey's brother, spoke first. "My Winter Princess, Apollo tells us you are still keen that we engage in a rescue effort to recover Queen Aurora."

"I am," I answered, and I wasn't the only one. Norfolk Ravenscroft and Olwen Lazarus, my mother's cousin and brother respectively, I knew felt the same.

"Would it not be a better use of our resources to focus our energy on crushing the rebellion?" Eirik Drakkar asked, as he would.

I had learned Frey's father didn't mind sending his men into battle although he himself got nowhere near it.

"I am no general," I answered, schooling my tone to sound respectful. "I simply expressed my wishes to Apollo. I leave the war business to you."

At this point, Walter Sinclair put in, "Our scouts have not found the witch, and I will repeat, I feel we should prioritize this mission. If she has the power to bind our Lavinia, and Lavinia tells me her foreign companion's magic rivals her own, we would be remiss not to seize this witch and claim her instruments for our own."

"You could send Balthazar and Quincy," I suggested. "They are both returned and my husband..." I faltered because, suddenly and against my will, my throat filled, making my voice husky. I forced myself to rally, recover, and I finished swiftly, "Told me they are very skilled."

"They are," Apollo added, his voice soft. "Frey told me the same."

"Then dispatch them instantly," Eirik ordered pompously.

"You forget, Father, that we still skirmish," Garik stated. "We need every blade we can get, and these men of Frey's are not only skilled at finding things, they are equally skilled with steel."

"Yes, this is true, Garik," Olwen Lazarus agreed. "But if we had these instruments *and* two extremely powerful witches, it might be they could use them to crush the rebellion with no more bloodshed on either side."

"No more blood, yes. No more loss of life, no," Apollo stated quietly, everyone looked to him, and I braced.

431

Apollo of the House of Ulfr was exceedingly gentle with me in a way that hurt since it reminded me of Frey. He was also exceedingly handsome in a way that also reminded me of Frey with his thick dark hair, big, muscular body and commanding presence (although his eyes were a stunning, pure, jade green).

However, in sitting in these meetings, which Apollo demanded I be included in, I had learned he might be gentle with me, but he was not a gentle man.

Not at all.

"Apollo," Norfolk Ravenscroft said low, and Apollo leveled his eyes on the older man.

"They hang, all of them," he declared.

"These *are* heads of Houses," Eirik put in. "Their actions were to unite Lunwyn, and we should—"

Apollo turned suddenly burning eyes on Frey's father and his deep voice was terse when he clipped, "They plotted to murder your daughter-in-law, kidnapped and imprisoned her. They killed your king. They hold your queen captive. And sir, might I remind you, *they murdered your son*."

I tried to fight it, but at his words, I couldn't stop myself from dipping my chin and staring at the rough carpets covering the snow under the tent.

Apollo went on, "He was Our Frey. He was Our Drakkar. The adelas are charred. The elves will never return. The dragons cannot aid us in our plight and will not wake unless Finnie births A Drakkar from Frey's seed, and even if she does, this will take years. And I hope I do not have to remind you of the lives already lost. The heads of those Houses are responsible for this. *All* of it. And they...will...*swing*."

Olwen Lazarus and Norfolk Ravenscroft immediately nodded. It took Walter Sinclair three seconds to agree (I counted). But Eirik Drakkar, who, with every encounter I disliked more, and who had lost more than anyone in that tent except me, glared at Apollo for long moments before he finally jerked up his chin.

But what surprised me was when Calder Drakkar muttered, "I claim hangman."

Then I was again surprised when Garik returned on his own mutter, "No, brother, I kick the lever."

"There will be enough that you both can share," Apollo declared then he ordered them, "Go to Balthazar and Quincy. Dispatch them to find the witch, scout the situation and give them leave to commence with capture if they feel it is safe or return if we need to send an outfit." He turned his eyes

432

to Ravenscroft. "The number of Frey's Raiders is diminished and those left will remain here for the princess's protection. But you have skilled Raiders amongst your troops. Choose those most stealthy to go forth and secure our queen. She, like our princess, grieves, and it is our duty to see to it she grieves amongst those who can offer her comfort, not alone and captive in an enemy camp."

"Hear, hear," Olwen Lazarus murmured.

My eyes moved to him, I smiled, and upon receiving it, my (kind of) uncle smiled back.

Apollo swept his gaze through the group and stated quietly, "Let us not delay," which I was learning was his way of suggesting people do what he said when he said it and telling them he was not pleased when they didn't.

Something else that reminded me of Frey.

Therefore, the men in the tent didn't hesitate further but filed out, Garik and Calder doing so after nodding to me, and I smiled at them, pleased at their show of loyalty for their brother and Lunwyn, and saddened he'd never know they'd shown it.

Eirik, as usual, didn't look at me which didn't bother me. I didn't like his eyes on me anyway.

Ravenscroft, Sinclair and Lazarus stopped to mutter polite words to me before taking their leave.

I watched the flaps of the tent swing closed behind Olwen then I stood, looked into Apollo's remarkable (it had to be said, because they truly were) green eyes and whispered, "I should get back to the wounded."

He crossed his arms on his chest and studied me. Then he said softly, "Finnie, we've not had a skirmish in days. Their wounds are healing and not one of them requires your constant attention."

"They bled for my son," I reminded him.

"They bled for Lunwyn," he corrected me.

I pressed my lips together and nodded because he was right.

He continued to study me before he pulled a breath in through his nose, closed his eyes and turned his head to the side. When he did this, I studied him, for this was unusual for Apollo. He rarely showed emotion and the only emotion I'd ever seen him show was gentleness to me.

And, sometimes, anger.

But now he looked conflicted.

He opened his eyes and returned them to me.

"It is early," he said gently. "For you, too early for such talk. For Lunwyn, however, it is not, and therefore it must be said. But I have concerns. Concerns I discussed with Lazarus and Ravenscroft. Concerns they share."

I felt my brows draw together as I felt a thrill up my spine. "What concerns?"

As was his way when he was with me, he continued speaking gently.

"You are vulnerable, Finnie, as is your child."

I knew this. Boy, did I know it.

Therefore, I nodded and reminded him, "I have Frey's men. They will stand behind me."

And I knew they would for Ruben told me they would. In fact, he vowed it.

"Indeed," he agreed. "And this is an alternative for you to consider."

I blinked.

An alternative?

"I have another choice?" I asked, sounding confused.

"I think, and Ravenscroft and Lazarus agree, that once this is done, the traitors are punished and Lunwyn is again at peace, you should wed me."

I blinked at the same time I drew in a sharp breath, but Apollo didn't stop speaking.

"I will vow to keep you and your child safe. I will vow to stand beside you and assist as you raise him king. And he will have a brother and sister who I've no doubt will dote on him."

I said nothing, just stared.

Apollo got closer, dipped his chin and held my eyes, but he didn't touch me.

He whispered, "We share something, you and I. Something no one but us understands. I do not offer you avowals of love and I think you understand I never will. I understand I will not receive the same from you. But our union would provide stability for our country, a mother for my children, a father for your child and company for us both. If your heart was to mend in such a way that you grow to find me pleasing, then perhaps we will create our own family. If not, I will understand and I will take my attentions elsewhere."

Eyes wide in shock, I opened my mouth to speak, but he shook his head and lifted a hand.

"This is not for now. This is for you to consider. This is for much later. This is simply an option, Finnie, nothing more. There will be no animosity should you refuse, and you leave this tent knowing, no matter what you chose, I stand behind you and always will."

434

I pressed my lips together again, this time for a different reason.

I let them go and forced out a heartfelt, "Thank you."

Apollo nodded, moved slightly away, and I knew by the look on his face his mind was on other things, and he was done with me.

But I wasn't done with him.

"Apollo," I called, he eyes focused on me, and then, haltingly, I asked, "Does it...I mean, I get the sense from you, um..." I stopped, his brows rose, and I finished on a whisper, "It doesn't get better, does it?"

His gaze grew soft, and his lids slightly lowered, but I still saw the flash of pain, the same pain I felt in my soul.

He whispered his reply, "No, sweet Finnie, it does not."

I nodded.

I knew that. I saw it in his eyes, felt it in my soul. I knew it.

It just sucked to have it confirmed.

I watched him suddenly tense, his torso twisting so he could look to the flaps of the tent, and he ordered, "Remain here," as he turned and walked to them.

I heard a restless commotion that seemed to come from all around before he made it to the flaps, and then they were thrown open and Lavinia rushed in followed by Valentine.

Their attention went to Apollo first (he was a big guy and standing in their way so they would do) then they both looked at me.

"We're bound," Valentine hissed, sounding pissed and worried at the same time but looking only pissed.

My body got tight.

"What?" Apollo clipped.

"We are bound," Lavinia repeated, her gaze moving to Apollo. "The witch is close. She's bound us. Something is—"

She didn't finish as shouts were heard, running feet, galloping horses, and Apollo turned to me.

"You and the witches, remain here. I will call Frey's men to your guard," he ordered and stalked quickly to a table, grabbed his sword in its scabbard and stalked even more quickly out of the tent.

Without word or movement, we all stared at the tent flaps after he left. The sound of shouting, running feet and galloping horses increased significantly within moments of his departure and this gave me a very bad feeling.

"We're under attack," I whispered.

"Do you think?" Valentine muttered drolly.

I glared at her. She held my glare and raised her brows.

I tore my eyes away.

Damn, shit, damn, shit, damn, shit, shit, *shit.*

I looked around Apollo's tent and saw his war chests, the quiver chock-full of arrows and the bow leaning against the wall of the tent, and I dashed to them.

"Finnie, what are you doing?" Lavinia asked.

"Arming myself," I answered, dropping to my knees and throwing open a chest to rummage inside.

"The Drakkar's men will—" Lavinia started.

But I cut her off, finding what I needed and pulling it out, I gained my feet while talking. "Frey's men will put their lives on the line to keep ours safe. That doesn't mean we can't help."

"Seoafin, I don't think—" Valentine started, but I turned to them and interrupted her too while strapping on the loaded knife belt.

"Come quickly to these chests and find daggers of a size and heft you're comfortable with. Don't bother with a belt, just take the dagger," I finished saying this to two wide-eyed witches as the noises outside grew louder. The increasingly alarmed vibe penetrated the tent and I reached for the quiver to strap it on, commanding, "Now, ladies."

Lavinia shook her head to shake herself out of her stupor and dashed to the trunk. Valentine stared at me clearly rethinking her show of remorse and not spiriting herself home before her magic was bound again, this time during what was sounding more and more like a battle zone.

"Valentine," I said warningly as I finished with the strap on the quiver and reached for the bow.

"*Merde,*" she muttered and stomped forward.

They got their daggers and we all stood by the tent flaps waiting, waiting, and then freaking waiting some more for one of Frey's men to come.

But the noise escalated outside the tent, grunts and clashes of steel, whizzing arrows, male cries of surprise or pain, galloping hooves.

None of it good.

All of it seriously fucking scary.

We all jumped as a sword tore into the side of the tent and slashed through. I turned to the sword, lifting an arm to yank an arrow from my quiver, setting it to the bow and pulling back the string, but the sword disappeared, and we heard the ring of steel against steel.

A mishit.

I released the tension on the bow but none of the tension left my body. I turned to face the tent flaps with the arrow at the ready and it was then I realized my breathing was not steady.

Not even close.

"My princess," Lavinia whispered. "The Drakkar's men, they are loyal to their Drakkar and to you. If they could have come to us—"

"They will come," I hissed, staring at the tent flaps, refusing to believe what I would have to believe if they didn't, and that was, they couldn't, and the only thing that would hold them back was something I would *not* think about.

No, I refused to believe that even as the vibe pounding against the sides of the tent became more desperate, the noises of war coming so fast, one on top of the other, it was impossible to distinguish them. Finally, two arrows tore through the tent walls on the opposite side to us, imbedding themselves in carpet and snow. But if we had been close, they would have imbedded themselves in one of us.

Shit!

"We're sitting ducks, Seoafin," Valentine snapped, and my eyes shot to her.

Crap. She was right.

I made my decision.

"Right, so, we fight our way to escape if we have to," I announced.

Valentine nodded instantly.

I looked to Lavinia, she did too, though hers was not instant.

I ordered, "I've had training, not a lot but some, so you stick with me, hands on me at all times so I know I've got you. You see a threat, you tell me, point it out, and I'll do what I can. You've got a shot to stick someone who seems to wish us ill, go for it. We are not on the offense, ladies. I carry the future king of this land and we must all do what we can to keep him safe so our goal is simply to get clear and get away. Got me?" More nods, I nodded back, looked to the tent flaps and whispered, "Okay, girls, let's go."

We went, and the minute we exited the tent, we saw chaos, blood, wounded men, dead men, dead horses, arrows in the ground and body pieces. The clashes of steel rung loud enough to deafen, the whispers of arrows whizzing one on top of the other.

It was hideous, extreme.

But I felt Valentine and Lavinia's hands on me, I thought of the little being in my belly, I blocked it all out, and I moved swiftly. Leading my witches, we skirted sparring men, ducked around tents when horses galloped through, picked our way over obstacles, but steadily and as quickly as we could, we kept moving.

Twice, I had to raise my bow, take aim and let fly as I caught a soldier's eye and knew he meant harm.

Twice, my aim was true.

More blood on my hands.

I still didn't care. The only thing I thought was I was pretty fucking pleased I'd practiced so goddamned much.

I kept moving, quickly, always vigilant, glancing left and right, up and down, over my shoulder, around tents, my witches always with me.

We got out of the tent area and into the forest, but it was happening there too.

God, there were so many of them. Men all around, beasts, dead, wounded, it was everywhere, blood staining the melting snow in what seemed like a river of red and pink.

But our way was clearer. We only had to look around trees, not tents, and we moved more swiftly, gaining ground.

I was feeling hopeful until I felt the loss of a grip on my gown. I heard Valentine cry out and I whirled, bow up, arrow at the ready, and I looked into a man's eyes. That man was holding Lavinia with a dagger at her throat while her hands were curled around his forearm, her back arched, her head pressed hard in his shoulder to get away from the blade, her eyes filled with terror.

I aimed my arrow at his face. "Drop the blade."

The battle raged on around us as Valentine pressed close to my back with hers, protecting it.

"Drop the bow, Winter Princess, or she dies then I take you," he replied, pressing his blade deeper.

Lavinia whimpered.

I pulled the bow back tighter.

"Drop the blade," I repeated.

"Your life for hers or I take both," he returned.

I closed one eye and lined my arrowhead to my target.

"Drop the blade," I whispered.

"Listen, princess, listen all around you. Your men lose. Die now or die at the noose. Our heads hold no affection for you as the prince had done. You will drop through the gallows," he whispered back. "Your choice."

He was wrong.

I had another choice.

And I took it.

I let my fingers loose and hit a bullseye. He fell back, dead instantly as my arrow shot through his eye socket and pierced his brain, his arms dropping, and Lavinia fell forward to her hands and knees.

"Let's go," I commanded, but suddenly Lavinia's head snapped up then twisted like she was listening to something, and Valentine whispered, "Oh my goddess," at my back.

I opened my mouth to tell them to get a move on when it happened.

I heard it.

Flapping.

Loud, leathery flapping that accompanied an enormous shadow that was sweeping quickly over us, so vast, it blotted out the sun.

Lavinia pushed up so she was on her knees, her head tilting back to look at the sky, her lips parting in shock as I felt Valentine tense behind me, and the noises of battle faded as men stopped to stare.

I looked up and that was when I saw them.

Dragons.

Dragons.

A delicate, delicious shiver slid over every inch of my skin as I watched the huge beasts fly through the air, webbed wing to webbed wing, hundreds of them, big as houses, their barbed tails snapping, their ferocious, horned heads tilted down, their beady eyes sweeping the landscape.

And it started.

They spewed fire.

Streams of it shafting out of their mouths, screams of shock silenced in nanoseconds when the flames hit their targets one after another after another.

It was terrifying.

It was awe-inspiring.

"*Run!*" Lavinia shrieked, gaining her feet.

Grabbing my hand and Valentine's, she tugged us, and we took off as the dragons flew, raining fire, incinerating men, leaving nothing but ashes and melted steel in their wake, trees burnt instantly to a cinder, snow melted straight to the earth, and through it, leaving a charred crater.

We all halted as one when a man combusted ten feet in front of us. We backed up several paces, shifted simultaneously and ran through the random shafts of flames, dodging this way and that, certain to get caught up in it as the fire streamed down all around us.

All of a sudden, we reached a clearing, halted at the vision before us and

instinctively huddled together, all of us staring at a line of standing dragons. Wings rolling and curling, long necks arching and writhing, tails snapping and thrashing, claws scoring the snow.

And then, as one, we turned to run, but halted dead in our tracks when
the next thing happened.

What appeared to be a large, white, sparkling meteor fell to the earth
one hundred yards away, exploding in a burst of white light from which a
misty ice-blue ring shot out moving so fast, if I'd blinked, I would have
missed it.

And it left in its wake two types of men. Those frozen completely in
their tracks in whatever position the ice-blue ring caught them in, and
those who still had the capacity to move, and did, running for their lives.

"We must go. We *must* go," Lavinia shouted, pulling at my hand, and I
felt Valentine grab my other one and tug.

But I couldn't move.

"I can't move," I forced through immobile lips.

"Pick her up!" Valentine yelled, sounding panicked, and when this
didn't work, she screamed, "*Drag her!*"

They pulled, tugged, pushed and yanked, but my body was rooted to
the snow.

I was caught in the ice ring, and I could tell by the frightful, restless
sounds of the dragons behind me they were about to blow.

"Go!" I cried through my frozen lips.

"My princess—"

"Go, go, *go!*" I screamed, but it came out weak for I couldn't make it
stronger.

"Seoafin—" Valentine whispered urgently, her body close, her mouth at
my ear, her hand still tugging at mine.

"Take her, Valentine. You know the beasts are preparing and you know
to look after your own neck. Take Lavinia, get her safe, and the minute you
can, go home," I implored.

"My goddess of—"

"Take her!" I cried, the words strange coming through unmoving lips,
but the tone easily read.

"Goddess!" Valentine exclaimed then she whispered, "You must know,
now, that I am sorry, my goddess of love, sorry for everything."

"Go!"

She hesitated then I felt both of my hands squeezed by both of theirs...

And they were gone.

I was alone.

I had thought when the dragons came...

Hoped...

But I was wrong.

I was alone.

Frozen, but my blood was singing with adrenaline.

This was it.

My last adventure.

And I was ending it alone.

At least Mom and Dad had each other.

But I was alone and terrified.

I couldn't even close my eyes.

Shit.

"I'm coming to you, baby," I whispered to Frey, but it came out naturally, my lips moved with my words, and I blinked.

I blinked!

Actually blinked, my eyelids moving and everything.

Holy moly!

"No, my love, I've come to you." I heard a beautiful, sweet, achingly familiar voice behind me.

In control of my body, I whirled and stared, mouth open, eyes wide, belly plummeting, heart in my throat, at my husband who was standing three feet away.

Then he lifted an arm and the dragons let loose. Their massive bodies bulged, necks extended, their fanged mouths opened, and flames erupted and shot forward. I stared as we were surrounded by an inferno over our heads, at our sides, my gown blowing with the force of it, the heat enveloping me, the bloody snow melting to a river rushing over my boots. But Frey's body, to my shock, was impervious and acted as a shield against the flames.

Then he dropped his arm and the flames immediately stopped.

I knew everything behind me was gone, reduced to ash.

But in front of me stood Frey backed by a line of fierce, colossal, terrifyingly beautiful dragons.

It couldn't be real.

"Are you a dream?" I whispered and his lips tipped up.

"No," he answered.

"A ghost?" I was still whispering.

"No, my wee one."

My wee one.

My wee one.

My heart squeezed.

"You're alive," I breathed.

"Yes," he stated the obvious, for there he was. Tall, broad, strong, powerful, beautiful and best of all...*breathing*.

"You're alive," I repeated on a whisper, my nose stinging, my eyes blinking against the wet because I didn't want him hazy. I wanted him clear.

I wanted to see him clear.

"Yes," he repeated.

"Alive," I breathed.

His handsome head tilted slightly to the side, his heavy brows drew together, and he asked, "Are you still frozen by the elfin magic, my Finnie, is that why you don't come to me?"

I stared at him.

Then I sprang from my feet, jumping into his arms and they closed around me, strong, safe, tight and definitely, *definitely* real.

I held on tight to his shoulders, shoved my face in his neck and burst out crying.

"They...they...the-the-they," I stammered into his neck, my arms convulsing, trying to hold him closer. "They told me you were dead."

"I am not," Frey's voice rumbled, and his arms squeezed.

I jerked my head back and glared at him before I shrieked, "*Where have you been?*"

He looked down at me and one of his hands came to my face, his thumb gliding through the wetness that was still coming, and he said gently, "I was injured, gravely, close to death. I convinced my men to leave me to my passing and see to business, something we had all agreed, should such occur, we would do. The elves sensed my injuries and the extent of them luckily before the adela burned. As I had arranged with them prior, they sought Kell and brought him to me. Kell had the adela branch, we used it, and he and I both went to the elfin realm where they healed me."

I blinked and stared.

Then I asked, "What?"

Frey's eyes went soft and slightly amused at my blink, and he explained, "The adelas are gone. But the magic of that bough and the reason it is so important is that it can be used by The Frey to move to the elfin realm and to bring the elves to our realm, say, should something happen to the adelas or he needs them urgently and cannot get to a tree."

"Wow," I whispered, and he grinned. "So they healed you?" I asked quietly.

"Their magic is strong, but my injuries were severe, so it took some time. But yes, my wee Finnie, they healed me."

"They healed you?" I repeated.

"Yes, my love."

"Like, good as new?"

He grinned and answered gently, "I'm clearly not a babe so, no. But fit as when you last saw me."

I closed my eyes at the memory, my head jerking at the power of it.

Frey's hand at my cheek moved to cup my jaw and his arm gave me a squeeze before I heard him amend on a murmur, "Or moments before the moment you last saw me."

I kept my eyes closed and dropped my forehead to his chest. "I thought you were dead."

"I'm sorry, my love, there was nothing I could do about that. I was in no state and Kell nor the elves could move between realms without me," Frey whispered into my hair.

But I shook my head as my frame started shaking with new tears and I repeated, "I thought you were dead."

"Finnie," he murmured as I held him tighter, my body pressing into his like I wanted him to absorb me.

"I said things—" I started, my voice hoarse, my throat clogged with tears.

"We will not discuss this now," he said quietly but firmly. "I wronged you, my love, but I will explain—"

My head shot back, and I whispered fervently, "You did, but it was me...*me* who said unforgiveable things and—"

I stopped when his thumb came to my lips and pressed as his face got close.

"It is for me to forgive or not to forgive and you said no less than I deserved," he stated, again soft but firm. "But I have an enemy to vanquish. Apollo and my men are standing behind you getting more and more impatient by the second having ceased being touched by lovers reunited about five minutes ago and now wishing my ear. So, we will discuss it later."

I stared in his beautiful, *beautiful* olive-green eyes with their thick, lush lashes.

Then I whispered, "Okay."

He grinned.

My eyes dropped to his mouth.

God, I loved his grin. I loved his eyes. I loved the feel of his arms around me.

And I loved *him*.

Therefore, I blurted, "I love you, Frey Drakkar."

He closed his eyes, dropped his forehead to mine and whispered, "And I you, Finnie Drakkar."

I closed my eyes too and sighed, my body relaxing into my husband's.

But my husband's body didn't relax against mine. His head tilted, his lips found mine, they opened, mine reciprocated and he kissed me. He took his time, he did it right and it was the best kiss I ever had.

Save one.

The one he gave me at our wedding.

That would always be at the top of the list.

Even if, with this one, cool-as-shit dragons were watching.

EPILOGUE
THE AFTERMATH

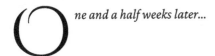 *ne and a half weeks later...*

MOTHER AND I STOOD, both of us wearing black suede cloaks, black leather gloves, our hair free around our shoulders, our crowns in place, our booted feet on the rocky shore, and we watched the boat with its square sail patterned in red and gold diamonds catching the wind, making it drift into the Winter Sea.

It was lined in red and gold silk, and in its middle, on a platform, my father's remains were shrouded in dark red and surrounded by flickering candles protected from the wind by red tinted glass.

Just behind me to my left, Frey stood so close I felt his chest brush my shoulder even through the cloak.

A vast gathering of silent Lunwynians stood behind the three of us, along the sweeping hill that met the icy sea, its glaciers drifting in the distance.

I stared at the boat and kept my shoulders straight, my head high and endured the burn in my chest as the boat and its precious cargo floated out to sea.

Frey raised his fisted hand and lowered it.

Thirty seconds later we heard the flap of powerful, huge, leathery wings.

Ten seconds after that we saw the approach of two dragons, one on each side.

Ten seconds after that, they bent their necks, and in unison, they spewed a stream of fire that struck the boat, incinerating it in the blink of an eye as they soared past each other so close their wings brushed.

Mother's hand reached out, her fingers curling around mine, and they clenched tight, but other than that, she didn't move.

Neither did I. Except to curl mine around hers.

The dragons flew off into the distance as my mother, my husband, myself and my father's subjects stared at the tranquil waves and peacefully drifting glaciers of the Winter Sea.

Many moments later, I heard my mother whisper to the wind in a voice filled with sorrow, "Good-bye, my beloved."

I pressed my lips together, locked my body, and when the tear came, there was only one.

And it was silent.

Even so, my husband shifted closer.

~

FOUR DAYS LATER...

WE MOVED through the forest slowly.

The snow gone with the thaw, wet, green turf in its place, the trees blossoming all around, we stopped at the small, ice marble pyre behind which were two seated dragons, their spiked tails swaying lazily, their wings tucked in, their long, slender, forked tongues drifting.

And on the pyre, swathed in brilliant, glimmering, ice-blue silk, only her pretty face exposed to the brilliant sun, was Alyssa.

Frey held my hand and stood by me, Aurora moving in at my other side, Bess next to her and Esther next to her. Skylar gently pushed between Mother and I, then leaned heavily against my side so I slid my arm around his shoulders. Jocelyn moved in at Frey's other side, and next to her, his gait slow, his hand that was not curled in Jocelyn's curled around a cane, was Thad. Frey's men and Alyssa's family and friends moved to their places and stopped.

When they did, Frey did not hesitate to touch the twirly tip of the long, glittering branch he held to the earth. At its end, a miniature elf sprung from the turf, she touched the branch and instantly grew to my height.

Without delay she gave Frey his salute. Her glowing ice-blue eyes touched on me then slid over the crowd.

She then walked to the pyre and around it, standing on the dragons' side. We watched as she looked down at Alyssa, her head tilted, her mouth went soft, she lifted her hands in prayer position to her lips for only a moment before she opened them so her pinkies were pressed together and then she dropped both slightly forward.

And when she dropped them, a flash of ice blue covered Alyssa's body, and at once a shock of bright-white sparks rose clear to the sky, and Alyssa's body disappeared.

Frey raised his fist and lowered it, the dragons straightened their long necks, aiming their mouths to the heavens, and there they sent a stream of fire.

I turned and pressed my face in my husband's chest as my fingers curled into his wool.

His arms moved around me and went tight.

~

Two days later...

In the State Dining Room, Rimée Keep, Snowdon.

"ARE YOU MAD?" Eirik Drakkar spat at his son from his seat mid-table flanked by his two other sons, the ones who were not married to me.

Before Frey could reply, Olwen Lazarus did. "I see the wisdom of this."

Eirik's furious gaze shot to the man, and he hissed, "You would, she's your bloody *sister*."

"This *is* highly unusual," Walter Sinclair muttered.

"It isn't *unusual*," Eirik snapped. "It's absurd!"

"I find nothing absurd about it," Apollo Ulfr drawled. He was leaned casually back in his chair and his green eyes were leveled on Eirik Drakkar. "Frey's suggestion is clearly sound."

"Clearly...clear...clear..." Eirik spluttered then pounded a fist on the table. "Clearly sound?" he shouted. "A woman has never ruled Lunwyn!"

447

"If any woman could, it would be Aurora," Norfolk Ravenscroft pointed out.

"And you would say that," Eirik returned hotly. "She's your cousin, you are close. You'd have her ear."

"You'd have her ear too, Eirik, if you weren't a horse's ass," Apollo put in smoothly, and from my seat to Frey's right where he sat at the head of the table, Mother to his left, I pressed my lips together to stifle my laugh.

Eirik glared at Apollo then stated sharply, "May I remind you that Lunwyn is just reunited. We have just been at war. Half the heads of half the Houses from both sides of Lunwyn were gods-damned *incinerated by my son*." He jerked a finger at Frey. "The other half are imprisoned awaiting trial for treason, and if you lot have anything to say about it, which you unfortunately do, they will hang. Now is *not* the time to audition womanly rule."

"It's hardly an audition considering I asked you all here in hopes of receiving your assent. But I will state at this point that I don't actually require it," Frey put in. "Until my princess births a son and he is of age to accept his responsibilities to his crown, Aurora of the House of Wilde will rule this land. She does it with my backing, which I'm certain I don't need to remind you includes my dragons and the elves. If, in the meantime, she were to be unable to command her throne, we will reconvene."

"Then, my son, I'm afraid you court further action like *we* saw while *you* slept with the elves," Eirik threatened with narrowed, flashing eyes.

I lost my humor and glared at the odious man who saw no action at all but had no problem hanging around in his tent while he ordered men to battle, some of them meeting their deaths while his grievously injured son was healed by the elves.

Jerk.

"Then, my sire, I'm afraid, if you threaten treason, I will be forced to remove you as the head of the House of Drakkar, transfer that privilege to my brother Calder, your second born, and wish you well with your retirement," Frey returned.

And just like that, my flare of temper disintegrated, and I was pressing my lips together again as I watched Eirik actually bounce in fury in his seat.

He crashed both his fists on the table and stammered an incensed, "I... you...you cannot...you can't do that!"

"I'm afraid I can. I am the true head of the House of Drakkar, and as is well known, if I do not wish to assume this role, then it is my due to transfer it to who I see fit. As I didn't give a gods damn who ran our House, I didn't take my due. Now, I give a damn, so I'll take my due." Eirik opened and closed his mouth like a fish as Frey's eyes moved to Calder. "Do you wish this responsibility, brother?"

"By all means," Calder muttered to Frey then he turned his head to his father. "If you would, I will ask you and Mother to make haste in your move to the dower house. Melba has long been telling me she thought new curtains would be lovely in the drawing room." Eirik blinked at his son while Calder finished, "And the study."

I couldn't help it, a snort escaped, and my eyes shot to Aurora who I saw gazing impassively at the sheen on the dining room table. But when she felt my regard, hers lifted to mine and I saw them twinkling.

"This is outrageous!" Eirik shrieked, and I turned back to him.

"No, this is done," Frey declared, standing and extending a hand to me. "Gentlemen," he dipped his chin to the table then turned to Mother as my fingers curled around his and I rose. "My queen," he murmured.

"Drakkar," she murmured back.

Frey moved me away from the table then flicked a hand at the chair he'd vacated, eyes still on his queen.

"Your seat," he whispered.

Her lips tipped up slightly before she rose gracefully, glided to the head and sat, her gaze moving to the men around the table and Frey moving me from the room.

When we were in the hall and out of earshot, I leaned into my husband and squeezed his hand, whispering, "Well done, my handsome husband."

"Mm," he murmured, eyes straight ahead. "I'm glad you think so, my wee wife, but this means no adventure for you for a time. We have word Baldur returns and I will need to stay close to show my support to our new leader."

I pointed my eyes straight ahead too and muttered, "I'm sure I'll find something I can do."

I felt Frey's attention on me, kept mine aimed at the hall then I heard Frey sigh.

"Indeed, you will, and this terrifies me," he muttered back and that was when I allowed myself to giggle.

So I did and I did it loud.

∾

THAT EVENING...

449

Late.

My body pressed to and straddling my husband's long, muscular frame, I kissed his throat as I felt his hands move up the skin of my back then I lifted my head and looked down at him.

"I don't believe I'm going to say this," I told him. "But I think I like your brothers."

His arms wrapped around me as he muttered, "It wasn't only me who sat at my Grandmother Eugenie's knee when I was wee."

I smiled at him and slid a hand up to curl around his neck. "I take it Franka didn't spend a lot of time with your grandmother."

"Franka was busy stealing her handmaids' hair pins and ear bobs, concealing them amongst her *other* handmaids' possessions, whispering in the right ears and then watching as false accusations were thrown, unbeknownst to the accuser they were false, and then watching tempers flare. She had little time for Granny's knee."

I could believe this.

Frey's arms gave me a squeeze and I watched his face grow serious.

Then he stated gently, "My wife does not sleep soundly."

I felt my face go soft even as the pads of my fingers dug into the skin of his neck.

He would notice, Frey would. He would notice and worry.

God, I loved this man.

"Baby," I whispered.

"Tell me," Frey whispered back.

My hand slid up and my thumb slid out to stroke his jaw as, stalling, I asked, "About what?"

"About what keeps you from a sound sleep," he answered patiently, knowing I was stalling.

I studied his beloved face.

We hadn't talked about this. Any of it. There wasn't time. Much was happening, we were traveling everywhere, I had a lot on my mind, and I had Frey back. All was well, I didn't want to relive it, any of it, and Frey had let this be.

But now I saw he'd been biding his time.

"What parts do you want to know?" I queried.

"All of them," he replied.

I held his gaze. Then I sighed.

"I thought you were dead," I whispered.

"I know," he whispered back.

I kept whispering. "I thought I said terrible, ugly words to you before you died."

He kept whispering too when he repeated, "I know."

"Frey," I murmured, not really wanting to go on.

"Finnie." He gave me a squeeze, not wanting me to keep it bottled in.

I looked at the pillow beside his head before my eyes went back to his.

"I took lives," I said softly.

"You did, wee one, and I am glad of it, for if you hadn't you might not be lying, naked, astride me."

This was true.

"I..." I faltered then confessed the worst of it, "After I killed Phobin, I not only rubbed Broderick's nose in it, I rubbed his nose in his defeat."

Frey grinned at me.

Yes, grinned.

Then he burst out laughing, pressing his head back into the pillows and everything before he rolled me so he was on top.

And after he did this, he was still laughing.

"Frey!" I snapped, his laughter died to chuckles, and he focused on me.

"I wish I was there to see that," he said through his dying mirth.

"It was not my crowning moment," I retorted sharply.

"Let us see, my wee one. He killed your father, Alyssa, and nearly killed Thad and me. You lived over a month thinking I was dead and drowning in sorrow and guilt for the last thing you did was shriek at me. He imprisoned your mother, was the architect of a number of faceless soldiers' deaths—"

"All right, all right," I cut him off. "I get it, but hello? Frey? Remember a while back when I lectured thousands of people about mercy? And there I was, getting in Broderick's face about—"

He lifted a hand to my jaw, thumb to my lips, and he pressed lightly.

Then he said quietly, "You will note it was not me who stood up when Viola was being pelted with ice missiles and demanded mercy for her. And it was not me because her actions meant I stood to lose you. With Broderick, you thought you had actually lost me, and you knew you again lost a father. I think succeeding in four short days in bringing him low and setting the rebellion into disarray, you can excuse yourself for gloating."

Well.

I had to admit, he had a point.

I decided not to respond.

Frey knew why and grinned.

His grin faded, his hand slid to my neck, and he said quietly, "We must speak of what I did to you."

I shook my head. "No," I replied. "All's well that ends well and thank God, it's ended well. So no, Frey, we never have to speak of it."

"You say this, Finnie, because you still hold the pain of guilt, all that time you thought I was lost. That dark shadow runs deep in you, my wee one. I see it at times, drifting across your eyes when you look at me."

"Frey—"

"But had we not been attacked in the middle of that episode, you would have been entitled to an explanation, wife, and you still are."

I tried to waylay him by explaining, "I know that it's, uh...law, um... here, in this world, for the man to decide if birth control is used or not and if the woman doesn't adhere to his, uh...decision, she can be sentenced to serve the realm." Frey stared at me, and I finished, "Uh...I told Aurora everything that night after Father...after we put Father...when his boat..." I sucked in breath. "Well, that night Mother drank two bottles of wine all by herself and I fell asleep while she did it, and so did she, and you had to carry both of us to bed. I told her what happened, and she explained it to me."

"This is not the same in your world," he guessed.

Women who did or did not take birth control against their male partner's wishes serving a term of nine months sentenced to do light work in castles, hospitals or orphanages?

Uh...crazy!

"No," I confirmed. "It's the woman's choice unless she's married and then they decide together, and until they do...well, she just takes it, mostly. I don't know, I've, uh...never been married until, well...now."

Carefully, Frey stated, "You hid taking it from me."

I blinked in confusion before, equally carefully, I replied, "No, honey, I didn't. I don't know why you'd think that, but I guess you just were never around when I took it."

He nodded before he reminded me gently, "All right, Finnie, but we discussed it with you approaching the subject within twenty-four hours of my return to you after I was at sea."

"I know, Frey, because we were set to have sex within twenty-four hours after your return to me, and at that time, I thought I was going home, and I didn't want to do it pregnant or with a newborn who'd never see his or her father again."

He studied me for long moments.

Then he muttered, "I misinterpreted this," but as he did, he held my eyes.

I smiled at him and said softly, "I gathered that."

His eyes dropped to my mouth and his hand shifted up so his thumb could stroke my cheekbone as his eyes lifted back to mine.

"I was in love with you when I ordered the elves to bind you to me," he said softly.

My body stiffened slightly under his, I shook my head and whispered, "Frey—"

"It is true I didn't know it," he interrupted me. "All I knew was when Nillen told me you were set to leave, I couldn't abide that. Nillen warned me there would be consequences, but I decided I would accept whatever they were as long as I knew you could never leave me." His face dipped closer, and his voice dipped lower when he went on, "You already had a hold on my heart, Finnie. You must believe I would not have done what I did if that wasn't true."

"You barely knew me," I pointed out.

"I knew you were beautiful. I knew you smelled good. I knew you filled out a gown very nicely. I knew you could cook. I knew your cheeks got pink and your eyes lit when you were excited. I knew in just weeks you made friends, you chattered brightly, you were interested in me, you smiled easily, you laughed readily, you would come to my defense when you thought I faced danger, you responded to my touch and," he grinned, "you did that wildly."

I rolled my eyes.

Frey kept talking so I rolled them back.

"And I left you alone in my cabin and you didn't just survive, you thrived, so I knew you were an uncommon woman. An uncommon woman who would match me. So I knew you, Finnie, and I bound you to me knowing I wanted to know you more and knowing I would like having a lifetime of that discovery."

Oh my God, did he just say that?

I stared at him, my heart in my throat.

He said it.

My voice husky, I started to threaten, "Frey Drakkar, if you make me cry—"

He cut me off. "But what I didn't know until later was when the elves bound you to this world, they also bound you to me, so when I returned from their realm, I knew where you were. I sensed you. I could find you. I went right to you, taking the dragons with me. I sent a messenger to bring my men to me so they would be safe from the dragon's fire then, as you ran with your witches through the forest, I knew exactly where you were so the fire I aimed from my beasts never got near you."

That was when I blinked and breathed, "Really?"

He grinned again and whispered, "Really."

"Cool." I whispered back and watched my husband's grin get bigger.

But his face grew soft, and his warm eyes roamed my own as he muttered, "By the gods, I hope you never lose your wonder for all that is life, my wee Finnie."

"Well, as long as I'm in a world with fire-breathing dragons, magical elves, hot guys who are impervious to extreme heat and fantastic ships straight out of a movie that are named after me, I don't think that's gonna happen," I told him, and his head tilted to the side.

"Straight out of a what?"

I cupped his jaw, lifted my head and touched my mouth to his.

I dropped my head back down to the pillow and whispered, "I'll explain later."

The look in his eyes shifted, that shift corresponded to a tingle some-place really good, and his hand slid from my jaw, down my neck, my chest and my side as he murmured, "You will?"

"Unh-hunh," I agreed, pressing my body to his as my hands moved on him and his head dipped closer, his nose sliding along mine.

"When?" he asked quietly.

"Later," I answered, hooking a leg around his hip.

His lips came so close I could feel his breath on mine, but his eyes stayed open and held mine captive.

"So then, what are we going to do now?" he asked.

"I don't know," I said breathily. "Do you have any ideas?"

"A few," he answered, his voice slightly gruff, his hand sliding back up my side to cup my breast.

I drew in a soft breath.

"I think I might like your ideas," I told him.

"I know you will," he told me.

"Sure of yourself?" I teased.

His thumb slid across my nipple, my back arched, and I drew in a breath that was not at all soft.

"Yes," he answered, his eyes smiling but still lit with that lazy, sexy light.

One of my hands slid up the sleek skin of his back and into his hair. "You could tell me what it's like in the elves' realm," I suggested.

"Later," he whispered, his lips still close, his thumb now circling my nipple.

I bit my lip as the sensations curled through me and I waited breathlessly for his mouth to take mine.

When I didn't get it, I prompted on a whisper, "Seriously, baby, are you going to kiss me, or what?"

My husband made me wait half a second while, super close, he looked deep in my eyes.

Then, just like Frey, he gave me what I wanted.

He kissed me.

~

INCIDENTALLY, I slept soundly that night, and except on a rare occasion, every night after.

~

ONE MONTH LATER...
  In the Queen's Study, Rimée Keep, Snowdon.

I STOOD SILENTLY at the window in my mother's study, my body facing it, but my head was turned so I could see the people at the desk.

Frey, Calder, Apollo, Olwen, Norfolk and Walter were standing at one side, the heads of three once Lunwynian, then Middlelandian, again Lunwynian Houses stood at the other side. All three had not participated in the rebellion, and for their refusal to support that campaign, they had all been imprisoned throughout the short war by Broderick then by the other heads.

Now, they were not.

Mother stood behind the desk, bent over it, signing a huge, poster board-sized piece of parchment.

Baldur stood next to her watching her with a stony face.

She straightened and offered her silver pen to him.

His lip curled as he looked at the pen.

"Do not delay, Baldur," Apollo said low. "Your carriage awaits and the rest of us have things to do."

Baldur glared at Apollo then he looked to Mother.

"It is my understanding, my son showed kindness to your daughter before she slaughtered him," he noted coldly.

Mother didn't show any reaction to this pointless comment, which was a miracle considering all the other things that were *not* kind that Broderick did, including ordering her (and my) husband to be murdered.

Instead, she stated blandly, "And it is my understanding she actually didn't slaughter him. She delivered a wound that was not lethal, but instead, it was one of the men of The Drakkar, acting correctly on what he felt would be his absent commander's wishes, who ran your son through." She paused then finished, not even trying to hide her pride, "But she did, of course, take the life of his lover."

Baldur's mouth got tight, and his eyes slid through the heads on either side, avoiding mine as they went, and he muttered, "This is preposterous. This woman does not even have the blood of a Wilde, and she's a *woman*, for the gods' sakes."

"Your options have been explained, Baldur," Frey reminded him. "You made your choice. With this delay, are you saying you're undecided?" Baldur's attention went to Frey and Frey concluded, "For if you are, I will be happy to make the choice for you."

"My choice has not changed," Baldur snapped.

I was guessing it wouldn't, for his choices were abdicating all claim to his throne by signing that paper and then immediately leaving on his journey to be exiled to a small island somewhere south, far away from here. Or a trial for impeachment that might end in a lifelong exile, not on a sunny isle, but in a cold dungeon.

He went on.

"But it is my due and I wish it to be known that you and your heads have acted well beyond the bounds of decency and respect. Dragon fire and trials of treason for heads of Houses? It is ridiculous. These are games of politics as they have been played for centuries."

"We are moving into a new era," Aurora announced softly, her eyes on Baldur. "Where politics do not include assassinations and clashes of steel but diplomacy. And the heads who remain are enthusiastic about Lunwyn's bright future."

Baldur's eyes narrowed on her, and he snapped, "At your command, you will lead the new Lunwyn to misery and my people will revolt."

"We shall see," Aurora murmured then her face brightened slightly. "Though, in opening your treasury, abolishing your paper currency and allowing our reunited citizens to trade their paper currency for coin, they seem to be quite content at the moment."

Baldur's face got red, and I pressed my lips together to stop myself from smiling and looked out the window, so I missed Baldur yanking the pen out of Aurora's hand. I heard the scribble of the squib on parchment, and I also heard movement as he stomped out.

I did not look back until Mother spoke.

"Gentlemen, if you would," she invited, and I watched her motion nobly to the oval table in the corner of the room.

The heads moved there with Mother. Frey and Apollo moved to me. When they arrived, they stopped close, and Frey's hand slid to the small of my back.

"Do you wish to stay, my Finnie?" he asked quietly, and I scrunched my nose.

"Attend a *meeting*?" I asked back, and he smiled at me before he turned his smile to an openly amused Apollo.

"Not exciting enough for my wee wife," he muttered to Apollo.

Apollo's response was an amused, rumbling, "Mm."

"You two enjoy," I mumbled.

"Right," Apollo murmured, looking like he wanted to attend this meeting about as much as I did.

"And your plans?" Frey asked and my gaze went to his.

"Check in on Sky. He's taking a test. He should be finishing up about now. And Bess is leaving."

He nodded. "Then you should be away."

"I should be away," I agreed.

His eyes warmed, his head dropped, and he touched his mouth to mine.

"I shall see you later," he muttered, looking over his shoulder at the conference table.

"Okay, honey," I whispered, drew up my hand, touched his chest and his eyes came back to me, so I smiled.

His hand tensed at my back then he moved away.

I turned to Apollo and smiled at him too, then my smile went wonky as he held my eyes but took hold of my hand and lifted it, knuckles up, to his lips. I watched as he brushed them with his lips and dropped our hands but kept firm hold of mine.

"Until we meet again, sweet Finnie," he whispered gently, and I felt my mouth go soft.

"Until we meet again, Apollo," I whispered back, squeezing his fingers.

He made to let go, but I held tight and moved slightly closer.

Once there, I said quietly, "A wise woman once told me happiness is a line with contentment at one end and bliss on the other." I squeezed his fingers again and went on fervently, "I hope you at least find a way to the middle of that line, Apollo."

His lips tipped up slightly before his head turned and I knew he was looking at Frey when he looked back to me and I saw his remarkable eyes lit with an appealing light before he replied, "I have, my princess, just knowing you have moved up that line to bliss."

My belly warmed.

"Apollo," I whispered.

"Hold tight to it, my sweet," he replied softly. "Every day is a gift."

He knew and so did I. We knew this to be very true.

I just wished there was some way this wonderful man would open his heart to a woman who would be generous to it. But I knew like I knew when I thought I had lost Frey that this was impossible.

I nodded, his lips tipped up more, his fingers squeezed mine then he let me go and moved away.

I watched and saw Frey watching us. I smiled at him as his eyes slid to Apollo then back to me, they warmed, and he smiled gently back. I looked to Mother who inclined her chin to me, her lips curled slightly, and she looked back at the table.

I left the room and hurried to the side entrance to Rimée Keep, hoping Bess was not yet away.

When I exited, I saw she was not, but the carriage was loaded, the horses put to, and she was standing beside it fretting.

Her head turned and her face lit when she saw me. "Oh Finnie! There you are!"

She rushed to me as I moved to her, and we took hold of each other's hands.

"Your trunks are packed, everything is ready and—" she started, but I interrupted her.

"Bess, I'll be fine," I told her.

"I know, but, the other girls—"

"The other girls are hopefully enjoying a much-needed break like you're about to."

She looked at me and grinned. So I grinned back because we both knew Jocelyn and Esther were undoubtedly enjoying their breaks for they were both in Houllebec in the company of their men, Thad and Oleg.

Where Frey and I were headed the next morning and I was glad of it.

My feet most definitely itched.

Her smile faded and she whispered, "I'll miss you, my sweet princess."

I dropped her hands but pulled her into my arms for a hug and whispered in her ear, "And I'll miss you, my sweet Bess. But it's only a short time, and soon we'll all be back together again and off to face our next adventure." I squeezed hard, let her go and stepped back. "Now, go. Spend time with your family and I'll see you very soon."

She nodded, grinned at me again then part skipped, part dashed to the carriage, taking the hand of the footman waiting there for her. He helped her in, closed the door and she leaned out the window and waved at me as the footman ordered the driver, "Away."

"Farewell, Finnie!" she called, waving as the carriage rolled forward.

"Farewell, Bess!" I called back, waving too.

I watched and waved as the carriage continued to move until it disappeared around the castle. And I kept looking in that direction, seeing the frost city of Snowdon now embedded in the deep green of the short Lunwyn summer. The ice and snow were gone, the land was lush and vibrant, and Frey told me this would be the way for another month or so before the snows again came and bound the nation in ice.

I turned to the doors, went through and immediately encountered a scowling Kell who was stomping toward me.

"Hey, Kell," I greeted when he got close, and we both stopped.

"Where's Frey?" he grunted, not greeting me when we both stopped.

"In a meeting," I informed him.

His eyebrows shot up and then his face returned to a scowl.

"A meeting?" he asked as if this concept was foreign to him, foreign and revolting.

"Yes, you know, where people sit down, discuss weighty issues, drink coffee, eat pastries and decide the future for hundreds of thousands of people," I stated. "A meeting."

He continued to scowl. Then he grunted. Then he turned on his boot without another word and stomped away.

I giggled to myself before I moved down the hall only to turn down another one and see a maid coming to me.

"My princess," she said and dropped in a quick curtsy before straightening and offering a creamy envelope to me. "This came in today's post."

"Thank you, Michelle," I said softly, taking the envelope.

She did another quick curtsy and scurried away.

I turned the envelope over and saw a bright-green wax seal, pressed with a scrolled, looped, double L.

Lavinia.

I smiled, ran my nail under the seal, opened the envelope and pulled out the thick, cream paper inside, opening it and reading.

My Winter Princess,

The adela takes root!

I cannot tell you how pleased I am. As you know, I planted three branches and all three have begun to glow. They send shoots into the earth, reaching to the elfin realm. It is very exciting to have this early success.

I am away to move through my beautiful Lunwyn and plant branches before the frost sets in. It will take decades for the trees to spread, but our great land will be graced by the glow of the adela once again, I will see to it.

I have received your letter and it is good to know your pregnancy does not cause you trouble as other women endure. I wish this for you for the entirety of it and I will be at your side when it is time for you to deliver our next king or our next Winter Princess to this world.

And I await stories of your next adventure, my princess.

Yours always,

Lavinia

I smiled at the paper then, folding it and sliding it back into its envelope, I moved to my mother's old office, a smaller room, more feminine and now unused.

The door was open, and I stopped in it to take in Skylar behind the desk, Penelope lying on top of it. He was bent over it with pencil in hand. She was sending her tail in wide sweeps, catching his papers.

"Stop it, cat," he muttered.

Penelope swept her tail away, then back over his papers.

He turned his head and glared at the feline. "Stop it, cat!"

She executed two more sweeps.

Skylar emitted a little boy growl that was alarmingly like the ones I'd heard from Frey's men on occasion and punished my cat by picking her up from the desk, cuddling her in his arms and torturing her with scratches behind her ears.

I could hear Penelope's purrs all the way across the room.

When I heard them, I smiled.

～

Two weeks later...
Houllebec.

I sat in Frey's lap shuffling the cards, my eyes on the occupants of the table.

Esther sat in Oleg's lap, and I was unsurprised to see, for I'd seen it before, that he was as gentle when he was with her as Frey was with me.

But, even so, he still didn't talk much, and when he did, it was mostly grunts.

Jocelyn sat beaming in Thad's lap. Although Esther and Oleg were testing the waters, clearly enjoyed each other and were becoming close, it didn't take a love doctor to see Jocelyn had fallen and when I say that, I mean *deep.*

Thad had too. It wasn't so much him showing it, though he, also like Frey, was not afraid of showing affection and he often teased her in a way I thought was super sweet. It was that Thad told Frey and Frey told me so I had the inside scoop that Thad had fallen, and hard, for my Jocelyn.

Thad was also recovered, or as much as he ever would be. He'd sustained an injury to his leg that would mean he'd always walk with a hint of a limp. But I had noticed he wasn't letting that slow him down. I also noticed that none of the other men said a thing about it, called attention to it or treated Thad any differently.

Ruben was with us too (his woman not there), as were Laurel, Ulysses and Frederick.

I stopped shuffling and smiled and chatted while I dealt the cards, every card I threw on my husband's pile I dealt from the bottom of the deck.

I set the deck down, picked up my cards and started to fiddle with them in my hand but didn't get very far.

Frey threw his hand down on the table face up and announced, "Finnie cheats."

I looked to the table at the fantastic hand I dealt him then lifted a fingers to touch my chest and my gaze moved to my husband.

"Me?" I asked with sham innocence.

Frey grinned. "You," he answered.

"Well, I never," I muttered.

"Yes, you do, Finnie. Every single time," Thad stated.

He was not wrong.

"Finnie?" I heard a voice that was familiar. A voice I hadn't heard in a long time. A voice I thought I'd never hear again, and I turned slowly in Frey's lap and looked at the woman standing behind him and my heart leapt into my throat.

"Claudia?" I whispered, taking in my friend wearing a Lunwynian style gown, her hair pulled back, a redhead, also in a Lunwynian gown, standing behind her, her lips tipped up in a cat's smile.

"*Claudia!*" I shrieked, jumped out of Frey's lap, rounded him and threw myself in my friend's arms. "Oh my God. Oh my God. Oh my God, *God*, *God!*" I chanted, holding on tight and swinging her side to side.

"Oh Finnie, honey, oh God," Claudia muttered in my ear then burst out crying, her arms spasming around me.

"Oh Claudia, honey," I muttered back then *I* burst out crying.

After we did this awhile, I pulled back, framed her face with my hands and grinned into her wet, twinkling eyes.

I let her go and threw myself at Valentine.

"Valentine," I whispered, holding on tight.

"My goddess of love," she whispered back, giving me a squeeze.

We said no more, just held on. I hadn't seen her in ages. She left shortly after Frey and his dragons routed the enemy and I hadn't heard from her since.

Finally, I pulled away, smiled at her and held her upper arms then my eyes caught on a flash at her throat. They dropped there and I saw a very, *very* large Sjofn ice diamond. What I had mistaken as aquamarines in my crown and the jewels I wore on my wedding night but what were actually very sought after, very expensive diamonds found only in the depths of Lunwyn. Diamonds that legend held were touched blue by the elves.

I looked at the diamond then at her.

When she had my gaze, she whispered, "I told you. Love is everything and your husband knows this."

I blinked.

Frey had given her that diamond. Somewhere along the line, Frey had given her an expensive diamond from another world in payment for her bringing Claudia to me.

In payment for her bringing things I loved from my old world to my new one.

I released her and slowly turned to Frey who was watching me.

"You did this," I whispered.

"Indeed," he replied.

I stared into his green-brown eyes.

Then I burst into tears.

About half a second later, I was in my husband's arms, my face shoved in his neck.

"Is that her husband?" Through my tears I heard Claudia stage-whisper to Valentine.

"Yes, dear Claudia," Valentine answered on a beleaguered sigh. "How, in your infinite insightfulness, did you fathom that?"

"Well, he's hot," Claudia shot back. "I mean, like, *hot* hot. Like *otherworldly* hot. Not that Finnie couldn't get hot, but...I've never seen that level of hot."

"Otherworldly hot," Valentine murmured, her two words sounding vaguely annoyed in a way that stated Valentine actually found them quite annoying, but she wasn't about to expend the effort to be *too* annoyed by the likes of Claudia.

Hmm.

Seemed things hadn't changed between Valentine and Claudia.

I pulled slightly away from Frey, wiped my face and smiled like a lunatic at my friends. "Find chairs, sit down, we're playing cards. I'll introduce you to everyone."

Claudia grinned at me.

Valentine looked aghast at the table like sitting in a pub, playing cards was akin to spending the night in a hotel that was any less than five stars.

I totally ignored this and shouted, "Lindy! We need horns!"

"Got it, Princess Finnie," Lindy called back.

"Awesome. *Princess* Finnie," Claudia whispered and smiled at me.

I smiled back.

Then my friend from my old world sat down with my friends from my new world. I introduced everyone. We played cards and drank ale.

Well, except me, I played cards.

But Lindy brought me apple juice in my horn.

～

LATER THAT NIGHT...

. . .

"WHAT IS THIS?" Frey asked as we sat on the mattress in the firelight and candlelight in the loft of his cabin, Penelope curled in a ball asleep at the end of the bed, all our friends gone home to soft beds and warm bodies with Claudia and Valentine staying at an inn in town.

I scooped out some peanut butter then set the jar aside and dipped it into the marshmallow fluff.

Claudia had talked Valentine into bringing gifts.

And she'd picked good ones.

I looked to my husband, who was warily inspecting my movements.

"Heaven on a spoon," I told him and turned the loaded spoon his way. "Try it," I encouraged, and his eyes came to me.

Then his mouth opened, and I fed him heaven on a spoon.

When he was working the delicious goo down his throat and I had started to dip the spoon back in the jars, I asked, "Do you like it?"

"It's...interesting," he replied.

I looked to him, grinned big, then shoved a giganto spoonful of peanut butter and fluff into my mouth.

My eyes closed slowly in abandoned rapture as I sucked the spoon clean.

"Gods," Frey muttered, and I suddenly found myself without spoon or jar and on my back in our bed with my husband on me.

"Frey, I wasn't done," I told him as his fingers pulled my nightgown up.

"You're done," he told me as my hands slid around his back.

"No, seriously, I wasn't—"

His lips came to mine, his hard hips pressed into my soft ones, and he growled, "You can have more later."

"Okay," I breathed against his mouth.

I felt his lips smile then he slanted his head, and he kissed me.

My handsome husband tasted of peanut butter and marshmallow fluff.

Kiss number three in the lineup of our best kisses.

Kisses, all of them, better than anything...absolutely anything...

Even my wildest dreams.

∾

VERY LATE THAT NIGHT...

The forest outside Houllebec.

. . .

Valentine Rousseau moved through the dark night until she saw the figure emerge from behind the tree and she stopped.

There wasn't a cloud in the sky. The moonlight was bright, and she saw his big, firm, muscular body, dark thick hair, strong jaw and jade-green eyes.

Delicious, she thought as she had always thought when she saw this gorgeous specimen.

"You are a powerful witch," his deep appealing voice rumbled.

"I am," she replied.

He hesitated.

Then he asked, "Is it true what Frey tells me?"

"About each world having twin?" she queried.

He didn't bother to reply, but she knew.

She knew.

She was pleased to bring her goddess of love jars of peanut butter, marshmallow fluff and even her tedious friend, for she had her delightful ice-blue diamond from The Drakkar.

But Valentine was multitasking.

"It is," she answered.

He moved a step closer, and she tipped her head back, keeping hold on those remarkable green eyes.

And what she read there made her draw in a delicate breath.

He held out a small leather pouch to her. She lifted her hand, palm up, and he dropped it in.

"Her name is Ilsa Ulfr," he growled then he turned and strode away.

She stared at his broad-shouldered, departing back.

Then she dipped her chin, pulled the leather band on the pouch to open it, and she tipped the stones into her palm.

They sparkled in the moonlight.

She smiled her cat's smile.

She looked to the distance and saw he was gone.

"Love is," she whispered to the night, "everything."

The End

GLOSSARY OF PARALLEL UNIVERSE

PLACES, SEAS, REGIONS IN THE KRISTEN ASHLEY'S FANTASYLAND SERIES

Bellebryn—(place) Small, peaceful, city-sized princedom located in the Northlands and fully within the boundaries of Hawkvale and the Green Sea (west)

Fleuridia—(place) Somewhat advanced, peaceful nation located in the Northlands; boundaries to Hawkvale (north and west) and the Marhac Sea (south)

Green Sea—(body of water) Ocean-like body of water with coastlines abutting Bellebryn, Hawkvale, Lunwyn and Middleland

Hawkvale—(place) Somewhat advanced, peaceful nation located in the Northlands; boundaries with Middleland (north), Fleuridia (south and east) and the Green Sea (west) and Marhac Sea (south)

Keenhak—(place) Primitive, warring nation located in the Southlands; boundaries with Korwahk (north) and Maroo (west)

Korwahk—(place) Primitive, warring nation located in the Southlands; boundaries with the Marhac Sea (north) and the nations of Keenhak (southeast) and Maroo (southwest)

Korwahn—(place) Large capital city of Korwahk

Lunwyn—(place) Somewhat advanced, peaceful nation in the farthest reaches of the Northlands; boundaries to Middleland (south), the Green Sea (west) and the Winter Sea (north)

Marhac Sea—(large body of water) Separates Korwahk and Hawkvale and Fleuridia

Maroo—(place) Primitive, warring nation located in the Southlands; boundaries to Korwahk (north) and Keenhak (east)

Middleland—(place) Somewhat advanced nation with tyrant king located in the Northlands; boundaries to Hawkvale (south), Fleuridia (south), Lunwyn (north) and the Green Sea (west)

[The] Northlands—(region) The region north of the equator on the alternate earth

[The] Southlands—(region) The region south of the equator on the alternate earth

Winter Sea—(large body of water) Arctic body of water that forms the northern coast of Lunwyn, filled with large glaciers

KEEP READING FOR MORE FANTASYLAND

The Golden Dynasty

Circe Quinn, the office manager of her father's moving company, goes to sleep at home and wakes up in a corral filled with women wearing sacrificial virgin attire—and she's one of them.

She figures (rightly) this is not good and soon finds she's not having a wild dream, she's living a frightening nightmare where she's been transported to a barren land populated by a primitive people. Then, in short order, she's installed very unwillingly on her white throne of horns as their queen.

Dax Lahn is the king of Suh Tunak, the Horde of the nation of Korwahk. With one look at Circe, he knows she will be his bride and together they will start the Golden Dynasty of legend.

Circe and Lahn are separated by language, culture and the small fact she's from a parallel universe and has no idea how she got there or how to get home. But facing challenge after challenge, Circe finds her footing as Queen of the brutal Korwahk Horde and wife to its King. Then she makes friends. Then she finds herself falling in love with this primitive land, its people and especially their savage leader.

Keep Reading for more of The Golden Dynasty.

THE GOLDEN DYNASTY
PROLOGUE

Running

I was running.

Running on those stupid, flimsy little sandals.

Running for my life.

He was on his horse, I could hear the beast's hooves pounding behind me, hear this mingled with my own panting, ragged, panicked breaths—and those hooves were getting closer.

I was covered in blood. Not mine. It was still warm from spurting from that man's body.

I didn't know where I was or how I got there. I wasn't certain what was happening. I went to sleep in my bed in a world I understood, and I woke up here in a world that was entirely foreign to me, everything about it, and not one thing about it was good.

And now I was running for my life.

The horse's hooves got closer. I knew they were almost upon me. Frantic, I glanced back and saw I was right. Not only were they close, the man—the rider, so huge he seemed giant—had leaned so deeply to the side, his body was in line with the horse's middle.

And his long arm was stretched out.

I faced forward and tried to run faster.

But I couldn't go any faster and I certainly couldn't go faster than a horse.

I cried out when the arm hooked me at the waist, closed around and lifted me clean off my feet before my ass was planted on the horse in front of him.

Without thinking, I screamed bloody murder, twisted on the horse and prepared—instead of running for my life—to fight for it.

The Golden Dynasty is Available Now.

ABOUT THE AUTHOR

Kristen Ashley is the *New York Times* bestselling author of over eighty romance novels including the *Rock Chick, Colorado Mountain, Dream Man, Chaos, Unfinished Heroes, The 'Burg, Magdalene, Fantasyland, The Three, Ghost and Reincarnation, The Rising, Dream Team, Moonlight and Motor Oil, River Rain, Wild West MC, Misted Pines* and *Honey* series along with several stand-alone novels. She's a hybrid author, publishing titles both independently and traditionally, her books have been translated in fourteen languages and she's sold over five million books.

Kristen's novel, *Law Man*, won the *RT Book Reviews* Reviewer's Choice Award for best Romantic Suspense, her independently published title *Hold On* was nominated for *RT Book Reviews* best Independent Contemporary Romance and her traditionally published title *Breathe* was nominated for best Contemporary Romance. Kristen's titles *Motorcycle Man, The Will*, and *Ride Steady* (which won the Reader's Choice award from *Romance Reviews*) all made the final rounds for Goodreads Choice Awards in the Romance category.

Kristen, born in Gary and raised in Brownsburg, Indiana, is a fourth-generation graduate of Purdue University. Since, she's lived in Denver, the West Country of England, and she now resides in Phoenix. She worked as a charity executive for eighteen years prior to beginning her independent publishing career. She now writes full-time.

Although romance is her genre, the prevailing themes running through all of Kristen's novels are friendship, family and a strong sisterhood. To this end, and as a way to thank her readers for their support, Kristen has created the Rock Chick Nation, a series of programs that are designed to give back to her readers and promote a strong female community.

The mission of the Rock Chick Nation is to live your best life, be true to your true self, recognize your beauty, and take your sister's back whether they're at your side as friends and family or if they're thousands of miles away and you don't know who they are.

The programs of the RC Nation include Rock Chick Rendezvous, weekends Kristen organizes full of parties and get-togethers to bring the sisterhood together, Rock Chick Recharges, evenings Kristen arranges for women who have been nominated to receive a special night, and Rock Chick Rewards, an ongoing program that raises funds for nonprofit women's organizations Kristen's readers nominate. Kristen's Rock Chick Rewards have donated hundreds of thousands of dollars to charity and this number continues to rise.

You can read more about Kristen, her titles and the Rock Chick Nation at KristenAshley.net.

facebook.com/kristenashleybooks

twitter.com/KristenAshley68

instagram.com/kristenashleybooks

pinterest.com/KristenAshleyBooks

goodreads.com/kristenashleybooks

bookbub.com/authors/kristen-ashley

ALSO BY KRISTEN ASHLEY

Free

Wild Fire

Wild Wind

The Colorado Mountain Series:

The Gamble

Sweet Dreams

Lady Luck

Breathe

Jagged

Kaleidoscope

Bounty

Dream Man Series:

Mystery Man

Wild Man

Law Man

Motorcycle Man

Quiet Man

Dream Team Series:

Dream Maker

Dream Chaser

Dream Bites Cookbook

Dream Spinner

Dream Keeper

The Fantasyland Series:

Wildest Dreams

The Golden Dynasty

Fantastical

Broken Dove

The Beginning of Everything

The Plan Commences

The Dawn of the End

The Rising

The River Rain Series:

After the Climb

After the Climb Special Edition

Chasing Serenity

Taking the Leap

Making the Match

The Three Series:

Until the Sun Falls from the Sky

With Everything I Am

Wild and Free

The Unfinished Hero Series:

Knight

Creed

Raid

Deacon

Sebring

Wild West MC Series:

Still Standing

Smoke and Steel

Other Titles by Kristen Ashley:

Heaven and Hell

Play It Safe

Three Wishes

www.ingramcontent.com/pod-product-compliance
Lightning Source LLC
LaVergne TN
LVHW091548070125
800737LV00006B/24